CARPET DIEM

OR HOW TO SAVE THE WORLD BY ACCIDENT

JUSTIN LEE ANDERSON

KING LOT PUBLISHING

For Juliet, Kieran, Nick, Adrienne, Grace and Jamie, who inspire me every day.

FIFTEEN YEARS AGO

Harriet woke on the floor; wet, confused and reeking of whisky. This was not unusual.

She wiggled her fingers and toes. They all seemed to be there. With a deep breath, she raised her head off the floor.

Ouch.

Carefully, she rolled onto her side to look around. The gentle crunch of shattered glass made her stop. The off license sparkled under a layer of the stuff. Rivulets of booze ran from the shelves, escaping shattered bottles to pool on the floor.

Sirens.

Harriet pressed herself up onto her elbows.

No glass in the window frame. That explained the floor.

Something was burning. Something big.

She grasped the counter, grunting with the effort of pulling herself up. Fragments of glass rained musically onto the floor. From the new angle, Harriet could see that the wet patch on her stomach was the Lagavulin she had been about to buy. She only briefly considered sucking it.

Her head pounded as her heart forced blood upwards; eyes black, ears squealing in protest. She waited, head hanging. After a moment, black turned to red and the world returned.

There was no sign of the assistant who'd been serving her.

She hobbled to the window. Her balance was less than perfect anyway, and the floor was slick as fresh ice. And her back hurt. A lot.

At least six fire engines across the road.

Blinking, she leaned against the door frame. The air reeked of acrid smoke and this wasn't the only building that had lost windows. Outside, scattered pockets of hushed witnesses held each other and stared at the chaos across the road.

Across the road.

The hotel restaurant.

The building where she had left her entire family yawned a gaping wound of flame, breathing thick black smoke into the night.

Oh, Hell.

Harriet lifted the nearest intact bottle – Malibu, more's the torture – and choked down a glug. She coughed so hard it almost came straight back up. Instead, she snorted black mucus over her hand.

Mindlessly wiping it on her trousers, Harriet sat on the destroyed window display.

Faced with the fact that she was probably the only surviving member of her family, and that she had been perilously close to joining them all in the choir immortal, Harriet muttered the only phrase that accurately reflected the gravity of the situation:

"Fuck me ragged."

Simon is falling.

This is not in the plan.

Of all the things he had expected to be doing this week, falling off a cliff was low on the list.

Though, to be precise, he isn't exactly falling *off* a cliff – he's falling *beside* one. He hadn't been on it to begin with – he'd been above it, and then been dropped. Quite unreasonably. In fact, the whole situation was unreasonable. What had he done to deserve a smashy death on huge, slimy rocks?

Still. It could be worse.

He could have been burned alive in his own living room, or had his head lopped off. At least he's still alive.

Sighing, Simon resigns himself to his helplessness and waits patiently for a sudden and messy stop – or for someone to catch him.

At what point should he have said 'no'? This afternoon? Yesterday? Tuesday?

There is no escaping it; the answer is clear. Simon had made one fundamental mistake a week ago, whence all of the ensuing tortures, misfortunes and calamities had emanated.

He should never have answered the bloody door.

CHAPTER ONE

Simon Debovar had come to a conclusion: he hated other people. Not any specific other people; just everyone who wasn't him.

He hated their demands on his time. He hated how they made him wait behind them in queues; got in his way on the street; filled up the bus before he could get on it; asked him questions and then expected answers. But most of all, he hated how they smelled: sweaty and sweet and spicy.

Simon Debovar had two baths a day and never smelled of anything but clean, and that's exactly how everyone else should smell, in his opinion. Anything else was inconsiderate. And lazy. Most inconsiderate people were lazy and most lazy people were inconsiderate, in Simon's experience. And most people were one or the other. Usually both.

Having given up hope of finding a quiet corner of Edinburgh that he could have entirely to himself, Simon had decided to lock out the rest of the world and create his own kingdom: the Royal Burgh of 42 Queen's Drive ("just past the Post Office with the two oaks outside, if you hit the Shell garage you've gone too far", as it was known to the local pizza, Chinese, Indian and Thai restaurants).

For thirteen years, Simon had lived a hermit's life in the middle of one of Scotland's busiest, most throbbing metropolises. Of course, he had to have some communication with the outside world, but he kept it to a minimum. When delivery drivers or repairmen necessarily came round, he would hide upstairs and shout directions. Had any of them ever challenged him as to why he remained a floor above, he was prepared to feign illness and/or injury as an excuse. In fact, he enjoyed dreaming up a new ailment each time such a visit was expected: "Today I shall have a broken toe, caused when I dropped a small antique clock in the shape of an elephant on it whilst visiting my Auntie Agnes." He hadn't dropped his Auntie Agnes' clock, of course. He didn't have an Auntie Agnes.

His living family consisted of, to his knowledge, a distant cousin called George, who'd married an Australian and moved to Switzerland (why an Australian would want to live in Switzerland bewildered Simon, sometimes keeping him awake at night wondering what Switzerland might have that Australia lacked), another called Sabrina, a lesbian who lived in New York, and Great Aunt Harriet, who, despite seeing all her peers and most of the generations after her pass on, had stubbornly refused to shuffle off her mortal coil.

Fifteen years ago, the rest of Simon's family had been killed in a tragic, pudding-related accident.

A huge family reunion had been organised for the Debovar clan. Simon's mother came from an unusually small Irish Catholic family, so they had been invited, too. The meal had been a huge success and everyone was just about drunk enough to throw themselves onto the dance floor when dessert was served.

Tragically, the chef had overloaded the flambés with alcohol at Harriet's insistence. When he set the first one alight, the fumes in the air went up like the Hindenburg.

Luckily for them, Sabrina and George were outside, in the

back of George's car, being seventeen. George was a second cousin once removed on Simon's father's side, while Sabrina was a great niece to Simon's mother's mother – or something. Suffice to say that, had they not been interrupted by the explosion and gone on to procreate, the fruit of their union would not have had to worry about its eyes being overly close together. George had later confessed to Simon, at one of the funerals (he couldn't remember which), that it would have been Sabrina's first time with a boy, and that they had been at a fairly crucial stage when the building exploded.

Simon had wondered whether it was psychologically significant that an Irish Catholic girl had turned out a lesbian after her entire family was blown to pieces the first time she touched a penis.

George and Sabrina had been saved by their rampaging hormones. Simon found that oddly romantic. But then, Simon found a lot of things odd.

Harriet, on the other hand, had fancied a whisky with her dessert. When the waiter offered her a choice of what she called "cheap, dirty water", she had barged out of the hotel and across the road to the off license for a bottle of Lagavulin. She had barely put her purse away when the fireball burst, shattering both the window of the shop and her newly purchased bottle. It took a protracted letter writing campaign, but Harriet had eventually managed to make the chain's head office accept that, while she had paid for the bottle, having not yet picked it up she had not, in fact, taken ownership of it and that, as such, they were obliged to send her a replacement. They eventually sent her a case, just to make her stop.

Harriet had been saved by her refusal to drink cheap whisky and her determination not to go without it. Or, as she liked to describe it, by her high standards and a steadfast refusal to compromise.

Simon had stayed home to watch *Friends*. He didn't like

crowds. In the end, it had turned out to be a flashback episode, so he almost wished he'd gone, just for the hell of it.

Until the police arrived.

He sometimes wondered whether the officers had stood outside debating how to break the news to him.

"Son, we've got good news and bad news. The good news is: Christmas will be cheap this year…"

Fortunately for Simon, his mother's brief resuscitation in the ambulance had made her officially the last to die, helpfully leaving him as the main heir to most of the wills, including his inexplicably wealthy Uncle Marvin. Thus, Simon hadn't had to work a day since. He largely survived on interest from the stupidly large sum of money in his account, and if he ever ran a little low, he only needed to sell one of the hideous 'artefacts' Marvin had 'collected' throughout his 'archaeological' career. (Whenever Simon's father had discussed his brother-in-law, there was always a proliferation of implied quotation marks left dangling in the air.)

George, Sabrina and Harriet were the only people Simon had any sort of normal contact with, and it was mainly to ensure the safe passage of regular payments he had promised them all after The Explosion. It only seemed fair that, with only the four of them left, he should share the wealth. Without the need to earn money, Sabrina had opted for life as a poet. Harriet had retired a few years before The Explosion, so only George had decided on a traditional career – as a lawyer. He had once tried to explain to Simon that he just couldn't accept not earning his own keep, even if his salary was effectively just a top up on the significant monthly allowance Simon paid him. Simon couldn't understand why anyone would choose an office over the comfort of their own living room, but there were a lot of things about people that Simon didn't understand.

He was probably closest to understanding Harriet. His great aunt had a unique vision of the world. She imagined herself much like Jimmy Stewart in her favourite movie,

Harvey – bumbling around the screen effortlessly while chaos cavorted around him. In reality, she bumbled around chaotically while the world occasionally stopped to scratch its head in bemusement. Sometimes, it got a black eye for its trouble.

Of all the people in the world Simon almost liked, he almost liked Harriet the most.

Simon kept the necessity for anyone other than himself to be in the house to an absolute minimum. Food shopping had initially been a problem. To begin with, he had paid a local child to get some groceries for him once a week. He would use the same child for a few years at a time, until they became curious beyond his tolerance. When Tesco announced home shopping over the internet, Simon threw himself a small party with a bag of 50 mini sausage rolls and a bottle of Dr Pepper.

Then he bought a computer. By phone.

During these 13 years, Simon became something of a mythical figure amongst his neighbours. Nicknamed 'Herman', after Herman's Hermits, they saw him as a comical, disgruntled little gnome. Rumours spread that he had a rare skin disease, which prevented him from coming out into the sunlight. Others said that he was a vampire and, thanks to the imagination of 8-year-old Mikey McCormack, that he was half goat and didn't want anyone to see his hooves. The neighbourhood children could sometimes be heard taunting each other with cries of "Herman's going to get you" or "You're going to be goat food".

Suffice to say, Simon Debovar was not about to appear on the FBI's Ten Most Wanted list, unless the FBI actually wanted a slightly tubby, greying man with a penchant for Eggs Benedict and an allergy to other people.

Incidentally, Simon did suspect Harriet might be the 'Mozzarella Mugger' who'd been terrorising the suburbs of Melton Mowbray this last year. Apparently, there had been a rash of pensioners knocked unconscious by a sharp blow to the back of the head with a blunt object – possibly an umbrella or walking stick – who later woke up to find their noses stuffed full of Italian cheese. Harriet seemed a likely candidate. She lived in Melton Mowbray, owned both an umbrella and a walking stick, and abhorred old people, since they reminded her that she, herself, was old. There was also the fact that she constantly referred to her peers as "stinking old cheesebags" and had vowed one day to make them all suffer as she did. Simon wasn't sure how seriously she meant that, but she was almost as committed to the cause of antisocialism as he was, and he respected her geriatric nod in his direction. Were she slightly more antisocial, Simon might even ask her round for dinner. Of course, he wouldn't, because she might actually come, and then he'd have to buy a load of new stuff: another plate, another fork, another knife – the things people selfishly expected a person to own purely for times when they came to visit.

Simon secretly hoped Harriet was the Mozzarella Mugger of Melton Mowbray because he was a big fan of alliteration. He respected her choice of cheese because of this. Ideally, she probably would have gone for a more pungent nose filling, but she'd have had to move and resort to murder to make the 'Camembert Killer of Cambridge' work, and even Simon agreed that was extreme.

Besides, people only smelled worse after they died.

It was not so much a surprise, then, as cause for serious alarm when Simon was awoken from his mid-afternoon siesta (as opposed to his mid-morning, mid-evening and mid-bath siestas) by what seemed for all intents and purposes to be the ringing of his doorbell.

He sat bolt upright in bed, shook his head in an attempt to inject some clarity into his still dozy brain, yawned and stretched.

Of course he hadn't heard the doorbell.

The doorbell didn't work. Simon had had it disconnected ten years ago as a birthday present to himself. (He'd enjoyed awarding himself the 'no-bell' prize and briefly lamented having nobody with whom to share the joke.)

Thus, having logically decided the noise that had awoken him was nothing more than a lingering dream, Simon swung his feet out from under the covers, stood up to his full 5 foot 9 inches and stretched for the ceiling.

He nearly threw out a vertebra when the doorbell rang again.

There was no denying it this time – it was definitely the doorbell. Could doorbells repair themselves? He really had no idea how they worked.

Was there such a thing as a door-to-door doorbell repairman?

Every fibre of his being was screaming at him to stay quiet; to pretend not to be in, just as he always did.

But the doorbell had *rung*.

Unfortunately, he *had* to know why.

Thus, despite desperately wanting the unexpected doorbell fixer to go away, he crept down the stairs in his dressing gown, carefully avoiding the squeaky steps – numbers 8 and 11. Slowly and carefully, he placed a foot onto the hall carpet. It was soft and welcoming. He liked a soft carpet. The fashion for hardwood floors was inexplicable to him. Why would anyone choose a cold, hard, slippy floor over a soft, warm, lush carpet? Especially on cold winter mornings. He was definitely a comfy, soft carpet kind of guy. He'd chosen the hall one because its slightly toasted cream colour reminded him of Andrex puppies. Of course, that meant he'd at least once pondered how many puppies would have been needed to make it.

Placing his second foot on the carpet, Simon took a deep breath and steeled himself for the short but ninja-like creep to the door, to see what his tormentor looked like.

"Mr Debovar? Hello?"

Simon jumped like a startled butterfly at his name and

nearly fell back onto the stairs. They knew his *name*! What kind of trickery was this? Now, in a panic, Simon had to decide what to do, quickly. Quick decisions were not really his forte – so he did what came naturally.

"Go'way!" he grunted, hoping his local reputation would be enough to see off the interloper.

"I'm sorry?" the voice politely answered. "What was that?"

Definitely male. Simon couldn't decide whether that was a good thing or not. It might not be a *thing* at all. Either way...

"F'koff!" he grumbled, croakily. Surely nobody hung around after that. He could investigate the doorbell once the nuisance caller had gone.

"I'm sorry, Mr Debovar, did you say you have a cough? Perhaps I could offer you a sweet?"

This was not going well.

Simon did not take sweets from strangers.

He decided on a new tack – take the initiative. It was not something he was used to, but then he'd never had someone refuse to leave the front step before.

"Whadayouwant?" he splurted.

"I have a proposition for you, Mr Debovar."

Ah. A salesman. The world made sense again.

"I'm not buying," he called decisively, heading for the kitchen. He had some hazelnut coffee he was looking forward to trying this morning.

"Oh no, and I'm not selling. Quite the contrary, actually."

Simon stopped. What was the opposite of selling? Buying? How could he know what Simon had that he might want to buy? Unless he'd broken into his house during the night, had a good look around and then left everything, in order to come back the next day and purchase it legally?

No, that was ridiculous.

Did he want to buy Simon? The thought of a troupe of white slavers barging down his door made him slightly light-headed. He suddenly longed to return to the comfort of his bed, where there were no people to confuse him and doorbells didn't ring – exactly as they were supposed to not.

Wait a minute.

"How did you ring my doorbell?"

"I... pressed the button."

"That bell hasn't worked in ten years," Simon answered triumphantly. He even had a little 'Ah-hah!' to himself, in his head.

"It hasn't?" Pause. "Oh."

Simon heard what he thought was another, softer voice whispering.

"I'm sorry to have bothered you, Mr Debovar," the male voice finally said. "We'll come again tomorrow perhaps – or maybe Monday."

Footsteps faded away down the path, then the gate swung open and shut.

Simon was elated. Having accidentally stumbled across the right question to make the possible white slave trader go away, he could get on with breakfast undisturbed.

Later, when the elation had passed, he would try the doorbell, which persistently would not ring.

Around the corner, a tall, thin man in a white suit, with mismatched eyes, turned to a dark-haired young woman in black leather and said: "How was I supposed to know the bell didn't work? Who has a doorbell that isn't connected? If you ask me, that shouldn't count."

CHAPTER TWO

The letterbox rattled.

Not in a 'you've got mail' way; definitely in a 'somebody's at the door' way.

Having had a whole day (and two sleepless nights) to think of a plan for this occasion, Simon was much less panicked than he'd been on Saturday. He'd thought through his options and decided that he knew exactly how to handle the situation. So, with a slight tremble of nerves he put his plan into action:

He sat very, very still.

After a minute, the letterbox banged again. Simon reminded himself to keep calm. He focused on the coffee he was holding and watched the hypnotic little ripples in the surface caused by the tremors in his hand.

"Mr Debovar?"

Simon spilled coffee.

"Mr Debovar, I know you're there. Can we talk, please?"

Something was deeply wrong with the world. Because not only did the voice apparently *know* he was there – it was *female*! What the hell was going on? Nobody ever came to visit him! One insistent doorbell fixer was unlikely enough, but *two* visitors in *three* days? As far as Simon was concerned, it was End of Days.

In panic and disarray, Simon considered shouting "No, I'm not!" in response. Thankfully, he quickly realised how stupid that was. He did, however, need to do something.

"Mr Debovar? *Please?*"

It was a nice voice. Soft. Viscous. Like honey. It actually made him want to answer the door, which was odd. He never wanted to answer the door.

"Mr Debovar, I really do just want to talk to you. Could you please let me in? It's cold out here and I'm not wearing very much."

...

She *"wasn't wearing very much"*.

It had been a very long time since Simon had seen a woman in the flesh. It had been a long time since he'd seen anyone in the flesh. He'd seen many, many women on his computer screen, but in the *actual* flesh?

He needed to calm down and think. She had a nice voice, but that didn't mean she would be as attractive as she sounded. After all, that was how all those sex lines made money, wasn't it? Charging men to pleasure themselves to the sound of someone's granny.

But on the other hand, she *might* be gorgeous. She *sounded* gorgeous.

He had to know. Wait, he had a spyhole in his door! He could see her without her even knowing! Simon realised with a guilty pang that he was dangerously close to voyeurism, but quickly decided that one can hardly be a Peeping Tom when the person at whom one is peeping is standing on one's front doorstep. Thus reinforced, he crept slowly towards the door, feeling nausea, elation and arousal, but mostly terror.

Halfway there, the voice came again.

"Well?" It tickled his earlobes. "Are you going to open the door?"

Simon stopped for a moment. He smacked his dry lips together and wondered where all the moisture in his body had suddenly gone.

"Maybe."

With excruciating care, he crept the rest of the way to the door.

"I suppose 'maybe' is better than 'fuck off'," the voice teased.

Simon stopped an inch from the door. He hadn't told her to fuck off. He hadn't even tried "go away".

Suddenly, Simon remembered the half heard whisper of Saturday. All of his arousal turned to panic. They'd come back to get him with a honey trap! A brothel girl, riddled with diseases and haggard with the ravages of the sea! (For some reason, Simon always thought of slave traders as sailors.)

Deciding that seeing the potential harridan before opening the door was even more important now, he leaned towards the spyglass, breathing heavily. He was so nervous that he initially closed the wrong eye, giving him a close up view of the eggshell blue on his door. It needed a new coat.

Blinking to regain his equilibrium, Simon leaned forward again and peered through the spyglass. Nothing but black. Damn. Could these things break?

"Nah-ah," sang the voice, "if you want to see me, then I get to see you too."

Damn this conniving seductress and her obstructive finger!

"How do I know you are who you say you are?" Simon asked, nervously.

"I haven't said who I am."

It was a fair point.

"Well then, who are you?"

"My name is Lily," she answered, softly. "I want to talk to you."

"About what?" Simon was very far out of his depth. But he seemed to be getting somewhere.

"Something you have, that I want; that I *need*."

"What?"

"Why don't you open the door, Simon?"

Simon's legs were rubber. What now? He was clearly going to have to open the door if he ever wanted to get rid of her, and if he ever wanted to sleep through another night without fear of the doorbell. Of the few people who had ever tried to see Simon, none of them had shown the one quality he wasn't prepared for: persistence.

So, after more than a dozen years in isolation, Simon braced himself for his first sight of unfiltered sunlight. He unlocked the door, took off the chain, removed the doorstop and turned off the alarm. Putting his hand up to shade his eyes from the glare, he opened the door slowly to reveal... grey. A cloudy, miserable, nothing.

In the split second before his eyes came to land on the temptress's cleavage, Simon felt a sense of immense anti-climax. Surely on such a momentous day, the sun could have had the decency to shine. The disappointment passed as he took in the woman before him.

Her midnight black hair hung in loose ringlets around her delicate, pale face, teasingly caressing her shoulders. She appeared to be wearing no makeup, yet her skin was utterly flawless, and her deep, soulful eyes were dark in contrast. Her full lips formed a relaxed smile and what little matt black leather she wore served to cover those parts of her that public decency required. The rest of her that was on display looked so smooth and firm that Simon found himself battling an extreme desire to *lick* her.

"Hello," she said. "Isn't this nicer?"

He had to agree; it was nice. And no slave traders in sight – just this beautiful, friendly, smiling woman.

"So, what do you want?" he spluttered.

"May I come in? I'd much rather talk about it in your living room," she answered.

Simon realised he'd come too far already. Opening the door to a beautiful woman was one thing, but letting her in, that was entirely something else. Then again, she was utterly stunning, and Simon found his eyes wandering south again, down the line of her lily-white, delicate shoulder, lower to her cleavage, then straying towards her pert...

"Nipples!"

"No I wasn't!" Simon spat in instinctive defence. But when he looked up, he saw that Lily was as startled as he was. And had he thought about it, Simon would have realised the voice was coming from his left. And was male.

"Nipples!" it bellowed again. "You've got nipples! You're not allowed nipples!"

A tall, thin man strode towards them from the side of the garden. His slightly too large white suit and white-blonde, short hair gave him a ghostly look, heightened by the mismatched eyes that provided the only splash of colour on his angular face.

Simon stood frozen.

"Sorry Mr Debovar, I don't mean to interrupt, but she really isn't allowed nipples."

"Oh, come on," replied the woman, "that's such a technicality – they're tiny!"

"Well *I* can see them, and *he* can clearly see them, so they're big enough," replied the man. "Now *that* is a much more worthy disqualification than a broken doorbell!"

Simon realised that this was the slave trader, but was oddly unafraid of him. In fact, he seemed vaguely familiar, and now that Simon could see him, his voice was even more melodic than it had been through the door. He looked less like a slave trader than a pop star, actually. Which was something.

"Oh come on, it's not like I did it intentionally. I just stuck my chest out and they... appeared!" she argued.

"No, no, no," replied the man. "You have no nipples. You

have absolutely no need for nipples. Only women who have children need nipples."

"Men have nipples," Simon offered, wondering what the hell they were arguing about.

"Ha!" chirped the woman, pointing at him. "He's right!"

The man turned to Simon: "Purely decorative. You just don't look right without them." He turned back to the woman. "Which is hardly the point. You had them a minute ago and you're not allowed them and now it's my turn!"

Simon wondered why the man wanted a turn with Lily's nipples and concluded that he really wasn't following this conversation.

The two stood staring at each other, fuming, for a moment, until Simon broke the silence with a rather pathetic little "ahem". Man and woman both turned to look at him.

"Why don't you have nipples?" he asked. "And why did you make my doorbell ring? Or rather, how?" he asked the man, who was now slightly red about the cheeks.

"Ah, yes. I suppose we've rather blown that, haven't we?" answered the man. He looked at the woman, seemingly for confirmation of something, and then said, "OK, Mr Debovar, it's time to come clean. Can we please step inside?"

"First you have to tell me who you are," demanded Simon. He realised in passing that neither of them smelled of anything. He could smell grass, flowers from next door, rubbish bags from the pavement and exhaust fumes from passing cars, but no perfume, deodorant, body odour, cigarettes – nothing at all, not even soap. They were like a scent vacuum.

"OK," answered the woman. "My name is Lily. I'm a demon."

Simon looked to the man, hoping for a laugh or a rebuttal, but he just smiled serenely and said, "And my name is Daniel. I'm an angel."

Bloody hell.

A phone rang.

A rugged, good-looking man of about 40, with sandy brown hair, light stubble and the beginnings of distinguished wrinkles around his blue eyes answered it, "Pizza Pizzazz," as he had done for the last three years. Prior to that, he had answered it "Perfect Pizza" for about six years, and before that, "Pizza Pour Vous", in an ill-fated attempt to fuse Italian cuisine with French.

Prior to that, it was a chip shop.

"It's time," the woman on the other end of the phone told him, urgently.

"What time?" he replied, confused.

"They're here."

"Who are?"

"Who do you think?"

His face fell. For her to sound so grave, so serious, there was only one 'they'.

"Already? It's only been, what, 15 years?"

"Yes." Pause. "They're good."

"I thought he'd be a lot harder to find. I thought we had more *time*."

"I know. What are we going to do?"

"What choice do we have? Are they there now?"

"Yes."

"How long have they been there? Did he let them in?"

"Yes – I don't know, I just got home – I was shopping."

"Damn it. He may already have agreed a deal. We could be too late. How did we not see this coming?"

"I don't know."

"OK," he said. "I'm coming home. I'll close up."

"Luke?"

"What?"

"I'm scared. Really scared."

"I know. I am too. We'll be OK."

"..."

"Gabby?"

"I'm here."

"It'll be OK. I'm sure."

"No, you're not."

A long cold pause hung in the air.

"No. I'm not. But I'm not giving up, either."

———

Simon sat on his couch, staring across his living room at the pair of lunatics he'd just invited in. On reflection, he had absolutely no idea *why* he'd invited them in. In fact, he was fairly sure he could specifically remember deciding *not* to invite them in, but to lock the door as tightly as possible, run away back to his bed and hide under the duvet. Because anyone who comes to your door and tells you that they are an angel or a demon is clearly a very long way off their rocker.

And yet, here they sat in his living room: two of them. He'd invited them in, and even offered them tea. Thankfully, they'd declined, avoiding the need for him to explain that they'd have to share a cup.

"What's happening?" he finally asked. "I'm a little confused."

"Yes, that's normal, Mr Debovar. We apologise for any disorientation." The man smiled at Simon as if he was an idiot child struggling to understand something that was really very simple.

The woman smiled too. Her smile was nicer. It felt more real – more genuine. The man's smile was a formality; a handshake before a business meeting.

"Yes, but, why are you here?" asked Simon.

"Ah, yes, well, that's a good question. You see, we need

something from you, Mr Debovar. If you are happy to give us a chance, we'd like to explain," the man answered.

"No, sorry, I mean: why are you *here*?" Simon gestured around his living room. As always, it was immaculately tidy, as he preferred, but it definitely had two too many people in it for his liking.

"You invited us in, Simon," said the still-very-much-honey-voiced-and-rather-sexy-too woman. "Don't you remember?"

"Yes, I do," Simon answered, "but I also remember having no intention of doing that."

"Ah," said the man. "Of course. Sorry, that is probably our fault."

Simon searched the room with his eyes, looking for things he could defend himself with when the nutters inevitably got violent and tried to do *things* to him. There wasn't much. Besides the furniture, there was a table lamp, his laptop and the wooden clock he particularly liked. It was the only decoration he'd kept from when his parents had lived here. He hadn't wanted to be reminded of them every day, wherever he looked, but at the same time, a piece of them was... nice.

They'd bought the clock on their honeymoon in Australia. He'd always liked the texture and smell of the wood. The gentle, lulling *tick-tock* had often been the only sound when he'd read comics here as a boy. The mechanical heartbeat made him feel safe. It had been an easy decision to keep it. It also helped with the guilt he felt for getting rid of everything else and replacing it with other things he'd inherited or bought himself with his unearned wealth.

In fact, that was another thing: his favourite piece of furniture – his leather recliner with the cooler in the arms – was currently occupied by the strange man who'd somehow blagged his way in here, while Simon was sitting on the sofa. How had *that* happened?

Then the penny dropped and Simon realised what was going on.

"Bloody hell!" he cried, holding his hands up to protect his eyes. "You're hypnotists!"

That was the only way they could have made him do something so ridiculously rash. They'd invaded his mind as well as his house! There must be a law against that, surely. He'd definitely be writing to his MP if not. Messing about inside people's heads without their permission was just not on.

"Get out!" He leapt to his feet, still shading his eyes from them both. "Get out, get out!"

"Mr Debovar," the man said, slowly and gently, "calm down."

Simon calmed down. He calmly sat back down and calmly lowered his hands.

"Honey," the woman began, "there are things you need to know."

That was definitely true.

"First of all," she carried on, "we have this sort of... power, to make things happen that we want to happen. It's part of who we are. Sometimes, we use it a little too freely – or accidentally. Like today."

Brilliant. The hypnotists believed they had magic powers. Simon had a sinking feeling that they were going to be more difficult to get rid of than the plague of ants he'd suffered after spilling a bag of sugar down the back of his washing machine last summer. But he stayed calm.

Unnaturally calm.

Why was he so *calm*?

Wait...

"I think..." he began, but then trailed off, as he realised he had no idea what to say.

The woman – Lily – walked towards him. She reached for his face and he meekly allowed her to put her hands on his cheeks, cradling them like a wounded bird.

"I'm sorry, honey. I realise this has all been very difficult for you. Let me fix that."

And, in a moment, she fixed it – insofar as she put an explanation directly into his brain. And explained how she was doing it.

Simon understood.

And it was terrifying.

CHAPTER THREE

Simon raised his head and looked in the mirror. He splashed some water on his face to clear the remnants of the breakfast he'd just *calmly* deposited in the sink.

The woman had done something awful to him. She'd given him *knowledge* – much more than he wanted.

Simon had always been something of an optimistic atheist – unable to believe in an afterlife, but hopeful he was wrong. Now, he knew the truth. And it was not as he expected.

He took a few deep breaths, splashed some more water on his face, then calmly walked back downstairs to continue his discussion with the angel and the demon.

"OK, let me just make sure I understand this, please?" Simon asked, sipping at his cup of sweet, milky tea. It was his mother's cure-all and he still fell back on it in times of crisis.

"Of course, Mr Debovar," said Daniel.

Simon tried hard to decide where to begin – and finally opted for the beginning.

"So, there is a God and a Satan, but not as we know them, because they're actually... *siblings*? Is that the right word?"

"It'll do," Lily answered.

"And they caused the big bang, but by accident?"

"It was not entirely... deliberate, that's true," said Daniel. "They were *experimenting* and, well, you know the rest. They initially tried to contain it, but decided it would be more interesting to see what became of the mass of gas and rock."

"And they seeded planets with life?"

Simon hesitated, not sure if he was actually about to say the next sentence.

"Then *bet* on which would become dominant?"

Daniel gave a sombre nod in reply. Simon looked to Lily for confirmation. She shifted uncomfortably as she also nodded. He hoped that meant at least *one* of them realised how ridiculous it was.

"OK," Simon continued, "so God and Satan are brothers who created life on Earth as a competition – to see whose species would win. Has God won, since humans are the dominant species? And what was Satan's species? Dolphins?"

"Ah," said Lily, "that's where we need to pick up. You see, God and Satan are not brothers."

"You said they were," Simon protested.

"No, I said they were *siblings*."

"What?"

"They're brother and sister."

...

"What?"

Simon shook his head, manfully trying to make his brain wrap around this newest piece of mind-boggling information.

"Brother and sister," Daniel confirmed. "Male and female."

"Are you saying that women are actually... a different *species*?"

Despite the fact that it actually explained a great many things, a little voice in Simon's head was screaming: *"You can't say that!"*

"It's true," Lily confirmed. "Men and women are *very* different."

Quite an understatement, apparently.

It occurred to Simon that he was taking all of this a little bit too well, and that reminded him of the other piece of information Lily had given him – and *how* she'd given it.

"This power you have – how does that work? Are you... mind controlling me?"

Lily took a deep breath and looked at Daniel.

"Do you remember when I accidentally rang your doorbell?" the angel asked.

"You '*accidentally*' rang it? What were you *trying* to do?" asked Simon.

"Sorry, of course I meant to ring it. I mean I accidentally *made it* ring."

Simon was staring. He was sure he was being at least a little bit thick.

"What's the difference?" he asked.

"Well, that's the rub," Daniel answered. "You see, the bell only rang because I wanted it to."

This explained absolutely nothing, obviously.

"What he's trying to say is that we can make things happen, by *wanting* it," Lily added.

"Yes," said Daniel, "that's a good way to put it."

"Right," Simon answered, feeling a deep, mortal terror rising again. "How does that work?"

"Well, when Daniel pressed your doorbell, he wanted it to ring. In fact, he expected it to ring. So when he pressed it and it didn't instantly ring, he subconsciously *made* it ring," Lily explained.

"We don't actually have to consciously make something happen, sometimes we simply have to want it and, if we're not thinking about it, our subconscious does it for us."

Simon closed his eyes and leaned his head back. He tried to envisage this ability, and found himself totally unable to do so without injecting personalities into both the doorbell and Daniel's subconscious.

What he came up with was an image of the doorbell being pressed and doing nothing. Daniel's subconscious then popped in to ask what on earth was going on – he'd clearly pressed the doorbell and why was there no ringing? The doorbell replied by pointing out that, what with not having his wiring connected, there was nothing he could do about it. Daniel's subconscious then pointed out that he very much needed the doorbell to ring, and if it didn't do its job, he'd report it to his boss, and that, quite frankly, if the doorbell wanted to argue the laws of physics with the being who co-wrote them, he was welcome to. At this point, the doorbell realised he was better off just to do as he was asked, rather than risk being retrospectively erased from existence. So he rang.

This little imaginary play helped Simon just about get his head round the concept. Just about. He decided it was one of those things he was just never going to understand.

"OK," he said, despite the fact that it was patently anything but, "why are you here? I mean why did you come here?" he finished, realising he was repeating his earlier question.

The demon stood. "The reason we wanted to see you, Simon, is that you have something we both need."

"I do?"

"Yes."

"What?"

Lily looked down at her feet, as if she were contemplating a response. She looked back up at Simon with a wide grin.

"Your carpet."

Simon wasn't certain, but he didn't think 'carpet' was slang for anything. He'd heard of 'rug' and 'underlay' having other meanings...

"I'm sorry, I don't follow. What do you mean by 'carpet'?"

"Your carpet, Mr Debovar," Daniel said, slowly and deliberately lifting his feet up and down. "*This* carpet."

Simon looked down. Ironically, the carpet was actually a

big rug, but it happened to fit the living room so exactly that it looked like a laid carpet. It had intricate patterns and designs that Simon often found himself absorbed in, only to realise that he'd made himself late for a bath, or a nap. Which reminded him – he had no idea what time it was, but he really felt like he needed a wash.

"Why do an angel and a demon want my carpet?" he asked.

"Have you ever heard of a side bet?" Daniel asked.

"Yes," said Simon instinctively. He hadn't, but that hardly mattered. Unless lying to an angel was some sort of sin. In which case, maybe he should be paying more attention to these sorts of things now.

"Well, that's what this is," Daniel continued. "You see, chances are that, yet again, this world is going to end in a draw, like most of the others before them. Man and woman always eventually strike a balance – a side effect of making them need each other to breed. One sometimes dominates for a while – as man has done here, until recently – but eventually, it all evens out."

"So, when is the end? When does the bet finish?"

"Same as all the others, honey," Lily answered, "when the timer runs out. Or in your case, when the sun goes red giant and wipes out all life on the planet. If you make it that far. You've already done more damage to the planet than any of your predecessors."

"Also assuming they don't wipe themselves out arguing about which religion is *exactly* right..." Daniel shook his head at Lily with a smile and she nodded wistfully in reply.

"Well, surely it's Christianity, isn't it?" Simon asked. "That's the one with God and Satan."

"We only called them that for you," Lily answered. "To make it easier. *We* call them something equivalent to your words 'Mother' and 'Father'."

"Oh," Simon answered, feeling less sure of his ground again.

"Here's the crux," Daniel continued, drawing himself up expectantly. "This time, they decided not to accept a draw; this time, they wanted a guaranteed winner, one way or another. So they made a side bet, just in case: one that had to produce a victor. And your carpet is the final piece."

Simon looked back and forth between Lily and Daniel. Both looked expectantly, and silently, back at him.

"So, *why* do you want my carpet?"

"It's like this," said Lily, "my Mother and his Father left thirteen different objects around in the early days. Their side bet was that their own people would find more than the other's. His team has six and so does mine. We're standing on number thirteen."

Daniel bristled slightly, but carried on: "We've had the hardest time tracking this piece. You see, the Holy Rug of Djoser was supposed to have been buried with a great king over four thousand years ago. Except it seems that his counsellor, Imhotep, salvaged it as a memento for Djoser's eldest daughter."

"Imhotep?" Simon recognised the name. "The *Mummy*?"

Daniel looked blankly at Lily.

"He means the movies. They used his name," she explained.

"They use the names of their great historical figures for *movies*?" Daniel raised his eyebrows.

"Sorry," Simon apologised on behalf of... everybody.

"These men were responsible for the pyramids, Mr Debovar, one of the great wonders of your world. Imhotep was a genius – an architect, engineer and the father of early medicine."

"Oh," said Simon. "Cool."

"Anyway," Daniel shook his head, "forty years ago, after a

lengthy history where it had passed through the hands of uncounted archaeological dealers and millions had been paid for it, the Rug came into the possession of Professor Donald M. Flannery."

"Uncle Marvin!" Simon was pleased to hear something he understood.

"Indeed. And then, fifteen years ago, you inherited it from your uncle and laid it in your living room."

Simon felt a surge of panic and nausea, much like the sudden remembrance that he had forgotten to turn off the oven. He had spilled, amongst other things, red wine, tea and golden syrup on the priceless artefact that would decide the biggest wager in existence.

"I think I'm going to be sick again," he blurted, cupping a hand over his mouth. "Should I stay off it?" he mumbled through the hand, before removing it to speak again. "I mean, am I being blasphemous by walking on it?"

"Honey, a carpet that you can't walk on would be quite pointless," Lily answered.

Simon tentatively put his feet down on the carpet he had casually walked all over for years. He was exceptionally aware of how soft it felt on his soles. At least, he congratulated himself, he had had the good taste not to put it into storage like so many of the '*objets d'art*' Uncle Marvin had left him.

"What happens now?" he asked, conscientiously lifting both feet back onto the sofa. "You both got here at the same time. Is it a draw?"

"Not at all," Daniel answered, "Lily and I have been working together for some time. We both realised that we weren't going to find this easily, so we set some rules and agreed to cooperate."

"Basically," Lily finished, "we agreed not to use our powers to influence the outcome and to accept the choice of the owner of the Rug, when we found it."

"The *choice*?" Simon asked, a cold stab of deep dread

spreading through him.

"Indeed. Your choice," said Daniel.

"My choice?"

"Yes."

"What choice?"

"You have to decide who gets it," Lily answered.

"Gets what?" Simon squeaked, desperately hoping that the answer wouldn't be...

"The Rug," said Daniel.

...

Simon ran for the sink.

———

Simon walked slowly back from the bathroom. Again.

"I have to choose which of the two creators of the universe gets to 'win'?" Of all the things Simon couldn't believe he'd said this morning, he couldn't believe this one the most. "On what basis do I make that decision? I mean, I'm a good person... I think. I want to give it to the good guys. Who are the good guys?"

Simon sat on the couch, pleased to no longer have to attempt to retain his utterly failing sense of balance.

"Well, it isn't that simple," said Lily.

Of course not.

"Indeed," Daniel added. "You see, your conventions of good and bad don't really apply. Father and Mother are less 'Good and Bad' and more like 'Yin and Yang'."

"What?" Simon asked, for the umpteenth time that morning.

"There's no good or bad in this," said Lily, standing again, "there's just *different*. So basically, it's not an easy choice between right and wrong, I'm afraid. You're going to have to figure out who you like more."

Lily smiled at Simon. He was pretty sure he knew who he liked more.

"No he's not, and stop flirting with him, demon. Remember Mr Debovar, for all that she looks good on the outside, underneath she's a Barbie doll. No innies or outies," Daniel grumbled.

"I can have innies and outies if I want to," Lily snapped, defensively.

"But then you'd be using your powers, wouldn't you?" Daniel replied. "And I'd win by default."

At this stage Simon was fairly sure that biological incompatibilities would not be an issue. If she even touched him, he'd probably burst.

"This is what it comes down to," Daniel continued, authoritatively, "we will each make you an offer for the Rug. It will be up to you to decide which offer you prefer. Does that sound fair?"

"I suppose so," Simon answered, after a moment.

"Excellent," Daniel replied. "In that case, I think we will leave you for now, and come back tomorrow, if we may?"

Simon was sure he'd misheard that. It was inconceivable that these people had just dropped the biggest bomb in creation and were now going to leave him alone with it.

"You look like you could use some rest, honey," said Lily, soothingly. "And please don't worry, I really want you to get a good night's sleep tonight."

At that, angel and demon both raised up and gathered themselves to leave.

"Wait a minute!" Simon blurted out. "You're actually leaving?"

"Yes," Daniel answered. "Why?"

"*Why?*" Simon suddenly found himself swelling with emotions he hadn't had in many years. "You're *leaving*?! You tell me I have to decide the fate of the world and then... *leave?* What am I supposed to do *now?*"

"Well, Mr Debovar, if I were you, I'd have something to

eat and then get some rest. You look a little – what's the word – peaky," said Daniel.

Simon gawped at the pair. Then, realising he was standing on the carpet again, yelped and leapt upwards as if plugged into an electrical main. He landed, kneeling, back on the couch.

"Really, honey, it is a rug," Lily said, soothingly. "You can stand on it."

"I know," said Simon, apologetically. "But it just doesn't seem right. I feel like I'm walking on the Turin Shroud or something."

"Oh, don't be silly," she giggled. "The Turin Shroud is a fake."

That didn't help. However, Simon did notice that her breasts jiggled very pleasantly when she laughed and silently resolved to be funny in her company as often as possible.

"So, that's it?" Simon asked, pleadingly.

"Pretty much," she answered.

"Yes. As long as you are happy to agree that you will choose to give your living room carpet to the one of us whose offer is most attractive to you, we'll come back tomorrow to make our offers," said Daniel.

"I suppose so," answered Simon. "Do I have to choose straight away?"

"I honestly hadn't thought about it," Daniel admitted.

"Of course not, honey. We'll give you, say, overnight to think about it?" Lily answered.

Simon considered the gravity of what was being asked of him before giving the only answer he could think of.

"OK."

He had a horrible feeling it wouldn't be.

———

Once outside, the unexpected and largely unwelcome visitors

climbed into a black car that glistened like wet rubber, with tinted windows and no visible marque.

"Must you keep calling him 'honey'? You sound like a prostitute."

Daniel touched the steering wheel and the car's engine purred into life.

"You think calling him 'Mr Debovar' is better?" she snarked.

"I was being respectful."

"You were being patronising."

"At least I'm not trying to seduce him with false hopes of grubby sex."

"It's not *my* fault he's heterosexual and... deprived," she smiled triumphantly. "And I'm *hot*."

Daniel sighed and looked heavenwards. This would all be over soon.

The sooner the better.

CHAPTER FOUR

That night, Simon took a particularly long bath, even by his standards. He had to reheat it twice. When he finally got into bed, near midnight, he was so exhausted and the bed so particularly comfortable and welcoming that he was asleep almost before his head hit the pillow.

Thus, he was utterly unaware of the conversation happening in his back garden, just an hour later.

"What do you mean you've never broken into a house before? You've been in and out of this house a million times," Gabby whispered, flicking her blonde, elfin hair out of her eyes.

Luke was carefully appraising the kitchen window, deciding whether he would fit through it. Even after all this time, he still found it hard to be annoyed at her when he looked in her eyes. She seemed to have only grown more elegant, more graceful with time. Sadly, she was not *actually* any more graceful than she'd ever been. And she was being annoying.

"That's because he's ordered *pizza*! The door is open and he's expecting me. And he stays upstairs."

"Well, surely you've seen it done on TV."

"I've seen the A-Team save an African country with a van and a garage full of crap, but that doesn't make me *MacGyver*."

"I liked him better in Stargate."

"What? Who?"

"MacGyver. Well, thingy double-barrel Anderson – you know, the actor. He was much better looking in Stargate.

...

"Sorry. I'm rambling. I'm nervous."

"I know," Luke said, as calmly as he could manage. "Can we concentrate on this, please?"

Gabby kissed him on the cheek, apologetically.

What happened next was... unusual.

While it was not inconceivable that Simon did not hear the breaking of his kitchen window, it was at least unlikely that he should have slept through the resounding thud of a man falling off his kitchen counter via a plate, a glass and a pizza cutter.

"Shh!" Gabby whispered helpfully, frantically waving her arms as if to blow the sound waves away.

Luke was afraid to move, convinced that any further noise would be guaranteed to alert Debovar to his presence. He waited for the sound of a creaking bed; of footsteps on the floor above. And all the while he tried not to think about the pain in his side, where his landing hand had punched the air from his lungs.

But the house was silent, except for a light snore.

Astonished, he gave Gabby a tentative 'thumbs up'. She began to climb in after him.

"No, wait!" he hissed, pointing at the back door.

"Oh," she mouthed, carefully extracting herself from the window pane.

Luke quietly opened the door. She stepped out of the dark into the faint green light of the microwave clock.

"Oh, you've broken his plate. Maybe we should leave him some money to replace it?"

Luke stared; still amazed that she could be so thoughtful and utterly inappropriate at the same time.

"Let's just get on with this, OK? If we survive, I'll buy him a tea set."

"OK," she answered, clearly hurt by his tone.

It was going to be a long night.

———

Coming downstairs after his morning bath, Simon wondered what time Daniel and Lily would return. As difficult as it was to accept, he was almost looking forward to it. Firstly, they had been polite, friendly and honest, as far as he could tell. And they didn't stink.

Although, now that Simon thought about it, he had a vague notion that Lily had smelled ever so slightly of vanilla ice cream by the time she left. He wondered briefly whether the mixture of food and sexuality in his subconscious was something to worry about.

Secondly, it was actually sort of exciting. The world was much more interesting than he had ever realised. And he was, albeit through no action of his own, right at the heart of something very important. He was living in 'interesting times'. If they ever made a biography of his life, now, it would definitely be on the SyFy channel. In fact, he'd probably be something of an internet hero. He wondered who else in the world might already know what he had learned.

He didn't wonder for long, though, as two things happened in quick succession that caused him to very nearly fall the rest of the way down the stairs.

Firstly, the doorbell rang. Having been afraid of hearing it for much of the weekend, Simon was instinctively jarred by the noise – which, of course, meant that Daniel and Lily were back.

Under other circumstances, Simon would have been

preparing to pay attention to the smell when he opened the door, to confirm his suspicion about Lily. However, now that he could see into the living room, he was too busy trying to comprehend what he could see. Or rather, what he couldn't see.

Simon's living room carpet was so out of style with the rest of his furnishings that it looked ridiculously out of place, but something about it had always drawn Simon to it and made him feel comfortable.

Looking now at bare boards, he felt a very long way from comfortable.

———

Across the road, two very tired carpet thieves were debating what to do next.

"Can it please be sleep?" Gabby asked, piteously.

"I don't know. If we have a shot of espresso each, once an hour, we could just stay up all day and not need to sleep," said Luke.

"That's not actually good for us, you know. What we should really do is get some sleep now – staying up all night is bad for our bodies."

"If this all goes wrong, our bodies are not going to be much use to anyone. Other than, perhaps, as fertiliser."

"What are they going to fertilise?"

"Exactly."

Luke paused before asking, "So, three sugars?"

———

Simon was struggling to regain his balance for long enough to finish walking down the stairs. After trying and failing a few times, he decided the best option was to sit down exactly where he was and call for assistance.

"Help," he yipped, quietly.

Thankfully, the ears he hoped would hear him were substantially more receptive than the most sensitive human ears, even on their best day, when they could hear an individual pin drop in an industrial pin-making factory.

Thus, Simon's front door flew past him and landed just inside the kitchen. Which was less unexpected than one might imagine, all things considered.

In the place where the door used to be stood the familiar and strangely reassuring figures of Daniel and Lily. Both looked concerned, yet confused as to why they had just removed the door somewhat forcibly from its hinges to rescue a man who, at this point, looked in danger of nothing more serious than a nasty carpet burn on his backside.

"What is it?" Lily asked, stepping into the house. "What's wrong?"

The best Simon could manage was a feeble "Eep!" and to point, meekly, toward the living room.

Taking this as a fairly clear indication that something was amiss in that area, and that this was an invitation to both of them to enter and see for themselves what had gone wrong (which was, in fact, exactly what Simon had been trying to convey), the angel and demon stepped into the archway between the hall and living room.

"Ah," said Daniel, matter-of-factly.

"Bollocks," said Lily.

The two turned to Simon, who was fervently wishing to wake up and find himself in bed, three days ago.

Several lifetimes seemed to pass before anyone moved. It was, unsurprisingly, Daniel who spoke first.

"Is it safe to assume that you did *not* spend last evening lifting the Rug, cleaning it and rolling it up neatly for us?"

"Ess," squeaked Simon, nodding.

"Right," the angel answered.

Simon felt himself starting to cry.

"It's OK, honey," said Lily, starting toward him.

"It is *not*," said Daniel, coldly.

Simon knew things were bad now. But at least Lily was stroking him. And he hadn't exploded. That was good.

———

Having made Simon a cup of milky tea and transported him to the sofa – which was a good foot further to the left than usual – Lily and Daniel had taken seats at opposite sides of the room. Again. Daniel stared intensely at the floorboards. Lily stared equally intensely at him.

After much contemplation of exactly what could have gone wrong, and after some time spent wondering what exactly the creators of the universe would do to the person who managed to lose the one thing in the world that they most wanted not to be lost, Simon finally managed to place the vast majority of his wits back where they belonged. There were one or two, he was sure, that had been scared away forever. Not really knowing where to start, he defaulted to instinct.

"Hello," he half whispered. "Sorry, I just realised, I haven't said hello. Very rude. Thank you for the tea."

Daniel glanced up at Lily, before replying. "Welcome back, Mr Debovar. I'm delighted you've rejoined us. Is there any chance that you can tell us what happened to your carpet?"

"It's not here," Simon replied.

"Yes, we'd realised that," he answered.

"I was asleep," Simon offered, pointing half-heartedly at the ceiling.

"I'm sorry, Mr Debovar," said Daniel, standing, "are you saying that you, who wakes up before his alarm every morning, slept soundly through the noise of someone completely rearranging your living room and removing your carpet?"

"Ah." It was Lily.

Daniel jerked his head toward her with a severity that Simon found disturbing.

"'Ah' what?"

"I think that's exactly what happened," Lily answered.

Daniel softened at this. "Really?"

Simon realised that the disbelief in Daniel's voice betrayed the fact that he really had thought Simon was hiding something, which rather unsettled him even further.

"I really wanted Simon to get a good night's sleep, so he'd be clear headed for today and, well..." she trailed off.

"And he was getting a good night's sleep under your influence, meaning nothing short of violent evisceration was going to wake him up," Daniel finished for her.

"Pretty much."

Simon was afraid that Daniel had considered violent evisceration an option a moment ago.

Another long silence ensued, during which Daniel occasionally sighed, before walking to the window, looking out for a while, and then sitting back down again. Lily sat back in her chair, playing with a strand of hair and looking at Daniel with something between irritation and guilt.

Finally, her patience wore out. "I presume it's not out the window, then?"

"Pardon?" Daniel looked confused.

"Well, since the obvious thing to do next is to start looking for the damned thing, I assume you've been discounting 'out the window' before we start looking somewhere else."

Daniel's face changed again. It was scary.

"Firstly, I'm not the one who put Sleeping Beauty out for the count and lost the Rug in the first place. Secondly, it's not a damned thing unless you get your hands on it; until then, it's just as likely to be a blessed thing!"

They seethed at each other. Simon imagined there would have been some major sexual tension between these two, had they been predisposed to having sex.

"Excuse me," Simon finally interjected. "You said neither of you was good or bad."

"Yes," said Daniel, visibly trying to calm down. "So?"

"Well, it's just that you said it would be damned if she got it, and blessed if you got it. Doesn't that mean she's bad and you're good?" Considering how wary he now was of the angel, Simon wasn't sure whether to hope he was right or not.

"No, honey," Lily answered. "Blessed and damned mean exactly the same thing – just from different perspectives."

"I don't understand," said Simon. "How can damned not be bad?"

"Think of it this way: haven't you ever had sex that was so sensuous, so absorbing, so completely mind-blowing that you described it as 'damned good'?"

Simon looked at her piteously, desperately trying not to give away that he hadn't, that he was now thinking about it with her, and that his penis was way ahead of him.

"Think who you're talking to," said Daniel.

Lily paused. "OK, haven't you ever had a buttery that was perfectly toasted, with just the right amount of butter and a perfect layer of melting Golden Syrup, so that when it disintegrated on your tongue, you thought 'damn, that's good'?"

"Oh, yes!" Simon was glad to be back on familiar territory.

"Damned is just a little more 'earthy' than blessed. Mother has a slightly more sensual notion of life. She doesn't have the celestial broom up her arse that his boss has." Lily nodded her head dismissively at Daniel.

Daniel rolled his eyes in a way that suggested he had had this discussion before. Simon was leaning quite heavily towards handing the carpet over in the sensual direction of Lily. If he ever got it back.

"Wait a minute!" Simon said. "Doesn't the fact that the carpet has been stolen from me mean that I am no longer the owner? And doesn't that mean that I don't have to make the decision anymore?"

He felt a sudden leap of elation as the burden lifted from him.

"Sadly not," answered Daniel. "Yesterday, when you agreed to give the Rug to one of us, we all officially entered into a contract which is binding for as long as we all remain alive or, in our case, exist."

Simon tried to swallow, but his tongue was huge.

"It's OK, we're not allowed to kill you," Lily reassured him, "unless you refuse to honour the contract."

The fact that they were not 'allowed' to kill him did not give Simon any peace of mind whatsoever, as it confirmed his suspicion that Daniel, at least, had certainly planned to kill him earlier, if not now.

"How do I honour the contract if I don't have the carpet to give you?"

"Well," said Daniel, "you'll have to get it back."

"Oh." Simon tried very hard not to cry again. "How do I do that?"

"First we have to find out where it is," said Daniel. "Thankfully, as the owner, you have certain rights regarding that information; rights which we, as seekers of the Rug, do not have. Therefore, all you need to do is find out who stole the Rug, find out where it is now and get it from them."

Simon resisted repeating himself, but there was no other way to say it:

"How do I do that?"

———

The caffeine was kicking in nicely. Gabby sat scribbling circles furiously on a sheet of newspaper, while Luke paced the floor like an expectant father.

"What will they do now?" Gabby asked, nervously.

"I don't know."

"Well, what would you do?"

"I don't know, I'd..." Luke trailed off, realising he knew exactly what he'd do. "Oh Hell." He closed his eyes as he said the name. "Faunt."

"They're not allowed to go to Faunt! It's in the Rules," Gabby protested.

"No, they're not," Luke agreed, "But *he* is."

———

"What, like letters, you mean?"

"No, Mr Debovar, 'Faunt', as in 'of information', sort of," Daniel answered. "Faunt is the only person who will definitely know where the carpet is."

"How?" asked Simon.

"It's... quite complicated. Faunt was empowered by a triptychal naming curse to know everything."

Lily groaned, frustrated. "I can't believe you're explaining the naming magic. Why does he need to know *that*?"

Of course, now that Simon knew there was something else to know, it transpired that he did, in fact, want to know what a triptychal naming curse was. It was the first time in a long time Simon had actually wanted to hear about something he knew nothing about.

"A *what* curse?"

Daniel smiled smugly.

"Well," Daniel began, "Faunt was once just a man who angered the wrong woman. In retaliation, she cursed him with a triptychal naming spell. She gave him the name 'Faunt'. Imbued in that name were three aspects. The first, and the one you know about, was from the word 'fount', as in 'fount of information', meaning he would know virtually everything. The second part was from the name 'Faust', the literary character who made a deal with 'the Devil', and lost his soul into the bargain. The third part... I'm going to let you see for yourself."

"Triptychal naming spells are quite common, as curses go," Lily added. "Names have a lot of power, and triptychal names have more than others."

"Oh," said Simon, who now very much wished he hadn't asked, because either he didn't really understand or he did understand and the world was even more terrifying than it had been five minutes ago.

As always, in time of stress, Simon fell back on his internal reserves. "I think I should eat something – it's nearly 11 o'clock."

"It's OK, honey," Lily stroked his arm. "We'll eat on the way to the airport."

CHAPTER FIVE

Having a credit card underwritten by the Bank of Creation means no fare is too big or too last minute. It also means first class. After all, who would travel economy if they usually flew with their own wings? Assuming they actually had wings, of course. Simon was taking nothing for granted.

Having never travelled first class before, he was sort of looking forward to the idea. Sort of, in that, of course, it was the least unpleasant and terrifying thing about making him leave his house for the first time in thirteen years. To do so, having given him all of an hour's warning to dress and prepare himself, and without actually telling him where they were going, seemed to Simon not a little unfair.

To help take his mind off it, Lily had nipples again.

In his old life, Simon had particularly hated driving. He'd often ranted at cars that had clearly been delivered without indicators. Taxis and buses also aggravated him, but the people he hated the most were, far and away, the stupid, suicidal pedestrians who regularly tried new and imaginative ways to throw themselves under his car.

He was relatively sure he'd only avoided jail by staying home.

As he sat in the back of Daniel and Lily's car – a huge, sleek black thing with leather seats and a stereo system that looked capable of everything short of performing oral sex on the driver (and there was a suspicious looking attachment that he hadn't worked out yet) – Simon looked out the tinted windows at the world passing by. He was acutely aware that he was on the outside of a giant curved ball. At any instant, he was convinced, gravity would cease to function and the car would lift right off the road and fall away up into space, beneath them. Thinking about it for too long made Simon feel gassy.

He decided to take his mind off it by concentrating on the matter at hand.

"Where are you taking me?" he asked.

"To the airport," Lily answered, chirpily.

Simon wondered if there was a level of Hell where people were tortured by overly literal demons. ("Yes I *can* stop it now, but surely what you want to know is am I *going* to stop it now?") But then he remembered that Hell wasn't actually his notion of Hell at all, which made him wonder what happened to bad people.

Surely it wasn't a case of all men going to Heaven and all women going to Hell? Then again, since Simon's idea of Heaven, prior to meeting Lily, would have been going somewhere entirely alone but for his TV and a bottomless jar of olives, it occurred to him that maybe there wasn't an ideal afterlife for everyone.

"I meant where are we going on the plane?"

"Oh, we can't tell you that," she answered, equally brightly.

"Why not?"

"Because you're not allowed to know."

"Know what?"

"Where we're going."

"But surely I'll know when we get there."

The conversation was making his head hurt.

"Actually, no, you won't," she countered.

"How?" Simon asked, growing a little frustrated that his seemingly obvious line of questioning appeared to be moving forward at a rate akin to that of a heavily drugged snail. "How is it possible for me to get on a plane, fly somewhere, get off at an airport and not know where I am?"

"Because we don't *want* you to," replied Lily.

...

The novelty was wearing off.

———

Some distance away, a man stared into a pool of water, tracing the ripples. The candlelight that brightened the room flickered on the tiny waves, and sparkled in his eyes. A chair brushed idly against his leg.

They should arrive this evening.

It was a stroke of luck that the Rug had been taken. It gave him an opportunity. There was only one thing he was going to ask for and, under the circumstances, they certainly couldn't call it unreasonable. And if they couldn't get it, it wouldn't be the end of the world.

Faunt pulled the plug out of the sink, dried his hands on a dishtowel and made himself a hot chocolate.

———

As they entered Edinburgh airport, Simon looked up at the departure screens, determined to memorise every flight. It helped take his mind off the fact that he was suddenly surrounded by a heaving mass of sweaty, sickly-perfumed, farty humanity. He felt dizzy at the sudden olfactory offensive.

14:30: Malaga; 14:35: Barcelona; 14:50: New York; 15:00: Amsterdam.

Simon memorised all the flights he could. As they queued for the check in, he looked forward to see which desk they were lined up in front of. Oddly, unlike all the other desks, he couldn't make out the destination name on the board. It was either slightly blurry, slightly obscured or misspelled – or all three.

Simon tried in vain to force his eyes to focus on the illegible name. He realised he was really quite irritated with his companions, and currently felt that, even if they did smell of occasional ice cream, they were showing the utmost in bad manners by dragging him out of his house and refusing to tell him where he was going. As such, he decided not to acknowledge their presence for a while. He was secretly irked by the knowledge that even if they noticed, they probably wouldn't care.

———

Outside, a taxi was arriving at the airport with two very tired passengers, one large and very hastily packed bag and a taxi driver who had spent much of the trip wondering if his passengers had accidentally been let out on their own.

"How will we know where they're going?" asked Gabby.

"We *know* where they're going!" answered Luke.

"Yes but, are you really sure? I mean, what if we're on the wrong flight?"

"If we're on the wrong flight, then we're going where we know they're going to end up at some point. Because they're flying *away* from the Rug, which means they don't know where it is. So, unless they know something we don't know, they have to go to Faunt. What we have to do is find out what Faunt's price is, then stop them paying it."

"Why don't we just ask him not to give it to them?" Gabby asked.

"He'd have to have a good reason for that or else he'd be considered to be interfering," Luke answered.

"Oh, yeah. I guess he wouldn't want that," she conceded.

There was silence for a moment as both realised the taxi was not moving. The driver had been watching the couple in the mirror, while holding the steering wheel straight. Which would have been fine, but for the roundabout they were now parked on top of.

"We'll walk from here," said Luke, handing over a £20 note. "Keep the change."

The two climbed out and, ignoring the stares from the surrounding drivers, walked the rest of the way into the airport, firstly by navigating the roundabout somewhat better than the taxi had.

Gabby changed the subject. "It's been too long since we made love."

Luke stopped mid-stride.

"What?"

"Well, it has. I mean, that's one of the biggest benefits of being alive, and yet here we are going, what is it now, five days?"

"We've been busy..."

"Well, yeah, but if we fail... Shouldn't we be doing it as much as we can, now?"

Faced with such a stunningly rational argument, Luke had little choice but to concede that yes, just in case the world was going to end, they should have as much sex as possible.

"Next chance we get," he smiled. "Promise."

Gabby broke into a grin and skipped towards the terminal. Luke stalked after her, thanking the universe again for this fabulous, kooky woman.

———

Simon woke up in an unfamiliar place. His first realisation was that his mouth was terribly dry. His second was that he had drool on his cheek. The third, that he was lying on someone's lap.

Knowing that the moment he sat up, a little wet pool of drool would be visible on Lily's skirt, he decided to stay where he was for a little while. Besides, it wasn't a bad place to be, all things considered.

From where he was, Simon could make out very little. He was in the back of another car with dark leather seats. The engine was barely audible and the ride was impossibly smooth.

Something was odd, though, and he took a moment to work it out, since his perception was somewhat skewed. Daniel and Lily were talking, but as hard as he focused, Simon couldn't understand them. It was gobbledygook. He sat upright with a jolt, embarrassing puddles be damned.

"Hoi!" Simon spat out. "What are we doing?"

"Well," Daniel replied calmly, "I am driving the car, Lily was, until a moment ago, serving as your pillow, and you were sleeping."

Only as he sat up had Simon realised Daniel was on the wrong side of the car. Or rather, not the right side of the car.

"Where are we?" Simon demanded, determined to plough ahead with his irritation before the realisation of who he was castigating sank in or the embarrassment about the drool caught up.

"Mr Debovar, I can certainly keep telling you that you're not allowed to know where we're going or, for that matter, where we are, but I'm fairly certain both of us will get tired of hearing it fairly soon."

With the dawning realisation that he had gone through an entire plane journey to somewhere, then been transported from the plane to this car without being able to remember any of it, Simon felt a sudden flip of nausea grab his stomach, shake it up and down a bit and poke him in the eye.

Then he realised he'd missed first class.

He rolled down the window and leaned out for some fresh air.

It was a less good idea than it had seemed, as he looked straight down a sheer cliff face to azure water below.

Simon couldn't recall exactly what came out of his mouth next, but the extremely sudden halting of the car and the look on Lily's face made him fairly certain it must have been something like: "Aggggggggghhhhhhh!"

Daniel slowly and deliberately stopped the car, removed the keys, turned around and, leaning his arms on the backs of the seats, said quietly: "Please don't do that."

"But, but..." Simon stuttered pathetically. Unable to form much in the way of actual language at this point, he pointed out the window and said, "Cliff!"

"Yes, honey, it's a cliff. You often find them on the sides of mountains." Lily smiled at him like a baby who had excitedly discovered his own head.

The calmness of the pair finally cracked Simon. Considering he hadn't had anyone to shout at for a very long time, there was thirteen years of bubbling irritation about the shortcomings of the human race looking for a way out.

"Is that supposed to be *funny*? You show up at my home, threaten me with the wrath of *two* gods, drag me to who knows where, knock me out on the way, and then when I am *disturbed* by the discovery that I'm halfway up a mountain with a sheer drop below, you *patronise* me?"

Everything was, momentarily, perfectly still.

Simon felt a warm ocean breeze drift in the car window to kiss the back of his neck. In the middle distance, seagulls were circling, arguing about who saw which fish first. Far below, the ocean waves lapped lazily against the cliffs, bobbing back and forth to an unheard bass rhythm.

It was beautiful. And calm.

"Feel better?" Lily asked, stroking his hair.

"Yes, I think so," said Simon, breathing more slowly.

"Marvellous," said Daniel, turning around to start the engine. "Let's carry on, then."

"Any chance of a drink of water?" Simon asked. "I've got a really dry mouth."

———

About five hundred yards back down the road, pulled into a small passing place where they had quickly concealed themselves when the car ahead came to a screeching halt, Gabby and Luke were doing a loose impression of slightly confused tourists.

"What if they see us?" Gabby asked.

"They won't. They won't even look behind them."

"Why not?"

"Because they're absolutely certain that nobody in the world could or would have any reason to be following them, and even if they did, they could hardly have anything to worry about, considering who they are. So, really, they wouldn't care if there *was* someone following them."

"OK. So, basically, they're not worried about it because, to be honest, what could anyone who caught up with them do anyway?"

"Correct."

"Luke?"

"Uh huh?"

"What *are* we going to do if we catch up with them?"

CHAPTER SIX

After a long, winding drive that was both breathtaking and nauseating for Simon, Daniel pulled the car up to a massive, wrought iron, decorative gate in a beautiful stone archway that had been completely hidden from view until they were right on top of it.

Many people had driven past it and thought they glimpsed something unusual in their rear view mirrors, but the close proximity of a two thousand foot drop to a watery death tends to focus the driver's mind on what's happening in front of them rather than strange gates that appear carved into the side of the mountain behind them.

The gates slowly swung open. Only then did Simon notice that there was an extremely tall, thin man, dressed in clothes the sandy-reddish colour of the mountainside, pulling them open.

"He's expecting you," the giant said as the car passed through.

"Of course," said Daniel, out his open window.

The car proceeded slowly up a carved stone tunnel, lit on both sides by torches that somehow left no scorch marks on the stone above them and didn't fill the tunnel with smoke. It was warm and inviting.

As the car bumped its way along the path, Lily offered Simon another drink of water. He took it gratefully. The dusty roads had kept his throat dry and it was, whether of its own quality or his thirst, the best water he'd ever tasted.

The car turned a final bend and the tunnel opened up into what was, effectively, a large front drive, carved completely inside the mountain. It was a half dome, the flat side of which faced them with what, under other circumstances, would have looked like a quaint little country cottage. It had a rounded wooden door with wrought iron studs, a wooden-framed window and a proliferation of plants and flowers in baskets, including a healthy ivy growing up the front. However, despite having been designed to *look* like it was made of stone bricks, the front was carved from solid rock.

They were looking at a cottage... in the heart of a mountain.

"I have a question," said Simon.

"Is it 'Where are we?'" asked Daniel.

"No." He had genuinely given up hope of that being answered.

"Shoot," said Lily.

"How do plants grow in here, where there's no sunlight? And how did those torches not give off smoke? And how is it so warm inside a mountain?" Simon paused. "Sorry, that's actually three questions, isn't it?"

"But only one answer," replied Daniel. "Because to those who have power and wealth, only information has value."

Oh, good. Another cryptic answer.

Daniel strode purposefully up to the door, but, instead of knocking, simply turned and said to Lily, "Come on."

Lily rolled her eyes and hurried Simon along to the door, where the three of them stood resolutely not knocking. Simon noticed there was, in fact, no knocker, which seemed an odd omission amongst the other iron door furniture.

"Come on..." said Daniel again, but this time, seemingly, to nobody.

"Who are you talking to?" asked Simon.

"He's waiting for Faunt to let us in," Lily explained.

"Wouldn't it help if he knew we were here?" Simon asked.

"He does, Mr Debovar. That's rather the point. He knows we're here and he knows what we want. The only question is what he might want from you."

"*Me?* I don't have anything valuable."

"Well, until yesterday, you had the Holy Rug of Djoser," Daniel said, in his condescending tone. "So it's safe to say that perhaps you don't know the exact value of everything you have."

It was a fair point. He'd sold quite a lot of the stuff he inherited, but there was still a lock up full of things he didn't know what to do with. Simon decided to shut up until something happened.

The door opened. A dishevelled, bohemian man wearing oversized pinstripe trousers drawn tight with a belt stood in the doorway. His white shirt was rolled up at the sleeves and the front hung open revealing a wiry, downy body. His feet were bare, and he had a shock of unkempt, over long hair that stood out at impossible angles. His stylish, round rimmed glasses looked like they might dive off at any second, but somehow still clung to his lean face. Faunt was odd-looking, but didn't strike Simon as the mythical creature he'd been led to expect.

"What kept you?" Daniel asked, clearly relieved to see him.

"Mr Debovar wasn't finished asking questions," Faunt replied, "and it would have been rude to interrupt him. Please come in."

Simon followed Daniel and Lily in the door, walking past

Faunt to do so. He noticed a faint odour from their host as he passed. It reminded him of forests.

"It's pine," whispered Faunt just behind him.

Simon stumbled forward. Daniel had said that Faunt knew everything, but not that he was a mind reader.

"I'm not, as such," said Faunt, as the four turned a corner into a candlelit, arched room, decorated in a sort of medieval style: wooden table; wooden stools; stone floor with some straw strewn around it. At one end, however, underneath a very rustic wooden kitchen counter, was a modern washer dryer, next to a *huge* double-door fridge. There was also a faint scraping noise, which seemed to be coming from everywhere.

"Because I like it," Faunt said, answering Simon's next unspoken question. "It's cosy, but convenient."

"Faunt," interrupted Daniel, "as a courtesy to the group, it would be nice if you would allow Mr Debovar to ask his questions out loud."

Faunt stopped and looked studiously at the angel.

"You don't always have to be the centre of attention, Daniel."

Daniel's face dropped. Faunt smiled benevolently.

Simon liked him immensely.

———

A short while later, the four sat around the wooden kitchen table, Faunt with a goblet of mead, Daniel with a gin and tonic, Lily with a pint of Guinness and Simon with a cup of Assam tea.

"So, Faunt," said Daniel, "you know why we're here and there is presumably something you want from Mr Debovar."

"Good lord, Daniel," replied Faunt. "Don't you know it's rude to cut straight to business? I don't get many social visitors you know, especially not as interesting as you three. A little 'schmoozing' would not go amiss."

"Listen, Accursed..." Daniel stopped mid flow thanks to the sharp pain in his leg; the result of a stiff kick from Lily, who had until now said very little.

Faunt turned to Daniel and smiled. "She wishes you would learn that, sometimes, the best thing is to allow the conversation to flow naturally." Then lifted his glass and said, "Cheers."

Lily raised hers in return.

Daniel stood up and limped out of the room, taking his drink with him.

Faunt turned back to Simon, who intended to say nothing whatsoever unless asked a direct question.

"So, Simon, the answer to the big question is this: I know everything that *is*, but not anything that *will be*. I know what you are thinking now, and I know what you have thought before now. When you think about something new, I'll know that. But I cannot predict what you will do when you have no time to think; reactions based on instinct, or decisions made in the heat of the moment."

Simon stopped sipping his tea. "Oh," he said, deciding to be very careful what he thought about Lily while they were both here. Of course, then Faunt knew he was thinking about not thinking about Lily, which made him think about her even more.

"Relax," said Faunt, "it's a common reaction. The moment people hear that I know what they're thinking, they immediately think of the things they don't want me to know. I already know them all and I'm very discreet."

Simon wasn't sure if he felt better or worse.

"Can I tempt you with Yahtzee?" their host asked cheerily.

Lily smiled. Simon wondered if it was possible for his life to get any weirder.

———

Luke and Gabby were hanging around the gate looking decidedly conspicuous.

"Oh, this is ridiculous," said Gabby. "How do we stop two of the hordes who..."

Luke grabbed Gabby firmly by both arms, pulled her up towards him and kissed her, deeply.

It took her mind off the problem for a moment.

As they separated, Luke answered, "By being in the right place at the right time to take advantage of the right thing."

"What does that mean?"

"It means if we have any chance at all, we need to be where they are."

"That's not a plan," came a voice from behind them, making them both jump in alarm. "That's... the opposite of a plan."

The gatekeeper stepped towards the bars, a shadow against the flickering light on the stone behind him.

"Follow them and hope something happens? That's not great."

"Well, what do *you* suggest?" Luke challenged him.

"That's not really my job, is it?" he replied.

"I take it he knows we're here?" asked Luke.

"Of course," said the gatekeeper. "He says to drive up the hill a few miles to the next village. The hotel there has a few rooms. He said to say: 'I agree. Have as much as you can. You never know.' Does that mean anything to you?"

Gabby turned a vivid shade of purple.

"I'll take that as a 'yes'," the giant smiled.

Luke turned to Gabby and shrugged his shoulders in resignation.

"OK," said Luke, turning back to the gatekeeper. "Thanks..."

"Bob," said Bob.

"Thanks, Bob," said Gabby, in a way she hoped belied her utter mortification at the knowledge that not only did Faunt know how they were planning to spend the evening, but Bob probably did too.

"Oh!" Bob shouted after them as they got back on their scooters, "He says get some sleep! Too much caffeine is bad for you!"

———

After four games of Yahtzee and three cups of tea, Simon got up the courage to speak a little more than just to answer questions.

"Erm, Mr Faunt? Do you play any other games? I mean, I assume Trivial Pursuit is out, but what about Scrabble? Or chess?"

"Both no good. I can't lose. In Scrabble, I always know what letters you have, I know what the best word is from my own letters, I know what letter I have in my hand inside the bag – for you, it would be like fighting Muhammed Ali blind-folded. Chess – same problem. I know all possible moves, including yours. I know the best move to make at all times. I know what you're most likely to do next.

"With dice, I have no idea. I don't know what numbers are going to come up. I know the best use of the numbers, but even that comes down to a gamble against what the dice produce next. I could play the perfect game of Yahtzee and still lose."

Faunt paused and smiled beatifically at Simon. "It's bliss. There is very little in the world that a man who knows every-thing appreciates more than being beaten. And for that oppor-tunity, I thank you both."

He raised his drink again, and Lily raised hers in return. She seemed very natural in this environment, whereas Daniel had not reappeared since walking off in a strop several hours before.

In the ensuing silence, Simon realised that, again, he could hear a slight scraping. Then he noticed one of the things it was coming from – the stool Daniel had been sitting on earlier was halfway across the floor towards the washing machine.

"Excuse me, but is it my imagination or is that stool moving?" Simon asked.

"Oh yes," said Faunt, "all the furniture does when it's not in use."

"Mmm," Lily replied, "teleporters?"

"Bloody nuisance they are," said Faunt. "It's the only way to keep them out."

Simon felt like he'd asked a bigger question than he intended to. Again. "Did you say 'teleporters'?" he asked Lily.

"Yep."

Simon took less time than usual to assimilate this piece of terrifying information.

"So," Simon replied, "why the moving furniture?"

"Ah, well," said Faunt. "The problem with teleporters is that they need to know the layout where they're teleporting, or they could materialize in a table. They can't teleport into anywhere things are moving around, just in case. So I had a very clever woman cast a little spell for me to have moving furniture. For every person prepared to trade for information, there are three who will try to take it by force.

"Of course, they wouldn't have much luck since I would know they were coming, when they were going to appear and what their plan was, but all the same, blood is difficult to clean out, you know? And it leaves an icky, irony smell about the place."

"OK," Simon said. It really was quite astounding what his mind was now prepared to accept without a Mexican wave of exploding brain cells.

"Ah," Faunt said, "I've reminded you that you'd quite like a bath, haven't I? And I would like some sleep. Simon, you're in the room at the top of the stairs on the left. A bath has been drawn for you in the en-suite. Lily, I was going to let you have the downstairs room, but Daniel has flopped off in there, so you'll have to have the other upstairs room, to the right. You'll find everything you need in there too – I had them moved."

"You're very kind," she said, nodding her head slightly in appreciation.

As she and Simon headed up the stairs, Simon allowed himself a flickering notion of her sneaking into his room in the night and the idea made him smile.

"You never know your luck!" shouted Faunt from the kitchen. Simon hoped Lily thought he was talking to her.

Probably not.

CHAPTER SEVEN

Faunt had to be the most considerate host on Earth. Simon was luxuriating in a mammoth bath with candles that gave off the sweet, light aroma of vanilla, with a hint of cinnamon. The bath itself was filled with rose petals, which Simon thought was classy, even if he was becoming slightly concerned for his masculinity.

There was a robe waiting for him, which he had grabbed a quick feel of before getting in – he trusted that it only *felt* like it was made of kittens. He was torn between sinking into the bath for longer or getting out just to snuggle into that robe and lounge on the bed, which he was certain had freshly washed Egyptian cotton sheets and would be just the right softness and length for him to get an idyllic night's sleep.

Faunt made Hugh Hefner look low rent. Hell, he made Hollywood look low rent.

The way things were going, he knew that he would wake up in the morning to a perfect cup of tea and some perfectly toasted butteries.

He felt not a single ache or discomfort anywhere in his body. It was as if someone had melted his insides into a comfy mess, then poured him into a bath full of yum.

Of course, the half bottle of Gran Reserva Rioja that he'd got through while he soaked had helped.

Simon's relaxed physical state was very much at odds with his mental state, however. Despite having engaged a function of his brain he hadn't previously been aware of – the 'fuck it' button – Simon was still desperately grasping for some form of perspective on everything. The fact that the world was not even remotely as banal as he had once imagined was actually something of a relief. He had little appetite for sharing the planet with the mass and throng of human chaos of which each imagined themself the most important thing in their worlds.

Now, he had met genuinely interesting people. Who *were* important.

Daniel, for all his posturing, seemed to have depth. The fact that he had a large pool of actually quite fascinating knowledge made him interesting, if patronising. It was also quite apparent that the angel's politeness was entirely born out of Simon's unearned importance to him.

Lily, Simon had very clear feelings about. He would like to feel her. She was sexy, sensuous and deliciously nice to him. But he had to bear in mind the probability that her niceties – and their implications – were just bribery.

Faunt, Simon just liked. As far as he could tell, he wanted nothing from him, so far, more than company. Having eschewed it for an age, Simon had been reminded of something long forgotten: *good* company was an absolute pleasure, and a person so thoughtful, obliging and pleasant was someone Simon could see himself spending a lot of time with. *If* he was invited, of course.

Simon wondered, as he poured another glass of wine, if perhaps the reason he'd locked himself away was because, in some way, he'd realised he was living in the wrong place. Perhaps he'd been *meant* to live amongst angels and demons and... accursed.

The thought of belonging somewhere was alien, but he was warming to it.

————

In another bed, not far away, Gabby lay awake. Just an hour ago, she and Luke had collapsed, exhausted, into bed, comforting each other with the unspoken reassurances of small caresses. For fifteen years they'd lived like this, having known each other for an eternity.

It had been a difficult adjustment, which came naturally to neither of them. But once they got used to their new life, and to each other, they quickly came to appreciate new pleasures. She loved Luke deeply, and not just because he was the only other person who could truly understand her and appreciate the world in the way she did.

Luke was putting on a brave face – trying to hide the fear – but she could see it. She felt it too. Neither of them knew how they were going to stop this thing from happening. But, lying next to him, stroking his chest and watching him sleep, she knew they had to try.

What else could they do?

————

Bob, unlike Simon, was not at all comfortable. Mostly because he was lying on a lumpy old mattress on a rocky shelf, inside a small room carved into the wall, just inside Faunt's gates.

How lucky the spider crossing the ceiling above him was. It might spend its life toiling away repetitively, spinning webs and eating flies, but at least it didn't know that its existence was completely pointless.

In another life, Bob had been a passably successful thief. His 6'7" frame did not lend itself to climbing in windows or crawling through ventilation shafts, but he had other skills that compensated.

Unfortunately, one night, he broke into the wrong home.

Antonio Calderon was an immortal – a legendary statesman and womaniser from northern Spain. Like many of his kind, he'd lived longer than he could remember and found that mere existence was too... mundane. In search of something, anything, to make him *feel*, he experimented with extreme pastimes. To his surprise, the one that gave him the greatest pleasure was sadism.

Bob could not help but cry out when he saw what the Spaniard was doing to the young man in the cage. But that was all he managed to do. Despite having almost a foot's advantage in height, the giant was quickly overpowered by the inhumanly quick torturer. Within minutes of entering the room, Bob was gagged and chained to the wall.

His initial panicked disbelief, his unwavering certainty that someone would come for him, faded as he listened to Calderon work. The screams were at first unbearable. Later, Bob was grateful that they drowned out the other sounds.

When the boy finally closed his eyes for the last time, Bob took his place in the cage.

Each day, he faded in and out of consciousness. Calderon was careful to keep him alive, but only just.

The Spaniard also liked port. And when he drank, he talked. He talked about fantastic creatures and impossible people, including a man who knew "the answer to everything". Bob listened.

After weeks – maybe months – the drunken Calderon left a sliver of metal in the thief's leg one night before passing out in a chair.

The main skill Bob had brought to thievery was his earlier training as a locksmith. He used the shard to free himself, and easily subdued his unconscious tormentor. Realising he could not kill the beast, but unable to leave him alive, Bob conceived of a way to use Calderon's immortality against him.

Tossing and turning on a slab of stone, Bob knew his bed was still infinitely more comfortable than Calderon's resting place – inside a supporting beam of one of Europe's longest bridges.

He trusted the boredom would be even worse, now.

Bob was no longer the man who had entered that apartment. Desperate for a way to reconnect with his life, he'd gone looking for the "man who knew everything". He would never have found him, but that Faunt knew he was looking, and found him interesting.

Bob had been prepared to swap anything for the answer to the question that now dragged at his soul: he needed to know the purpose of life.

Finding out that he was simply supposed to enjoy it had been an oddly liberating answer, rendered bittersweet by the price: that he spend the next decade acting as Faunt's servant.

At least there was the occasional game of Yahtzee to lighten things up.

Faunt smiled to himself, perusing the thoughts of the three who remained awake along with him. He *did* like Simon; he was a little jealous of Gabrielle; and he knew he was doing the best thing for Bob.

That certainty helped him to relax. He crossed his hooves, placed his head on the straw and closed his eyes.

CHAPTER EIGHT

The next morning, Simon woke rested and refreshed.

In fact, he felt reinvigorated, as if gently roused from a half-waking dream by a Listerine wash to the brain. He was wide awake, alert, thinking clearly, and ready to face the very strange world.

He had somehow had another contender for the most restful night of his life. Long used to waking up stiff and sluggish in the morning and waiting until his muscles decided they were prepared to move comfortably enough to make coffee and breakfast, this sensation of waking up awake was extremely pleasant.

He liked it so much that as he wandered down the stairs, happily wrapped in his big, white bathrobe, he wondered what he might be able to do to become a permanent resident chez Faunt.

"It's the pine," said a slightly muffled, nasal voice, followed by what sounded a lot like someone sucking on the end of a cigar.

This was strange, because the only other living thing Simon could see appeared to be a small deer at the bottom of the stairs, standing on wobbly little twig legs. With everything that had happened, the otherwise intriguing appearance of Bambi didn't even strike him as worth wondering about. It explained the straw, though.

In fact, as he searched the bottom of the stairs and their surrounds for the source of the answer to his question (which he had assumed was Faunt), he almost didn't look at the deer at all.

Except, of course, that its head appeared to be on fire. On closer inspection, it quickly became clear to Simon that the deer was not, in fact, spontaneously combusting but was in fact sucking on a fat cigar.

This definitely qualified as weird enough for further investigation.

"Yeah, it's a bitch," the deer said, through partially gritted teeth, "but I'm sort of used to it."

There are things life can prepare you for and things they cannot. On this scale, a mind-reading, talking deer with a cigar may not rank quite as highly on the unprepared scale as, say, discovering that your carpet is the key to existence, but still...

As such, Simon pedalling backwards and screaming like a particularly timid small girl was perhaps not unreasonable. Treading on the hem of his dressing gown – simultaneously pulling it open at the front and ending any chance of him staying upright – he tumbled backwards, cracking his head on the steps just hard enough to put him back to sleep.

———

As he came round, finding himself staring at the same ceiling he'd awoken to that morning, Simon could have been forgiven for assuming he'd had an odd dream about meeting a highly unlikely small animal and collapsing in a heap. The evidence, however, refused to play along: the smell of cigar smoke and the severe pounding at the back of his head meant either the dream had been real, or he was having a stroke. All things considered, he hoped it was the first thing.

"It's the third part," he heard someone say, "of the naming curse. I spend midnight to noon as a fawn."

"Oh," Simon answered. "OK." It really wasn't.

"It was a pain to begin with. Using these legs is like walking drunk across custard. I won't go into all the adjustments I've had to make, but suffice to say Bob helps a lot. He carried you back up here. I hope you don't mind."

Of all the things Simon might have minded, being carried to bed like a wedding day bride by a surly giant was low on his list today. Slowly, like the Titanic groaning its way from the ocean bed, Simon lifted his head. Seeing Faunt, indeed still a small deer, but with a shorter cigar stub than before, brought the reality of the situation crashing home to him and subconsciously took smoked venison off the menu for the rest of his life.

"I had to give you some painkillers, they're the best available. I'd have just had Lily sort you out but, actually, I wanted a word with you alone. I hope that's OK. They should work pretty quickly."

True enough, someone had turned down the volume in Simon's head a little bit already.

"Daniel and Lily told you that there are rules," Faunt said, matter-of-factly.

Simon began to nod, then decided he preferred keeping his head still and gave a simple, "Yeah," instead.

"I know everything," Faunt continued, his hooves clicking on the tiled floor beside the bed, "but that doesn't mean I can tell you everything. We all have to abide by the Rules."

Simon's stomach flip-flopped for the umpteenth time in a few days. Faunt looked contemplative as he spat out his cigar and stomped it out with a hoof.

"I'm going to tell you the price for the answer to your question this morning. Lily and Daniel won't like it, but I promise

71

you, it is not unfair. In fact, under the circumstances, it is an extremely reasonable price. They still won't like it.

"But I couldn't live with myself if I didn't at least give you a little bit of advice first. It's generic but, trust me, you'll appreciate it eventually."

"OK," Simon said, again.

"Those who help you are not always your friends; those who oppose you are not always your enemies."

Simon let the words roll around in the silence for a while. After some thought, he finally asked, "What?"

"Sorry kid, that's the most I can give you."

Simon's headache was coming back.

———

After breakfast, during which Simon did indeed glut himself on butteries, Faunt invited him to his study. In keeping with the rest of the cottage, it was a huge, stone-walled cave of a room with a peat-burning fire at its heart. Three walls were lined with a menagerie of brightly-coloured leather-bound books, which seemed to breathe and stretch on the shelves.

The remaining wall was decorated with reverential paintings of some very ordinary looking people. There was a young soldier, an Oriental man and a woman in Victorian dress standing next to a man in what seemed to Simon to be roughly 1960s-style clothes. On closer inspection, the paintings all had brass plaques on them. Simon was standing closest to the soldier, whose plaque read: 'Sergeant Michael Edward Hicks, World War II'.

"Excuse me," Simon asked, as he caught himself a chair to sit on, "who are these people?"

"Ah," said Faunt. "These are some of the most important people of the last 200 years."

"Really?" asked Simon, who felt he really should have heard of them if they were that important.

"Oh yes," said Faunt. "Take that young man: Mickey Hicks – ended World War II."

"Ended it?" Simon asked. "How can one person end a war?"

"By cutting off the snake's head."

Simon didn't remember there being snakes in World War II. In fact, the only story he could think of with snakes had something to do with Cleopatra, who he was absolutely sure was dead by the Forties.

"He shot Hitler. Blew the back of his head right off."

"Really?" Simon asked. "I thought nobody knew for sure if Hitler was even dead."

"That's because a few seconds after Michael pulled the trigger, his platoon were blown up. Every one of them was killed. But he'd already fired the bullet."

"Wow.

"So who's that then?" Simon asked, pointing to the man and woman.

"Mary Shelley and Bill Kowalski. She wrote Frankenstein, he ended the Cuban missile crisis."

Simon knew fine well there was a big gap between those two things.

"It's a little-known fact that on the final day of the crisis, JKF had decided to bomb Cuba, which would have ignited a devastating nuclear war. Kowalski had been reading Frankenstein and was giving an impassioned account of the book's warning against man playing God to a fellow White House janitor. Kennedy was passing and heard the conversation. It made him think again."

Simon was beginning to see a pattern. "Right. And him?"

"He is the biggest of them all," said Faunt. "The perfectly incompetent Doctor Xian Chu.

"During his training as a medical student, he found himself stuck in an elevator with a pregnant, claustrophobic woman, who panicked and went into labour."

"And he delivered the baby?"

"Nope. He completely botched it. Mother and baby both died. But the baby would have been Kim Hum So, the most brutal military commander in Chinese history. Under his leadership, the Chinese army would have staged a coup, reignited the nuclear arms race and conquered or laid waste to much of Asia by the end of the 20th century."

Something about this last story bothered Simon and, surprisingly, it didn't take him long to work out what it was.

"Hang on, you said you couldn't see the future. And that didn't even happen. How could you know what *would* have happened to that baby?"

"Excellent!" said Faunt, almost clicking his hooves together as he stood abruptly upright. "Excellent question! You're absolutely right; I can't see the future – especially not alternate futures."

Faunt lowered his head slightly and smiled conspiratorially.

"But I know a woman who can."

———

Bob had spent a lot of time doing things for other people in the last few years. It was not something that came naturally to him. Being a thief required a natural proclivity to dismissing the needs and desires of others fairly casually – particularly their desire not to have their homes broken into and their things stolen.

What he had gradually discovered while working for Faunt was that he sort of enjoyed it. Having spent most of his adult life taking things from others for his own benefit, it turned out that Bob actually managed to find some pleasure and contentment in doing things for other people. Not a lot; but some.

Initially, in Faunt's service, he had tried to plan for his own future by stealing small trinkets. Occasionally, he'd take something that appeared both odd and pointless enough that it must have some kind of inherent value beyond his understanding. He'd hide it in a hastily dug safe in his room by the gate.

The next morning, it was always gone. Trying to steal from a man who always knew what you'd stolen and where you'd put it was something of an exercise in futility. Still, it was something to do. When the novelty of waking up each morning just to see if maybe this was the morning his treasure would still be there had worn off, he'd finally resigned himself to an immediate future of making the best hot chocolate possible and discreetly clearing up deer droppings. Having done the latter already this morning, he was now focused on the former.

"Hi there," said Lily, entering the kitchen. "How are you this morning?"

Bob stopped mid pour. How was he? It had been a while since anyone had asked. Now, here was a very attractive young woman, or at least what appeared to be a very attractive young woman, smelling rather deliciously of jasmine, he noticed, asking after his wellbeing.

"Well," Bob replied, "I spend half my time fetching and carrying for a small deer and the rest between looking after the front gate, doing housework and playing Yahtzee."

"But how *are* you?" Lily asked again, frowning slightly at his answer.

"Not sure," said Bob. "Ask Faunt."

"Are you unhappy?" she asked.

"Wouldn't you be? I'm a slave."

"Are you?"

This irritated Bob. It seemed so obvious that he was, that he didn't understand why she was asking him such a pointless question. Perhaps she was a bit slow.

"Well, I do everything I'm told to do and I can't leave. What would you call it?"

"Interesting," Lily replied, leadingly.

"Is it?"

"Isn't it?"

Bob had already lost patience with this line of conversation. He sighed and returned to the hot chocolate, turning his back on the annoyingly inquisitive demon.

"I'm taking these to the study for Faunt and Mr Debovar. Would you like one?" he asked.

"Would *you* like one?"

Bob stopped again. This was becoming annoying. He turned to Lily, wishing he didn't know fine well that she could turn him into a gelatinous puddle with a thought, because he really wanted to throw things at her.

"Why are you bothering me?" he asked through tight lips.

"Am I bothering you?" she replied innocently. "I was just making conversation."

"Well, please don't," he answered, again turning his back and picking up the two full cups.

"What would you like me to do, instead?"

Had Bob been able to jump a few seconds into the future, see the results of his next decision and leap back to advise himself on the best course of action, he would have said that while the cups did make a satisfying 'thunk' as he slammed them both back down on the counter, the flying hot chocolate which accompanied the gesture was possibly not worth it, all things considered. Sadly bereft of time travelling talent, Bob's little temper tantrum left him with two shoulders dripping with warm, brown liquid, and a splattering of metaphorical egg all over his face. At this point in time, the only thing that could have made him feel any worse would have been if the annoying demon had been stupid enough to say something like...

"You probably didn't want to do that."

Anger has a tipping point. A person can only take so much before they hit a pressure valve, which opens and releases the excess build up. Were this process visible, Bob would have had multitudes of steam coming out of various orifices. He eventually reached a moment of perfect calm and turned slowly to his tormentor.

"No. Not really."

Lily was still smiling sweetly at him, as though they had just spent five minutes discussing the comparative merits of puppies and kittens.

"Can I ask you something?" she asked.

Bob considered for a moment whether there was any way he could stop her.

"Why not?"

"When you came here, were you happy?"

"No, not very."

"And what did you want when you came here?"

"Answers."

"To what?"

"Everything."

"Did you get them?"

"Yes."

"And did they make you happy?"

"No. Life is pointless."

"So you were unhappy."

"Yes."

"And you still are?"

"Yes."

"When *will* you be happy?"

"When I get the hell out of this place!"

"Why?"

"So I can do whatever I want."

"And you're looking forward to that?"

"Of course!"

"So working for Faunt has given you something to look *forward* to? A time when you will be happy again?"

...

A domino fell over in Bob's head.

Lily smiled sweetly back at him. At least he knew why now. He smiled back.

"I didn't... understand." Bob's world view had gone somewhat askew.

"I'll make some more hot chocolate if you'd like to get changed," offered Bob's new friend. "I'm very good at it."

He was happy to let her.

————

"Come in," called Faunt, just before Daniel knocked on the study door. He turned to Simon and smiled. "You'd think it would get old, but wait 'til you see his face."

The door opened in a seriously disgruntled manner. How Daniel managed to actually make the door itself seem so utterly dischuffed with having being knocked on *after* the knocker had already received a reply was a matter of interest to Simon. It reminded him how much he didn't want to annoy someone who could make a slab of wood looked pissed off.

Daniel entered, scowling. Faunt grinned.

"Good morning Faunt. Mr Debovar. I trust everyone slept well?"

"We did, thank you," answered Faunt. "Have a seat. Lily is making hot chocolate and will be with us shortly. Should I ask her to make you one?"

Daniel looked at a nearby armchair, which promptly shuffled towards him. "No, thank you," he said, sitting down. "I'd rather we could just get to business, if you don't mind."

"He never lets up, does he?" asked Lily, entering with the hot chocolates on a tray. "Years I've been trying to get him to relax. I'm not sure he's capable."

Daniel sighed and leaned back in his chair.

Lily handed Simon a mug. As she reached down to put a

mug in front of Faunt, on the floor, he reached up a hoof to touch her hand.

"Thank you. That was kind," he said pointedly.

"You're welcome. I'm glad to be able to repay your hospitality."

It seemed an awfully intense exchange over a hot chocolate, Simon noted. Then he tasted it.

"Wow," he said. "He's right; this is wonderful. Thanks."

Lily smiled. "You're welcome, honey. I'm glad you like it." She took a seat in a nearby chair and drank from her own mug.

"So," Daniel began. "As you know, Faunt, Mr Debovar is the rightful owner of the Holy Rug of Djoser. It was recently stolen from him after he agreed to give it to either Lily or me. He needs to retrieve the Rug in order to fulfil his part of our agreement. In order to do that, he needs to know where it is. What price would you charge for that information?"

Faunt stopped lapping at his mug and looked up at Daniel. "You know fine well I can't answer that," he chastised.

It was clear from Daniel's expression that he was not used to being rebuffed – particularly not by a deer with a chocolate beard.

"I can't tell you anything about the Rug and I can't offer you a price for information about it. It's not yours."

Lily and Daniel both turned to look at Simon, who suddenly felt like a young boy who'd accidentally wandered into his father's business meeting with a lolly in one hand and his penis in the other.

"What?" he asked.

"Honey, we need you to ask Faunt the price for the information on your carpet."

"Oh. OK." He turned to Faunt, who had returned to his mug.

"Mr Faunt, how much will it cost for you to tell me where my carpet is, please?"

Faunt looked up at Simon, breathed deeply and stood up to his full two and a half foot height.

"I want my wife back."

...

Daniel was first to break the stunned silence.

"We're not a dating service."

"And you know we're not allowed to make people act against their wills either, right?" added Lily. It was the closest Simon had seen her to being rattled since they'd met.

"I do," Faunt answered casually. "But she is, I think, being kept against her will. What I want you to do, Simon, is free her, so that she can choose whether to come back to me or not."

Simon had two completely different sinking feelings. One: he was being asked to perform some kind of Rambo rescue mission to the deepest jungle, killing guerillas with ad hoc weapons made from bamboo and chewing gum. Two: Faunt had said "I think". The second was more terrifying than the first.

"You '*think*' she's being held against her will? Why don't you know?"

"You really are much sharper than you give yourself credit for, Simon," replied the deer.

"Crap, I hadn't even thought of that," Lily added. "Why don't you know?"

Faunt turned to Daniel. "Would you like to explain it, since you've already figured it out?"

Daniel sighed. He was being tossed a bone. But it also meant he knew where Faunt's wife was.

"She's with Priest?"

"Correct. As far as I know."

Lily's face fell. She was definitely rattled. Simon's sphincter hit DEFCON-1.

If he was supposed to rescue Faunt's wife from a priest who made Lily look like someone had just violently murdered her puppy, he'd rather stay home, all things considered.

"Right, I'm leaving," he said, standing up abruptly and making for the door.

It was Faunt's voice that stopped him.

"No, Simon, you're not. I'm really sorry, but you're not. If you don't get the Rug back and give it to one of these two, they can't finish their jobs. If they can't finish their jobs, they'll both be punished. And the only way to avoid that would be for you to be dead, so that they can declare the contract null and void. If you leave, they pretty much *have* to kill you."

Simon could feel tears welling up.

"Again, I'm truly sorry. But you should know, it's not a jungle rescue mission and there will be no guerillas. It's actually a very nice island holiday resort, I understand."

The tears stopped.

"It's a what?"

"Priest's Island," Daniel answered, "is a beautiful location. It is said to be the inspiration for most of man's traditional images of Heaven."

"But it's got a prison?"

"Not that I know of," Daniel answered. "But there could be one, I suppose."

Simon was getting that exasperated feeling again. There was information here to which he was the only one in the room who was not privy.

"Would someone please just tell me why Mrs Faunt is being held against her will and why none of you seem to have much information about this priest and his bloody island?"

"Good Simon; very good," said Faunt. His hitherto encouraging words felt a lot more patronising than they had previously. Maybe supernatural types weren't that much better than real people after all, pleasant aromas notwithstanding.

Lily stood up and crossed the room to Simon.

"The answer to both questions is because of Priest. If you

sit down, I'll explain."

"All of it? No stupid riddles or literal answers?"

"All of it, I promise."

Simon retrieved his chair from behind Faunt and sat, but left it further away from the others than it had been previously. He hoped he was conveying the fact that he was prepared to walk out in a serious huff at any moment. Well, as well as he could in a room with one person who knew fine well that he wouldn't and two others whose determination to kill him before he reached the door was the main reason why not.

"Priest is The Exception," Lily began.

"To what?"

"To everything. Laws. Physics. Everything. He did a deal with Mother and Father a long time ago. Rules don't apply to him. Which is why Faunt doesn't know for certain anything about what's happening on his island. And why we can't come with you."

"Right. Excellent. Well, that's brilliant."

"There's more."

Of course there was more. Every time Simon was absolutely sure things couldn't get any worse, there was more.

"Priest has an incredible effect on women. They can't resist him. He's like living chocolate. If he wants a woman, he gets her. For as long as he wants her."

"And Mrs Faunt is his latest woman?"

Faunt half snorted and half laughed. It was an odd sound for a deer.

"Latest?" he said, raising his eyebrows – well, the furry bits of his face above his eyes where he should have had eyebrows. "Not by a long way. By the best estimate I can make, there's probably something like 300 women currently on Priest's Island. He picks them up as and when he fancies one and just keeps them all there so that he can have whichever one he wants when he wants her.

"Oh, and my wife's name is Cassandra, by the way. She

would object quite strongly to being called Mrs Faunt. Best you know that before you meet her."

Simon had the feeling there were a lot more things he would need to know before he met Cassandra. Not least, how on Earth he, Simon Debovar, professional hider and accomplished bather, was supposed to go to an idyllic island and rescue a woman he'd never met from a man who, it seemed, was capable of doing pretty much anything.

"We're not going to send you alone," Faunt assured him. "You can take someone with you, if you want to – just not one of us."

"Why not?" Simon asked. Although, right now, the last people Simon wanted anywhere near him were these three.

"Because all angels and demons are barred from Priest's Island," Lily answered.

"What about you?" Simon asked Faunt.

"Well, my leaving here would attract a great deal of attention, unfortunately. However, even were that not so, Priest and I are not on the best of terms."

"Because he stole your wife?"

"Actually, not really," the deer answered. "But that hasn't helped, I suppose. However, we do have an *understanding*. We leave each other alone."

Simon was starting to feel like a pawn about to be sacrificed to save the queen.

"I understand that, Simon, and I am sorry," said Faunt. "If it helps, I've had a bath drawn for you upstairs. As it's coming up for noon, I plan to retire to my room to change, so you could take some time to think about who you should take, if you like."

He definitely liked. Hopefully there would be more Rioja. He badly needed Rioja. And maybe some drugs.

Prozac might be nice.

———

Luke had awoken to the sound of birdsong and the smell of coffee. Despite living on the stuff for several days previously, it was a welcome aroma.

"Morning gorgeous," he heard Gabby say.

Luke squinted against the sunlight streaming in through the window. There had been a time when he took such things for granted, but not now. Bathed in the warmth of the light, he took a moment to appreciate the delicious sensation before sitting up and lifting his cup.

"Morning, gorgeous. What time is it?"

"Nearly twelve."

It was unfortunate that the little hotel had chosen white bed linen, as it was really going to show the stains from the projectile coffee.

"What?"

He jumped from his position, vaguely aiming the cup at the bedside table.

"Why didn't you *wake* me? They could already be *gone!*"

Gabby smiled calmly back at him, holding out a piece of paper.

"I've been up since 8, sweetheart."

Luke took the piece of paper, wondering what on Earth could be on it that would make the fact they had risked losing Debovar not such a cause for concern.

On it was written, in an archaic ink scrawl:

> *Gabby,*
> *Pleased you're feeling better for the rest.*
> > *Stay here for now. I'll let you know*
> > *when you need to move.*
> *Best,*
> *F*
> *PS – I should let Luke sleep if I were*
> > *you – he was exhausted last night.*

"It was slid under the door this morning just after I woke up. I looked outside, but there was nobody there."

Luke considered the possibilities. Was Faunt genuinely helping them?

"What do you think?" he asked.

"Well, I see it like this. He knows everything. If he's against us, we're screwed. If he's with us, he's an incredible ally and we might as well take his advice."

It was a surprisingly clear piece of thinking. Luke smiled.

"OK, then I guess we're staying here."

"Well, 'here-ish'. The hotel has a hot tub downstairs." She smiled devilishly. "It's not like he won't know where to find us."

"Fair point," Luke answered. "Did we pack swimming costumes?"

"Nope..." she answered, giggling slightly.

He had to save the world. This woman was just too good to die.

CHAPTER NINE

Simon sank down in the bath. Who did he want to come with him? He was fairly sure that Batman wouldn't be allowed – though it did take him longer than it once would have to rule him out.

Who else?

Simon had always wanted to meet Tori Amos. He loved her music and had always found her rather intoxicating, as if there was something elemental about her. In fact, now he came to think about it, he wondered if she was altogether human. But having a kooky, sensuous singer/pianist with him seemed likely to be more of a distraction than an aid – though the idea was appealing.

For a man who had no friends, choosing someone to help keep him alive was not an easy task.

What would he need from his companion? They'd need to be wily, clever and cool under pressure. They'd need to be pretty much fearless, to compensate for Simon's utter failing in that area, and also be at least a little familiar with violence. Most of all, Simon would have to trust them.

Once he thought about it like that, he knew exactly who he

wanted. She was the only possible choice. The only thing he had to do was figure out how to convince her to come.

———

Simon was delighted to find an open bottle of Campo Viejo Gran Reserva on the kitchen table, waiting patiently for him.

"Help yourself," said the human-again Faunt. "It's for you."

Simon did not need to be asked twice.

"So, you've chosen a partner for your adventure."

Simon rankled at the description of what was being asked of him. Calling it an adventure seemed akin to calling D-Day a bit of a lark at the beach.

"Erm, yes," he answered. "But I don't know if she'll come."

Simon poured himself a glass and sat at the table.

Faunt turned to the hall and called out, "Cherry!"

Simon stared. Who the hell was Cherry? *What* the hell was Cherry?

A woman in her twenties waltzed in ('walked' did not do justice to the casual disdain with which she regarded everything in the room). Her name matched the colour of her spiky hair, which clashed with her pink, tiger-print jeans. Or what was left of them. She had topped off the look with what seemed to have started life as a Stiff Little Fingers t-shirt, which she had industriously converted into something between a bra and a vest. It had the pleasant and distracting habit of falling open under her arms to reveal tantalising glimpses of her ludicrously pert breasts.

Simon baulked. Lovely as she was, it was clear why she was here – to him, anyway. He stood and turned to address his host.

"Faunt, you really have been an excellent host, but this is a step too far, even for me."

Faunt put a hand up as if to interrupt, but Simon was not for stopping, afraid that if he did, he wouldn't get to start again.

"I'm sure you've thought about my attraction to Lily affecting my decision, but I'm really not comfortable with you providing me with a prostitute."

The last word hung in the air a moment as Faunt visibly winced. Simon realised why when he felt the 'thwack' of the punk's palm rattle against his left ear.

"Owwww!" he howled. Why had she hit him? He'd been studiously careful not to call her a whore... Then another thought occurred to him: maybe she was a dominatrix. The thought excited and terrified him in roughly equal measures.

It honestly didn't cross his mind that perhaps Cherry was not the woman of the night he had assumed she must be. Only prostitutes and exotic dancers were called Cherry, and he was quite sure that Faunt would not have been cruel enough to book a lap dance for the horniest man in Europe.

"Cherry, please help yourself to a drink," said Faunt. The girl retrieved a bottle of beer and opened it with one of the contraptions hanging from her belt.

"Simon, assuming a woman is a prostitute is even worse than assuming she's pregnant," Faunt said, smiling in a way that Simon thought clearly suggested he was suppressing a laugh.

"Oh dear," Simon mumbled, feeling a terrible cad. "I'm so sorry, I couldn't possibly feel any worse."

"So, you got a hard on for the demon, huh?" she asked.

Incredibly, he felt worse.

But at least he understood the name now – she was American.

"Cherry is a teleporter, Simon. She works for me," Faunt explained.

The punk smiled and lifted the front of her vest, exposing her stomach.

"And just so we're clear," she said, "*not* pregnant."

Simon wished very hard to die. Or to touch that stomach. Either one.

"I asked her to collect your companion as soon as you made a decision," Faunt continued.

"Oh." A teleporter. Because, why not? "Did she agree to come?"

Before Faunt could answer, a voice of chargrilled gravel did so for him.

"Has my fud of a nephew been making a flying prick of himself again, then?"

Harriet was here.

"Harriet," said Faunt, extending a hand to greet the newcomer as she entered the kitchen, "it's a pleasure to meet such an extraordinary woman."

Harriet took his hand and returned the pleasant smile.

"No need to blow smoke up my backside, hairy boy. I hear you've got an impressive stock of single malts here somewhere."

"It's the only reason she came," Cherry piped in, as if any explanation were needed. Simon knew Harriet, and Faunt knew everyone.

"Hello Harriet," Simon finally said. "It's... nice to see you."

Harriet turned and grabbed Simon's cheeks in one iron claw, lifting his face toward her for inspection. It shouldn't have been physically possible for a woman of that age to have such a grip. Simon felt his teeth digging into his skin.

"You've still been hiding in that bloody house, haven't you, you pasty bugger? What are you so afraid of?"

Tears instantly welled in Simon's eyes and his lip trembled imperceptibly to anyone but Faunt. He felt like he'd just had his shorts removed and his bare arse skelped for the world to see.

"Aunt Harriet," his voice was trembling too, "I am not *afraid* of anything. I choose to stay at home because I find the human race to be selfish, rude, inconsiderate, stinking slobs whose purpose has always been making my life more difficult!"

"I'll drink to that, buddy," said Cherry, as she did exactly that.

Harriet roared like a Viking King at an orgy.

"Good for you, boy. You might be a tubby little wuss, but at least you've got the Debovar stones in there somewhere! Now," she turned to Faunt, "where's the whisky?"

"Cherry, would you please show our guest down to the cellar?"

"You're the boss," said Cherry, saluting. She knocked back the last of her drink and led Harriet out to the hall. The octogenarian followed at a pace that was slightly indecent. But then, for Harriet, decent was rarely a useful adjective.

"She's quite something, isn't she?" Faunt asked, once she was out of earshot.

"Yes," Simon answered, "but she's family, and if I have to rely on someone, I can't think of anyone else. Unless *you* want to change your mind?"

Faunt smiled wryly. "I'd love to, Simon, but there are a lot of reasons why I can't. I'm touched you might have chosen me, though. Personally, I understand your choice. I might have gone for Tori Amos, though."

He laughed and, as much of a surprise to him as anyone else, so did Simon. A deep, hearty laugh. It had been a while, and it felt good. He poured another glass of wine for himself and topped up the glass Faunt offered. Simon was having a drink with a friend.

It was Christmas.

———

"What's wrong with those books?" Harriet barked. "Am I drunk or are they fucking moving?"

She sat in a luxurious, medieval armchair by the library

90

fire, holding court as only she could, even in the company of an angel, a demon, an immortal and a teleporter. And Simon.

"No, you're right," answered Faunt, "they are. They're being written."

"You what?" she snapped.

"Well, as I know the full contents of every book ever written, there are none I can read for pleasure. These, therefore, are books currently being written by their authors."

"Fantastic," Simon heard himself say, in genuine wonder. "You get to read books before they're even finished! How brilliant."

"Well, you'd be surprised by how some of the greatest books ever written started life. Hemingway's first drafts were, in his own words, 'shit'. The first draft of *Wuthering Heights* had a happy ending."

Simon hadn't read *Wuthering Heights*. Now that he could assume it ended badly, he probably wouldn't bother.

"Now," Faunt said, moving the conversation on, "since those of us who *need* to eat are at least peckish, I've asked Bob to bring in some tapas." Faunt gestured to the door as it opened to indeed reveal Bob and a tray of stuff.

Simon was delighted; he liked tapas. He also tried to remember, in passing, whether Faunt had a spyglass on his front door. If so, it must have been the only one in the world that saw less action than his own.

"Not for me," said Harriet, brandishing her glass in defence, "don't want too much blood in my alcohol stream." She laughed at her own joke, seemingly unaware it was older than her.

As often happened, Daniel broke the silence as Bob passed round the patatas bravas.

"So, you both understand your mission?"

"Get his missus back off a magic island," Harriet replied, jerking a thumb at Faunt, "and try not to have any fun at all while we're doing it."

Daniel didn't like Harriet.

"Good. So, we've made arrangements. You both need invites to get onto Priest's island, which Faunt has secured for you." Daniel threw two envelopes onto the central coffee table, which was one of the only pieces of furniture that stayed put all the time. "Cherry will take you both to the jetty, where the speedboat will take you to the island. Once there, you'll find Cassandra and bring her back here."

"Yeah, I get the theory, sunshine, but you've yet to tell me this: why should I?" Harriet asked.

"Pardon?" Daniel was taken aback.

"You heard me, posh cock. What's in it for us?"

Cherry giggled.

Simon wondered whether mentioning that his head would maintain its close relationship with his neck if they did would be enough to persuade her. He hoped not to have to find out.

Daniel turned a shade of pink and a small vein appeared on his neck. He seemed to share more anatomy with humans than he cared to admit.

"Actually Harriet, there is an important element that Daniel hasn't yet explained," Lily interjected.

Harriet sipped her Ardbeg. "I'm listening."

"Priest's Island has very strict entry credentials. He likes to maintain a certain level of aesthetic standards amongst his guests."

"And in English, girlie?"

"Only the young and beautiful are allowed in."

Simon was confused. He was neither young nor beautiful. He was quite sure of it.

"How the hell do you intend to get round that then? Me and Captain Couch Potato over there don't exactly qualify, do we?" she asked.

"Well, we are allowed a certain amount of leeway when something like this is required."

"Again with the English, please?"

"We'll make you and Simon young and attractive."

Harriet's eyes lit up. She nearly dropped her glass. Nearly.

"How young?" she asked, barely able to stay seated.

"How does 23 grab you?"

Harriet burst from her seat and threw her arms around the demon.

"Hell, girly, make it 21 and I'll do you and the angel at the same time before we go!"

Lily, Faunt and Cherry laughed. Even Bob cracked a smile. Daniel's eyes opened wide. Whether through surprise or terror was difficult to say.

Simon interrupted. "I don't want to be younger or look different. I'm happy as I am."

Faunt smiled. "Simon, in many ways, you are a role model, my friend."

Harriet was dancing with Lily.

"Well, unfortunately Mr Debovar, it will be necessary," Daniel piped up, happy to move on from Harriet's proposal. "However, we will only change you as much as is necessary, and I promise we will return you to your natural state when you're done."

Simon sighed. "I suppose." Young and gorgeous was more attractive than headless.

"When do we start?" Harriet asked, with more enthusiasm than Simon felt was appropriate.

"You're booked onto the morning boat tomorrow," answered Faunt. Then he paused, as if noticing something unexpected.

"Excuse me, but could I go? I'd like to help." It was Bob.

Faunt turned and smiled. "Really?"

"Yes. I'd like to help you get your wife back."

Faunt looked at Lily and the two exchanged smiles. Lily nodded.

"Yes, Bob, if you'd like to go, you are welcome. I take it you don't mind, Simon? I can vouch for Bob."

Simon thought for a moment. What harm could it do?

"Sure," he shrugged.

"Thank you," Bob smiled. "I'll go and pack, if that's OK?"

"Certainly," said Faunt.

Bob left the remaining snacks on the table and left the room.

"Thank Christ, we're taking a real man with us," said Harriet, pouring herself another large measure.

Cherry stood up as if to leave, but instead stopped in front of Simon's chair and leaned forward. He was transfixed, wondering where she was going to hit him this time. What she did was even more astonishing, pulling his face toward her and kissing him.

The room went silent as Simon felt her soft, moist lips caressing his own, gently, before her tongue slid between them and lightly flicked the end of his. She actually tasted of cherry.

As the kiss ended and she pulled her face back, it took Simon a moment to regain his focus – not least because a great deal of the blood that should have been servicing his brain had suddenly found itself required elsewhere.

"I like a guy who's comfortable with who he is," she said, pointedly. "Don't ever change for somebody else."

"And you," she spat as she turned to Harriet, "are a grade-A bitch."

Cherry marched pointedly out of the room – most likely to the kitchen for more beer.

Simon was aware he was sitting very still and probably had a deeply goofy smile. He couldn't have cared less.

"I like her," said Harriet. "Can she come too?"

"No," said Faunt, decisively. "I have things I need her to do."

"Shame," she replied.

For the first time that day, Simon agreed with her.

CHAPTER TEN

Faunt had arranged a formal dinner for everyone. Daniel had opted not to attend in favour of visiting a karaoke night at a local bar. This ranked as the most surprising thing Simon had heard all day.

The dining room was, like the rest of the house, a strange mix of old and modern. A huge, medieval oak table, stained with red wine crescents and the rippled remnants of candles, dominated the room. Bolted to the table were half a dozen huge metal candlesticks. Simon suspected they were some kind of engine parts, but never having had the inclination to learn more about the workings of a car than "turn key", he couldn't be sure. They were occupied by intimidatingly phallic candles. The long flames lapped upwards, providing the only light in the room.

The chairs Simon recognised as having Rennie Mackintosh wrought-iron backs. On the stone wall was a dormant plasma screen, hooked up to surround sound speakers around the room. Also, on an oak sideboard was a musical device attached to the same speakers. It had a flat silver front, which opened when Faunt waved at it to reveal some impressive buttons and lights. It was currently playing a selection of extremely soothing and elegant classical music.

Simon looked across the table at Cherry and Bob. The three of them had arrived about the same time, eight o'clock – when Faunt had asked them to. Harriet and Lily were as yet unaccounted for at almost quarter past. Simon was unimpressed.

"So Bobby, why'd you decide you wanted to help?" asked Cherry. "You've never struck me as a 'team' kinda guy."

Bob smiled gently and looked down. Candlelight flickered across his features. It was bloody eerie.

Simon suddenly felt like he was in a Gothic horror, about to hear that they were all, in fact, dead. Then their meal would arrive and they'd all begin eating, only to discover that they were feasting on their own roasted corpses.

"Actually," Bob raised his spooky head, "I finally recognised something. A friend. And I owe him."

Faunt smiled. That also looked creepy. Simon resolved to read less Edgar Allan Poe.

The door opened, letting in a swathe of electric light that changed the mood entirely. A shapely young blonde girl paraded in, wearing an evening gown that clung where it should and floated everywhere else. Simon could smell her light, floral perfume from the table. Her features were delicate, almost sculpted, and her skin looked fresh and vibrant. He couldn't remember seeing a woman so breathtaking outside of his television.

Dear God, she was fabulous.

"What do you think of this then, boys? Got your tackle twitching?"

Dear God, she was Harriet.

Lily entered behind her, smiling. "What *do* you think?"

"Well," said Bob, appreciatively.

"Fuckin' A!" said Cherry.

"Um," said Simon.

Harriet strolled over behind her nephew. She leaned forward and he could feel her breasts against the back of his shoulders. "It's OK, kiddo, you're allowed to fantasise about me," she whispered in his ear, "I'm not really your aunt, I was just good mates with your granny."

This was news to Simon. Whether it was good or not, he wasn't sure yet. He took a swig of his wine.

"Really?" he asked, nervously.

"No!" Harriet laughed. "You really have got the horn for your own great aunt, ma boy!" She snorted raucously.

Cherry spluttered a laugh despite herself. Bob and Faunt both smiled.

Simon wondered if he could still change his mind.

Harriet took her place at the head of the table, opposite Faunt. Lily sat next to Simon.

"You're late," Simon grumbled, without looking at Harriet. "It's extremely rude. Faunt has been an exceptional host and you can't even be on time."

Harriet took a deep breath and sighed.

"Son, I've spent twenty years becoming more incontinent by the day. I've pissed myself in the supermarket and again in the car. As of one hour ago, I've got a pelvic floor that could crush coal into diamonds. I couldn't give a flying monkey fuck if I'm three days late for dinner."

She flashed a dazzling, defiant grin before draining a full cup of Faunt's homemade mead and burping in appreciation.

Even Cherry's mouth hung open. "God damn, woman..." She shook her head in something between astonishment and respect.

Bob's eyebrows had gone in search of his hairline. He decided it was time to top up the drinks, and began with Faunt's – the furthest from Harriet.

"And if Little Lord Faunty-boy is really offended," she carried on, "I'll be happy to show him just how tight it is!"

Simon wished with all of his being that he had a less vivid

imagination. It was his turn to knock back his drink. Bob helpfully refilled it immediately. And left the bottle.

"What do you think, Simon?" Lily asked.

"About what?" he replied, the irritated tone in his voice betraying that he was starting to feel the effects of the alcohol.

"About Harriet. Being young. Not bad, is it?"

"Not bad? Have you been listening?"

"No, I mean she looks good, doesn't she?"

"Oh. I suppose." Simon wondered why Lily had taken it upon herself to torture him.

"So maybe you won't find it so terrible, right?"

Simon looked down at himself. He was a little soft about the middle, but not so much that anyone would mistake him for a bouncy castle. His skin was beginning to wrinkle, a little. Avoiding the sun for a long time had preserved it better than most. He looked OK.

"I've always believed that people are the shape they deserve to be."

"Easy for you to say, boy. When did you last burn your nipple on a candle reaching for your drink?"

Cherry started the giggling, of course. Faunt quickly joined in and, before long, the whole table were laughing heartily – even Bob. Simon was fairly sure it was some form of collective euphoria, but it was better than hearing about his great aunt's genital improvements.

The ice broken, dinner arrived and, of course, Faunt had everyone's favourite dish prepared.

As he lay in bed later, fidgeting and praying to fall asleep, Simon tried in vain not to think of it as a condemned man's last meal.

He touched his face, feeling the familiar contours. He hoped he'd still recognise it tomorrow.

CHAPTER ELEVEN

Gabby trembled slightly as she poured her coffee. Her head ached. She was in good condition. She knew the value of taking care of her body. It would inevitably degrade. But a professional athlete would be sore after last night.

Luke reached out and steadied her hand, gently stroking it at the same time. He was feeling rough, too. But it was worth it. Who knew how many more nights like that they would get?

The hotel breakfast was good. Food was another benefit of being mortal, and one neither of them took for granted. It was one of the reasons they'd chosen a pizza delivery business. Pepperoni pizza is perfect food.

The meal before them might not have been a traditional Scottish heart attack on a plate, but the Continental mix of fresh croissants and good coffee was a nice way to start the day in the current heat – and with their current hangovers.

"You'll be the lovebirds then, huh?"

Luke and Gabby both jumped at the voice. They had been alone in the dining room a moment ago. Now there was an audaciously dressed young woman looming over the table. Several croissants now had more coffee on them than usual.

Cherry pulled up a chair from another table. "So, how's

the food? I always find this European stuff a little light, you know? Gimme a half dozen donuts any day."

Luke reached for the bag beside him. He doubted he could get the gun inside it without her noticing. This girl was either inhumanly fast or a teleporter. If it was the latter, he had a chance.

"Who are you? What do you want? Where did you come from?" Gabby apparently wasn't in the mood to wait for answers. Or, for that matter, to breathe.

"The big guy sent me."

Luke stopped with his hand on the gun, still inside the bag.

"*The* big guy?" he asked.

"Ha! No, not him. The other big guy. The furry one."

"Faunt," Gabby realised. Luke kept his hand on the gun all the same. He didn't like people appearing out of nowhere.

Cherry helped herself to a slightly soggy croissant, and poured herself a coffee in a cup stolen from the next table. "I have to tell you when to go and give you these," she said, producing an envelope from a pocket somewhere on her body. Luke attempted to ascertain exactly where from – there wasn't a lot of material that looked capable of sustaining a pocket.

"But there's a condition," the girl added.

Gabby looked apprehensively up at Luke. Was Faunt about to tip his hand? Were they even in the game? Faunt was an information broker. His help did not normally come without a fee. What was this going to cost them? She knew Luke would understand all of her concerns from her glance.

Unfortunately, he was looking intently at Cherry's thigh and missed it. Gabby made a mental note to beat him later. With sticks.

"He says you can stop them, but Simon is not to be hurt."

"Why would we want to hurt him?" Luke asked, defensively. "We've been looking after him for years."

"Have you?" she asked, seeming genuinely interested.

"Sweetheart, it's not that unreasonable, is it?" said Gabby.

"I mean..." She gave him a pointed look, not wanting to have to finish the sentence.

Her words knocked the wind out of Luke. He hated being reminded of *that*. He hated that she'd reminded him.

And he hated that she was absolutely right.

"OK," he said, staring at the table. "What are we stopping them from doing?"

"Bringing back Faunt's wife. She's called Cassandra. You know her?"

"I know *of* her," Luke answered. "Where is she?"

"Priest has her," Cherry answered.

Luke and Gabby looked at each other across the table. Gabby raised her eyebrows. Maybe they could just leave Debovar to fail all by himself.

"OK," Luke finally said. "Anything else we should know?"

"He says if Simon gets hurt, he'll hold you two personally responsible and that regardless of who else you have to answer to, he'll make you pay for it."

This was obviously not a point Faunt wanted to be taken lightly. To be targeted by a man with absolute knowledge was an unappealing thought.

"OK," said Luke. "You have my word."

Cherry turned to Gabby. "And yours?"

She nodded, silently.

"Cool. Everything you need to know is in here. You have to get the second boat. Simon won't recognise you. Faunt says he's never seen your faces, but Bob has and will."

"Who's Bob?" Gabby asked, perplexed.

"Tall guy – looks after Faunt's place."

Gabby remembered. The gatekeeper.

With that, Cherry threw the envelope towards the table and was gone before it landed, with a gentle, sucking breath of air.

Gabby looked at the envelope. She no longer had an appetite. She stood, lifting it from the table and headed for the stairs back to their room. "Come on, we need to read. And talk."

Luke stood after a moment's pause. She seemed... annoyed... or at the very least disgruntled. Had he done something wrong?

Well, he'd find out eventually.

———

Simon looked at himself in the mirror. He was naked.

This was not an uncommon state of affairs for him. What was unusual was that he was, as he'd heard it described on TV, 'buff'. His slightly wobbly spare tyre had been replaced with a fully-ripped six pack. The beginnings of man boobs were now rock hard pecs. His legs had gone from pale and awkward to tanned and toned. And one particular increase in both length and width assured him that it had been Lily who'd designed his new look – Daniel would not have bothered with that particular detail.

His face, however, was the change he could not tear himself away from. He'd never really considered himself to be unattractive, but neither was he anything special to look at. In short, impeccable manners aside, he believed himself to be comprehensively mediocre. And yet, while the face looking back at him was still very clearly him, it was also, somehow, *better*.

A few wrinkles had gone, along with a few old acne scars, leaving skin that looked as young and vibrant as a baby's, but with a slightly rugged, manly tone. His nose was a little more narrow; his jaw a little more square. Even the best cosmetic surgeon would struggle to identify each tiny tweak that had been made to Simon's appearance, but the overall effect was of turning a largely unremarkable man into one who would stop women in their tracks. And some men, he imagined.

In the closet, Simon also found an entirely new wardrobe.

The baggy, comfortable clothes he'd hidden in for years were replaced with tight long-sleeved tops and jeans measured to show every taut muscle on his newly improved body. Even his shoes were a fashionable pair of brown leather trainers, instead of the nondescript black shoes he'd arrived in.

Faced with the difficulty of deciding exactly what he should put on and how he was going to cope when people might actually *look* at him, Simon had run himself a bath. He had noted that he smelled fresh and musky, rather than the normal, dank, stale morning smell he was accustomed to. But still – a bath was a bath.

"Nice ass!"

Simon's new look had done nothing for his nervous disposition. Thus, startled and, indeed, naked, he shrieked and dived into the wardrobe, pulling half of the clothes off the rails and on top of him.

"Wow. Didn't mean to scare you," Cherry giggled.

"I'm naked!" Simon blurted from under an Armani shirt.

"I can see that," Cherry replied.

Simon realised with chagrin that while his upper half was buried in clothes, his lower regions could still feel the unmistakeable tingle of clear air.

"And real nice it is too, can I say?"

Simon's face flushed as he scrambled to draw himself into the closet, clawing at clothes, while all too aware of the shoes that were trying to insinuate themselves between his buttocks.

"Go away! This is a terrible invasion of privacy and totally unfair!" he grumbled.

"Would it be fairer if I was naked too?" Cherry asked in return.

Simon stopped clawing and peeked out from the depths of his makeshift cavern. If he said yes, would she undress? Regardless of the consequences, that was definitely worth a shot.

"Maybe," he mumbled, trying to sound indignant rather

than ridiculously excited at the prospect. The last woman he'd seen naked had been on a computer screen. Hell, the last hundred women he'd seen naked had been on a computer screen. The last one he'd seen naked in the flesh had been a very, *very* long time ago.

"Fair enough," she answered, and immediately disappeared, leaving her clothes to crumple into a heap on the floor. She reappeared a few feet further away as gloriously naked as Simon had dared to hope. The reality of that was every bit as wonderful as he had imagined from the stolen glimpses and flights of imagination he'd indulged in recently. Suddenly, he had something new to worry about concealing – and it was more substantial than he was used to.

"Better?" Simon's new favourite person in the world asked.

"Aggmff," he replied, chewing on a tie he'd found over his shoulder.

"OK, good." She strode towards the cupboard and sat cross-legged on the floor directly in front of Simon, who at the same time wished both that the back of the cupboard would fall open and deposit him in Narnia, and that he could somewhere find the courage to reach out and touch that magnificent skin.

"So here's the thing," said Cherry. "I like you, and I think you're being taken advantage of."

"I am?" Simon whimpered.

"Yeah. That demon has you twisted around her little finger and she knows it. And it's not cool. You're a decent guy, Simon Debovar, and there ain't a lot of you around.

"We've got two hours before I have to take you to the jetty to catch your boat. And you are *seriously* hot, right now. Instead of a bath," she nodded to the open bathroom door, "would you consider taking a shower? With *me*?"

Simon started to hyperventilate. She was a prostitute after all. Faunt had *lied* to him!

"Did Faunt send you? Does he know you're here?"

"Well, of course he knows! But no, he didn't send me. I promise, this is my decision. Because I like you. And I don't like *them*."

Simon's breathing slowed down. This was the situation, as he could see it: he had a brand new, ripped body, including some formidable sexual apparatus, and a hot, naked young girl sitting a foot away who wanted to take a shower with him. He, conversely, was hiding in a closet under a mountain of designer clothes and terrified of touching her. What was *wrong* with him?

Cherry reached out her hand. Slowly, trembling, Simon lifted his own arm and reached back. When his hand brushed her skin, he felt a crackle of electricity.

He gasped and his heart jumped.

———

An hour later, Simon Debovar had a whole new appreciation for showers and a much-improved opinion of Americans in general. He was also entirely in lust with a teleporting punk and no longer drooling like a puppy over the demon who'd given him his new look.

Cherry was entirely satisfied.

———

Simon and Cherry arrived at the kitchen together for a late breakfast before setting off for the boat. He was quite certain there was a large sign on his forehead saying "I've just had sex!" He could feel it burning. Then again, his whole face was burning.

It didn't help that he'd known Faunt was aware of the whole thing. He'd once seen a stand-up comedian talking about his dead ancestors watching him have sex. Now he could sort of relate.

"Morning," Cherry announced herself.

Bob and Harriet sat at the table. The giant, who looked a little younger and a little *better*, was working on a full English breakfast, while Harriet had what Simon assumed was a buck's fizz – alcohol with a hint of breakfast. Bob rose quickly to retrieve a plate of Eggs Benedict for Simon and a stack of pancakes for Cherry.

"Made to order," he smiled as he placed them on the table. "I hope you like them."

As Bob sat back down next to Harriet, there was the slightest hint of familiarity between the pair. Simon had a horrible feeling that perhaps he and Cherry had not been the only ones enjoying themselves in the last 12 hours. He resolved to stop thinking about it immediately on the basis that he was not prepared for anything to put him off his breakfast.

"So, you're looking pretty snazzy too," said Harriet. "Happy with the look or still whining about not being yourself?"

Simon looked up at her and smiled, perhaps a little too confidently. "Actually, it's OK."

"Thank Christ for that. I was half expecting to have to wipe your eyes for you. Have you seen these?" she grasped her breasts, firmly. "They're like honest to God cantaloupes!"

Simon focused on the food. And the memories of that morning. Cherry brushed his leg with her foot, under the table. Harriet's taunts were meaningless noise.

———

"Listen Accursed, all I want to know is: why *this*? Why did you choose *this* thing? Debovar barely qualifies as a sentient human being. He's socially inept! How do you expect him to overcome Priest?"

Daniel was in full flow. Faunt grazed peacefully on a pot of grass by the library fire.

106

Lily put her hand on Daniel's shoulder, encouraging him to sit. He did, reluctantly.

"I think what Daniel is trying to say is, there are more reasonable things you could have asked for. This is pretty near a lost cause. Simon will be lucky to come back at all, never mind with your wife."

Faunt finished his mouthful and trotted over to a chair, jumping up on it before answering.

"Firstly, you underestimate Simon. There's much more to him than you realise. Either of you."

Daniel harrumphed.

"Secondly, if he doesn't come back, it will be because he is dead, and you will be free to pursue the Rug of Djoser."

"Not necessarily," Daniel interrupted. "He could just choose to stay on the island, couldn't he? Is that what you're planning?"

Faunt tilted his head. "Planning? You think I'm planning something, Daniel?"

"Oh for Heaven's sake, you already know what I think."

Lily's eyes darted to Daniel and back to Faunt. She wondered, apprehensively, how far he was prepared to push their host.

"Yes, I do know. And you should know that if he does decide to stay on the island, you only need to remove the charm you've placed upon Harriet and him. Return them to their natural state and Priest will expel them."

"True," Lily nodded.

"So you see, Daniel, there would be little point in my plotting anything against you, would there?"

"You're not telling us something. Why have you chosen this *particular* price?"

Faunt raised himself up. The hairs on his back were bristling. It was the first time Lily had seen him seem genuinely irritated. She didn't like it. Regardless of the power she and Daniel held, Faunt was not to be taken lightly – by anyone.

"Because, 'angel'," he said, "we three all know exactly what's riding on this, don't we? And if it goes the way it might, then the value of what you're asking far exceeds the price I've asked, wouldn't you agree?"

Daniel simmered, but looked down.

"And in the circumstances," Faunt continued, "is it really unreasonable for me to want to see my wife again?"

"OK, fine," Daniel assented. "But I don't like it."

Daniel rose and left the room.

"I'm sorry, Faunt," Lily apologised. "He takes this very seriously. He's under a lot of pressure, you know? He's not bad, really. His boss is... pretty uptight."

"I've heard that. However, I am a patient man and your company has been most pleasant, Lily. And I can only thank you again for your help with Bob. I believe it would have taken him the full ten years to realise why he was here, otherwise."

"Well, you gave him back his life and he'd never have thanked you for it, I don't think. Seemed a little unfair to me. Why'd you do it, by the way?"

Faunt hesitated. "He was... damaged. By someone with whom I share a mutual dislike."

"And you can't tell me who, right?"

Faunt shook his head in confirmation.

"Gotta love the Rules, eh?" the demon smiled.

"You are a lady, 'demon'," Faunt smiled. "Will you join me in saying *bon voyage* to our intrepid adventurers?"

"I will."

The sensation of being teleported was entirely bizarre. Cherry could only carry one person at a time, so she'd deposited Simon in a small copse of trees, just out of sight of the jetty, before going back for Harriet. She'd also paused for a quick snog before going back, which had done nothing to help steady Simon's wobbly legs. Feeling like someone had pumped lead into his stomach and emptied his limbs of bones at the same time, Simon collapsed unceremoniously against a tree.

A few moments later, Cherry and Harriet appeared out of thin air. In passing, Simon wondered what constituted 'fat air'.

To Simon's secret delight, Harriet wobbled sideways and caught herself on another tree before her stomach expelled 'breakfast'.

Cherry shot Simon a smile, then blinked out again.

"Ah well," Harriet grumbled, "more room for lunch..."

Lily had explained to Harriet before they left that, having restored her body to its 21-year-old state, her digestive system was no longer inured to her regular intake of alcohol. In short, she would need to eat. Regularly.

As Harriet regained her composure, Cherry reappeared with Bob. He seemed slightly less rattled by the experience and Simon assumed, with an unexpected twinge of jealousy, that she had teleported him before.

"OK, you guys. Good luck," she said, smiling broadly. "I'll make sure the fridge is stocked for when you get back."

With that, she was gone.

The three pulled themselves together and headed for the dock.

With the distraction of Cherry gone, Simon finally started to think about what was ahead. They were getting on a boat to a mythical island. What would it be like? A broken old cripple, wrapped in ancient cloths and smelling of rancid death, guiding them across on a raft made from the broken bones of the damned? A Viking ship, piloted by a ghostly warrior? Perhaps the *Marie Celeste* itself, unmanned and floating eerily on its path?

It was something of a disappointment when it transpired that their transport was being provided by a badly-dressed, balding man who most closely resembled the Captain of the Love Boat.

"G'day," cried the speedboat captain, pulling at his orange and red Hawaiian shirt to fan himself in the heat. "You folks heading out this morning?"

Of course, he was Australian. Why wouldn't he be?

"We are," Bob answered. He had been elected spokesman on the basis that he was the most socially capable of the three. It hadn't been a long discussion.

"I'll just need to see your invitations then, please?" The Captain smiled a shark smile, which said 'If you're genuine guests, I'll do anything you ask, but if you're chancing your arms, I'll eat your lungs'. He reached out his hand towards Bob, who carefully placed an envelope in his hands.

While Simon and Bob trusted Faunt, neither of them felt entirely comfortable with the wait. The captain perused their invites closely, examining the photographs attached and peering intently at each of them in turn. It was akin to that uneasy feeling Simon always got around police officers: a desperate urge to confess to the packet of Polos he'd stolen aged 12 and throw himself on their mercy. Simon began to sweat even more. Bob looked shiftily at him as the wait lasted forever.

Harriet had already worked out that she could take the Aussie wanker with a sleeper hold and drive the boat herself.

He finally looked up from the paperwork and smiled, minus the shark.

"Welcome aboard," he invited them, removing the rope band that had previously blocked the gangway. "I'm Captain Alexander and I'll be escorting you all to Priest's Island this morning. Have any of you visited before?"

"No," Bob answered as he led the way on to the boat.

Alexander eyed Harriet from top to toe as she stepped on to the boat. Simon wished he'd gone before her so as to avoid seeing the way she deliberately hitched her skirt just a touch higher than necessary as she passed him. It was slightly less upsetting now that he wasn't labouring under a decade's worth of celibacy, but it was still *wrong*.

Simon followed on board. He looked towards the Captain, expecting to nod politely and smile at him, but the idiot was still watching Harriet fumble around and bend over too far. She wasn't actually interested in the poor man. For a start, she had always said that Hawaiian shirts were only bought by men who were devoid of personality, so attempted to wear one instead. But she was clearly enjoying both the attention and the fact that she was torturing a colonial.

Simon hoped he would survive Harriet's twenties.

CHAPTER TWELVE

The journey took 45 minutes. Harriet's casual vomiting made it feel nearer a week. ("It's not my fault, it's that bloody shirt, it's making my eyes go funny!")

As they neared the island, the turquoise waters of the bay gave way to virgin-white sand along a two-mile crescent of beach. Beyond the sun-bleached wooden jetty stood an arch of terracotta stones that looked like it had grown straight out of the earth. The possibility that it had done just that was not lost on Simon. Beyond the coast was a welcoming flourish of trees bearing brightly-coloured, exotic fruit; a natural fireworks display to greet them. As the engine stopped, the comforting serenade of birdsong mingled with the gentle lapping of the waves against the boat.

Daniel was right. This *could* be Heaven. It was beautiful. It was breathtaking. It was...

"Fucking magnificent! I can smell the piña coladas from here!"

It was fucking magnificent, apparently.

Captain Alexander flashed a Cheshire Cat grin. It had probably been a while since he'd met a young lady with

Harriet's 'spunk'. In fact, there may never have been such a woman.

"Damn right it is, girlie. And I guarantee you, you won't want to leave."

"I wouldn't bet on that," Bob muttered under his breath.

Harriet played with the necklace Faunt had given her that morning. The leather strap carried an eclectic blend of small wooden carvings.

"Never take this off," he had warned. "Even to sleep. It should protect you from Priest's influence – keep your mind clear."

"My mind is never clear," Harriet had joked. "But OK. If this keeps off the voodoo, I'll do my best not to lose it."

Any time Simon started to feel a little too relaxed, he knew he'd only have to look at that necklace to remember that this was anything but a holiday.

The captain finished tying off the mooring rope and offered a hand to Simon. He took it and stepped up out of the boat, relieved to be on solid footing again. He'd never been one for the sea. He thought too much about what was underneath.

Harriet followed, but the novelty of torturing the Australian seemed to have worn off. Bob disembarked last, shaking Alexander's hand. Simon thought he noticed Bob slip something to him as he did – probably a tip. It made him a little more glad to have Bob along. He'd really never understood tipping culture, and the question of whether he should have tipped a hotel concierge had once kept him awake wondering if he'd spend the weekend eating saliva.

"Welcome to our island!" The voice seemed to come from nowhere. As the three turned away from the boat, a figure emerged from the shadow of the arch. His midnight-dark skin starkly contrasted with the cream linen of his shirt and trousers. He cracked a broad, charismatic smile. Was this Priest?

"Hello, my friends! My name is Carlos. Welcome..." he flung his arms theatrically wide, "...to Paradise!"

"You can take me to Paradise later, gorgeous," said Harriet. "For now, just show me the bar."

Carlos laughed. "I like you, mademoiselle. Could I just see your invitations, please?"

Again with the papers. What was this, Nazi Germany? Bob handed over the envelope and, again, the visitors stood like gift horses waiting to have their teeth poked. Carlos took his time, wandering a few feet away to speak into a walkie-talkie. Simon started to sweat again. What didn't he want them to hear? Were they already busted? Had Faunt given them duff paperwork? Surely not...

Carlos returned, looking serious.

"I'm very sorry, there's been a problem. I understand your booking was changed at the last minute to add Mr Carter," he said, nodding at Bob.

"Yes, that's right," Bob replied. "Didn't think I was going to come, but at the last minute, things changed."

"Well, it seems our receptionist took down the wrong details of your credit card, so the payment was rejected. I'm sorry, but is there any chance I could ask you for the card so as to process it properly?"

Shit.

Shit. Shit. Shit.

Faunt had organised everything. But he couldn't allow for this. What would they do?

"Erm, actually, I didn't pay for it myself," Bob explained. "A friend did, so it was his card."

"Ah," replied Carlos. "So could we call him, possibly?"

"Erm, he doesn't take calls, really. It's hard to explain."

What need did Faunt have for a phone number? If anyone wanted to speak to him, he knew it immediately, and he could contact them if he wanted to.

Carlos frowned. This was clearly not a good thing.

"Give me a moment, please," he asked, backing away again and talking quietly into the walkie-talkie.

This was bad. They did not need to draw attention to themselves. And on this island, Faunt couldn't help. He wouldn't even know they were in trouble.

"Oi," Harriet nudged Simon.

"What?" Simon asked, in a panicked hush.

"Sort it out," she said, gesturing to Carlos with her head.

"What am I supposed to do? I can't get in touch with Faunt!"

Harriet took a deep breath.

"Pay for it, you *nipple*. You're loaded!"

"Oh yes, so I am!" Simon answered, surprised. He never really thought of himself as wealthy, just that he always had money in his account when he needed it. He needed it a lot right now.

"Erm, excuse me, Mr Carlos?" he called.

Carlos looked up and grumbled something into the walkie-talkie. A smile returned to his face as he approached one of the *paying* customers.

"Yes, Mr Debovar?"

"Is it OK if I pay for Bob?" He proffered his platinum credit card.

Carlos's smile broadened and his eyes lit up again.

"Of course, Mr Debovar! That is a most satisfactory solution. Please follow me."

"Thanks," Bob whispered to Simon as he passed. "I thought we were in trouble. I didn't realise you were rich."

"Neither did I," Simon answered, following him.

It was Harriet's turn to sigh. She'd put her perky new body in the hands of a buffoon. Well, if nothing else, she was determined to have some fun with it before he got it pulped.

———

Gabby had a conundrum. She knew they needed to get to the jetty for their boat. She also knew that Cherry, who was standing here before them waiting for an answer to what seemed to her to be a very simple question, was the best way for them to get there. She equally knew that there was not a chance in hell that she was leaving her alone with Luke. OK, it was entirely irrational and she trusted Luke completely – but still.

"So?" Cherry prompted. "Who's going first?"

Luke looked to Gabby. He knew he was on thin ice, he just didn't know where the weak spots were. "Erm, why don't you go first darling?"

Gabby shot him with a look. "OK," she answered. For some reason, it definitely wasn't.

Cherry took her hand and they blinked out. Moments later, Cherry was back, smirking.

"Your lady says I better not touch any more of you than I have to, and we better be back within 30 seconds. *Coming?*" She grinned mischievously, reaching out her hand.

He took it, resolving not to enjoy it in the slightest. As he did, the hotel room faded away and Gabby appeared before him. He dropped Cherry's hand like a jellyfish, struck with guilt despite his innocence. Women, he had noticed, had an uncanny ability to cause this reaction in men. It was one of those things that one could never appreciate without being human.

"OK, so you guys have everything, right?"

"Yes," Gabby answered.

"OK. Faunt says 'good luck'. As far as he knows, they made it to the island. And just so you know, hurt Simon and Faunt's not the only one you'll have to look out for." She stared intently at the pair, and was gone.

"How have we managed to find the most popular hermit on the planet?" Luke asked.

"I have to admit, I like him," Gabby answered.

"Me too," Luke nodded. "So let's go screw up his day in the nicest possible way."

They headed down the jetty as a bald man in a ludicrous orange shirt pulled up in a speedboat.

———

"Well, I'm glad they're gone," said Cherry, putting her feet up on the kitchen table and opening a beer.

Daniel, having pressed Faunt's hospitality as far, if not farther, than was sensible, had been keen to leave once Simon and his entourage had been on their way. Lily had duly gone with him, though Faunt had offered her the opportunity to stay on should she wish. Crucially, he knew she'd say no.

"So am I," Faunt replied, drinking his own beer. "Now we can only hope that they all manage to figure out the solution themselves."

"Are you sure you're doing the right thing?"

"I've done as much as I can, for now," Faunt answered pensively. "Simply giving them the solution would break the Rules and, as I said, the Rules are what really matter here – but if I compromise them, we've already lost."

Cherry looked intensely at the deer. "Well, Christ, if I can't trust that you know what you're doing, what can I trust?" she asked, taking a long slug of beer.

Faunt wished he shared her confidence.

———

"It can't be," Simon thought to himself as he surveyed his room. It was designed for absolute comfort, with bamboo walls allowing a delicate, temperate breeze to flow through. A door led directly onto a small, secluded balcony, which was made private by a few palm trees, but still afforded a view of the ocean. The mini-bar was stocked with Dr Pepper and there

117

were six bottles of Rioja in the wine rack. The television in the room received British satellite TV and there was a bath the size of Bath. Faunt had ordered ahead for him and actually produced a room that was – surely not – as good as the one he had just stayed in.

There was not so much a knock at the door as a battering, and Harriet pushed her way in.

"Holy crap! Have you got a half dozen bottles of malt too?" she asked, surveying the room like a starving hyena with the scent of carrion in her nostrils.

"No," Simon answered, a note of irritation in his voice. "And even if I did, it would be mine."

"You don't bloody drink whisky, anyway."

It was true, but hardly the point.

"Come on, we're going down to the bar," she said, tugging at his arm.

"I don't want to go to the bar," Simon objected. "We're here for a reason, remember?"

"Oh for fuck's sake, have you never been on holiday?" Harriet almost immediately realised her mistake. "Listen, if you want to meet people on holiday, you have to get drunk with them. And get in good with the barmen. Trust me!"

Simon was reticent. It sounded plausible, but at the end of the day, Harriet wanted to go to a bar. There was a fairly clear ulterior motive here.

"She's right," said Bob, who had appeared at the door completely unheard.

Simon had previously thought Bob unobtrusive. He was beginning to think him sneaky, which was a little disturbing. With the options of seeing him either as a creepy Peeping Tom or a useful ally in their current predicament, Simon plumped for the latter.

Harriet smiled smugly.

"OK," Simon conceded, "but I'm having a bath first."

"Fuck that, m'boy. Bobby and I will be in the bar." Harriet

turned on her heels and stomped out, grabbing Bob's arm as she passed. The door slammed closed behind them, punctuating her dramatic flounce rather well, Simon thought.

He headed for the bathroom, peeled off his top, and turned on the bath. It had been uncomfortably hot all day and the steam from the bath only made him warmer. He was starting to feel a little funny in the head. Simon realised with alarm that he was in a deeply unsettling position. He didn't want a hot bath. But his body was slick with sweat. He needed to be clean. Now.

Then he noticed something in the corner of the room. While there was no screen, or curtain, there was a showerhead sticking straight down from the ceiling. The whole room was tiled. Simon had heard about wet rooms, but he'd never been in one. A cool shower – he never imagined it would seem so appealing. His memories of his previous shower that morning gave him a familiar tingle, too, which was not unpleasant.

Incredibly, Simon was going to have a shower.

———

"Oh. Dear. God," thought Simon, before quickly adding, "and Satan!" for fear of seeming biased and incurring the wrath of Lily's superior.

The showerhead had the word 'Amazon' engraved on the side. It was, essentially, a big metal circle suspended from the ceiling by a pipe. You wouldn't imagine something so nondescript could provide the sheer ecstasy which it was currently bestowing all over Simon Debovar. He knew exactly where the name came from: he was standing in an Amazon rainforest downpour, as the sweet, sweet water cooled, cleaned and did a damn good job of massaging him. Muscles throbbed with the gorgeous pain of relief. Simon had heard women on TV (notably in *Sex and the City*, if he recalled correctly) talk about falling in love with their showerheads. While he was sure the specifics differed, he finally saw the attraction. If he ever decided to get out of this shower, he was having one fitted at home within minutes of getting back.

A wolf whistle shook Simon from his reverie. He felt a pang of masculine guilt at the thought of some Neanderthal harassing a poor woman outside. But the whistle was followed by a cry of "Hello!" which was distinctly feminine. And, more disturbingly, clearly audible. Audible in the sense that it didn't sound as if it was being filtered by the glass of his bathroom window.

This was, he realised with a hideous, sickening pang of terror, because he'd left it open.

Rinsing the shampoo off his head and frantically wiping at his eyes, Simon prayed he was going to be wrong, but he knew in his heart what he would see when he finally could. Which was, as it transpired, three women standing outside his bathroom window, smiling and waving appreciatively. Instinctively, Simon put one hand down to cover his crotch and his other arm across his chest. The women giggled. Firstly, because this was a deeply feminine reaction – and he wondered why he had felt the need to hide his nipples – but secondly, because his hand was having some difficulty coping with the entire capacity of his new appendage. Sidling towards the window, Simon opted to use both hands for the weightier issue and accept that his nipples would have to get used to public display. He was on a tropical island, after all.

He forced a smile at the ladies as he pushed the window closed. He knew his face was beaming and only hoped that the suitcases the women carried meant they were on their way home. Sod's law dictated, of course, that they had just arrived. They booed dramatically as Simon clicked the window lock.

Instead of the horrendous embarrassment and indignity he naturally expected to wallow in for a few days, Simon found himself smiling at the attention. Cherry had said he was 'hot'. He had subconsciously chosen to believe she was being kind out of pity and the fact that she liked him. It seemed that perhaps he had been mistaken and he actually was now sexually attractive to women. Certainly, he was fairly sure that had he accidentally left a window open at home and been showering visible to the neighbourhood, the only women outside shouting at him would have been mothers throwing eggs at the local pervert.

Things had changed.

———

"So what are we going to do?" Gabby asked.

"I'm working on it," Luke answered, unpacking his bag.

"How can we have come this far and *still* not have a plan?"

Luke stopped packing and looked up.

"OK, what's your plan, then?"

This was not a question Gabby had been expecting. She was naturally inclined towards occasionally pointing out glaring flaws in plans, but not so well inclined towards instigating plans of her own. In short, she could tell what was wrong, but not how to fix it. It was not chief among the reasons Luke loved her.

"That's not fair! You know I don't do plans."

Luke smiled, patiently.

"Then please stop harassing me to come up with one. We're here. Honestly, I thought we'd be toast by now. If not for Faunt's help we probably would be. We'll get a chance. We just have to take it."

"OK," Gabby answered. "So, now what?"

"Now, we check out the lie of the land. If possible, we get in with Priest."

"Why?"

Luke fixed her with a pointed stare.

"In case we end up having to stay here."

CHAPTER THIRTEEN

"Where are you, you spineless little... little... ah, hell I can't think of a word. Simon!"

Harriet burst unbidden into the room and staggered towards Simon. Well, mostly towards him – also quite a lot towards the floor. Bob followed her in, looking fuzzy around the edges.

Harriet grabbed a pillow from Simon's bed, placed it on the floor and carefully collapsed next to it.

"Hello, Simon," Bob smiled, sitting on the end of the bed. "You didn't come to the bar."

It was true. He hadn't. He'd showered, dressed and even done his hair. In the mirror! But when it came to the crunch, he just couldn't go out on his own. So he'd sat on his bed eating pistachios from the mini bar and watching TV, trying to forget that his life was at stake.

"No, I didn't."

"Pussy!" Harriet grumbled from the floor.

"Well, I've got British satellite in here and there was a *M.A.S.H.* marathon on and it was the version without the laugh tracks, so I sort of got into it and..."

Bob smiled understandingly.

"It's OK," Bob said, standing up. "We found out some things." He walked to the bathroom and Simon could hear him pouring a glass of water.

"Oh. Good."

"Well," Bob came back into the room and stood just next to Harriet, "it's not all good, actually. Priest is not here."

"Isn't that good?" Simon asked, suddenly hopeful that fate had been kind to him. He was also vaguely aware of snuffling noises coming from the floor. Bob took a drink of his water, and casually tipped the rest onto Harriet's head.

"Fuh say!" she complained, through a mouthful of wet pillow. "You could've used vodka!"

"Actually, no," Bob answered Simon's question, "because Cassandra is with him."

"Oh," said Simon. "Why is she with him?"

"Well, that's the bad news. The staff call her his 'first wife'. He takes her everywhere, apparently."

"Oh." Simon felt a bit sick. Not in his stomach, though. He felt sick in the depths of his soul, where his certainties lay. They'd had a good kicking of late, and were prone to disorientation.

He decided to change the subject.

"How much have you drunk?"

"Well, that's a good question," said Bob. "The local alcohol is rather potent. Someone told Harriet. She took it as a challenge. And her body..."

"...isn't used to alcohol, anymore," Simon finished for him.

"I have only found a few. *Had* a few..." Bob was swaying gently, like a sapling in a light wind. Simon determined not to drink the local stuff.

"Who did you speak to?"

Bob broke into a broad smile.

"Actually, a really nice girl called Amelia. She was born here. And she was lovely."

Bob's eyes had gone slightly glassy.

"Nutsack!" Harriet bellowed into the floor. "Nutsack is a good word!"

Simon sighed and raised his eyebrows at Bob.

"Shall I take her away?" Bob offered.

It hadn't occurred to Simon that leaving her there was an option. Regardless of what she'd said previously, he was unnervingly certain he'd be awakened by her drunkenly attempting to mount him during the night.

She had to go.

"Yes, please."

Simon helped get her to her feet and propped her on Bob's arm. This was the kind of thing Simon had always despised doing and he was grateful to Bob for taking the responsibility.

As he closed the door behind them, he heard Harriet ask, "Are we going to shout at Simon, now?"

Things could only get better, he hoped, tomorrow.

"Have you seen my tits?" Harriet bellowed from along the corridor.

The answer was probably "yes", whomever she was asking.

CHAPTER FOURTEEN

"Fucking sit still," Harriet spat in the general direction of the walls.

She'd managed to open her eyes almost halfway, but the damned room was lurching and spinning like a belly dancer on jelly.

Hangovers were, for Harriet, an utterly foreign experience. First of all, she rarely drank so little that she woke up sober. Secondly, once she was awake, she never waited for the hangover to kick in before starting the day's imbibing.

After several minutes of thinking as quietly as she could, considering the various merits of a frontal assault (head for the sink), a rearguard action (head for the toilet) or a pincer movement (the toilet/bath combination), Harriet realised that the furry sensation in her mouth was not only punishment for last night's excesses, but also a quite literal clue to the fact that she was lying face down on someone's pedestal mat. It could well have been her pedestal mat, but there was no way to tell from this angle.

This also explained the cold, hard mattress she had been considering complaining about. Still wearing yesterday's clothes and some of yesterday's dinner, Harriet reached up to the edges of the toilet bowl and hauled herself into a drunk-ard's push up. After twenty minutes of deep and meaningful conversation with the toilet, she crawled to the mini-bar and ate every salty snack she could reach, washed down with mineral water.

It was bitter.

———

Bob breathed in deeply. He'd woken just before dawn and watched as the sun blushed the sky before rising over the hills. The warmth on his face; the sweet scents of the flowers; the sound of the wind caressing the trees – he was drinking every drop. His shoulders hung loose; relaxed. He was a man reborn and the world was reborn with him.

After a succulent breakfast, he had asked his waiter for a recommendation of a good place for a walk. The sunken garden he now had to himself was the answer. There were plants here beyond his imagination, defying both logic and gravity, growing within stone ruins that breathed with history.

Bob's mind was quiet.

Rising from the stone bench he had paused on, he wandered lazily along the makeshift 'path' through the grass. With Priest and Cassandra away, there was little to be done beyond enjoying themselves for a while. And this was a very enjoyable place. Plus, it was nice to be away from Hurricane Harriet. Regardless of her newly refined looks, she was a menace. Bob had been fortunate to require very little work in that regard. He was already tall and dark. It took only a few tweaks here and there – mostly removing a few visible scars – to add handsome to the stereotype.

"Argh! Sorry!" he yelped as he turned a corner and very nearly careered straight into a young woman picking fruit from a tree.

"I thought I was alone," he began to apologise, before recognising the girl as Amelia from the night before.

"Oh, hello. I didn't recognise you," he said, composing himself and placing both feet back firmly on the ground.

Amelia had not been as rattled by the chance encounter. She was perfectly calm. And still. Completely and utterly still.

"Hello?" Bob asked, confused. He waved a hand before her face, and noticed important things. Her eyes didn't move, even to blink. She wasn't breathing.

But she was stunning – a work of art carved from flesh and cloth. Though she did not move, even minutely, her white summer dress flapped gently in the breeze, hugging then fleeing from her legs.

Bob was transfixed. He felt an immediate and desperate urge to touch her. He stood in a museum, inches from a Pre-Raphaelite Angel, knowing he wasn't allowed to reach over the velvet rope. And yet, his hand crept slowly toward the pale, delicate skin of her face as he also stopped breathing...

"Bloody odd, isn't it?"

Bob jumped the jump of a guilty man. The voice had come from behind him – yet another place he had been certain there was nobody standing.

He turned to find a swarthy, stubbled young man, with hair that was part surfer, part pirate, smiling broadly at him.

Bob reeled for a moment, before his priorities returned to him.

"Odd?" he answered. "Is she... I mean... what's...?" Bob shrugged his shoulders and nodded at Amelia, certain his questions were self-evident.

"It's OK," the stranger replied in a soothing Irish brogue, "she's not dead. She's just stopped." He smiled at Bob as if this explained everything.

It didn't.

"Stopped?" Bob asked, wondering if this meant she had

been able to see him reaching towards her like a cat with a candle. "Stopped what?"

"Just stopped. She does it all the time. Has done since she turned 14. Something to do with her and them witches, I think."

Bob took in the information as quickly as possible. Firstly: witches? Bloody hell. Secondly: 14! Bloody, bloody hell! He hoped that had been some years ago. He desperately wanted to turn and look closely at her to confirm his belief that she was somewhat older, but was terrified that one glance would give away his thoughts to the Irish pirate.

Clearly, his eyes betrayed him anyway.

"Don't worry, she's well over 20 now," the pirate smiled, patting Bob on the arm. "You can stop beating yourself. Unless you like that sort of thing."

That grin again.

"I'm Sean, by the way. Sean O'Halloran. Pleased to meet you."

"Bob," Bob replied, taking the hand offered to him. "Are you a guest?"

"Used to be. But I ran out of cash, so I asked if there was any way I could stay. Now I'm a barman."

"A barman? I could use a drink."

Sean threw his arm around Bob. "Done and dusted, sir."

Bob paused, looking back at Amelia. "What about...?"

"I'll tell you about it in the bar, once you're sitting down."

"Will she be OK?"

"Aye, she'll be grand. It's not like it ever rains here. The worst she'll get is a bit dusty."

Bob allowed himself to be dragged towards an explanation and something to put his weight on besides his uncertain legs.

———

There were many sounds to which Simon had become unaccustomed during his solitary confinement. Several had presented themselves unexpectedly in recent days. His doorbell was, of course, first amongst them. Following this had been the sound of conversation in his living room, the chatter of a busy airport and the sound of friends laughing together.

Cherry had made sounds he'd never heard before. He liked those. She'd also made him make some noises he'd never made before and that he was entirely unsure he knew how he'd made in the first place. He was, however, prepared to repeat the experiment to see if they happened again.

One sound that was completely alien to Simon was that of a ringing telephone.

He only had a telephone line connected in his house for emergencies and takeaways but, no matter how he tried, he couldn't seem to avoid sales calls. Initially, as a small revenge and rebellion against these intrusions, he took some pleasure in playing with the callers. He would allow them to finish some elaborate and clearly scripted speech before saying, "I'm sorry, I wasn't paying attention. Could you repeat that?"

But even that became tedious, so he eventually just stopped paying his phone bill in protest. When a British Telecom operator called to cut him off and told him he'd be placed on a service which allowed "emergency calls out only", she was somewhat surprised with Simon's whoop of delight. He then offered to pay the outstanding balance immediately, but only after securing the woman's solemn word that she would leave him on a service which did not accept incoming calls.

The poor woman was so bemused by this that she took it upon herself to look up Simon's call records. In five years, there were only three local numbers he had called with anything resembling regularity – all around dinner time.

Other than that, he had made half a dozen calls to each of three numbers: one in Melton Mowbray, one in New York and one in Geneva. The pity she felt in seeing this was slightly alleviated by her passing amusement at the thought that his high percentage of overseas numbers would have flagged him up for regular sales calls from the long distance team.

Out of compassion, she misguidedly called the local Samaritans and gave them Simon's details, suggesting he could do with a visit. This caused great irritation to Simon as they knocked on his door in the middle of an episode of *Lost*. Having to duck behind the couch and turn down the volume on the TV made it even more difficult than usual to follow what the hell was going on. It did, however, finally convince him to get a Sky+ box.

When Simon heard a phone ringing while brushing his teeth, then, it was not entirely inexplicable that his first thought was, "Next door's phone is loud." Having quickly decided that the noise was definitely coming from his room, his next thought was, "Who put the telly on?" A quick glance out of the bathroom door confirmed that this, too, was wrong.

Bewildered, Simon wandered into the room and called out, "Hello?" through a mouthful of Aquafresh. With the next ring, the phone next to Simon's bed clearly vibrated slightly, confirming the inconceivable fact that, yes, someone actually wanted to speak to him. Shambling around the bed, Simon lifted the phone and put it tentatively to his ear, the way one might pick up a furry bundle of teeth and claws whose owner has just cheerily assured you not to worry, because it hardly ever bites.

"Yes?" Simon enquired of the phone.

"Hell... me."

The voice was gravelly and spoke from the depths of the earth. Worms crawled in it and death rattled around it. "Help... me," it repeated, this time including the missing consonant. Simon was frozen with terror. On this magical island, he was being called from beyond the grave to avenge a murder.

It was the only thing that made sense.

Simon was to be Hamlet, relentlessly seeking revenge on this poor, bereft zombie's tormentor. He even had a ready-made lunatic to be his Ophelia – which also neatly took care of Shakespeare's incestuous undertones.

"Wah-tur," the voice came again. "Wah-tur."

"Walter?" Simon asked. "Is that the name of your murderer?"

There was a pause as the zombie processed the question.

It then cleared its inhuman throat and replied, "Water, you fuckwit. Bring water. Now." The line went dead.

Simon's shoulders slumped. Ophelia was the zombie. As usual, his life was less Shakespeare; more pantomime.

Resigned, he finished dressing, emptied his bag and refilled it with the bottles of water from his minibar. With a deep breath, he opened the door and slowly left his room, off to rescue a dipsomaniac from dehydration.

———

"I don't usually drink this early," said Bob, "but..."

The empty glass that had, moments earlier, carried vodka to his lips, now stared accusingly up at him.

"Sure, you're on your holidays," replied Sean, pouring himself a Jameson behind the bar. The Irishman gestured to the vodka bottle, silently offering a top up. Bob shook his head. He was still a little tender from the night before and genuinely felt uncomfortable about the early hour.

"So every now and then she just... stops, like that?"

"That's about it, mate," replied the barman, seating himself beside Bob at the bar. "She's one of the very few people to have been born on this island. Her mother is one of the witches. I don't know who her da is, but I have my suspicions."

"Witches?" Bob asked. "Like, real witches?"

"Well, I dunno. They call themselves 'socialites', which is, frankly, silly, because I've never met a less sociable pack of bitches in me life."

"They have magic powers?"

"Well, let's just say that some bloody weird stuff happens around them. For example, from a distance, you'd think you were looking at the tastiest bunch of fluff you'd ever been lucky enough to set eyes on. Get close though..." Sean's voice trailed off as he shuddered and knocked back the last of his whiskey.

"Oh," said Bob. He wanted an explanation, but Sean didn't look like he wanted to expand on the topic. "Is Amelia a witch?"

"Don't think so. Sure, the closer you get to *her*, the *prettier* she is."

Bob winced at the reminder of how Sean had found him earlier. He was right though; she was beautiful.

"Boo!" Bob jumped in his seat as fingers dug into each of his sides. That small shock, however, was merely a tremor compared with the seismic quake of seeing who his assailant was. He was suddenly glad he hadn't agreed with Sean out loud.

"Jesus! Hello Amelia!" Sean said, warmly throwing open his arms to the now entirely mobile girl. "We were just talking about you."

Bob wondered if his face was as pale as it felt. How much had she heard?

"Oh, really?" The girl smiled angelically and looked at Bob. "All good, I hope?"

"Well, yeah..." Bob spluttered like a teenager. It was an unfamiliar position for him. He was a confident man, but this girl turned him to jelly. What the hell?

"I was just explaining to Bob about your condition, you know? He was out in the garden and bumped into you, then I bumped into him, and now we're here."

"Well thank heavens you were there Sean, otherwise Bob

might have ravaged me!" She patted Bob's knee playfully and laughed.

Bob forced a smile. 'Ravaging' her had genuinely not occurred to him. Until now.

"You're up early this morning. What happened to your girlfriend from last night?"

"My... *Harriet?*" Bob sputtered. "God no, she's not my girlfriend! She's a..." *Companion? Accomplice? Lunatic?* "...friend."

"You don't sound very sure, mate. *Is* she a friend?" Sean asked.

"Yeah. She's a friend."

"Oh, really? Well then there's nothing to stop us two singles from going for a walk in the garden together later, is there? I can show you my favourite flowers," said Amelia, "there are some great little alcoves and hidden spots."

Bob's internal sensors did a quick rewind. Had he heard that right? Had the beautiful enigma just asked him to go for a walk in the amazing garden, looking for hidden alcoves?

"I guess not," he answered, grinning widely.

"Lovely," Amelia smiled. "Right, I need some breakfast. See you both later!" With a wave, she bounced through the terrace doors and out to join the growing throng of people breaking their fast.

"Bob, close yer mouth, son," said Sean, pouring himself another whiskey.

"She's..."

"She's something else, isn't she?"

"She's amazing," Bob finally said, reaching for the whiskey Sean had just poured and knocking it back in one.

Sean grinned, pulled Bob's empty glass to him and started pouring again.

———

"For God's sake, slow down!" Harriet barked.

"Harriet," Simon replied as calmly as he could manage, "we're standing still."

"Bollocks," she murmured, her eyes closed and her head hanging like a sack of onions as she leaned on her nephew for support.

Simon had arrived at her room and found the door ajar. Inside, he'd found his great aunt face down in the remains of the mini bar: mainly empty water bottles and crisp packets. He'd managed to prop her up and pour water into her mouth (mostly), for which she'd seemed a little grateful and a little annoyed.

After she tried and failed to fall asleep because "the bloody room won't sit still!" they decided that food was the order of the day to combat the hangover from Hell.

"Come on," Simon coaxed, "we're nearly there." He hated this with every fibre of his sober being.

Harriet lifted her head groggily and peered out through tiny slits. After a moment, they opened wide.

"Are you mental?! That's the bar!"

"Harriet, the map said the breakfast terrace is through the bar."

Harriet used every ounce of her strength to grab Simon's face with both hands and raised her head to look him in the eyes.

"You have no idea what you're asking me to do," she said, with an intensity rarely felt outside of prison.

Simon sighed. It was too much to hope she'd learn something from this experience.

They shuffled onwards, finally negotiating the swinging double doors. Expecting to find the room empty, Simon was surprised to see two figures sitting at the bar. As they turned to see who was joining them, Simon was even more surprised to see that it was Bob. And a pirate.

He wondered if alcoholism was contagious.

134

"Bloody hell mate, what did you do to *her*?" the pirate asked, advancing on them.

"Sean, this is Harriet and her... cousin, Simon," said Bob, also getting up and moving towards them. "This is Sean. He works here."

Simon relaxed a little at the thought that Bob was simply doing what he'd said he was going to do – getting to know the staff. "Hello," he said, as cheerily as he could muster.

"Ugh," said Harriet, vaguely moving one hand in his direction.

"Harriet drank a lot of the local spirit last night," Bob explained.

"Ah, right," said Sean, lifting her free arm and guiding her to a seat. "Now what would make a fine young girl like you think you could handle that kind of nonsense?"

"Ugh," Harriet replied again. Simon and Bob swapped a conspiratorial look that also contained no small amount of amusement for them both.

"Well, what kind of barman would I be if I didn't have a hangover cure on hand?"

Sean marched jauntily behind the bar and began pouring things into a blender.

Harriet motioned to Simon to come closer. As he leaned in, she whispered as loudly as she could, "Kill me."

Simon sat down next to his not-so-great aunt.

"Isn't it a little early for drinks?" Simon asked Bob. He hoped the disapproval wasn't too evident on his face.

Unfortunately, it was.

Fortunately, Bob didn't care. He was still swimming in the warm waters of Amelia's smile.

"I've only had a couple. Had a bit of a shock."

"Good shock or bad shock?" Simon worried that things had gotten worse while he played nursemaid. Though what would be worse was hard to imagine.

"Good, I think. I'll tell you later," Bob reassured him.

Simon cocked his head with interest.

Sean arrived back at the table with what could best be described as a pint of pure blue. He placed it carefully in front of Harriet.

"Get that down you, love. You'll be right as rain in 15 minutes."

Harriet's pathetic attempt to grab the glass didn't last long. Without skipping a beat, Sean produced a straw from somewhere and dropped it in the glass, which he then placed right under Harriet's face.

She got her mouth around the straw and began to suck, slowly at first, then, as if gripped by a fervent desire, faster and faster. She eventually grabbed the glass violently from Sean and, throwing the straw away, glugged back the last of the drink. When it was completely drained, she stood up abruptly and loudly announced to the empty room, "Monkey suffering fuck!" before collapsing on the table.

Sean walked calmly back behind the bar. Bob and Simon looked to each other for some explanation of what had just occurred.

"Is that supposed to happen?" Bob asked.

"It's not unheard of," Sean answered casually. "Anyone else for coffee?"

———

Ten minutes later, Bob, Sean and Simon sat around a table in the vast, empty bar. Harriet remained out cold, but now propped carefully up in her chair. This had been necessary to make room on the table for the cafetière and cups.

"So what do you think of the place?" Sean asked Simon.

"It's very pretty," Simon answered, hoping not to be asked for specifics.

"What have you done so far?"

Damn.

Simon hesitated to answer, since "I sat in my room all evening watching *M.A.S.H.* and eating nuts" sounded so pathetic in his head that he was terrified of finding out how it sounded out loud. Especially not in the company of this gregarious, charming and virile Irishman.

Thankfully, Bob rescued him.

"Well, we only arrived yesterday and, as you know, Harriet and I hit the bar. We had a chat with Amelia and the barmaid."

"Oh aye? Who was on last night?"

"Star, I think her name was," Bob replied

"Ah, the lovely Star. Now there's a heavenly body." Sean's faraway look suggested he had examined it in some detail. Bob looked at him with what seemed to Simon like admiration and a little jealousy. He understood. It was hard not to like this man – and not to want him to like you back.

"And what about you?" Sean turned back to Simon. Crap. He thought he'd been forgotten.

"Simon had a big night on Wednesday, so he crashed out early last night."

It was Harriet's voice. All three turned to see the previously comatose hellcat sitting serenely in her seat, smiling beatifically at them all. She winked at Simon.

Harriet had just helped him. He had to let that sink in.

What did she *want*?

"Welcome back," said Sean. "It's nice to see your gorgeous eyes rather than the top of your head."

Smooth.

"Really?" Harriet replied sweetly. "A lot of men have enjoyed looking at the top of my head."

There was a moment of brilliant silence as all three pennies dropped.

Sean burst into raucous laughter. Bob joined him, shaking his head, and even Simon chortled nervously.

"So tell me," Harriet began, leaning towards Sean, "am I

dreaming, or am I really looking at a gorgeous, Irish barman who comes with his own hangover cure?"

Sean beamed.

"My Lord, girlie, you've the heart of a lion and the mind of a harlot!"

"That may be my favourite ever compliment," she answered. "So, who's hungry? I should eat."

"Yes!" Simon exploded from his seat, keen to escape Harriet's foreplay.

"I could eat," Sean agreed.

All four raised themselves and carried their coffees to the terrace.

———

Luke examined himself in the mirror. He'd left a few nicks here and there, but mostly, it looked OK, considering he'd never shaved his head before.

"How is it?" Gabby called from the bedroom.

"Well, you know how Bruce Willis looks better without hair?"

"Yeah, I guess."

"Not like that."

"Oh."

Luke walked back into the room where Gabby sat, brushing her hair in the mirror. Her previously short blonde hair was now a jet black bob. She actually suited the wig, he thought, with only a small tinge of jealousy.

"Oh, that's not that bad at all, you know!" she said, turning towards him. "In fact, it's kind of sexy."

"You're just saying that..." Luke smiled sheepishly.

"Seriously, if you just let that stubble grow out into a light beard..." She stroked his newly shaven head, smiling affectionately.

"OK," he smiled back. "So shall we risk venturing out of our room, then?"

"I suppose we'd better, or else there wasn't much point in coming, was there?"

———

Cherry sat on the plush sofa in her room, wrapped in a luxurious dressing gown and drinking coffee. Faunt was an excellent host to everyone who stayed in his home – even those working for him. She hadn't slept particularly well the night before, but then she often didn't. As a child, she'd suffered night terrors and as an adult she never found sleep easy to come by.

Usually, beer helped; but not last night.

She'd had an ominous sense of foreboding – the strange, indefinable feeling that something was about to go badly wrong. Watching the news since she'd given up on sleep at about 5:30, there had been nothing to particularly worry her.

There was a political scandal over a French government official sleeping with a male model; a sudden, inexplicable decline in the fish population off the coast of Norway; some equally unexplained damage to a Danish bridge, which might have been a failed terrorist attack, and a missing Lord in Britain, who, it seemed, had some 'misunderstandings' over his tax returns, going back some years.

Nothing to be overly worried about. And yet... here she was, glued to the television with that horrible feeling that something was not right.

CHAPTER FIFTEEN

Gabby was starting to feel decidedly conspicuous. She wasn't actually pretending to read a newspaper, or wearing dark glasses, but she was absolutely certain that anyone who looked at her and Luke would instantly know that they were watching Simon and his friends. After breakfast that morning, they followed them down to the beach. The barman had gone back to work. The three of them had then lounged on the beach, Harriet occasionally barking directions at Simon on how to enjoy himself "properly". He had, to his credit, awkwardly tried his best to follow the instructions, even having a few piña coladas with her.

Here they were, though, back at the castle-cum-hotel, watching them having lunch. And, she was sure, wearing big signs that said "SPIES" around their necks.

"What's wrong?" Luke asked.

"Nothing," she answered. "Why do you think something's wrong?"

Luke nodded towards her hands, which contained the remains of the napkin she'd been unconsciously making confetti with.

"Oh. I'm just, you know..." she grimaced.

Luke smiled reassuringly back at her.

"What do you think it'll be like? Being dead?" she asked.

"What do you mean? You know what it's like."

"I know what it's like now. I mean, you know, after. What will it be like?"

Luke's face fell. He opened his mouth to answer, but he had no words.

"I hope it's like a dreamless sleep – you know?" said Gabby.

Luke nodded.

"We're not done, yet," he whispered. "We're not beat."

"Yet," Gabby repeated.

At that moment, a young girl they didn't recognise arrived at the other table. She didn't look like a waitress. She was pretty and had an air of invincibility about her. After a moment's conversation, Bob got up from the table and followed the girl back into the hotel. As he passed their table, both Luke and Gabby suddenly found their menus unusually fascinating – particularly considering they'd already eaten.

"Now what?" Gabby asked Luke when she was sure Bob was out of earshot.

"We stay with these two," Luke answered. Which, of course, would have been somewhat easier, had Harriet not at that very point decided to get up and walk into the bar, leaving Simon alone at the table.

"*Now* what?" Gabby asked, aware she was being repetitive.

"Um, right." Luke scanned the room for an answer. "You follow her. I'll stay with him."

Gabby's eyes opened wide. This was bad enough *with* Luke. *On her own?* Following the *mad* woman?

"OK," she answered nervously, getting up from the table.

She silently resolved to punish Luke later for not coming up with a better plan.

"I don't like this."

Daniel was pacing. He'd been doing it for some time.

"I know you don't."

Lily was draped over a very comfortable armchair, engrossed in the television.

"They're totally out of our control. They could come up with a plan to stay in there. What if they just tell Priest everything and he grants them sanctuary? *Then* what?"

"Will you please just relax? Come watch this with me. It's not bad."

Daniel exploded. "Are you serious? Do you know what kind of pressure I'm under? Do you know how much this *means*? If we screw this up, if we lose him... remember what happened to the last one?"

"Of course I do," Lily turned away from the TV for the first time in the conversation. "But what do you propose that we do, right now, that will make the slightest bit of difference? We've already brought a boat out to the edge of Priest's waters. This is as close as we are allowed get. We've got surveillance covering the area all around the island. As soon as he leaves, in any direction, we'll know. Until then, we know where he is. So as there's absolutely nothing else we can do right now, why don't you sit down and watch TV with me?"

A look crossed Daniel's face that Lily was not accustomed to seeing. He was a businesslike, serious and fairly obsessive personality. 'Fun' was not a concept that would often find itself in close proximity to the angel, unless 'Fun' took a second job as an accountant. But Daniel had a look that, on any other face, she'd have considered to be... devilment.

"What are you *thinking*?" she asked.

"I'm thinking," he smiled, "that what we *can* do is remind them of the consequences if they stay there too long..."

Simon was doing something unusual. He was exploring. He had to do something to take his mind off the ridiculous situation he was in. His life depended on kidnapping the wife of the apparently all-powerful ruler of this actually rather nice island. Them not being here was sort of a relief, but it was only delaying the inevitable. He actually just wanted them to come back so he could get it over with, despite being simultaneously completely terrified of the idea. And every time his mind wasn't occupied, Simon drove himself insane thinking about all the ways he could end up dead.

Hence the exploring.

The vast, old castle of a hotel was full of interesting nooks and crannies. In fact, if Wikipedia needed pictures to illustrate the phrase 'nooks and crannies', every variety of the species could most likely be found within this very building. There were suits of armour lining a ridiculously long hallway, in which hung the kind of paintings Simon suspected were each worth substantially more than his life, and, collectively, probably more than Britain's Gross Domestic Product. Some of them looked sort of familiar, while others were totally foreign to him.

There was a small cinema, with plush, suede-covered seats and a bar, into which Simon very much hoped he would be invited later. There was also a stunning, huge swimming pool, which was half under cover and half open to the sky, on a balcony, which looked out off a cliff top down to the sea.

It was here that he discovered the group of ladies, sitting around a table, under the shade of a parasol. They were sipping what looked like very exotic cocktails and chattering away at the same time in the way that women can. They were – every one of them – classically elegant.

The six of them were completely different, and yet they each shared flawless skin, perfectly symmetrical features, silky, luxurious hair and smiles that would melt glaciers. It was as if God or, he presumed, in this instance, Satan, had opened each of them in Photoshop and made liberal use of the airbrush.

Had they appeared on a magazine cover, he'd have scoffed at them as an unrealistic idealisation of feminine beauty. And yet, here they were, *looking* at him.

Being Simon, he did the most natural thing in the world when he realised a group of women were looking his way. He looked over his shoulder to see who was behind him.

Once he realised there was nobody else around, the phrase 'bunny in headlights' did little to reach the extremes to which Simon suddenly plummeted in his lack of social skills. It was more akin to one of those googly-eyed bush babies in a force ten gale, under floodlights.

Then, in a completely unexpected and unpredictable way, it got worse. One of the women got up from the table, smiled, and glided towards him.

"Hello," she said, as she drew near.

What the hell was he supposed to do now?

———

Gabby was pacing. She'd followed Harriet and Sean. It hadn't been difficult. They went straight to Harriet's room. She'd hung around outside feeling horribly conspicuous just long enough to hear that the pair were clearly going to be engaged in private activity for some time. As it was loud enough for her to hear through the door in the hall, she assumed that the occupants of the adjacent rooms would also be aware of the situation. If they happened to stick their nose out of their door, as people sometimes do in these situations, she had no desire to be left trying to explain what she was doing loitering in the hall listening intently.

Sensibly, she buggered off.

Having spent some time trying to find Luke and being

afraid to call him in case his ringing phone alerted Debovar to his presence, she had found herself here, in an upper hallway, wondering what to do next. With a large sigh of frustration, she threw herself down in a chair and leaned on the adjacent window ledge, looking out at the beautiful garden below.

As serendipity would have it, she found herself looking down on Bob and Amelia, who were sitting on a bench not far below her. Fantastic! Now she could tell Luke she had tracked down the gatekeeper and the girl when she'd had to abandon the other two!

Pleased with her fortuitous competence, she settled quietly to watch her new subjects.

They spoke softly to each other, laughing often. They looked happy. In fact, they reminded her of Luke and herself, in better times; before they were on the verge of losing everything. In fact, she realised, she'd been unfair to Luke. After all, he was only human. Now. Sort of.

She would apologise for being so hard on him, later.

Smiling, Gabby's thoughts returned to her unwitting subjects below. The girl twirled her hair and giggled. He cleared his throat and looked her in the eyes.

Wait a minute.

If Gabby didn't know better she'd think they were... Wait a minute! Wait a minute! She was leaning towards him. He leaned toward her. "They're kissing!" she very nearly yelped out loud, jumping up from her seat. This was an unexpected twist – even in this odd story.

It wasn't a quick peck either. It was a long, intense, deep kiss – the kind between two souls reunited after a lengthy absence. Between two people, lost and alone, who have unexpectedly found something they didn't know they were looking for. It was beautiful.

Suddenly, Gabby realised her afternoon's activity was in danger of qualifying her for Voyeurs Anonymous. Hoping no one had been watching *her*, she quietly got up from the seat and moved on. That was it, she'd done her bit. Both of the people she'd been watching were getting busy and she was starting to feel a little neglected, herself. It was time to go back to the room and prepare Luke's apology.

Time stopped.

Simon had reached the absolute peak of social awkwardness. Worse than accidentally flashing the neighbours. Worse than farting in church. Only moments ago, as the slinky, liquid blonde had moved toward him, he had been in a state of sheer terror.

He was alone. She was going to speak to him. It was obviously terrifying.

And then it got worse. As the woman stepped within a few feet of Simon and stretched out a hand to greet him, she seemed to wither, age and decay in front of him. The sophisticated beauty became a cretinous hag. She said something. He definitely saw her mouth move – but all brain function had clearly been diverted from his ears to where it was busily screaming "What the bloody, buggering hell is that?!" and desperately doing its best not to let the shock, horror and disgust register on his face.

That would be rude.

What he definitely was not prepared for – which is not to say that he was prepared for the melted-faced monstrosity reaching for his hand – was to see the same shock and horror on her face as she looked back at him. Why on earth would this Gorgon be scared of him? He was barely retaining control of his sphincter as it was.

Simon looked down. He couldn't see his feet.

It wasn't because of the new trouser bulge to which he was still becoming accustomed. It was his belly.

He was back to normal.

At first, seeing such a familiar sight seemed natural – almost comforting. Then he realised where he was and that, if he were seen like this by the wrong person, he could well be thrown off the island. Then he'd have no Cassandra, no carpet and, eventually, no lungs, he was pretty sure. Unusually for Simon, this all occurred to him quite quickly. It's amazing what mortal terror can do to speed up one's mental faculties.

The screaming in his head got louder and he moved to run away. As he took a step back, however, the woman instantly returned to her previous, beautiful state. She stood there, looking utterly bemused at him, but without the disgust of a moment ago. Over her shoulder, Simon caught sight of himself in a wall mirror and was deeply relieved to see himself returned to his previous, Adonis-like condition.

Thus, here they were. Standing looking at each other, confused, befuddled and wondering what the hell was going on. After a few moments of looking for an explanation on the floor, which stubbornly refused to offer one, Simon looked up to see the woman walking slowly back to her table, still looking confused.

He knew how she felt. It was time to be somewhere else. He wondered if there was any more *M.A.S.H.* on.

———

Sean sat huddled against the door, backed up against it like a cat that had accidentally stumbled into an illicit late-night cat-eating club. His eyes were wide and staring, and he pointed, limply, back at Harriet, who sat up, gloriously naked in the bed.

"Wh... wh..." he panted, trying in vain to get out more than one syllable.

It was a fairly understandable reaction from a man who'd just seen his latest bedroom gymnastics partner instantly age 60 years mid-stroke. The speed with which he'd extricated himself from the situation, bounded out of bed and found the nearest hard surface to back up against would have put that cat to shame. Language, however, had not quite come back to him yet.

"Right, so..." said Harriet, "there's probably something I should explain."

––––––

"You did *what*? Are you *serious*?" Lily's mouth gaped.

"Just for a few seconds," Daniel shrugged his shoulders. "Five, at the most."

Lily couldn't decide whether to scream at him for being so reckless or roar with laughter.

"You know something? I think you're loosening up."

"Don't be silly," said Daniel, turning away from her. "It was a sound tactical decision. To remind them we're here."

"Well, you better hope they're the only ones you reminded of anything, that's all I'm saying..."

Daniel smiled. Just a little.

––––––

"Right. OK. So you're not a witch?" Sean asked.

"I've been called a lot worse than that!" laughed Harriet.

"No, but seriously. You're not. Right?"

"Seriously? There are witches? Bugger me."

"Oh aye. And you don't want to be getting on the wrong side of them. I made that mistake once."

"Right. Well, no, not a witch. Just the other thing that rhymes with it. Is that going to be OK with you or am I going to need to look for another toy boy?"

"Toy boy?" It was Sean's turn to smile. "Heh, well, that's funny, you see. I'm a little older than I look too."

"Oh really?" Harriet braced herself for being under-whelmed by his admission of being over 30.

"1812," said Sean.

"What about it?"

"That's when my boat landed here."

It wasn't often that Harriet was speechless. Scratch that – Harriet had never been speechless in her entire life. It was an odd experience.

Sean grinned. "So technically, I'm the one robbing the cradle here."

Harriet grabbed at the whisky on the bedside table and knocked back what was left of it. "OK. You can explain that later. For now, since we've sorted that out and I seem to be 21 again – do you think we could get that working?" She nodded toward Sean's crotch.

"Get it *working*? Jesus woman, we'll have to coax the thing back out of me diaphragm, first!"

———

Luke burst into the room.

"Something weird happened!" he announced.

Gabby wondered what he would consider weird. This could be interesting.

"He changed! Just for a moment, but he definitely changed."

"Who did?"

"Debovar! He was talking to one of the witches and just for a moment, he went back to himself! What do you think it means?"

"Back to himself? You mean, what, older?"

"Back to normal."

"I don't know. What do you think?"

"I think maybe their powers aren't entirely working here. I think maybe they can't keep them young for long."

"Really? Is that possible?"

"I think so. Maybe. They're banned from coming here, aren't they? Do you know what that means?"

"Not really."

"If they can't keep Debovar and his aunt young indefinitely, then all we have to do is keep them here long enough for them to turn back to normal. Then they'll be thrown off the island."

"But don't we want them off the island as quickly as possible?"

"Well, we want them out of the way, where they can't do their job."

"So how do we do that?"

Luke finally paused, his energy depleted, and sat on the edge of the bed.

"Well, that's the thing, isn't it? How can we keep them tied up?"

Now and again, when everything came together and the stars were in the correct alignment, or in this case, as she looked across the room at the massage oil she'd lovingly prepared for Luke's return, something sparked for Gabby.

"There's a prison downstairs! We just need to get them arrested for something!" She brandished the bottle of oil at him, as if to confirm the point.

Luke's eyes widened. It wasn't a bad idea.

"Why did the bottle make you think of prison?" he asked.

Gabby looked down at it as if it had just appeared in her hand.

"I dunno. Massage oil... prison? It just did."

"Right. So we just have to get them to do something wrong," said Luke. "Well, something illegal, anyway."

"OK, so what can we get them for?" Gabby asked, seemingly having exhausted her planning contribution for the year.

"Well, Simon barely leaves his room. After the little

wobble this afternoon, he went back and hasn't left since, I don't think."

"So where have you been?" Gabby asked, trying not to sound too suspicious. "It's nearly dinner time."

Luke had a moment of that particularly male experience when a woman asks him a small question, which he knows fine well has a much bigger question hiding inside it; when she asks "Where have you been?" but she means "Who were you with?"

No matter how innocent he is, the man has an unmistakeable moment of guilt, before being able to answer, as if the collective male subconscious has been inexorably emblazoned with the fact that, at heart, all men are dogs and should be sorry.

He explained and, after some discussion, they actually had a plan. It was a good plan.

They hoped.

CHAPTER SIXTEEN

Dinner on Priest's Island was an opulent, decadent affair. The breakfast terrace, also used for lunch, was abandoned as the whole event moved up on to the roof. On a huge, terracotta stone floor were dozens of large round tables covered in white linen tablecloths and adorned with elegant candles, silver cutlery and flowers. They were only a sample of the foliage though, with the tables surrounded by plants, vines and flowers. Overhead, some old wooden bars, which seemed once to have held grape vines, were draped in a spectacular array of fairy lights and paper lanterns – all in white.

At the end furthest from the door that led back down to the kitchen lay one long main table, where six of the 'witches' sat, three at either side of two empty seats.

"Do you think this is where they filmed *Mamma Mia?*" Gabby asked.

"What?" Luke asked. It was more 'What the hell are you on about?' than 'I'm sorry, what did you say?'

"You know: *Mamma Mia*. I wonder if they filmed it here?"

"You're babbling again," he said, affectionately.

"I suppose I am, a bit. Sorry."

"It's OK," Luke smiled, looking nervously toward the table

across the terrace where Simon, Harriet and Bob sat with the barman and Amelia.

He wondered how they'd managed to become so friendly with two of the island's inhabitants so quickly. It was also risky for Amelia to be sitting with Bob, he thought. It made no difference now, anyway, since he and Gabby had, just an hour ago, walked "casually" past one of the witches – a red-haired one – and "casually" discussed a few things. It was only a matter of time.

"Do you know what I want to know?" Gabby piped up again.

"What?" Luke asked, scratching his head, which had begun to itch all over.

"What does 'I smell like I sound' mean?"

It was a non sequitur of epic proportions, even for her.

"Pardon?"

"In 'Hungry like the Wolf'. Duran Duran. How can you smell like you sound? That's stupid."

Luke stared.

Thankfully, a waiter arrived and delivered their starters, which appeared to be some kind of roast pigeon.

"Brazil?" Gabby added, gesturing to the surrounds, as if this explained everything.

She had become less and less comprehensible since they became human.

———

To say that Simon was uncomfortable surrounded by strangers was an understatement worthy of awards.

To add to that existing discomfort, he had somehow become the fifth wheel when his travelling companions had both paired off, with somewhat undue haste. Harriet had assured him the timescale was "normal for holidays". He wished she'd stop calling it that. It wasn't a holiday, it was a highly dangerous, secret mission to save his life – but he seemed to be the only one focused on that goal.

Despite his discomfort, the meal was, overall, enjoyable. A main course of seafood paella was well done and the dessert was some kind of chocolate mousse cake thing, which was excellent. Even Harriet had eaten it enthusiastically, though she did dribble some of her whisky over it first. Intentionally.

Just as Simon was thinking he'd be able to go back to his room soon, having survived a whole day, the chatter died down when a spoon was clinked repeatedly against a glass. He looked up to see something terrifying – the gorgeous monstrosity he'd come across that afternoon was standing up, glass in hand. Simon did his best impression of an empty chair as she looked at their table.

"Oh God," said Amelia, smiling and wincing in equal measure. "It's mother."

"That's your mother?" Bob asked.

If he was under the impression this meant that the girl by his side was going to turn into a classic beauty, Simon had bad news for him – unless he was prepared to remain outside a five-foot perimeter. Which seemed unlikely, what with the way he had mooned over her all evening.

"Ladies and Gentleman," Amelia's witch-mother began, hushing the assembled diners completely, "may I welcome our most recent arrivals to Priest's Island. I hope you will enjoy your stay."

Her voice was like a young Katherine Hepburn's. She had a sensuous Southern drawl that made Simon think of hot summer nights, white cotton shirts, repressed homosexuality and insidious racism.

"As most of you know, our host is away from the island on personal business at the moment, meaning that control of the island is left to us. This means we are here to make your stay as enjoyable as possible, but also that we have to deal with any legal issues that arise."

Simon's heart sank even further. He'd been revealed in true form right in front of the highest-ranked person on the island.

He might as well have wobbled his danglies at the Pope.

"Unfortunately," Amelia's mother continued, "an issue has arisen which needs to be addressed."

Simon's left arm developed a nasty twitch. With any luck, he'd have a heart attack and avoid the rest of this announcement.

"As you all know, we have some local laws here which, while our island is both exclusive and dedicated to your pleasure, must still be obeyed. Breaches of these laws are taken very seriously."

Simon felt a sudden and urgent need for a toilet. As they were sitting fairly far away from the head table, he wondered whether he could creep away unnoticed, before she finally got to the point she clearly intended to make. Harriet kicked him under the table. He looked up to see her mouth, "What's wrong?" at him. Apparently, he wasn't disguising his nerves as well as he imagined.

———

Harriet scowled at her nephew. He was either having some sort of fit or just being a dolt in public again, shaking like a particularly pathetic leaf in a slight breeze.

So some authoritarian bitch was making a statement about keeping to the rules. There was no reason for any of them to think they'd been compromised. It wasn't as if one of them had done something stupid...

She'd been away from Simon all afternoon.

She kicked him again under the table, harder. This time, as he looked round, she hissed at him, "What have you done?"

He looked pathetically back at her.

Bollocks.

Harriet started to pay attention to the bitch's statement – she was still wittering on about rules and obligations. Reaching across the table, Harriet picked up an almost finished bottle of wine and casually drained it into her glass. Then, feigning a cough, she put the empty bottle down on the floor next to her bag, from which she retrieved a tissue and blew her nose. Putting the tissue away again, she grabbed the bottle and placed it between her knees under the table, within easy reach.

She took a deep breath, lifted her large Caol Ila from the table and necked the contents.

Right. She was full of adrenaline and single malt.

Game on.

———

"So, I'm afraid there is an issue that we're going to have address," the witch continued. "And I'm going to have to ask someone to come up here and make a statement in front of all of you, as witnesses to the openness and fairness of our system."

She looked straight at their table. In that long, long moment of silence, Simon could hear his bowels loosening. At any moment, she was going to say his name and he would have to walk up to the front of the room and be humiliated. And possibly disembowelled.

But the worst thing was that every single person on this rooftop would be looking at him.

She paused forever. The woman seemed to be adding to the drama, just for the hell of it. Simon hated her more than most.

"Amelia," the witch finally said, "would you come forward, please?"

Simon shook uncontrollably.

———

This was unexpected. Perhaps her calamitous nephew had not done anything wrong after all. It seemed to be some kind of family tiff, which was certainly none of Harriet's business.

She relaxed a little and watched as a confused Amelia smiled and exchanged a look with Bob, before standing and demurely making her way towards her mother. Bob looked around at the rest of the table and shrugged, smiling. So the giant had no idea what was happening, which suggested he hadn't done anything disastrous either.

All good. She poured herself another measure and breathed in its aroma.

Amelia arrived beside her mother, smiling that same awkward smile.

"Yes, mother?" she asked in a tone that was clearly half obedience and half irritation.

"Amelia, where were you this afternoon, at approximately three o'clock?" she asked, authoritatively.

"I think I was in the stone garden. Why?"

"And who were you there with?"

"A friend – Bob," Amelia answered, nodding towards their table.

"Oh shit," Sean muttered under his breath. He looked at Bob and then at Harriet. "Something's wrong."

Harriet went back to high alert, clenching the bottle between her thighs.

Amelia was saying something quietly to her mother in the pleading way that only a daughter who has been dragged in front of a crowd of strangers to be questioned can do. Her face was scarlet.

"And Amelia," her mother asked aloud, so that the whole audience could clearly hear, "is it true that you were seen kissing this man?"

Amelia went from scarlet to pale white as she realised where this was going.

"Oh, mother, no,' she whimpered. "Please, you can't..."

Earlier, Luke had been explaining his afternoon whereabouts to his lover, whose look was currently saying: "I'm not angry; I'm fine. But if you don't have a very good answer for where you've been in the next thirty seconds I'm going to fricassee your testicles."

"Well," he answered, "after I saw that Simon had locked himself back in his room, I went to see what I could find out about the others. First I looked for the giant, but I couldn't find him. But I did find out something interesting. There are these women here – they're... very beautiful."

Luke knew he was on thin ice again and that he'd better get quickly to the other side if he was to have any chance of seeing that massage oil in action. Gabby's face confirmed this suspicion.

"But actually, they're not. When you get close to them, they become, well, hideous. I think they're witches."

Phew – he'd made it to the point.

"*How* close?"

Damn.

How did he not see that coming?

"Well, within a few feet."

"Why were you that close to them?"

The massage was fading away.

"Well, I went to speak to them about what happened. With Simon. To see if they knew anything."

"And what happened?"

Luke pondered a moment. While the absolute truth was slightly damaging to his ego, it was also just possible that it would get him out of trouble.

"They called me 'baldy' and told me to polish my *own* head."

Gabby rose up indignantly.

Brilliant.

"They said what?! What did you say to them?"

"I just asked if they'd noticed anything odd about the guy they'd just seen."

"And that's how they responded?"

"Well, I think they assumed it was a pick up line."

"Oh they did, did they?"

Excellent, the witches were now firmly the enemy.

"Right, we'll see about that." Gabby stood up and started getting dressed.

"Wait." Luke put his hand on her arm. "I don't think we want to annoy these women. I think they're kind of in charge when Priest's not here. And I think they're powerful."

"Ah," she said. "Right."

She sat back down.

"So do we need to get Simon in trouble with them?"

Luke perked up again. That's exactly what they needed.

"Yes, yes, that's perfect. They'll have to put them in jail until Priest comes back. With any luck, by then Debovar and his aunt will have changed back to normal and they'll be thrown out!"

"OK. So how do we get them in trouble?"

"Well, from listening to them, they seem to pretty much only care about themselves, their looks and gin. The only time I heard any of them talk positively about another person was when one of them was talking about her daughter – that Amelia girl."

"Amelia? Is that the pretty girl? The young one in the floaty dresses?"

"I think so," Luke answered, keen not to confirm the 'pretty' description too enthusiastically.

"So, if I had happened to see her kissing the big guy, Bob, in the garden this afternoon, then that would be interesting, would it?"

"Seriously? Like a friendly kiss or...?"

"If you kissed a friend like that we'd have a problem."

"Right. That *is* interesting."

While a light bulb did not actually appear over Luke's head and burst into life, it was patently obvious to Gabby that he'd had an idea – and it was a doozy. He smiled broadly at her.

"What? *What?*" she asked, barely able to wait as long as it took Luke to draw breath.

"Well, how old would you say Bob is?"

"I don't know. Mid thirties? Maybe a bit younger."

"And Amelia?"

"Early twenties, I'd say."

"And witches – they tend to live a very long time don't they?"

"Yes."

"So if these witches are like most witches, they probably live about 200 years, yeah?"

"Yes." Gabby did not see where this was going.

"Which means that they have a different perspective on time. Under witch law, a girl does not become a woman until..."

"Thirty!" Gabby shouted, finishing the thought for him. "She's underage!"

"Exactly," Luke answered, pleased with himself. "We've got him for indecent assault of an underage witch."

"Oooh, wait though. That's pretty serious. What if they execute him or something?"

"This is Priest's island. They'll have to wait for him to come back to try him, I'm sure. And unless he abides by witch law, then Bob's done nothing wrong, so he'll get off free. And as a guest of the island, he'll be protected from the witches doing anything themselves."

"And what if Priest abides by witch law?"

"As far as I know, he abides by doing whatever he likes – especially here."

"OK, so that takes care of Bob – what about the other two?"

"Well, I was thinking – what if they thought that Bob *was* in danger of being executed? And what if someone suggested to them a plan to break him out of the dungeons? And what if that same someone happened to tip off a guard about it so that they got caught – and ended up in jail too?"

Gabby nodded in appreciation. "Oh, that is good. Well done."

"Thank you."

"One thing though," Gabby added. "What if you're wrong? What if the witches take this on themselves and we end up getting all three of them killed?"

"Then Faunt's going to shish kebab us."

"Exactly."

"It'll be fine, I'm sure," Luke said confidently.

As was often the case, he wasn't.

———

Two men who looked a bit like guards and a bit like the mice from Cinderella – when they'd been turned into coachmen – stood behind Bob.

Bob looked stunned.

The whole rooftop had just heard how he had allegedly indecently assaulted Amelia in the garden. The girl stood helplessly weeping beside her mother.

Simon sat in equally stunned silence. He'd been sure he was about to be exposed and humiliated but, instead, it was Bob who'd been exposed and Amelia humiliated. His brief feeling of relief was now replaced with another: indignation. This was unfair! Bob had no idea Amelia was not of legal age in her culture! He'd done nothing wrong. It was an outrage. Simon stood up and began to open his mouth to complain, but as he did so, he got another stiff kick under the table, which made him yelp. He looked round, expecting to see Harriet glowering at him, but instead she was staring at him with what almost looked like respect. In fact, it was Sean who was looking at him with wide eyes, which were clearly screaming, "Sit down and shut up!"

Screaming eyes rarely being an encouragement to carry on, Simon duly obliged, noticing as he did that Sean also had a very firm grip of Harriet's arm. He shut up.

Bob stood up and allowed the two coachmen/guards to walk him away, mouthing a sheepish, "Sorry," to Harriet and Simon as he left.

Amelia ran for another door. She was crying and obviously distressed. Once they were out of sight, Amelia's mother continued.

"Thank you all for your time and understanding. We will now serve more coffee."

She sat down as if she had just given a short speech on fire safety. The music resumed and the rooftop was suddenly alive with chatter.

Harriet turned to Sean as all three leaned in together.

"What the fucking fuck was that all about?" Harriet asked. "How can the girl be underage? She's the same age as me for Christ's sake!"

"Listen, seriously," Sean replied, "now is not the time. We need to sit tight for the moment. While Priest's away, these women are in charge and they do not take well to people questioning them. We need to have our coffees and go back to your room. We can talk then."

"But what..." Harriet was interrupted as a waiter arrived and placed coffee and chocolates on their table. He studiously avoided Bob and Amelia's places, as if there had never been anyone sitting there. Simon felt an unreasonable hatred for the man. He scowled after him as he moved on to the next table.

"What exactly were you going to do?" Harriet asked him.

Simon realised he had no idea.

"I don't know. I don't suppose I could have done much. I mean, look at me."

Sean looked confused.

"Exactly," Harriet replied. "Look at you." She lifted a silver tray holding chocolates and dumped them all into her lap before holding it up to show Simon his reflection.

It did not reflect the Simon Debovar that he held in his head. He had muscles and a firmness of frame to which he was totally unaccustomed. This was the first time it had even occurred to him that, had he wanted to physically intervene, he probably could have. The thought sunk in and he smiled. Harriet smiled back at him.

"That's my boy," she said, popping a chocolate in her mouth.

———

Across the roof, Gabby had turned pale.

"I feel terrible now. Maybe this wasn't a great plan. Did you see how upset she was?"

"Of course I did," Luke snapped.

Gabby looked hurt, but Luke carried on.

"We're trying to save the world."

His tone was harsh, but his face pleaded with her to be on his side, to forgive him and not to have second thoughts. He badly needed her to put on the same brave face. She did her best.

It wasn't very good.

CHAPTER SEVENTEEN

The man climbed out of the taxi and stretched. His limbs were still stiff. It would take time. He had time.

The bitter winter air was fresh in his lungs and sharp on his tongue. His feet crunched in the snow, the black leather shoes quickly showing distress at the wet. They had begun to let in water at the airport. He didn't mind. It was pleasant to feel the sting of the cold again.

The door of the chalet opened a few moments after he knocked. A strikingly beautiful young black woman with deep, ice-blue eyes looked up at him. As they recognised him, the ice turned to steel.

"What do you want?"

"Hello Maya," he leered. "I've come to collect on your debt."

———

Cherry had been indulging herself. Faunt had given her the day off. It was nice.

To take her mind off the bad feeling she'd woken with, she'd spent the morning on a beach in Thailand. After a shower in an Amazon waterfall, she had popped over to Venice for a lunch of wood fire-baked pizza and a few glasses of Barolo. In the afternoon, she had walked some of the Inca trail, and then visited her mother for dinner (lunch, for her mother). She'd ended the night watching Green Day play Wembley from backstage and was now back at home, making herself a hot chocolate before bed. She'd automatically made one for Faunt too.

She jumped as she turned to leave the kitchen, finding Faunt standing in the doorway. He could move impossibly quietly when he chose to.

Her smile as she recovered her composure faded as she saw her boss's grey complexion and the thunderous look in his eyes.

"We have a problem," he said, darkly.

Cherry couldn't remember the last time she'd seen him look so serious – or so worried. It was nearly midnight and time for him to change, so he was usually in his room now, preparing.

"What's up?" she asked. "Have I done something wrong?"

"Oh, no." Faunt softened, realising he'd given her the wrong impression. "It's not you. But I'm going to have to ask something of you, something which I'd really rather not. However, I've thought about it every way I can, and I simply don't see another solution."

Cherry felt her stomach flip. Faunt did not spook easily, and she had never, ever seen him stumped. This could be bad.

In the fifteen minutes before midnight, Faunt explained the situation to her over hot chocolate.

She was right.

It was bad.

———

"So, you thought *this* was a good idea?"

Sean sat in the chair by the window of Simon's room. He had sat quietly and listened as Simon and Harriet had argued about what they should tell him, how much they should tell him and, eventually, how they should tell him. By the time they had come to a decision, he already had a pretty good idea of what they were going to tell him.

The extent of the explanation was limited to the fact that they needed to rescue someone from the island, including the information that her husband had sent them and that Simon's life depended on their success.

Sean looked quizzically amazed.

"Seriously, you hardly fucking know me! I could be *anyone*. What if I grass you up? Then what?" he asked.

Simon looked slightly piteously at Harriet. It was a reasonable point.

"Look, boy toy, we need your help to get Bob out. We might be able to get whatserface off the island without him, but if we have to leave him behind, then we leave the possibility of Priest being able to track us down, and that's not something I fancy. Now I may not have known you long, but I have known you biblically and frankly, sunshine, no man who's made the noises you've made underneath me is going to grass me up to anyone, are you?"

Sean grinned.

"Yeah, OK. But still, you two have got a lot to learn about secret missions. Secrets, for a start."

"Yeah, well, your poker face sucks," said Harriet, cocking an eyebrow at him.

The look between them was lasting a little longer than Simon was comfortable with.

"So, em, how do we get Bob out?" he asked, hoping to get the conversation going again.

"Right, well, firstly, Amelia's mum is basically in charge, but unless there are exceptional circumstances, she can't do anything until Priest gets back."

"So what, we just leave him in jail the rest of the time we're here?" Harriet asked. "Seems a bit…"

"Harsh," Simon finished for her. "It's totally unfair. We can't leave him in there. He hasn't done anything wrong. These women are…"

"Bitches," Harriet finished for him. "I agree with the moral compass. Bob's OK and that little prick tease has got him in trouble. We have to get him out."

Sean frowned. "Firstly, Amelia's a good girl. This isn't her fault, either. In fact, she's had a few holiday flings, that I know of, and this hasn't happened before. When we add that to what you've told me, I wonder if something else isn't going on here."

"Like what?" Simon felt his insides going mushy again. He disliked the idea that there were any other goings on that he didn't understand beyond the goings on that he was directly involved in not understanding.

"I dunno, mate," Sean answered. "But it's a bit odd, isn't it?"

The barman stood and looked out the window. "How important is all this? Seriously."

Harriet and Simon looked at each other.

"What do you mean?" the ex-hermit asked.

"Well, if it gets bad, there is one thing I could try. But it's costly."

"Oh, we've got money!" Simon interrupted, excited that he had remembered the fact all by himself this time. "Lots of it."

"Unfortunately, I don't mean money," Sean said, smiling slightly. "But that's good to know. Anyway, hopefully it won't come to that. As long as Ingrid doesn't do anything stupid, maybe we can get Bobby sorted out without any major hassles."

"Ingrid – that's Amelia's mum?" Simon confirmed.

"Yeah, that's right."

"Bloody Scandinavians," Harriet interjected. "Never met

one who didn't have a superiority complex. Bunch of Nazis and sex addicts."

Simon wondered if Harriet was even vaguely aware of the irony.

"Actually, I think her family background is German," said Sean.

Harriet rolled her eyes. "For fuck's sake. That's worse."

Simon had a horrible feeling it couldn't get worse. Then again, he had learned not to trust any of his assumptions in the last week.

As long as Amelia's mother didn't do anything rash, they might be OK.

———

"How dare you?!" Ingrid bellowed at her daughter, who stood staring at her defiantly while tears streamed down her florid cheeks.

"How *dare* I?" the girl retorted. "How *dare* I? What have *I* done? You just publicly humiliated me in front of..." Her sobbing became too intense for words. She collapsed dramatically into a nearby chair.

"*I* embarrassed *you*?" Ingrid seemed to grow several inches with indignation. "I am in charge of this island in the absence of our Patron. Do you remember that?"

"So what?" Amelia spat through her tears.

"So what? So how do you think it looks when the daughter of the island's Host Prime is whoring it around with some overgrown lackey who couldn't even pay his own way onto the resort?"

"What?" Amelia was often confused by her mother, so this was nothing new.

"Exactly as I said. I spoke to Carlos after hearing about your little tryst. The giant idiot was paid for by a 'friend' and when there was a problem with that, the moron with him had to pay the bill. I'm pretty sure he's a *servant*. How do you think that reflects upon me?"

Amelia was stunned into silence. Not because she gave a damn either way about Bob's social standing, but because she'd managed to forget just how obsessed her mother was with appearances. This was an untimely and unwelcome reminder.

"Mother," she said, making sure to add some humility and pleading into her tone, "I don't know what he does, or how much money he does or doesn't have, but I do know that he is a lovely, kind man. He has the most gentle eyes, and he lights up like a child at the smallest things. You should have seen him in the garden. It was beautiful. I've never seen another person take as much pleasure from it as I do."

Despite her intense focus on self-aggrandisement, Ingrid's minimal maternal instincts roused themselves at her daughter's heartfelt plea. She relaxed slightly.

"Tell me about him."

Amelia grabbed a tissue from her bedside table and blew her nose, composing herself and trying very hard to remember who she was speaking to.

"Well, I was down in the garden and I had stopped for a while as I was picking some fruit for a cheesecake."

"You had stopped?" Ingrid raised an eyebrow.

"Yes, and Bob – his name is Bob – bumped into me. He was kind of transfixed, apparently. It was sweet. I'd met him the night before in the bar, and..."

"Wait," her mother interrupted, "'apparently'? What do you mean, 'apparently'?"

"Well, Sean told me. I didn't..."

"O'Halloran? The pirate? Are you telling me that you had stopped and you didn't see this happen?"

Amelia suddenly regretted sharing what she considered a sweet introduction to Bob's character.

"Well, yes, but..."

"And how do you know exactly what did happen, then?

For all you know, the pirate found the idiot stripping you naked and pleasuring himself! In fact, that's a hell of a lot more likely than that he was standing staring sweetly at you!"

Ingrid rose to her full, unnatural height again.

"And then you allowed him to molest you *again*? How naïve are you, you stupid, *stupid* girl?"

"Molest? Mother, it was a kiss!" Amelia's voice was desperate and the tears were running again. Her mother was turning this innocent, pure thing into something dark and horrible.

"Just a kiss," Ingrid hissed back at her now inconsolable daughter. "Honestly girl, the man is twice your age and you think he's some idyllic Romeo? He's an incorrigible letch, who's taken advantage of you, you idiot child."

Amelia was now struggling to breathe through the sobs.

"We must make an example of this disgusting pervert. We can't have people thinking that their servants can come to the island and take advantage of our children. He'll be tried in the morning and flayed by lunch. Zero tolerance."

Amelia had stopped sobbing. Ingrid turned on her heel and marched for the door, slamming it dramatically behind her and turning a key in the lock.

Amelia's tears dripped onto her dress as she sat staring after her mother, completely and utterly still. And silent.

———

Cherry materialised in the back garden, ankle deep in snow. The neighbourhood was quiet, except for a couple of drunks singing about something on their way home.

She slipped her hand into her pocket and held down the button that silenced her phone. The last thing she needed was her mother texting her while she was trying to sneak into a house.

As the voices disappeared down the road, Cherry crept

close to the kitchen window. Her breath fogged it up as she peered inside. Ordinarily, she'd have popped right into the house after Faunt gave her a rundown of the layout. But not this house.

Faunt's story had been difficult. All he'd been able to tell her was that a man had been freed who was going to do something that could see Bob, Simon and Harriet dead. Messily dead. But, since he apparently had a 'non-interference pact' with this man, he couldn't even tell her his name. In fact, he couldn't even directly ask her to help. All he could do was give her another name, Maya Constantine, an address, and the fact that she was in danger. Now.

The kitchen was dark. But a faint light bled through from another room. She crept slowly across the grass to a set of double glass doors. They were locked. Damn. Through the curtains, though, she could see some vague shadows in a far room. Someone was still up.

She could also see enough of the room to know it was safe to enter, so pictured herself standing inside the glass doors. The reverberation knocked her off her feet. Damn it; a teleport shield. Either Maya Constantine was a witch, or she knew one.

Around the side of the building was a half-open window on the first floor. She may not have been able to teleport inside the house, but she could certainly teleport twenty feet up in the air. Checking nobody was watching, she blinked out.

She climbed in from the window ledge and quietly shut the window. Slowly, she tiptoed to the door of the bathroom and listened for sound outside. Nothing.

As delicately as she could, she grabbed and turned the old brass handle. As the bolt slipped free, there was a tiny 'click' – the kind of sound that would never be heard in any normal situation by any reasonable human being. But, of course, exactly the kind of sound that Cherry knew would probably have been heard by the as yet unnamed murderer she'd come here to find in the snow and the dark.

Fuck.

She breathed as quietly as possible, waiting for the slightest sound from outside the door; any hint that the snick of metal had given her away. She could feel the sweat beginning to bead on her forehead and under her arms, despite the cold.

Shit, shit, shit.

CHAPTER EIGHTEEN

Sean stood in front of the door. It was almost one o'clock, which made it 'the witching hour' – appropriate considering whose door he was about to knock on.

It had been a weird day. This morning, his biggest concern had been the prospect of facing that stale, morning-after smell that the bar inevitably had every single day. To clear his head and get a break from it, he'd popped into the garden for a quick blast of nature.

The day had not exactly gone 'downhill' from there; it was more of a rollercoaster. And now, here he was, about to engage in conversation with one of the specifically few people whom he strictly avoided at all costs.

The Socialites were anything but social, and very well known for disliking everyone – including each other. And he was about to put himself directly in the firing line to help a couple of blokes and a woman he hadn't even heard of 48 hours ago.

Then again, what a woman.

Taking a deep breath, he knocked on the door, secretly hoping that maybe she was out or asleep – or both.

The door flew open with a pace and ferocity that

suggested strongly to Sean that he'd better have a bloody good reason for knocking on it and, frankly, it had best be some very good news.

"What?" Ingrid barked at him.

"Hiya, Ingrid," Sean began, "I was wondering..."

"You were wondering *what*?" she cut him off, stepping forward to give him an eyeful of her brutal ugliness. "Wondering if I know what that disgusting old pervert did to my daughter? Wondering if I know that you most likely had a hand in it? Wondering if I can prove it?"

With each question she moved closer and closer, forcing Sean back until he was pressed firmly against the opposite door, with her gruesome visage just inches from his own. Her breath was as bad as her face.

"You'd better hope I can't, because I don't give a damn what your contract says – if I think you're trying to help that letch get away with molesting my daughter, then I'll stand you right beside him tomorrow, and strip your flesh too."

Saliva dripped from the corner of her mouth, landing on Sean's chest. Her breath was hot, and he could feel it beginning to condense on his lips.

"Erm, I was wondering," he recovered, "if you'd like anything from the bar before I close it for the night." He smiled as agreeably as possible.

For a long, awful moment, Ingrid stared into his eyes, searching for any trace of treason. But, as they say, when Irish eyes are smiling...

The witch moved back slowly, until she reached her own threshold and, having moved sufficiently far away, returned to her beautiful façade. She smiled at him like a minister's daughter at Sunday School.

"No, thank you, but it was very kind of you to offer."

The door slammed shut.

After a few moments of composing himself, Sean peeled

his back off the door. Watching Ingrid's room carefully, he turned and walked back down the corridor towards Simon's.

"Right," he muttered to himself, "that's Plan A fucked, then."

———

Cherry's breath turned to mist in front of her. The room had suddenly become so cold that she turned to check she definitely had closed the window behind her.

She touched the small radiator next to the sink – it was hot. Inches away from it, her fingers felt the bite of the cold again.

Deciding that sudden, inexplicable cold was not usually a good thing, Cherry had to make a choice. She wanted out of that room. Two options: back out the window and play safe, or open the door and see what and who was on the other side.

"What the hell," she decided, "can't live *forever*."

She crept back to the door and placed her fingers on the handle. Then something unexpected happened.

The bathroom was about 7 feet by 5 feet. The shower curtain was open, and there was not a cupboard or any type of door to be seen. There was, definitively, nobody else in the room.

With this in mind, what Cherry very much wanted to know was: who the hell had just whispered, "Wait," in her ear?

———

"Right. Let's fillet the bitch."

As always, Harriet's solution cut to the crux of the matter.

"You really, really don't want to try that," Sean warned her. "I mean, you know, be my guest, but don't come crawling to me afterwards. In fact, you'll be lucky if there's enough of you left to crawl. You'll probably need to be dragged."

"I'm not afraid of that skinny old cow. She could do with a bloody good beating. Might remind her to crack a smile now and again."

"No, Harriet, please." Simon asked. "You haven't seen her, really. She's..." he searched for the correct words, "...she's not *right*."

"That is one fucker of an understatement, mate," Sean agreed.

Harriet sat back on the bed. "OK, so what *is* the plan?"

"Best thing I can think of is we sneak down to the cells tonight, break Bob out and get him the hell off the island. Can you guys do what you came to do without him?" Sean asked.

Simon looked at Harriet.

"Course we can," she answered. "He's only here for the jolly."

"Right. How tired are you?" he asked Simon.

Simon realised that, actually, he was very tired. And he hadn't had a shower since lunchtime.

"I could sleep," he answered.

"OK. Let's go get some kip. There are only a few guards on overnight downstairs. There's usually nobody down there, so they don't tend to guard the cells too hard, you know? I think they change over at 4:00. Our best option is probably to go down there about 3:30 – with any luck they'll be out cold themselves by then and we can hopefully sneak past them without any confrontation."

"Hopefully," Simon repeated.

"Well, to be honest mate, this whole plan is pretty dependent on hope. The guard rotas are extremely secret. Nobody outside the guards themselves knows who's on when. But we might get lucky."

———

Cherry hadn't so much felt the breath as felt the absence of air where breath might have been, making the hairs on the back of her neck stand abruptly to attention.

There was only one explanation: she'd broken into a haunted house. Brilliant.

"Now," she heard the voice again. It was creepy, yet somehow reassuring at the same time. So, despite feeling every sinew of her being tell her to get the hell out of this nuthouse, Cherry slowly turned the handle. This time, it made no sound.

There were no lights on, but someone had lit a fire downstairs. From the glow, she could make out a corridor with three other doors. The two farthest away were closed, but the nearest one, about five feet to her left, was open. The ambient light only penetrated about a foot into the gloom and thereafter it was black.

She stared intently into the dark. If anyone was in there, she'd be more visible to them the closer she got to the top of the stairs. She held her breath, at the same time trying to focus all her energy on listening for the faintest sound – a shuffling foot or any other sign of life. There was none, except the persistent crackle of the fire and the growing smell of something cooking. Hopefully, that meant that at least one of the two people she expected to find here was in the kitchen and maybe she'd have the chance to catch the woman alone more easily than she expected.

At the bottom of the stairs, the wall stuck out a few feet before the archway. Theoretically, that meant she could port down to the foot of the stairs and remain hidden, avoiding walking past the open room on the way. If the house was haunted, it was also a damn good bet the stairs were creaky. Then again, maybe just the bathroom was haunted. She'd heard of stranger things. She *was* a stranger thing.

At the bottom of the stairs, the glow from the fire was much more intense and, from a mirror on the wall opposite, she could see there was nobody immediately around the corner.

She took a deep breath and, preparing to jump straight back upstairs if she needed to, leaned forward.

She retched involuntarily, covering her mouth instinctively and praying she hadn't made a sound.

The hearth was cold and black. Next to it, strapped to an armchair, the body of a woman was burning. Her face was turned upwards, permanently held in a grotesque snarl, as if she were cursing the skies.

"Me," the voice whispered. "Sorry."

"*I'm* sorry," Cherry replied, realising that her mission to save this poor woman, whoever she was, had taken too long. Cherry walked across the room and stood in front of the burning carcass, wondering if she could have done anything more and why Maya had been so important that Faunt would send her here. Only when she felt a tear touch her lip did Cherry realise she was crying.

The cold whipped in again like a winter storm, and the flames flickered violently.

"Run," whispered the voice again – urgently this time. "Run!"

Cherry turned without question and headed for the door. Halfway across the room, her feet stuck to ground, as if she'd stepped in superglue. Her forward motion had the effect of sending her tumbling forwards when her feet stopped moving, painfully jarring both ankles as she landed on her hands, arms outstretched. Instinctively, she tried to stand but, with her feet frozen to the ground, her balance was off. She was stuck. But it was fine, she could just port herself across the room and position herself upright again that way.

Except she couldn't. For the first time in her life, Cherry envisaged herself somewhere and found that she was still rooted to the spot. Fear tightened her chest.

"No, no!" she heard the voice pleading. She had a horrible feeling it wasn't her it was pleading with.

"*Hola, señorita,*" said a voice from behind her.

178

She'd assumed the murderer had left, since his victim was clearly dead. She'd never checked the kitchen.

"Do you know, I thought Faunt might send his teleporter after me. I honestly didn't know if the immobilising charm would work on a jumper. I am delighted to find that it has."

Cherry didn't answer. She was reeling with panic at losing her ability, like a fish suddenly suffocating in water. And she was bent double at the mercy of a maniac. What the hell had Faunt sent her into?

She was shocked into focus by the feel of a hand slowly stroking her back, under her top. She could just about see her assailant's face by the firelight, upside down. It looked weird, and he seemed to be drooling.

Whatever else he might eventually do, she was not about to let him perv all over her first. Bending her knees as much as she could, Cherry pushed up with all her strength and managed to bring herself jerkily upright, catching her balance, just, as she reached vertical.

"Keep your fucking hands off me," she spat over her shoulder.

The low, guttural "Heh" sounded almost respectful. Mostly, it was terrifying.

Slowly, he walked around Cherry, stalking her like a spider, and moving almost as silently. Finally, he stopped in front of her.

By the flickering light of the flames, she could see his face was a mass of scar tissue and his eyes were pale – too pale – as if he hadn't seen the sun for a long time.

"It's something, is it not?" he asked, stroking his hand down his face. "I was a work of art, once. The most lusted after boy in Barcelona. Now, I am this."

"You're doing better than her." Cherry nodded towards the still burning corpse.

The man grinned, but it was more like a tear across his face, showing perfect white teeth.

Cherry felt a sharp pain against her neck. She'd hardly seen him move, but he held a knife against her throat. He took a phone from his pocket with the other hand. She could feel the edge digging in and winced away, but the action nicked her skin. A trickle of blood ran down her neck.

He replaced the weapon against the wound. It stung. Cherry glowered defiantly at him, despite her growing fears that she was probably going to die here, alone.

"Stand still. I am expecting a call, and I would not want to *accidentally* cut you." His tone was viscous. Oily. Evil.

The phone rang.

"Hello, Faunt," he said, putting the phone on loudspeaker. "I seem to have something of yours."

"Cherry, I'm so sorry," her employer's voice said. "This is my fault."

"Of course it's your fault," Scarface replied. "You're a predictable man. I may not have known how to reach you, but I knew how to get your attention..." He flashed that fleshy rip at Cherry again. Bile rose in her throat.

"You know what I want," he continued. "Where *is* he?"

"You know you deserved it, don't you? What he did to you?" Faunt answered.

The Spaniard didn't answer. In that moment of silence, Cherry heard a faint whisper: "Ignite."

Ignite what?

"You have two choices, my friend," he finally said. "Tell me where he is and I will slit her throat."

"I think you mean 'or'," Cherry sneered at his mistake.

"No," Faunt replied, solemnly, "he doesn't."

"If he does not tell me," the man continued, addressing Cherry now, "then I will keep you alive. For a long time."

He drew the knife slightly across the cut he'd made earlier and Cherry winced again.

Another long silence. Again, Cherry heard the whisper: "Ignite."

The ghost presumably had a plan to help her, but there was nothing in reach that she could start a fire with. She could just about reach the sideboard to her right, on which were some photos of exotic landscapes and... a candlestick. But no candle. Still, if she could reach that, maybe she could use it as a weapon. At the moment, she couldn't even move without cutting her own throat.

"Faunt, *mi amigo*, we both know what I am going to do to this girl if you do not tell me. However, for her benefit, perhaps I shall run through some of my ideas now."

His eyes were black as death. Cherry looked into them and saw the end. Her knees began to give way. Unless she could get him to step away from her, she had no chance.

"All right," Faunt said. "He's on Priest's Island."

He looked perturbed. Cherry was shocked. Faunt had just given up Simon, Bob and Harriet with barely an argument. Why didn't he lie?

Worse, he'd given up on saving *her*.

The man sighed heavily, lowering the knife to his side. "That is extremely inconvenient, you know?" He stepped away from Cherry and moved to the window. This was her chance, and probably her only one. She leaned as far right as she could, stretching for the candlestick.

"I do know," Faunt answered. "Cherry?"

"Yeah?" she answered, her voice trembling.

"Say it out loud."

The man cocked his head and jammed his finger at the phone, hanging up. He glowered angrily at Cherry. Whatever Faunt had planned, it hadn't worked.

She had seconds before he reached her. What did he mean, "Say it out loud?" Say what out loud? Why was everyone being so freaking cryptic?

Then she remembered his curse. He knew everything. He knew what was happening. He knew her predicament. He knew what she was thinking.

And what she was hearing.

Scarface placed the phone in his pocket and moved towards her, raising his knife to strike.

Cherry stood up defiantly, gritted her teeth and loudly said:

"Ignite."

The world burst into flames.

CHAPTER NINETEEN

Cherry instinctively ducked and curled herself into a ball. Her would-be murderer lunged towards her, screaming venomously in the fire. Blinded by the flames, he swiped wildly and tripped over her, landing on his back a few feet away. His nudge knocked the teleporter off balance and her foot moved.

She was free.

Instantly, she pictured herself in the front garden, in a spot she could see through the rapidly melting window, and was standing in the snow. The cold pierced her lungs as she gulped it in frantically.

Looking back into the fire, Cherry watched as the man picked himself up and stumbled towards the door, howling like a wounded animal. He still held the knife in his hand.

She was tempted to stay and watch him burn, but a voice inside was screaming at her to get as far from that man as possible, to never let him touch her again.

Mouthing a "Thank you," to the ghost, she pictured her shower at home and blinked out just as the burning body burst out of the front door and lunged awkwardly into the cooling salvation of the snow.

He sizzled and popped as the fire went out, a ringlet of smoke trailing above him and puddles of melted snow pooling on the singed grass. Rolling over, his lidless eyes staring maniacally at the sky, he seethed, "Fuck you, *puta*."

In the fire, the ghost smiled.

———

With trembling hands, Cherry switched her shower on and collapsed into a ball under the calming water, sobbing uncontrollably.

She was alive.

———

Simon wasn't good at being woken up from a deep sleep. Conversely, he was very good at sleeping.

When a subtle knocking on his door roused him from his happy slumber, his first instinct was to ignore it and hope it would go away. After all, what could be so important that he needed to wake up when he was this tired? Plus, he was having a nice dream about Heather Graham and a game of shuffleboard to save Africa from being deleted. It made sense in the dream.

Sadly, the knocking persisted.

The problem now, of course, was that he was awake enough to realise he needed to pee. He lay for a few moments, hoping the feeling would go away, but instead, he started to feel hungry. There are many things a man can sleep through, but when he consciously realises he is both hungry and in need of the toilet, the game is up. Salvation lies in a slice of buttered bread, via the bathroom.

Some persistent men will lie for an age, vainly trying to recapture their dream; to incorporate their hunger into it and ignore their bladder.

It doesn't work.

Simon switched on his bedside lamp, then promptly knocked it over as he realised he wasn't at home. He let out a fairly unmanly yelp, before the memory of where he was came back to him. He remembered why he had to get up. It was just after 3 am. Nobody who wasn't watching a full season of 24 on DVD in real time should be up at this hour.

He stumbled out of bed and opened the door to let Sean and Harriet in. When he emerged from the toilet a few minutes later, Sean was pouring coffee. Simon picked up a packet of biscuits from the table and sat on the bed.

"You back with us, then?" Sean smiled, handing him a cup.

Simon was amazed at how the Irish could smile in any situation. Come Armageddon, the nation of Ireland would surely be found in the pub, laughing like children and beckoning the horsemen in for a Guinness.

"I suppose so," he answered. "I probably shouldn't have gone to sleep."

"Yeah, we didn't bother in the end," said Sean.

That was as much as Simon was prepared to think about that, so he focused on the less disturbing idea of breaking a giant out of a castle dungeon.

Then he had a quick shower.

———

Luke couldn't sleep.

Guilt was nothing new to him. He lived with it every day and, while it never got better, he managed to spend more and more of his life not thinking about it. When he did, however, it gnawed at him. With something fresh to feed his guilt tonight, he had little chance of respite.

It didn't help that Gabby had obviously been disappointed in him. She hadn't said so, but it was hanging in the air all night like a raincloud waiting to burst.

She wanted him to find another solution. So did he.

They could manage this situation. Tomorrow, they'd suggest to Debovar and his aunt that they should break their friend out of the dungeon, then tip off the guards. For Bob's indiscretion, he'd probably get a slap on the wrist when Priest came back. For attempting to break him out, Simon and his aunt would be held long enough for them to change back to normal, and be evicted.

This would effectively put an end to their attempt to locate the Rug. And yet, here he was, staring at the damned ceiling.

———

When Cherry finally came out of her bathroom, wrapped in a towelling robe after leaving her soaking clothes on the floor, Faunt was waiting for her. It was hard to tell, what with him being a deer, but it looked like he'd been crying.

"I'm so sorry," he said.

She didn't have the energy to shout, or even to question him. She shrugged and sat gently on the bed. There was a cup of hot chocolate on the bedside table. She wondered how he'd made it with hooves.

"Maya says 'thank you'," he said.

Cherry looked up with watery eyes.

"For what? I got her burned to death."

"She's grateful because you tried. And because you set off her self-destruct spell to take some revenge on her killer."

"Is *that* what that was?" Her voice was monotone and frail. "Why didn't she just do it herself?"

"She wasn't allowed to. She owed him her life. He claimed it. You, on the other hand, were not in debt to him, so she gave you the trigger."

"Why didn't it burn *me*?"

"The spell is designed to protect the caster."

Cherry was understanding everything, but feeling nothing. Part of her had shut down. Faunt was looking at her with, almost literally, big doe eyes. She realised she was crying again.

"I shouldn't have sent you," Faunt said. "I walked into his trap."

"No," Cherry whispered. "*I* did."

It was cold.

"Is Maya *here*?" Cherry asked, louder.

"Yes," Faunt replied.

"Will she stay?"

Faunt looked surprised.

"She will, if you want her to."

"I'd like that," Cherry answered, sliding under the sheets. "Is it OK if I crash now, please?"

"Of course, I'm sorry," Faunt apologised again and backed out of the room.

"You still can't tell me his name, can you?" Cherry asked.

Faunt paused outside the door and hung his head.

"No."

"Goodnight," said Cherry, with no trace of emotion.

"Goodnight," said Faunt. As he left the room, he flicked his head, indicating to the door to follow him. It swung closed.

Cherry collapsed, her exhaustion outweighing her insomnia.

Maya watched her sleep.

―――――

Faunt stood outside the door, his eyes closed. He dropped his head and sighed.

When he raised it and opened them again, the sadness was replaced with anger.

―――――

Simon watched a lot of television and had seen a lot of movies. From this, he had learned many things.

Guards in a castle dungeon, for example, are lazy and stupid. Thus, their plan of sneaking down to the dungeon when the guards were coming to the end of their shift made perfect sense, as they were bound to be asleep.

Of course, when the three of them had crept down the staircase, which Simon was delighted to note was actually lit by a succession of flaming torches, they found the two guards on duty fully awake and debating the merits of their new uniforms.

When Sean had seen who they were, he had frantically gestured to his companions to turn back. Harriet had shushed him and quietly told him not to be such a pussy.

A hastily and silently organised new plan had ended with Simon sneaking around to the guards' right, while Harriet moved to their left. She would distract them so that Simon could sneak up behind them and smack them both over the head with the nearest heavy object. Sean vehemently tried to convince them it was a bad idea and that *he* couldn't be seen, but his explanation was limited to gestures and small whispers. Simon half suspected he was just trying to keep himself out of trouble, but he hoped that wasn't the case.

Harriet had shrugged at Sean and shoved Simon on his way. The lady was not for turning. Simon dutifully crept his way down the edge of the gloom.

Sadly, Harriet's attempt at distraction had been A/ predictable, B/ based on another false guard-related stereotype and C/ wholly unsuccessful. Which was why Simon now stood shaking with nerves to the side of two guards who had not moved an inch from their positions in front of the main gate to the cells, but who *had* moved their attention to Harriet's exposed breasts.

"What do you think of these, boys?" she bellowed.

"Well, they're certainly firm-looking... well-balanced... and the nipples are a nice shade of pink, wouldn't you say, Ki?" the first guard replied.

"Yes, like cherry blossom," the other answered, with a soft Oriental accent.

Harriet stood frozen in silence. It was a rare event.

"Is there anything else we can help you with, Madam?" the first guard continued. "Because you shouldn't really be down here."

Simon had come to read his aunt's expressions very well in the short time they'd spent together, so he was fairly sure that what then went through her head consisted of: "Shit. Now what? Can I take them? Yeah, I can. Fuck it."

Pausing only to put her breasts away, Harriet grabbed a torch off the wall and ran at the nearest guard, the one who had spoken first. As both guards turned towards her, Simon jolted into action himself, picking up a stool and running, very, very quietly, towards the back of Ki's head. This attempted combination of speed, stealth and the flagstones beneath him left him looking somewhat like a drunken gazelle on hot coals... carrying a stool.

Simon reached the spot a few feet behind Ki and swung the stool with all his strength, which was, now, not insubstantial. Inexplicably, Ki's head had ceased to be where it was when he started swinging it, leaving him lunging forwards after the stool, which then smashed against the stone wall. Adding insult to injury, Simon had fallen after the stool, carried by his own momentum, and as it bounced back off the wall, it smashed against his forehead. Simon's eyes flashed red on impact, then he blacked out for a few seconds, collapsing face first onto the floor. By the time he regained his equilibrium and turned over to see what had happened, his head was pounding furiously. Ki looked down at him with a confused and piteous expression.

"Why did you do that?" the guard asked.

Simon had no idea how to answer the question, so decided

just to remain silent and hope someone else would speak up for him. He looked around for Harriet. She was sort of frozen in mid-run, mouth open in what would probably have been a scream, had she still been able to scream. The first guard was simply holding up a hand towards her, and this seemed to be keeping her in place.

Simon mentally added a new note to his preconceptions about prison guards: sometimes, if you're very unlucky, they'll turn out to be a wizard and a ninja. In this instance, do not attempt to sneak up on them.

"What do we do with them, Edoard?" Ki asked his colleague. He was now holding a very pretty, but very, very sharp looking sword to Simon's chest.

"Well," the wizard answered, "much as I hate to say it, they do seem to have been trying to attack us. Since we so rarely have new guests down here, I can only assume that they are somehow connected to the tall gentleman who was brought down last evening.

"Is that the case?" He turned to Simon for an answer.

Gripped with mortal fear, Simon resorted to every child's response in the face of being caught utterly red-handed and presented with their own crime. He nodded piteously, looked at the ground and hoped for mercy.

He also noticed, with some irritation, that there was still no sign of Sean. Well, if they were on their own, then so be it. At least they knew where they stood.

Probably.

"Well," Edoard continued, "in that case, I'm afraid we are obliged to also place you both in custody until you can face trial for this attack. Would you both be so kind as to come along quietly, please? It will be much easier all round."

Simon nodded again. Harriet, on the other hand, struggled and let out a muffled grunt.

"I'll take that as a no, miss, shall I? Fair enough, I'll just move you as you are."

He made a twisting gesture with his hand and Harriet was suddenly turned sideways, suspended in midair like a statue transported through a museum on an invisible trolley. Ki opened the gate and Edoard walked through, 'pushing' Harriet in front of him. Ki gestured to Simon, smiling good-naturedly at him, as though he was showing him to his table. Simon got up and docilely walked through the gate, following Edoard. The other side of the gate was gloomy and cramped. The walls were arched stone, damp and mouldy and there was a faint stench of sulphur.

This part of the island was clearly not intended to be on the tour.

CHAPTER TWENTY

Harriet moved her fingers. Slightly. She'd been unceremoniously propped against the wall of her cell, which was both extremely uncomfortable and dripping with some kind of ooze. She'd also listened to about half an hour's worth of Simon lamenting the injustice of their situation to her and Bob, who was in the cell to her left. He hadn't said much.

"Ffffff..." She wasn't yet in full control of her mouth. She did, however, get Simon's attention.

"I think she's coming to," said her nephew.

"She'll be right as rain a few minutes, just you wait."

The voice came from the corridor. Simon swung around to look for its source. Harriet tilted her head.

While their cells were fronted with bars, leaving an open view of the corridor and the adjacent cells, the opposite stone wall was punctuated with heavy, oaken doors. In the small, arched window opposite Harriet's cell, green eyes peered out of the dark.

"See? She's moving more already." The voice was deep and resonant, but raspy, as if it hadn't been used for some time.

None of them had realised they weren't alone.

"Hello?" asked Bob, suspiciously.

"Hello," the voice answered. There was an awkward silence.

"Hello," said Simon feebly.

More silence.

"You boys are real social butterflies," the voice started up again. "I ain't had any company down here in a long time. Whatever happened to the art of conversation?"

The accent was difficult to place through the phlegm, but it also sounded Deep South American, maybe Cajun.

"Erm, hello," Simon started, lapsing into his best 'polite conversation' mode, "my name's Simon. What's yours?"

"It's been a long time since anyone asked me that. I *definitely* used to have a name. Started with a D, I think. Or maybe a P. Anyways, only thing people called me in as long as I can remember is 'Prisoner'. So I guess you can call me that."

Simon looked confused. As usual.

"Well, nice to meet you," said Bob, in a way that also implied, "Goodbye."

"So, you all made kind of a mess, huh?" the voice persisted.

Simon exhaled. "I suppose we did."

"Guess that's how everyone ends up in a dungeon, huh?" the voice continued.

"I suppose it is," Bob answered, again with that 'end of conversation' tone.

"But getting yourself mixed up with the daughter of the head witch and attacking a couple of guards are pretty impressive ways to get yourself thrown down here, I'da said."

They froze. How had he known that? Who was behind the door?

"So," Harriet asked, sighing with relief as she finally managed to sit down on her bunk, "who the fuck are *you* and how the fuck did you know *that*?"

Simon involuntarily jumped away from the wall of bars he'd been leaning against, since he shared them with Harriet.

"Hey, look at you, all moving and talking," the voice answered.

"Let's go, Wizard of Oz," said Harriet. "Pull back the curtain."

"And rude too. Quite an attitude for such a fine young lady."

"I'm older than I look."

"Funny how that's true of a lot of folk here, ain't it?"

"So, you going to tell us who you are or not?" Harriet cut to the heart of the matter with her usual subtlety.

"Well, I suppose the thing you want to know is not who I am, but why I'm here. You see, this is my island."

———

Faunt paced around his straw bed. He wasn't going to get any sleep. The problem with knowing everything is that you also know when there isn't a solution to a problem. However Faunt looked at it, he couldn't see a way around the Rules. As long as he was alive, Faunt's non-aggression pact with the Spaniard was binding, at the cost of his life. While, currently, he was angry enough to risk that eventuality, he was aware of his own importance in events and not angry enough to take all leave of his senses.

Faunt's limitations in knowing everything were few. But the biggest, and most frustrating, were in not knowing things that were directly beneficial to him specifically. For example, he didn't know how to reverse the curse that turned him into a deer at midnight. He also didn't know how to prevent Bob from... he preferred not to finish that thought.

Of course, in the big picture, the worrying thing was that Simon might end up hurt, or even dead.

Wait.

Simon.

Of course!

Simon was under his protection – he'd announced it in no uncertain terms to Luke and Gabby. Therefore, he was justified in sending protection for Simon. And if that help happened to help someone he was with, as a consequence, that was not under Faunt's jurisdiction, surely?

As loopholes went, it was tenuous. But it was a plan.

In the morning, Faunt would ask a favour he had no right to ask. He knew they'd both say yes.

In fact, he'd barely have to ask.

———

"You're Priest?" Simon asked.

"That *diable?*" the voice answered. "I wouldn't spit on that boy if he was on fire. Again."

This was a confusing turn of events. This was Priest's island. Priest was nowhere to be seen and a man with no name in a dungeon was claiming ownership of the place. If nothing else, he'd made an odd choice of accommodation. Crazy, some might say.

"No, that big side of beef stole the island from me. It was mine for years, you see, and once, while I was away on vacation, the fat rogue set up camp here, changed the whole place around and claimed it for himself!

"When I came back, he even had the gall to tell me I was in the wrong place! As if I didn't know my own home. I grew up here. Every tree, every blade of grass, every waterfall, I know 'em all. And he stole 'em."

Prisoner's accent was getting thicker the more excited he got.

"What did you do?" asked Bob.

"What could I do? I challenged that boy to a duel for ownership of the island, and do you know what he said?"

195

Silence. It soon became clear that he actually wanted an answer.

"No." Simon filled the uncomfortable gap.

"He said, 'I don't need to have no duel, I'm The Omission'. And he threw me down here."

"Are you sure he didn't say 'Exception'?" Simon asked.

"That's right; 'The Exception'."

"Right." Harriet stood up. "So you're about as much use as non-alcoholic beer." She turned to look at each of the boys. "How are we going to get out of here?"

Bob looked uncomfortable. "I don't know."

He was trembling and seemed to be repeatedly counting his fingers.

"You OK?" Harriet asked.

"I... don't like cages," the giant answered. "I'd like to get out."

"Aye, well, seeing as Amelia's mum is planning to skin you alive tomorrow, we thought that'd be best, too."

Harriet had broken the news gently, as usual. Bob's face drained of colour. Simon found himself singing 'Whiter Shade of Pale' to himself. Sometimes his mind did really inappropriate things. Actually, it was quite often.

"Well, well, sounds like maybe you all need my help after all," said Prisoner.

"And what good are you likely to be?" Harriet asked. "You can't even remember your own name."

"Ah, but I can remember which one of these cells I dug a hole in the wall of. All we have to do is get into it."

"*We*? You're coming with us, are you sunshine?" Harriet asked.

"You don't think I'd help you escape and stay here on my own, do you?"

"Wait," Simon interrupted, "it's all well and good you saying there's a way out in one of the other cells, but how are we supposed to get out of our own cells? The guards don't strike me as the type we're going to be able to trick into letting us out."

Bob cleared his throat. The colour was beginning to return to his face.

"I can help with that."

CHAPTER TWENTY-ONE

"Wait. You're a locksmith?" Harriet asked. "So, you could have let yourself out at any time? What the fuck?"

Harriet was less impressed than Bob had imagined at the news of his lock picking skills.

"I thought escaping might just make it worse. And where would I *go*?"

Bob's face confirmed his genuine belief that there had been no point in letting himself out. And he clearly would have, given half a chance.

"OK, so you can pick locks. Get us out of here." She stood up, unable to sit still any longer.

"Well, that's the other thing. I need tools. I left mine in my room. I didn't expect to need them for dinner."

"So what, would a hairpin do?" she asked.

"Probably." Bob brightened. Harriet put her hands into her hair.

"Oh, wait, I don't *have* any hairpins because it's not 19 *fucking* 53!"

Bob shrank again.

"So you need, what, something long, thin and sturdy?" came the voice from the darkness.

"Yeah," Bob answered.

"Would these do?"

A hail of white and grey came through the window, clattering over the stone floor and spreading into Harriet's cell.

"Are those what I think they are?" Harriet asked with distaste.

"Bones," Prisoner confirmed.

"Of what?" Simon asked, sounding a little more horrified than he intended.

"A few birds; a few rats. Maybe a vole."

Harriet picked up the bones in her cell and the few that she could reach outside it. She handed them to Bob.

"Remind me to wash my hands," she said.

Bob turned the small pile of dusty bones over in his hands. They weren't the best tools he'd ever used. Then again, they weren't the worst either.

An hour, a lot of concentration, and a great deal of swearing from Harriet later, the three of them were gathered in front of the door of Prisoner's cell. Simon kept glancing nervously along the corridor towards the main gate and the guard station, but there was no sign of activity or of anyone considering coming down to check on the prisoners. Despite their individual skills, it had been a while since they actually had anyone new to guard.

Bob finally clicked open the lock on Prisoner's door. He turned the rusty iron handle, which squeaked in protest. All three stopped, staring intently down the corridor, afraid to breathe. Still no movement. Slowly, Bob pulled the heavy door open to reveal a thick, damp gloom.

Simon waited expectantly to see the ragged, dirty form of Prisoner emerge from the gloom, like a particularly old and dirty baby being born back into the light. As a shape began to take form, a foot emerged first.

To Simon's surprise, the foot that appeared was not a foot, per se, at all. It was, in his best estimation, an expensive and beautifully polished Italian black leather shoe, draped in crisp, clean white trousers.

Of course.

Out of the dark stepped a small, immaculately dressed man. He had shaved, his clothes were clean and pressed and he looked for all the world like a businessman on his way to his daily commute. To New Orleans, admittedly, but still.

Based on their expressions, the other two were also a little surprised.

"What?" Prisoner asked. "I ain't been outside in an age. Thought I best make an effort."

His grin was infectious.

Simon added it to the list entitled 'Things to Worry About Later.'

———

"So, have you decided what you're going to offer him?"

Lily had exhausted *Final Fantasy* on the stupidly huge plasma screen. She had to keep reminding herself to use the XBox controls and not just will the characters to do what she wanted.

Daniel looked up from his book. He'd finally stopped pacing at around 3 am and settled down with it. The silence had been welcome for a while, but Lily had reached the stage where she needed to hear someone's voice, even if it was her own.

"Of course. I've known for some time. Why?" Daniel's reply was cordial, with just a little hint of niggle. He liked the idea that Lily wasn't sure what to offer, yet.

"Just wondered. What do you think you'll do next?"

"After I win, you mean?"

Lily half snorted. "Yes, Daniel, after you win."

"I don't care really. I just want to get out of this place, to be honest. It's so... uncivilised, don't you think?"

"Really? Huh."

"You don't think so?"

"I think it's kind of fun, if you let it be."

"Fun? Look at the way they treat each other. They start wars over nothing. The rich throw away the lives of their poor in pursuit of ever more money. They're savages."

"To be fair, isn't that mostly your lot?"

Daniel took a deep breath. "I suppose it is. But that's largely because we're dominant."

"Yeah, but that's only because you got to have your guy down here first. If we'd carried on for long enough to have our girl come out..."

"Isn't she already here?"

"Yeah, but Mother got so distracted going after this thing, I think she just shelved it. Plus, I think she's kind of complacent about it. She's pretty sure she can force a draw, even without playing her ace."

"Typically arrogant," Daniel laughed. "Always thinking she's got it all in hand, isn't she?"

"Unlike you, you mean?" Lily smiled sweetly.

"*Touché*," the angel answered.

"So, you know what you're going to offer?" he asked after a silence.

She knew he couldn't resist asking.

"Oh yeah," Lily answered chirpily, "I've known since before we met him."

The demon smiled angelically at her partner cum enemy. Daniel smiled back.

He didn't mean it.

———

Simon's heart was pounding. He could feel the pulse of the veins in his hands as they pressed against the rough stone floor. Whether this was more due to him being slightly claustrophobic and therefore uncomfortable in the currently cramped confines of the tunnel they were crawling through or to the adrenaline that had begun coursing recklessly around his body on the realisation that he was taking part in a genuine jailbreak was hard to say.

While one might imagine the latter would distract him from the former, Simon was more than capable of being excited and terrified at the same time. Like a mouse, he could live perpetually on the edge of a significant coronary event.

"Hope you're not getting too excited back there, kiddo!"

Harriet was crawling ahead of Simon. She'd already joked about him not staring at her arse.

"Are we nearly out?" he called towards Prisoner, who was leading the merry band of moles.

"Pardon?" he shouted back.

"I said, are we nearly there?"

"Sorry, son, I can't hear you over the wind. We're almost at the end of the tunnel!"

Moving just a little further forward, the howling wind indeed drowned out all other noise. Ahead, Simon saw Prisoner disappear out into the darkness, followed by Bob, then Harriet. As he reached the end, Simon could smell the salt in the air and felt the whip of the wind across his face. He stopped a moment before moving out of the end of the tunnel and breathed deeply.

Sea. Salt. Crisp, clean air. Rain.

Rain?

What was it doing raining on Priest's Island? The place was supposed to be paradise. And come to think of it, that was no gentle summer breeze – it was proper, full on wind. The kind more commonly found battering North Sea oil rigs than meandering lazily through palm trees.

Then Simon focused in on something else. A deep, rumbling sound: rhythmic, crashing waves. As he crawled the last foot to exit the cave and stood up, a distant lightning flash briefly lit the scene, showing the sheer drop to weather-beaten, behemoth rocks below. For a moment, his balance deserted him as his brain struggled to come to terms with what he was seeing.

At the same moment, the thunder from the gathering storm rumbled through, taking Simon's final equilibrium with it. Suddenly, there was nothing beneath his feet and a long drop in front of him.

———

"Good lord, boy, whoever gave you the impression you were a damn bird?"

Prisoner hauled Simon up by his collar. The old man was deceptively strong. He set Simon back on his feet on the wet, grassy cliff ledge, just above the tunnel's exit. There was a persistent drizzle, which stung when the wind drove it across his face. Lightning flashed again at sea, and the rumble of the waves on the rocks below mixed with another growl of thunder.

"What the fuck is this?" Harriet asked nobody in particular, gesticulating at the world in general. "I thought this was an island paradise! What's with the Moby Dick set?"

The four stood on a ledge no more than ten feet long and about the same width. Above them rose a sheer cliff, slick with torrents of water and moss. Below: rocks. Lots and lots of rocks.

"I'm *so* sorry."

The words came out of Bob's mouth like the last, dry gasp of a dying man. His shoulders hung low. His face was pale and there were dark circles under his eyes. It was hard to tell in the insistent drizzle, but Simon suspected he may even have been crying.

Harriet stepped towards him like a gladiator braced for battle.

"Fuck sorry, sunshine. Listen, you didn't do a damn thing wrong."

"Hey," Simon piped up. "Sean! Sean said he thought there was something weird about all this. He thinks maybe this isn't really about you at all!"

Bob looked confused. "What?"

"Yeah, that's right, actually. He said it was all a bit odd," said Harriet, "like some bastard was trying to get at us, through you."

"But..." Bob hesitated as he took in the full implications of this news, "wouldn't that mean that there was somebody here, on the island, who knows why you're here and is trying to stop you?"

Simon felt a little colder. "That does seem likely, doesn't it?"

Harriet took a deep breath. "OK, well at least we know, right? So we can go back to vinegar wings and the tart and tell them that we tried, but we were sabotaged. Then it'll be up to them to sort something out."

Simon hoped that was right, but he couldn't get rid of the memory of Daniel's face when he discovered the missing carpet. All things being equal, he'd rather have to own up to Lily. Preferably in Faunt's house, which, right now, felt like the only place in the world he might be safe.

"If you three are done jawing, I've remembered where we go next," Prisoner announced.

He stood at the far side of the ledge, holding what appeared to once have been some kind of rope ladder, anchored to the cliff face.

"Remembered?" Harriet asked. "You've been here before?"

"Yep, at least once," Prisoner confirmed.

"What happened?" asked Bob.

"I got caught."

"You got caught?" Harriet was doing a pretty good impression of a tripped land mine. "You've brought us on an escape route that you got caught on before?"

"Well, yeah, but don't worry. We're as good as free. There's a boat at the bottom of this ladder. We get in that and we're gone," he reassured her.

Harriet looked murderous. Which was a worry...

"How did they catch you?" Simon asked, hoping the answer would calm her, at least slightly.

"Can't remember," Prisoner answered chirpily, as he climbed onto the remains of the ladder and began his descent, "but I can't be that unlucky twice, right?"

This answer was not good for Harriet. Lightning flashed again in the distance. Whatever threat she mouthed in reply was lost in the rolling thunder.

———

Cherry woke early, annoyingly. She felt as if she'd spent the night drinking tequila on an empty stomach rather than sleeping like a corpse. Her back and shoulders ached and her lips were cracked. Her dry tongue stuck to the roof of her mouth and her head throbbed. Still, at least she wasn't *actually* a corpse.

Her pillow was damp.

She found a bottle of water and painkillers on her bedside table. He might almost have gotten her killed, but she still had a pretty awesome boss. The smell of coffee wafted into the room. With a grunt, she pulled herself out of bed and stumbled for the shower.

———

By the time she got downstairs, the coffee aroma was dancing with pancakes. Faunt was definitely feeling guilty. She smiled to herself, wondering how long she was going to get the royal treatment.

"Probably until I feel better."

Faunt appeared at the bottom of the stairs, still in deer-form.

Cherry laughed. "You'd think I'd be used to that, by now. Hang on. If you're out here, who's in the kitchen?"

"Jean-Claude. He owes me a favour. Since Bob is away and I can't cook like this..." he nodded down towards his hooves, "I called it in. He's going to stay until Bob gets back."

A few hours later, in Paris, Michel Baudry would wake up to the nightmare of his head chef having taken indefinite sick leave in the week a Michelin inspector was expected. It would be the worst day since he was arrested for inappropriate interference in a public sporting event. He'd stopped drinking absinthe for a while after that. It blurred his distinction between 'funny' and 'public indecency'.

"OK." Cherry had learned to take things in her stride with Faunt. It was the only way, really. "So, where's breakfast?"

"Where would you like it to be?"

"In the TV room?"

"Of course. I'll follow you through."

———

The descent had been perilous – much like the rest of Simon's life lately. Wet, mouldy rope did not make for anything much resembling a sound hand hold. But at the bottom, there was indeed a boat. Though it definitely stretched the definition of 'boat'. It was more of a ramshackle collection of floating wood and nails.

"Are you winding me up?" As always, Harriet succinctly expressed the thoughts of the group.

"It floats, little lady, and surely that's all we need, right?" Prisoner argued.

Harriet's glare would have felled a water buffalo.

"You're welcome to stay here if you like and take your chances with the trial. If you're lucky, maybe she won't flay all of you," he said.

Prisoner smiled as if he'd just invited them all into Santa's grotto and held his hand out to Harriet. The boys both held their positions, waiting for her to take the lead. Irritatingly, in that moment, Simon realised he needed to pee again.

"I must be off my fucking rocker." Harriet took Prisoner's hand and stepped into the boat. The others followed, relieved. Prisoner untied the tattered rope that held the boat in place, before expertly guiding the little vessel through a barely noticeable gap in the rocks. They were away.

"OK, now what?" Bob asked, once they were well clear.

"Well," Prisoner stood and the boat rocked slightly in protest, "if we head straight that way, I'm pretty sure we'll hit Greece some time tomorrow."

Simon took a deep breath. "Pretty sure?"

"Almost entirely."

Lightning flashed and lit them again for a moment. Harriet's hair was plastered to her head and rivulets of water ran down her face. Had anyone taken a photo of her now, Simon imagined it being used to scare children into bed.

"Prisoner, sorry to ask, but is your leg flashing?"

It was Bob. And he was right. Around his calf, a red light flashed rhythmically through Prisoner's wet, white trousers.

Prisoner looked down at it curiously, like an old acquaintance whose name would not quite come to him.

"Ah hell," he finally said, "I remember how they caught me..."

CHAPTER TWENTY-TWO

Cherry sat back and sighed, full of pancakes and maple syrup. She sipped at her hazelnut coffee, appreciating the luxurious softness of the leather armchair she was sinking into. Yep, major perks to working for Faunt.

"Would you like some more?" Faunt asked.

Cherry looked at him quizzically. "I'm full, thanks. Why don't you know that?"

Faunt smiled. "I do, but, you know, sometimes people like to be asked..."

"Fair enough." She sank back again. "I'm good."

"Are you?"

Cherry took a deep breath. "No. I'm not. There's no point in me telling you how scared I was, or how angry I am at you, because you already know that. And I'm pissed at you for already knowing that, so that I can't tell you."

Faunt looked sadly at her.

"And now, you're biting your damn tongue from saying, 'I know', aren't you?"

Faunt closed his eyes and nodded.

"See? I can't even shout at you!"

"Well... you sort of are."

Cherry paused for a moment, and then burst into a huge, hearty laugh. "I am, aren't I?"

The laugh quickly transformed into sobs, and tears welled in her eyes.

"I think maybe I can help, a little, though..." said the deer.

"Yeah? How you gonna do that?" she challenged him.

"Well, the thing that bothers you the most is not that you nearly died, it's the realisation that you're mortal. You've always felt like no matter what trouble you got into, you could always get out of it by teleporting, so you've often been reckless. Careless, sometimes.

"This time, you discovered what it's like to be in danger and to not be able to teleport out of it. Which terrified you. And now you're worried that it might happen again. Which makes you scared to leave the house. And that makes you angry at yourself for being a coward, because now you think all your bravery came from relying on your power. But you're wrong. You're still brave, even without it. And I'll prove it to you."

Cherry's mouth hung open. Everything Faunt had said cut straight to her core. He was, of course, right. And, hearing it spoken, hearing her inner torment given form, somehow *had* made it better.

"You'd have figured this all out eventually yourself, of course, but unfortunately I don't have time to let you. I have to ask more of you, I'm afraid."

"*Seriously?*" Cherry was surprised again.

"I'll put it as simply as possible. Simon needs protection. Maya is prepared to do the job, but she can't go alone. She can only hold her form in this world with a human anchor to keep her here."

"Right. And you want me to be the anchor, yeah?"

"Yes, I do."

Cherry looked up at the ceiling.

"Where do you want me to go?"

"Daniel and Lily have a boat anchored off Priest's Island. If you're onboard, that's close enough for Maya to spend a significant amount of time on the island."

"OK. So what happens when Maya needs someone solid to do something for her?"

"She's very resourceful."

Cherry looked at the giant TV screen on the wall. It was off, and reflected a darkened version of the room, which she found apt. The world was a bit darker today.

"OK. I'll do it. On one condition. Tell me his name."

Faunt knew everything and was therefore rarely surprised. With this in mind, he was rarely rattled. So to see him visibly shaken, as he was now, actually upset Cherry even more. She regretted asking.

"You have to understand. It's not just my life..."

"Seriously? You're so important that the world can't live without you?"

"Maybe not," he answered, quietly.

It was Cherry's turn to be shaken. He was serious. Inexplicably, Faunt looked up, with a relieved smile.

"Thank you," he said to the air.

The hairs stood up on Cherry's neck in a familiar way and an icy draft blew over her ear:

"Calderon."

———

"What the fuck are you going to do if I don't?"

Prisoner, Simon and Bob had all recognised the futility of arguing with heavily armed men in a helicopter. Harriet, not so much. Which was why she was now standing in the rickety excuse for a boat, holding herself up with the end of the rope ladder, and screaming into a torrent of rain.

In reply, one of the gunmen took three shots. All three

missed Harriet – and hit the boat. Water instantly bubbled in to lap at Harriet's ankles.

"We're leaving now, Miss," he shouted through a loud-speaker after the bullets. "You can come if you want."

Harriet grabbed hold of the ladder with both hands and climbed up two rungs. She stopped and glowered. That was as far as she was going. The head soldier shrugged and indicated to the helicopter pilot to carry on.

"Sorry, folks," Prisoner shouted over the motor. "Guess it wasn't a great plan after all!"

Simon hoped they locked Prisoner up again before Harriet got hold of him.

The Cajun turned to the soldier next to him. "Hey, do I know you?"

"Yes, sir. Billy. Nice to see you again."

Simon turned to the soldier on the other side.

"I don't suppose there's a toilet on board?"

———

Luke burst into the room like the Devil herself was chasing him.

He'd gone out to pick up some pastries for breakfast, and to see if he could move forward their plan to get Debovar and his aunt safely locked away. Gabby had pretended to be asleep when he got up, because she didn't know what to say to him.

She had the nagging feeling she was being unfair. She had Luke on a pedestal. He was her hero. And at the moment, he was being particularly... fallible. Human. She was sad that he wasn't living up to her ideal of what he was, and could be. Reality, as it does, was screwing up her world.

So as he came bursting back into the room, she decided she had to act, now, before another word was said. She sat up in bed and firmly held up her hand. Luke stopped in his tracks, and looked at her in pleading astonishment.

"But..."

"No, sweetheart, I have something I absolutely have to say right now and no matter what you're going to tell me next, I have to say this first."

Luke shrugged, but the panicked look remained. "OK."

"I've been unfair to you. I adore you. And I expect you to be able to move mountains – not literally, these days, but you know what I mean – and I guess seeing you not be perfect is difficult. But I know you're doing your best, and I know you're doing it for the right reasons. And just so I've said it, I think your plan is great. I'm sure it's going to work and we'll all get out of here safely."

Luke's eyes filled with tears. This was not entirely the reaction Gabby had expected.

"I would give anything," he said, "to not have to tell you this..."

———

"Holy shit."

Gabby was not overly given to swearing, but it was more than appropriate, all things considered.

"I know," Luke answered.

"What can we do? We can't let them be killed! Especially not – what did you say? Flayed? What does that even mean?"

"Having all their skin torn off."

"Why would anybody *do* that?"

"The Assyrians were big on it. And the Mings. Lots of nailing skin to doors, wasn't there? It was supposed to be a warning. Like a head on a spike."

Luke caught the look of horror on Gabby's face. He'd missed the point.

"Sorry, yes, it's horrible."

"So. What can we do?"

"Well, as long shots go, this is a big one. But I spoke to the waitress, Star. Apparently, in case of emergency, there is a system in place to notify Priest when he is required back on the Island urgently. But it's only supposed to be available to the custodians."

"The witches?"

"Exactly. But I was thinking, if they're all at the trial later on – surely the guards and everyone will be focused there too, right? So maybe we can get to the signal and set it off?"

"OK. And what happens if it takes him too long to get here?"

"In that case, I think we're in a lot of trouble."

"Oh. That's what I thought, too."

CHAPTER TWENTY-THREE

"Jesus bloody wept."

Harriet looked up in the darkness as the sound of drums became louder and louder, rattling the floorboards above them. Light shone in around the edges of a square, illuminating the dislodged dust and dirt falling into their eyes.

Simon, Bob and Harriet stood back to back in a triangle, their wrists tied to a central post with rope that Simon thought must have been specially designed to rub skin off. There was no other rational explanation for the amount of pain it was causing.

Plus, they'd been under here for hours waiting for someone to tell them what was happening. With no food or drink. It was inhumane. And past lunchtime.

"They don't half do a bit of drama, do they?" she asked nobody in particular. "You'd think we were in a bloody Roman colosseum."

Now Simon was imagining lions. He whimpered piteously.

"We're dead, aren't we?" he asked.

"Would you please get it together?" Harriet roared at him in the dark. "We're *not* dead, but I'll tell you what, if we are going to end up cooked for these bitches' Sunday lunch, I'm going to make damn sure they have to chew. So how about you harden the fuck up?"

It wasn't quite 'Once more unto the breach', but it did have an effect. Simon took a deep breath. This was unfair and unjust. They were being put on trial for something totally unreasonable. If there was any justice at all in the world, they would see out the rest of the day. It was a substantial 'if', admittedly...

"You're right," said Bob. "We have to hold our heads up."

Above them, the trapdoor banged open and light flooded into their cell. The sound of the drums hit them like a wave. Winches screeched as ropes were pulled and the platform they stood on was hauled up towards the flickering light, which, as their eyes adjusted, they could all see was provided by huge, flaming torches.

As their heads rose through the floor, Simon was disconcerted to see the ankles of the guards at eye-level. For a moment, he lost his equilibrium and the room went sideways. He wobbled and leaned, but immediately found a hand supporting each side. Harriet and Bob had grabbed an arm each. He looked over his shoulder to thank them and saw the trails of dried tears in the dust on Bob's face. Harriet's, of course, was dry – except around her mouth, where there may have been traces of spittle. Simon had always thought of her as a bulldog. He wondered just how much damage his great aunt was capable of.

The platform banged into place, filling the hole on the floor. They were in another room they hadn't seen before. It was, essentially, a windowless stone cube, with several large wooden doors, and a balcony along one wall. The dozen carved stone pillars on the balustrade seemed to be moving or, in fact, writhing. As his eyes focused in the torchlight, Simon could see that each one depicted a person in the throes of one of various hideous tortures. Their little stone mouths cried out in mute agony. It was really quite disturbing.

The other three walls were hung with blood-red, heavy, dark tapestries, all depicting vast images of battle and death. There were old, dark liquid stains on the floor and a thick aroma of burnt meat in the air.

"I like what they've done with the place," Harriet grinned.

The three were surrounded by a bizarre concoction of witnesses and gawkers. Simon wondered where they had all come from, because very few of them came anywhere near to the beauty standards required for visitors to the island. Facial tattoos, scars and unorthodox hairstyles were everywhere.

Maybe they were the staff – the ones that were usually hidden from the public.

"Ladies and gentlemen!" A heavy cane banged hard on the balcony floor, stopping the drums and the chatter. Even the little torture victims were still.

"That's a bloody liberal use of the phrase," Harriet whispered.

Ingrid stepped forward and leaned over to glower at her prisoners. Behind her, Simon could just make out the other Socialites, including Amelia. She looked emotionless – almost dead. But she was there.

"Today, I ask you all to bear witness as we pursue the unfortunate task of punishing someone who was a guest of this island, for the despicable act of taking advantage of a child for his own sexual perversions," Ingrid spoke slowly and deliberately.

"Bloody hell." Harriet rolled her eyes. Ingrid looked at her murderously.

"And also," the witch spat, "the accomplices who tried to help the perverted rapist escape from the island. Including," she looked up to the ceiling, where a cage hung directly above them, "the insane old idiot we've kindly been keeping safe here."

Looking up, Simon saw the round, rusty bottom of a cage. It swayed slightly as Prisoner answered.

"That, madame, is unkind. Ain't nobody ever diagnosed me insane. Not that I can remember."

"Oh, hell," said Bob, through gritted teeth, "not him too."

"So, by the power vested in me by the Constitution of this Island, I hereby confer the following sentences," Ingrid announced.

The crowd breathed in anticipation.

"Wait a minute!" It was Simon. Unexpectedly. Not least by Simon. "You can't just move to sentencing! We haven't had a trial!"

Ingrid smiled. Despite her outward beauty, every ounce of her inner ugly was on display.

"This is how our trials work. We already know you're guilty, *don't* we?"

"But that's not... fair!" Simon bellowed up at her. "Who do you think you are?"

"I'm the person who's in charge, boy, and I'm also the person who is about to pass sentence on you. So unless someone here wants to challenge my authority, I strongly suggest you shut up and pray."

Simon breathed deeply. "I challenge your authority!"

Ingrid laughed and the Socialites joined her in a group cackle.

"*You* don't get to challenge my authority. Only a member of the ruling council can."

Simon's shoulders slumped. He had run out of ideas.

"So, *does* anyone from the council want to challenge my authority?" Ingrid spread her arms wide, arrogantly defying anyone to answer.

The room returned to hushed silence. Simon looked around, begging for someone, anyone, to speak up. Harriet glowered at Ingrid. Bob struggled against the ropes on his wrists.

"Actually, *I* do, ye mad old whore," said a voice from the crowd.

Pins dropped all over the place.

———

Gabby couldn't believe their luck. So far, every guard station they'd passed on the way up the tower had been abandoned. It looked like Luke was going to turn out to be completely right, this time. They hadn't even had to be particularly quiet, since the drums had been reverberating around the whole building.

Even so, they'd crept carefully up the steps, peeking round every corner, prepared to put their ingenious 'Where's the toilet?' charade into effect. But after three guard posts, they'd not seen a single person. Luke peeked around the final corner to scope out the route to the room Star had told him housed the emergency button – the Priest Signal.

"Crap," he whispered.

"What?" Gabby asked, nervously.

They were expecting at least one guard, so if it was bad, there must be more. Two, three, maybe four.

"How many are there?" she asked.

Luke turned around. "None."

"What?"

"None. Nobody. Just... a door."

"Is that bad?"

"Well, it seems odd, don't you think? There must be some sort of security, but we can't see it."

The drums stopped, leaving them looking at each other in silence.

"That can't be good," said Luke.

Gabby knew they were running out of time. She launched herself past Luke and headed for the door.

"Wait!" he yelped, grabbing at the air behind her.

By the time he caught her, she had already reached the door and was turning the handle. It swung open with a creak.

Neither of them saw what was behind it – Luke, because, having desperately tackled Gabby, he was face down on the stone floor; Gabby, because she had a faceful of Luke.

"Are you mad?!" They shouted in unison.

"You could have killed yourself!" Luke shouted, bringing himself up to his knees.

"Well, we're out of time, right?"

"That's no excuse!"

"Well, nothing happened, did it?" Gabby gestured wildly at the open door as evidence of the perfectly safe nature of her actions.

As there was, conspicuously, absolutely nothing pointy, hungry or otherwise violent emerging from the door, Luke decided not to argue. He sighed and helped Gabby to her feet. Slowly, the two of them crept towards the door until they could see inside.

What they saw was not quite what they had been expecting.

Firstly, there were four unconscious guards tied up on the floor. One was snoring. Two were going to be slightly uncomfortable when they woke up, unless they actually had that kind of relationship.

Above them was a button. Like all the best ones, it was fat and red, with EMERGENCY ONLY proudly printed on it in big white letters. That was, in fact, pretty much exactly what they were expecting to see. But it was the flashing light above the button that really spoke to Luke and Gabby. What it said was:

"Somebody already pressed the button."

———

"Who was that?" Ingrid literally spat into the throng below her. Several people were repulsed.

"I fucking knew he was a good 'un," Harriet smiled.

The crowd moved to leave Sean standing alone in a circle of abandonment. Those who had been standing directly next to him had clearly not wished to be mistaken for having been the one who had called the crazy lady a bad word. They all shrank back, trying to blend into the person next to them.

"The barman?" Ingrid laughed, followed by familiar cackling behind her. Amelia, however, smiled. Her limpid eyes moved for the first time since the trial began, to look appreciatively at the Irishman, who had, for some reason, come dressed in even more extravagant pirate regalia than usual.

"You don't get a say either, you idiot bottom feeder. Council members only."

"Actually," said Sean, smiling that smile, "I think you'll find that on December 13th, 1814, I was appointed Special Advisor to the Council on all matters of and relating to Piracy. To my knowledge, that appointment has never been repealed, so I am, in fact, a member of the Council."

Ingrid's face was thunder. "Is that true?" she hissed indiscriminately at the women behind her, who looked hopelessly at each other for an answer. Finally, one looked back at Ingrid and shrugged.

"I don't believe you!" Ingrid barked.

"Well, no problem," Sean answered, calmly, "We can just wait until Priest gets back and ask him."

This was not the response Ingrid had desired, clearly. She was literally foaming at the mouth.

"Fine," she barked. "Your challenge is accepted. Choose your weapon for a trial by combat."

Sean took a breath. Simon suspected he had been hoping she would wait. After a pause, he reached down and drew a beautifully engraved cutlass from its scabbard.

"I'll have this, ta," he said.

Simon turned to Harriet. "Is he any good?"

"He's a fabulous swordsman," she answered.

Simon deeply regretted asking the question. As was often the case.

"Simon," Bob whispered, "Move your hands to mine."

Simon was puzzled, but did as he was told, and was surprised to find Bob's hands moving, largely unrestricted, to work on his binds. Harriet moved closer to them both, positioning herself to hide them from the witches' lines of sight.

Finished conferring with her coven, Ingrid finally turned back towards the pirate and spoke.

"As a lady, I, of course, exercise my right to select a champion. I nominate Ki."

Ingrid gestured with a flourish toward the guard, who stepped forward, bowed slightly, and drew his katana from its place on his back.

"Aw, shite," Sean muttered.

The crowd had begun to thin out, creating a large space in the middle of the room. Sean walked casually toward Harriet.

"I am so hot for you, right now," she whispered at him.

"Hang onto those ropes," he grinned back at her, "and you can thank me later."

"Oh my God!" Simon had realised something fairly awesome – certainly in his estimation.

Bob and Harriet both turned to him in alarm.

"Sshhh," Bob warned him, "Don't draw attention to us."

"Sorry," Simon replied, hushed now, "but do you realise what's about to happen?"

The pair looked at each other blankly.

"Pirates versus Ninjas!"

———

Sean had not entirely thought this through. His first plan had not been great. His fallback plan, to call Priest back and stall the trial, had seemed like a great idea. He hadn't expected Ingrid to agree to the challenge so easily. And he'd been pretty sure he'd be a match for any of her private guard when it came to swords. But he'd forgotten she could call on Priest's private guards while he was off the island – and, therefore, Ki.

They were friends. They'd spent many nights up late, drinking sake and talking about which Empire would win in fantasy combat. Ming versus Byzantine. Rome versus America. He was a quiet, thoughtful man. And Sean was either going to have to kill him or, more likely, be killed by him.

"Ki." Sean nodded in acknowledgement.

"Sean." Ki bowed slightly.

Sean moved in close, touching swords with Ki in an apparent gesture of readiness.

"Any chance we could just spin this out as long as possible?" he asked quietly, when their faces were only a few feet apart.

Ki looked confused. "What are you up to, my friend?"

"I just need..."

"Hoi!" Ingrid barked to interrupt. "No talking. If you two are thinking of fixing this, let me make the rules very clear. One of you dies or you both die."

Ki and Sean looked hard at each other. Ki shrugged.

"Pirate rules?" Sean grinned.

"What are pirate rules?" the ninja asked.

"Ever seen an Errol Flynn movie?"

"Of course."

"Dirtier than that."

"OK," Ki smiled back.

Sean pushed Ki away with his sword and the two began to circle around each other. Ki moved fluidly, like a cat. Sean's movement was more deliberate, more cautious. It had been a long time since he'd had to do this, and even longer since he'd done it on solid footing. Still, like riding a horse, right? You never forget.

"Are you two going to fight or dance?" the witch bellowed again.

With that, Sean swung high over his head and brought the sword down in a crashing arc onto the cobblestones, where Ki had been standing. Ki, on the other hand, was now behind him, having somersaulted over him from a standing position. The two turned and faced each other again.

"Cool," whispered Simon.

Harriet glowered at him. The two fighters began again, their swords clashing repeatedly as they moved around inside the circle of witnesses. Both were feeling their way, pulling their punches. There was no bloodlust between the two, but it was certainly more convincing than Errol Flynn.

And without the straining tights.

———

Simon felt the binds of his rope come loose – loose enough for him to slide one hand free from the other. He was free, but carefully kept his hands behind him, maintaining the illusion of captivity. The urge to stretch his shoulder muscles was horrendous. He had to settle for cricking his neck, which was blissful in itself.

Bob moved on to Harriet's binds.

"Hurry," she prompted him. "I'm not sure how long toyboy's going to last."

"I know," said Bob. "Try to stay still."

Bob looked up as he worked and paused as he realised he was being watched. Intently.

Amelia had come to the edge of the balcony. She looked sad and scared. And sorry. Bob wondered how long she'd been watching and if she knew what he was doing. He wanted to let her know, but dare not risk any of the witches seeing. Instead, he beamed a broad smile and winked.

———

Amelia was stunned. She had no idea why he was smiling. But the idea that there was some reason for hope, some glimmer of a possible way out of this, was all she needed. She was reinvigorated.

If her mother was going to try to kill her new friends, she wasn't going to let her do it easily.

———

Sean and Ki continued to cross swords below, feinting, parrying and carrying on their melee to the delight of the crowd. It was a spectacular show and only those genuinely trained in the art would have been able to tell that's exactly what it was. Ki's acrobatics were particularly impressive, though Sean used the surrounds to his advantage.

As he was knocked against a member of the crowd, he reached back and grabbed the man's belt, pulling him round as a human shield. Ki, naturally, stopped. Sean poked his sword under the man's armpit, nicking his opponent's sword arm. Ki stepped back in surprise.

"*Touché*," he nodded to Sean.

"Ta," Sean answered as the panicked witness dragged himself away to the back of the crowd, rattled, but unhurt.

———

As the spectator crept away, he bumped into a couple trying to worm their way in the other direction. They were trying to get in closer, but the crowd was tight knit this close in.

"What can you see?" Gabby asked, urgently.

"It's the barman, the one Debovar's aunt was with. He's fighting... a ninja, I think. And he's dressed like Johnny Depp in that pirate film."

"What the hell is going on?"

———

Ingrid was growing more incandescent with rage by the minute. Regardless of her stunning beauty, not a man (or woman, for that matter) would want to get within 100 yards of her right now, for fear of being melted by sheer malice.

Unfortunately for all concerned, she was about to get more bad news.

"Madam." A guard tugged at her shoulder.

She spun round to face him. "What?!"

The guard paused briefly to wipe the saliva from his eye.

"Someone has activated the emergency button. They assaulted the guards, but left them unharmed. I thought you should know."

Ingrid stood up to her full height, which looked a good six inches more than it was.

She turned to watch the fight with murder in her veins.

"They're stalling," she hissed to nobody in particular.

———

Amelia hadn't heard what the guard said to her mother, but she knew the look on her face. Somebody was about to be very sorry for something. She crept closer, making a show of trying to get a better view of the action. As she neared her mother's shoulder, she heard her muttering. It didn't sound like any language she'd heard.

Which was a worry.

As was the fact that her eyes were glowing blue.

Sean was getting tired. They'd been at this for a good fifteen minutes now and, while it surely looked good, they were going to have to come up with an exit strategy soon. He and Ki were managing to look like they were trying to kill each other, and both had a few flesh wounds for dramatic effect but, if Priest didn't show up soon, they were going to have to find a way out of this.

Then, as he turned away from one of Ki's lunges, he glimpsed a face in the crowd, and an idea formed.

He leaned in towards the ninja, preparing to tell him his idea. But something weird happened: Ki's eyes flashed blue. Then looked very, very angry.

"Ki?" he asked, hopefully.

Ki's mouth contorted into a malicious grin as he slowly shook his head.

Oh, bollocks.

———

"Wow, they've really stepped it up!" Simon whispered. "I mean, it was amazing before, but... wow!"

"Could you please remember what's at stake here?" Harriet snapped at him.

Bob finished freeing her hands.

"Right," she said, "everybody ready?"

"For what?" Simon asked.

"I've no bloody idea, sunshine, but whatever it is, we'd better be ready for it."

———

Sean was parrying with everything he had. Whatever had possessed Ki – literally, by the look of it – he had retained his martial arts skills, which meant he was now fighting an extremely capable ninja who was actually trying to kill him. A different proposition entirely.

He was coping, but only just, and it was only a matter of time before he slipped up.

New plan.

Sean began staggering, as if his legs were about to give way, feigning a pain in his ankle.

Ki smiled broadly and closed in, like a lioness stalking a wounded antelope. He slashed again and again at Sean, who parried and dodged, but stumbled backwards.

"Shit," said Harriet, "he's going over. Get ready."

Sean circled past them and glanced up to see Harriet poised to strike as Ki advanced toward him. She wrapped the rope around her fist, ready to pound the ninja unconscious as soon as he passed her. But the look on Sean's face made her pause. In fact, she thought he mouthed, "No." She furrowed her eyebrows at him quizzically.

If she had been unsure about the word, the definite shake of his head made it very clear: he wanted her to stay out of it.

The chivalrous idiot was going to get himself killed. Harriet was unused to men being prepared to die for her and part of her found this exceptionally romantic. However, Harriet being Harriet, mostly she thought it was bloody stupid.

Bob placed a hand on her wrist.

"Wait, I think he knows what he's doing," he said.

Harriet turned to him. "You better be pretty damn sure, mate, or else it won't be the bitch up there you need to worry about," she gestured towards Ingrid, "it'll be the one down here."

"I know," said Bob, "so trust him, not me."

Harriet was unused to putting her faith in anyone other

than herself. Mainly because most other people were imbeciles. This was a lot to ask. But what the hell, this was one weird-ass holiday.

She relaxed her muscles and returned to watching the fight play out. Besides, the ninja was out of her reach, for now, and even she wasn't stupid enough to think she could cover several yards to reach him before he filleted her with the big sushi knife.

———

Sean finally lost his footing and fell, somewhat harder than he intended. That was going to hurt tomorrow. Assuming he was alive tomorrow. His sword clattered away from him. For all intents and purposes, he was at the mercy of his opponent, who closed in with his sword raised high. Sean rolled onto his side and put up a hand in defence.

"Wait," he panted.

Ki looked down at him curiously. "No," he replied, tensing to bring the sword down and end the fight.

———

Amelia grabbed her mother's shoulder and shook it.

"Mother," she asked, with faux concern, "is everything OK?"

Ingrid jolted as if from a dream and turned to look at her daughter. Had it been anyone else in the world, they would most likely have spent the few remaining moments of their life in agony.

Amelia escaped with a firm slap in the face.

"Not now," Ingrid growled.

———

Ki paused, looking unsure of where he was and, to be honest, exactly how he'd gotten there. This was not, however, to be the most unexpected thing to happen in that moment, as he felt something hammer into his stomach, knocking the air from him.

He looked down to see smoke rising from the ancient pistol in Sean's hand.

"Sorry, mate. Pirate rules."

Ki, with a new appreciation for the merits of understanding the rules one is playing by, collapsed in a crumpled heap and bled on the floor.

CHAPTER TWENTY-FOUR

"Yes!" Harriet bellowed.

She'd been certain Sean was mincemeat, but the bugger had a gun on him all along! She liked him more and more. It was all she could do not to run to him and give away the fact that they were all no longer tied up. But her sense of self-preservation kept her still. Just.

"No!" Ingrid howled. "Cheat!"

Sean pulled himself to his feet, looking as sprightly and uninjured as he really was.

"Actually, he and I agreed in advance to pirate rules. Under those rules, concealed pistols are not so much allowed, love, as downright expected. Nobody cheated."

He leaned close over Ki and placed two fingers on his neck.

"He's dead," he pronounced solemnly, looking up. "Which makes me keeper of the Island until Priest returns, right?"

The hush was a mix of awe and disbelief.

"It does," said an older man, stepping from the crowd. He was dressed like one of the guards, but in a more decorative uniform than the others. Which was an achievement.

"I place my men at your disposal, sir. What are your orders?"

The Captain seemed pretty happy to have had his mistress usurped and Harriet wondered just how popular the old bat had been with, well, anybody.

"Disperse this crowd and place Ingrid under house arrest until Priest returns. And release the prisoners. All of them," he said, nodding towards Prisoner, whom Harriet had completely forgotten was still rattling around above them.

"What about the body, sir?" the Captain asked.

"I'll handle that," Sean answered, solemnly.

The Irishman found Edoard in the crowd and beckoned him forward.

A pair of guards approached the supposedly restrained threesome.

"This could be awkward." Bob nodded towards their free hands.

"In the grand scheme of things, Bobby, I think they might let that one slip."

Harriet shook the ropes off her wrists and held them up to the guards.

"Shite rope!" she said, grinning.

———

Edoard stepped up to Sean. His eyes were glassy with pain and anger. The pirate did his best to look positive, without giving anything away.

"Yes, sir?" The wizard spat the second word like it burned in his mouth.

Sean spoke quietly and deliberately.

"Listen carefully to what I say. I want you to take Ki to his quarters and... *deal* with him. I believe you have the skills to do what is necessary." He lowered his voice to a whisper and added, "Quickly."

Edoard was an extremely intelligent man. There was no need for him to hurry to deal with a corpse.

He moved quickly towards Ki, casting the same spell he'd used the previous day on the mad woman with the breasts. Ki, suddenly rigid, floated off the ground and the crowd parted for the wizard to push him out of the hall. As they cleared the room and rounded a corner, Edoard broke into a run, bringing Ki with him. His own room was closer than Ki's; they'd go there.

———

Ki was exceptionally disciplined. So, when Sean knelt over him and whispered, "Play dead," it was an easy task. He was, after all, already feeling pretty exhausted, what with having had his body invaded by a witch and a pellet of lead in quick succession. So lying very still and slowing his heartbeat with meditation hadn't been a huge difficulty.

He did, however, expect a very fine bottle of sake from the Irishman for his trouble.

———

Harriet ran to Sean and threw herself the last few feet at him.

"My hero!" she said, with not as much mockery as Sean might have expected. "Take me away and ravish me, you beast!"

"Steady, girl. I've just staged a bloody coup, in case you missed it. Let's get you and your mates off the island before we do anything else."

"Excuse me," Prisoner called politely from above.

"We can't leave! We still need what we came for." Simon had followed Harriet to thank the Irishman.

"Shite, *seriously*?" he answered. "D'you know how bloody lucky we are to be alive?"

"Unfortunately," Harriet answered, "if we leave now, *he's* probably still dead."

"Oh," said Sean, the wind gone from his sails. "Well that's bollocksed plan B."

"Hello?" Prisoner called again.

Amelia had come to the edge of the balcony.

"Are you all right?" she called to Bob. "I'm so sorry!"

Bob smiled up at her.

"I'm fine. We all are," he answered.

"Oh thank God. I'd never have forgiven myself if mother had..." She couldn't find the words to finish the sentence.

"Hey." Bob changed the subject. "What light through yonder window breaks?"

Amelia stepped back, took in the balcony and herself, and giggled.

"Anybody know what *that* is?" Prisoner asked everybody and nobody.

"What's that smell?" Simon asked. "Is something burning?"

Harriet and Sean sniffed the air. There was a faint whiff of... something unpleasant.

"Christ. What *is* that?" Harriet asked.

"Will one of you damned fools please *look up*?!" Prisoner begged, with a distinct note of terror.

A burning yellow hole had materialised in the ceiling, no more than ten feet from Prisoner. But the real worry was the gloriously ugly head that poked through, resembling the bastard love child of a hag and a hawk, with teeth like jagged rocks.

"What the *fuck* is that?" asked Sean.

And then it screamed.

———

Ingrid was a bad loser. To lose control of the island, so publicly and officially, was embarrassing. But to lose the right to punish the lecherous oaf who had abused her daughter was unacceptable. What would the ladies think?

She'd easily killed the guards and slipped back into the lower chamber, to conjure something that would properly finish the job. She may not have jurisdiction over the island any more, but she was damned if she was giving up jurisdiction over her own flesh and blood.

The Furies would see to that.

———

"Can someone get me down please?" Prisoner yelled, urgently.

Simon reacted first, running for the winch supporting the cage. He worked to release it, trusting that someone would give him a warning if he were in imminent danger of being eaten. The winch was stiff, but he got it moving. Sean quickly arrived to help.

The remnants of the crowd that had gathered to watch the festivities beat a hasty exit. As the last of them cleared the room, the heavy wooden doors slammed shut, leaving only Simon, Harriet, Sean, Bob and Ingrid in the main chamber, with Prisoner in his cage and Amelia on the balcony.

"Get out!" Bob called up to her. "Amelia!"

She didn't answer. She stared, frozen, at the hole from which another two heads had appeared on long, serpentine necks. The three beasts grunted and grated their teeth, struggling to push through the burning, sulphurous portal. Ingrid stepped from the shadows and shouted something unintelligible. All three heads calmed and turned to her.

She pointed at Bob.

The giant gulped back a mouthful of bile.

The heads turned on him, pulling and jerking with a manic intensity, growling and shrieking at Bob like wolverines caught in a snare. They strained to be free, desperate to reach the object of their summoning.

Prisoner's cage hit the ground with a loud clang.

Bob had nowhere to run. If he moved towards the others he was only going to put them in danger, too.

The heads were almost within reach. He shuffled backwards under the balcony, never taking his eyes off the drooling mouths, praying for some miracle to distract them.

"Oi! Ugly! Over here!"

Harriet threw something at the monsters, catching one on the side of the head. It shrieked, and all three heads turned towards her, teeth bared with rage. Harriet grabbed a burning torch from the wall.

"What are you doing?" Simon shouted, as Sean fumbled with the keys to Prisoner's cage.

"No idea!" she answered. "But I got their attention!"

"Now what?" he shouted back.

"Well, if I may," Prisoner said, stepping from his cage, "perhaps your friend ought to make his way up to the balcony. There ain't no doors up there."

Simon looked up. Prisoner was right. He could just see the tops of the archways at the back of the balcony, and there didn't seem to be any doors on them.

"Bob!" he shouted, pointing. "Balcony!"

From underneath the balcony, Bob had no idea why he was supposed to get up there, but anywhere was better than where he was. He tugged on a nearby tapestry. It held. He grabbed two handfuls and began to climb.

Sean rejoined Harriet with his sword drawn. The more she threw things at the dripping maws, the more they danced and weaved in front of her, darting forward and snapping with each lull in the projectiles.

With Bob on his way to safety, Simon decided that splitting the things' attention might be helpful. Following Harriet's lead, he began hurling anything he could lay his hands on. He hit the nearest head with a loose chunk of stone, and it turned towards him. As it bared his teeth and reared back, Simon realised he'd made a horrible error: he had nothing to defend himself with.

The head lurched towards him and Simon instinctively dived for the only obstacle in reach – the empty cage. The beast's teeth clanged off the metal as Simon ducked inside. It screeched with frustration, biting and nudging the bars, rattling the cage until it finally tipped over. Simon went with it, banging his head hard on a bar. For a moment, everything went black. As his eyesight returned, he saw the head looming above him. Something was wrong. Even *more* wrong.

There was nothing between them.

The cage door hung open, dangling down towards him. The monster's eyes glinted with delight at its imminent kill. Simon glanced around, still dizzy. He was trapped. The only way out was up past the head full of teeth. His defence had become his tomb.

With an excited grunt, the beast jerked downwards. Simon instinctively pulled his feet under him and forced himself upwards, slamming the cage door up against its face. It shrieked and banged repeatedly against the bars, incandescent that its prey had escaped again. Simon pushed upwards with all he had, crouched inside his metal shield. Only his newly perfected muscles were keeping him alive – and he doubted even they would hold out for long against the barrage.

———

Bob had nearly reached the height of the balcony, but he still faced a significant leap to get to it.

As he began to sway, building momentum, the one head not engaged with Harriet, Sean or Simon seemed to suddenly remember its reason for being there, pulled around and launched itself towards the giant. The lunge fell just short, managing only to rip the arse out of Bob's trousers, but taking flesh with it. Bob jerked at the pain, his fists closing tight on the tapestry, which finally ripped from its moorings. With a howl, he disappeared into the folding material as it collapsed to the floor.

———

"Bob!" Simon shouted, as the frantic beast banged against the cage again.

Bob pulled himself out from the tapestry, but was still well within striking distance of the monster. The head bobbed back and forth with a fluid grace, slowly bearing down on its target, gurgling with the joy of an impending kill. Bob tried desperately to shuffle back under the balcony, but the monster was playing with him, cutting him off each time he shifted left or right.

"Hey! Hey!" Simon shouted again, vainly trying to get its attention, all the while resisting his own imminent death. But it was focused on its prey. There was nothing he could do but watch.

Bob's chest heaved with his panicked breathing. The adrenaline was keeping him from feeling the pain of his wounds, but he literally had nowhere to go. He scraped at the wall, desperately trying to pull loose a stone he could use in defence.

He raised his hands, pulling his legs up as the drooling *thing* reared back and threw its head forward with a screech of delight. The giant winced as its jaws clamped down.

On steel.

———

The beast roared in pain as it sliced its mouth open on Sean's blade. He'd slipped away from Harriet and thrown himself along the ground, sliding backwards into Bob, sword raised.

The other two heads also recoiled with the shock, giving Simon a moment's reprieve. His hands shook, bloody from the repeated battering and exhausted from the strain of holding the door closed.

———

A moment of reprieve was all Harriet needed.

Breaking what cover she had, she darted toward the mumbling witch, who stared blankly at the hole the beast had almost finished coming through. Passing a table, Harriet dropped her torch and picked up a discarded bottle. The last of its contents splashed against the wall as she broke off the neck and drove it into Ingrid's throat.

The witch staggered and focused long enough to stare, astonished, at her killer. At this range, Harriet could see her true face, but as her last breath escaped in a bubbling gurgle, her glamour disappeared. She slumped on the floor, her face a mask of surprise and hatred. Harriet stood over her, panting.

"I *told* you I'd get you, *bitch*."

"Harriet!" Simon cried, urgently.

She turned. While the portal had vanished, the beasts had not died with their master. Or, in fact, beast, since she could now see that the three heads were all connected to one enormous body, which stood upright in its full, murderous glory, pissed off and with nobody to control it.

Harriet dived away from the head that lunged at her, towards her discarded torch, still burning on the stone floor.

———

Prisoner had made his way to the balcony unnoticed. He had

no idea how, as he'd been right above Bob, but the head that was so intent on eating the giant hadn't even glanced at him.

On the balcony, he found Amelia still frozen and defenceless. He tried to lift her over his shoulder, but she was utterly rigid and awkward to move. Instead, he settled for pulling her by the waist out into the hall. Then he looked for some rope.

———

"Thank you," Bob shouted at Sean. He was aware of the woeful inadequacy of the phrase, but hoped he'd live to show his gratitude later.

"Can you stand?" the pirate asked.

He was engaged in a thrust and parry with the nearest head. The blood that dripped from its mouth bubbled like boiling tar on the floor.

Bob pulled himself up. Pain seared through him now, every time he tried to use the muscles at the top of his legs. He brought himself upright behind Sean.

"What do we do?" he asked.

"To be honest," Sean answered, parrying the teeth away, "I was hoping you'd have an idea!"

The head darted at them again, and Sean landed a blow across its nose.

Almost simultaneously, Harriet grabbed her torch and lifted it in defence, jamming it directly into the mouth of her attacker.

All three heads reared back toward their shared body, took a deep breath... and screamed.

The world went black.

———

The hurricane of sound extinguished every light in the room and knocked everyone off their feet. Simon covered his ears, praying that the noise would stop but, when it did, it was replaced with a loud ringing and the terror of complete darkness.

They were deaf, blind, sealed in a room with a monster that very much wanted to kill them all, and which Simon knew – absolutely *knew* – could see in the dark.

He fumbled for the cage door, aware he had to keep it shut if he had any chance of surviving, but he'd lost all sense of perspective. He barely knew which way was up.

A low rumble began to pierce the ringing in his head, and he winced as a hot, wet breath brushed his face.

———

There is a common understanding that things are usually at their worst just before they start to get better. Or, to use the common phrase, that it is 'darkest just before the dawn'. Often, this translates as heroes arriving at the last minute. It is an understandable belief, because it is almost unavoidably true.

If a hero does arrive and save the day, then it must be at, effectively, the last minute, as the danger is then over.

If they arrive too late, then they are not particularly useful heroes and are forgotten.

Those who arrive and are killed while saving others are considered even greater heroes, to be eulogised and martyred by those they made 'the ultimate sacrifice' to save.

Those who arrive, die and fail to save anyone have nobody left to remember them either way.

Thus the rule remains intact.

What it hides, however, is an utterly true fact.

The best heroes have immaculate timing.

———

A door burst off its hinges and flew across the room, landing somewhere between Simon's and Harriet's positions. Nobody heard it land, but everyone turned toward the new source of light, including all three of the heads, interrupted as they prepared to feast.

Framed in the light was the silhouette of a large, well-muscled man. Simon thought he must be at least six foot five – almost as tall as Bob. He strode into the room as if he owned it, everything and everyone in it. He walked directly to the beast's nearest face, which contorted in confusion.

The man breathed deeply and, in a voice so resonant it seemed to come from the depths of the Earth beneath him, spoke one word:

"Out!"

The beast quivered and, with a befuddled grunt of confusion, blinked out in a puff of yellow smoke.

———

Not only had the man's voice been audible, it had restored their hearing too. In the eerie, ambient light, Simon could see his friends, backed up against walls around the room and all, miraculously, alive. And sweating. There was a lot of sweating.

He looked to their saviour, who was smiling warmly back at him as if Simon was a long lost relative who'd arrived for Christmas dinner. He was just as mountainous as his shadow suggested. Simon could now see his ebony skin and elegant black suit. He exuded magnetism, not so much owning the room as dominating it, until it begged for a kind word or a smile.

"Father!"

Amelia had regained her movement and appeared back at the edge of the balcony.

The man looked up at her and smiled.

"Hello, angel," he said in that same orotund voice. "You OK?"

"Yes! Thank God you're back!" she shouted, tears of relief and happiness welling in her eyes.

"Well," Sean said to Bob, "that sorts that out."

"What?" asked Bob.

"I always reckoned she was Priest's daughter."

CHAPTER TWENTY-FIVE

Calderon closed his eyes and leaned back in his chair, his mood becoming blacker by the minute. Firstly, he was very tired of being stared at by the scum he was forced to share the flight with. It only reminded him of the damage to his face – once a source of considerable pride to him. His mother would have told him it served him right; it was just reward for his hubris. But she'd been dead a long time, and he had long since abandoned the strict morals she'd attempted to instil in him on the streets of Barcelona.

Also, he was too hot. The damned heating was stuck on, despite it being far too warm onboard, and when he turned the air on overhead, it dried his lips and face.

If it weren't for the fact he'd probably be arrested on landing, which would irritatingly delay his journey by at least a few hours, he most likely would have slaughtered one of the lowing cattle in the toilet, to make himself feel better.

He decided to settle for spiking the gin of the elderly woman next to him with a slow-acting poison, which would leave her perfectly healthy for a good hour or two after the flight.

By then, he'd be well beyond the reach of the local law.

Harriet was in lust. First, she had Sean, who had saved her life at least once in the last few hours and very possibly twice. Then there was this new guy, who she wanted very little more from than for him to allow her to cover him in whipped cream and lick it all off.

Now.

She reached up to reassuringly touch her necklace. This *had* to be Priest, and Dear God Almighty, even with the Priest-resistant necklace on, she wanted him. He smiled and she melted, the aches and bruises of the battle disappearing as she imagined the two of them in a deep, warm bubble bath together.

Then it occurred to her that perhaps, if she asked nicely, she could have both men at the same time and make them into one big pretzel.

She looked down at her blood-spattered hand and realised the evidence of her recent murderous activity was fairly... evident. Perhaps her lascivious thoughts were less than appropriate, just at the moment. Especially considering she'd just killed the mother of his daughter.

Still, she was optimistic.

Simon sidled up to her. He looked uncomfortable.

"You all right?" she asked, without a hint of condescension.

"I think so. Though I might have wet myself a little," he joked.

Harriet cracked a smile and resisted torturing her nephew. Just this once.

———

"I found some rope!"

Prisoner came barrelling back onto the balcony, panting heavily and dropping an end of rope over the edge. It took him a moment to realise that his frantic hunt, while noble, had been somewhat redundant.

Sean and Bob looked up at him. The giant was leaning heavily on the Irishman as they moved across the room towards Harriet, Simon and... him! The usurper who'd stolen his island!

"Thanks, mate," Sean called up to him, "but I think we're grand now, ta."

A crowd had started to form, milling back into the room now that all the roaring and crashing and bleeding had stopped.

Priest stood over Ingrid's body. He hugged his daughter as she sobbed into his chest.

"It's my understanding that you three are legitimate guests on the Island and that you annoyed my ex-wife. My daughter tells me it wasn't your fault and, honestly, that's no surprise. Could I invite you to join my wife and I for dinner, this evening? After you've had a chance to rest, of course.

"Oh, and you, sir," he said, turning to Bob, "should see Edoard. He'll fix that for you." He nodded toward Bob's wounded posterior.

Sean looked as if he'd been punched in the chest.

"Boss, do you know where Edoard is?"

Priest removed a sleek and sexy little tablet device from a pocket and tapped the screen. Simon wondered how all these magical / immortal / weird people managed to get hold of all the great gadgets. Maybe they all shopped at Amazon.omg.

"In his room," Priest replied.

"Come on," Sean said, supporting Bob, "I'll take you."

———

Daniel was in a huff. Again.

Faunt's teleporter had shown up out of nowhere and said Faunt would be "obliged" if they would show her the same hospitality they would have shown him. If he ever left his house.

"What harm can it do?" Lily turned to Cherry. "What are your thoughts on *True Blood*?"

"Ooo. What season?"

"Three, I think."

"Awesome. Got any beer?"

"I'm sure there must be some in that kitchen. Wait until you see this TV!"

The girls wandered off without even a "by your leave" to Daniel.

He had the distinct feeling that Lily wasn't taking this nearly as seriously as he was. Which was probably a good thing. He'd already seen what happened when someone failed his father. And he wasn't going to end up living like *that*.

He was going to claim the Rug. He knew exactly how to get it – and have a little fun with the Demon in the process.

He couldn't wait to see her face.

———

"I am so sorry, mate," said Sean.

"Me too," added Bob.

Ki sat in a chair in the corner of Edoard's room, sipping at something that appeared to be tea.

The room was as opulent and garish as Bob would probably have expected from a wizard. The plush furniture was a rich purple, often laced in gold. The four-poster bed, on which he now lay with his wounded buttocks exposed, was intricately carved in dark oak, and the sheets were of the softest cotton. Around the walls were a number of aged, wooden bookshelves holding a combination of old leather-bound books and what Bob could best sum up as 'trinkets' – little carvings, bottles and statues which seemed to follow no pattern of taste or style whatsoever.

There were also elaborate oil paintings on the wall which, while he couldn't actually see them moving, he was almost certain were not quite the same each time he looked at them. Some were of battles; a few seemed to be royal courts, while one was just a motley collection of characters standing around a candle, in a cave.

"It seems that I will live," Ki said, gently, "so I suppose there is no harm done. Would you mind, however, telling me what it was all about?"

Sean grinned. "If I just say 'a woman', is that going to be enough?"

Ki sipped his tea.

"From most people, no. From you, my friend, I expect no less. The one with the nice breasts?"

Sean nodded. "If it helps, she was the one who skewered the auld bitch – with a beer bottle."

"Do you know," Ki said, closing his eyes and smiling, "that does help."

Edoard appeared back from the side room he'd disappeared into just after Bob and Sean arrived.

"This is going to hurt, I'm afraid. I had another serum, which is painless, but I used it all on Ki and it takes eleven hours to make more."

"It's OK," said Bob, "to be honest, I'm glad to be alive to feel it."

"Amen to that, son," said Sean.

"And to be fair, it was my fault."

"It was not!" cried an indignant, female voice.

Edoard jumped as he began emptying the bottle onto Bob's exposed rump, spilling some of the potion on the bed sheets.

"Damn!" he yelped, and ran back into the side room.

Bob took a sharp breath as the liquid that did land on him bit hard into his wounds. He also lifted his head to see Amelia, who was standing in the doorway. She rushed to the side of the bed and knelt down, facing him.

"I'm so sorry," she said, tears welling in her eyes. "You didn't do anything wrong. It was all my stupid mother. She can be so horrible! Do you know, she was most upset about the fact that she thinks you are somebody's servant? I swear, she's going to have to do a lot of grovelling to make up for *this*."

Rooms can fall into comfortable silences, when old friends sit by a fire, come to the natural end of a conversation over a glass of wine and feel no need to fill the quiet with meaningless words.

There are nervous silences, when a couple who have finished a date and retired to one of their houses for 'coffee' run out of witty bravado and both know that the next thing they do will either lead to pleasant fumbling or fumbling embarrassment.

There are odd silences in elevators, when one of those present loudly breaks wind and the rest of the strangers desperately try to pretend they didn't hear anything. And even if they had, in fact, heard something, it certainly wasn't funny. Not a bit.

Then there are *those* silences; the painful, awkward, somebody-please-God-say-something silences.

These come in many forms and can range from disconcerting to utterly crucifying. But it is difficult to beat the silence that descends when a room full of men don't know how to remind a nice young girl that they recently played a significant role in the violent death of her mother. Not without making her cry, anyway. And making attractive young women cry comes quite high on the list of things said men would prefer to avoid.

The three men were dumbstruck, jaws metaphorically agape, looking at each other for some hint as to how to broach the subject of her mother's mortal coil being well and truly shuffled off.

Thankfully, Edoard came bustling back into the room with another bottle and a cloth to attack the spill on his bedsheets.

"Oh, Amelia," he said, "I'm sorry about your mother."

"Oh, don't worry," she answered chirpily. "She totally deserved it. She has no right to hold it against any of you. I mean, summoning the Furies; what was she thinking?"

This response served only to further confuse the men. Including, now, the wizard, who spilled rather more of the new liquid than he intended, yelped again, and started frantically dabbing at the sheets with the cloth.

"Erm..." Bob started, and then realised he had no idea what was going to come out of his mouth next.

"I'm sorry," Ki eventually said, calmly, "I understood she'd been killed."

"Oh yes," Amelia agreed enthusiastically. "And she will be *very* embarrassed about that."

More silence.

"Ah," Edoard looked up from his sheets, which he had apparently decided were either fine or beyond saving, "I take it she was under a preservation order?"

"Oh, yeah," Amelia answered, "her and all her friends. They're like weeds – always popping back up again when you think you're rid of them."

"A preservation order?" Bob found some words, at last.

"Yes," Edoard explained. "It's a peculiarity of the island. Priest has the – I suppose 'right' is the correct word – to grant virtual immortality to anyone he chooses while they are here, by slowing their ageing process to virtually nil. In some cases, however, he can also have them resurrected should they be killed by violent means. It's part of his 'deal'."

"Yeah, I've got one, too," Amelia chipped in. "It's nice to know you've got a safety net, you know?"

"Really?" Sean asked with interest. "Sure, I didn't know it could extend to that."

"Nor I," said Ki.

"Anyway," Amelia said, keen to change the subject, "how are you?"

Bob stood up.

"Better, I think."

"Yes, those wounds are healing nicely," Edoard agreed. "But you should get some rest. And some trousers."

He handed Bob what appeared to be a sarong, which the giant wrapped around his waist.

"Yeah. First, I think I need sleep," he said.

"Would you like me to come with you?" Amelia offered. "Just to keep an eye on you, I mean," she quickly clarified.

Bob breathed deeply.

"Please don't think I'm holding any of this against you, because I'm not, but I think I need just need some time to... recover."

Amelia nodded, but her smile betrayed her disappointment.

"Of course," she said, her voice quivering slightly.

With that, she turned to Sean and put her hand on his arm.

"Thank you," she said, quietly, "all of you." She looked at Ki and Edoard individually, then left almost as suddenly as she had arrived.

Luckily, she made it out before the men saw the tears welling in her eyes and awkwardly felt they had to do something about it.

———

Gabby slammed the door shut behind them as they stumbled back into their room.

"Holy Mother!" she panted. "That was... wow!"

Luke sat down on the bed.

"I know," he nodded sagely.

"It was... wow!"

250

"It was almost a disaster. But it was almost an answer too, wasn't it?"

"What do you mean?" Gabby started to come back down. "Didn't you see them, with the swords and the torch... and the *Furies*?"

After being shut out of the chamber in the rush of the crowd when The Furies appeared, the pair had managed to find themselves a vantage point into the room from the side of the balcony. They'd nearly been seen by the strange man from the cage when he moved Amelia, which would have drawn more attention to them than would have been ideal, but he'd been so busy looking for rope that he didn't even look in their direction. Thankfully, it hadn't occurred to him that the drape they hid behind would have made a pretty decent rope substitute.

"Yes, I saw it."

"Wasn't it... exhilarating?"

"Well, I suppose so, but... I think we need to talk about something."

"What is it?" she asked, sitting beside him.

"Maybe that's the only solution."

"How do you mean? Debovar was almost killed."

"I know."

Luke left the silence to fill the empty carriages in Gabby's train of thought.

"You mean, you think he *should* have died?"

"Well, it's an answer, isn't it? If he's dead, they can't get the location of the Rug from Faunt, and they have to start again."

"OK, but then Faunt kills us, right?"

"Probably. But isn't it worth that?"

Gabby sat in stunned silence. While she'd always said she was willing to risk her life for this cause, she hadn't expected to come to a point where she actually had to decide her own life was expendable. Luke stood and paced.

"No," she finally said, firmly.

"No, it's not worth it?"

"Yes, it's worth it, but no, it's not a solution."

"Why not?"

"Who owns the Rug if we're dead?"

"Well, whoever Debovar leaves it to in his will, I suppose."

"Yes, but they're not going to find it, are they? I doubt he has everything listed somewhere. Which means it'll stay right where it is, in our attic. And when we're dead?"

"The house will be sold, I guess."

"And the new owners will find the Rug. It'll be theirs by default. Now, with it being so close to where they were already looking, how long do you think it will take them to find it?"

Luke sighed. "Not long."

"And without us to protect it?"

"OK, I see your point."

"If we die, we're just putting off the inevitable, not stopping it."

She was right. God, he loved her.

She walked to him, placed her hands gently on his face and looked deep into his eyes, smiling. Tears ran down her cheeks as she said, "We're still alive. We're. Still. *Alive*. While we are, there's hope. There's *always* hope."

CHAPTER TWENTY-SIX

Simon had badly needed the shower. Between the prison, the tunnel, the cliff, the boat, the helicopter, the prison again, the fight and the monster, he smelt wholly unholy.

Of course, the more badly one needs to shower, the more pleasant it is when one does, and Simon had thoroughly enjoyed his return to the Amazon, staying under its massaging waters for a good half hour. He found himself thinking of Cherry and wondering what she was doing. And wishing she was there with him. The memory made him smile. He wondered when he would see her again, and what would happen.

He came out of the bathroom with a towel draped around his waist. He usually tended towards a dressing gown, but was actually rather enjoying the shape and sight of his new body now, and was therefore comfortable with showing it off, even if it was just to himself in the mirror.

"Hey, Narcissus..."

Simon jumped a proverbial mile, grabbing at his towel to prevent it falling down.

Harriet grinned. She sat in a dressing gown, her hair wrapped in a towel.

"God, Harriet, don't you knock?"

"I did, but you were in there forever. So I let myself in."

"How?"

She held up a white, plastic card.

"Housekeeping card. Swiped it from the maid."

That wouldn't even have occurred to Simon. He was, again, glad she was on his side.

"Listen, I'm going to tell you something, but if you ever repeat it, I'll kill you."

It was an idle threat from most people. Simon knew well enough to take her at her word.

"OK."

"I was impressed."

Simon grinned awkwardly.

"Really? Why?"

"Because you reacted instinctively, and the things you did were to rescue the nutjob and then put yourself in danger to help Bob. You may be a huge dweeb, my boy, but your subconscious might just be a hero."

Simon felt himself reddening. Praise was, to be understated about it, not something to which he was accustomed.

"I just did what you did," he shrugged, trying to hide the full extent of his pleasure, and having to avoid her eyes to do so.

"No, you didn't. I had a torch. Sean had a sword. You didn't have anything except that cage between you and that thing. You were in a much more vulnerable position, but you did it anyway. That was brave, Simon."

Looking at his feet, Simon wasn't sure what made him more unsteady: the praise, the realisation that she was right about how much danger he'd put himself in, or the fact that Aunt Harriet, who was the most insulting, caustic person he could imagine, had just called him by his first name, with no sense of irony or insult. He smiled, despite his best efforts.

"Like I said," she continued, standing up, "repeat that and I'll rip your bollocks off."

But she laughed, and so did he.

There was a knock at the door. Both were still on their guard, despite the apparent safety of their immediate situation. Simon looked for Harriet to take her lead. She shrugged.

"Hello?" Simon called. He was still fairly unaccustomed to answering doors.

With a roll of her eyes, Harriet crossed to the door and opened it. There stood an attractive young girl with a trolley, on which was perched a silver platter and an ice bucket with a bottle of champagne in it. Harriet looked at Simon, whose face showed no knowledge of having ordered anything.

"Good afternoon," the girl said with a smile. "Your host sends this with his compliments. He hopes you are both feeling better."

"Dancer!" said Harriet, stepping back into the room to allow the girl in.

She wheeled the trolley in to the table at the window, placed the platter and the bucket on it, then turned to the pair.

"Is there anything else I can do for you while I'm here?" she asked, pleasantly.

Harriet smiled mischievously at Simon and raised her eyebrows toward the girl. Realising what she was suggesting, he immediately reddened again, and headed for the bathroom.

"No, thanks!" he sputtered over his shoulder as he closed the door behind him.

"Don't mind him," Harriet said, "he's a little shy around women."

"I don't know why," the girl responded with a smile.

"What have we got?" Harriet asked, lifting the bottle out of the ice to examine it.

"Bollinger," the girl took the lid off the platter, "and a selection of tapas."

Harriet looked down at the collection of olives, potato

things and meats. Simon would probably like that. She'd have the bubbles.

"Cheers," Harriet said, popping the cork. A little of the champagne bubbled over the top, so she quickly put the bottle to her mouth for a large glug.

"Can't go wasting it, now, can we?" she said, wiping her lips.

"Of course not," the girl smiled.

"What's your name, missy?"

"Star."

"Well, Star, do you by any chance do massages?"

"I do."

"Fantastic. My whole body is killing me!"

Harriet dropped her robe and flumped forward on the bed, bottle still in hand. Three-headed monsters notwithstanding, this was some hotel.

———

An extremely uncomfortable half hour later, Simon emerged from the bathroom after hearing Star leave. He was hopeful that Harriet's moans and groans had simply been the result of an excellent massage, but he couldn't be entirely sure, so had decided to stay well out of sight until it all stopped. Harriet sat up on his bed, dressed again in the gown, but now with her damp hair hanging over her shoulders.

"This place is bloody magnificent, isn't it? Oh, I asked her to bring back another one," she said, noting his disapproving look at the empty bottle.

Simon had dressed and shaved while hiding. He was delighted to find the tapas and sat down to begin nibbling his way through them.

"So, I actually came round to tell you I've had an idea," said Harriet.

"Oh?" Simon said through a mouthful of chorizo.

"This," she said, holding out her hands to show each wrist sporting a brown, wooden bracelet.

"What are those?" Simon asked.

By way of an answer, Harriet pulled open the dressing gown to further expose her unadorned cleavage.

Simon scowled at her in confusion before realising her necklace was missing.

"You made it into bracelets? Why?"

"Well, we need to get Mrs Faunt off the island, right? And as it stands, that would mean kidnapping her. But if I can get her to wear one of these, maybe it would break Priest's control over her, and she could decide to leave all by herself."

Harriet crossed to the table and casually picked at Simon's food.

"Do you think that would work?" he asked.

"I have no bleeding idea. But at the moment, I can tell you that, wearing both of them, I still feel like I could tell Priesty to go fuck himself, if I wanted to, despite the fact I spent the last half hour fantasising about him."

Simon found himself slightly indignant on Sean's behalf.

"OK, but what if you were only wearing one of them?"

"I dunno," she answered, thoughtfully.

Simon's hands began to tremble slightly. He hoped the girl came back soon. Maybe she would bring two bottles.

———

Bob knocked at Amelia's door. He'd washed, slept and generally pampered himself all afternoon. The wounds on his body had largely healed thanks to Edoard's potion. He'd have a few new scars to add to his collection, but no more than that. And, ridiculously, he'd been through worse...

The girl opened the door slowly, as if she was afraid of what she'd find. When she saw him, she visibly relaxed, then tensed again.

"Hi. How are you?" she asked, in a failed attempt at casual.

"Better," he smiled. "I'm on my way to dinner with your father and I was wondering... if you're coming?"

"Do you want me to?" she asked, quietly.

"Very much," Bob answered.

Amelia stood up to her full height and smiled.

"Give me five minutes!"

She closed the door in a hurry. Bob moved across the hallway and looked out the window at the sea. It was beautiful, and smelled of summer and potential.

————

Seven minutes of urgent primping later, Amelia emerged.

"Wow," said Bob. Thankfully, she got her looks from her father's side.

"Thank you," Amelia smiled up at him.

Bob offered his arm, and the girl took it enthusiastically.

Small talk, the common staple of an early date, is often most difficult to begin. Once you broach a topic, conversation usually flows naturally, if the couple are at all compatible. If it doesn't, they're most likely in for a long night and several bottles of wine.

When your day has included the death of your date's mother after your own near death at her hands, and the evening ahead is going to be spent with your date's father and the step-mother you're actually here to kidnap, finding any kind of starting point which does not leave a great, galumphing elephant in the room is somewhat of a challenge.

"So," Bob began, "your mother..."

"What about her?"

"She'll be back *soon*, will she?"

"Oh, she already is!"

Bob had been fairly confident the evening couldn't get

more awkward. It was a stupid assumption, in retrospect.

"She is?"

"Yeah, but don't worry, she's not coming tonight. They're stoning her."

"They're... what?"

"Stoning her," Amelia answered chirpily. "Look, we'll probably see it from here."

She pulled him toward a window and, true enough, on the concourse below, a woman was handcuffed to a wall, having stones thrown at her by a group of about ten other women.

"But... why?"

"It's her punishment," Amelia answered.

"For trying to kill us?"

"Oh no! For *failing*!"

Bob felt like he was on the right end of the wrong conversation.

"For failing?"

"Yeah, the Socialites are not big on being made to look bad and her losing the challenge and then summoning The Furies and getting herself killed without even taking one of you with her? They're way unimpressed. She'll seriously have to work her way up again. She may even have to do the drinks runs for a while."

The light-hearted way that Amelia relayed this information to Bob was disarming and, instead of finding himself appalled, he decided just to trust her judgement. What was to be gained from pointing out to her that the whole situation was barbaric, medieval and disgusting? Sleeping dogs and all that.

Plus, Mummy definitely wasn't coming to dinner.

———

Simon was not scared of heights. But riding up to the top of a mountain in a cable car constructed entirely of glass was definitely testing his agoraphobia.

259

The other three seemed absolutely fine with being pulled through the air in a see-through box. Bob and Amelia were utterly engrossed in each other. She was enthusiastically telling him stories as she pointed out far off parts of the island, and he was a wide-eyed schoolboy, drinking in every word.

All Simon saw when he looked down was an awful lot of nothing with a very hard something at the bottom.

Harriet, on the other hand, was drunk. Well, in so much as she was well into her third bottle of champagne and, to be fair, was probably well used to seeing her surroundings wobbling around. Simon wondered whether the combination of her inebriation and the movement of the cable car would cancel each other out. She certainly looked fairly steady, standing almost gracefully at the rear in her flowing white dress, her hair elegantly adorned with flowers.

Harriet had visited the island's complimentary hairdresser after her massage. Having her hair tied back and looking good was both pleasant and practical, in that it would be out of her way if she threw up later.

Simon moved next to her, hoping she could distract him from the view.

"You know what's nice?" she asked, rhetorically. "Having someone cut your hair. I'd forgotten. I've forgotten a lot."

"Have you?" Simon asked, in that polite way that people do.

"Yeah." She looked down. "I'm going to miss this body..."

She paused, leaving just a moment's more silence than was comfortable, then looked at Simon.

"You could pretty much get yourself looking like this again, though, ay? Join a gym. Hell, buy a gym."

Simon hadn't really thought about 'after'; what he would do next. He had been very much focused on the immediate priority of not dying.

"I suppose I could – well, as much as a man of my age can."

"A lot more than a woman of my age can, sunshine."

Simon nodded in silent acknowledgement.

Harriet sighed. "People take things for granted, you know? Today, I can put both feet behind my head. A week ago, I'd have needed two new hips, a heart massage and a mop if I'd tried to touch my toes."

She looked straight in his eyes.

"Be grateful."

She raised her glass in salute, then knocked back the remaining liquid in one gulp.

"Eat, drink and be merry..." she said, looking wistfully down at herself.

Simon couldn't help but finish the adage in his head.

Calderon looked down at the hideous shirt and wished he'd thought to pack some spares for himself. It looked like a rainbow had thrown up on him.

The thing that had been driving the boat had been insistent that he wasn't getting on without an invite. Calderon had been equally insistent that he was, and that the thing had the option of driving the boat for him or swimming. In the end, it had done more sinking than swimming.

Still, its teeth were sharp, and the damage it had done to his shirt made it unwearable, unless he wanted to announce to the first people he saw on the island that he'd been in a nasty disagreement.

On the other hand, Calderon's efficiency with his knives had left the Captain's shirt largely intact, and the few spatters of blood were lost amongst the maelstrom of colour.

Still, wearing the hideous thing offended his every sensibility. He'd find a shop as soon as he reached the island and take something less abhorrent to wear. In fact, he'd take two.

One was certain to end up covered in blood again.

CHAPTER TWENTY-SEVEN

Disembarking the cable car, Simon found himself, yet again, surprised. He had expected a grand, palatial residence of some sort for a man of Priest's standing. Instead, he was looking at a fairly simple log cabin, with an impressively large balcony, which was built onto the side of the mountain in a way that suggested gravity was another of the laws to which Priest was immune.

A set of wind chimes danced in the breeze as they approached the door. Simon's left arm began to twitch involuntarily. He grabbed it with his right hand, hoping to squeeze it still.

Amelia knocked briefly and opened the door.

"Hello? We're here!"

A lithe blonde woman with intensely green eyes appeared from a doorway. She looked maybe a few years older than Amelia at best. Maybe less. She gave a warm smile and opened her arms to embrace the girl.

"Hello, darling. I hear you've had a few days of it."

"Hi Cass," Amelia answered, returning the embrace. "Yeah, it's been kinda mental."

They kissed on the cheek before separating.

Amelia turned to Bob, who was hovering politely behind her.

"Cassandra, this is Bob. Bob, this is my step-mother, Cassandra."

Bob glanced at Harriet before taking her hand gently.

"It's a real pleasure to meet you," he said.

"You *are* tall, aren't you?" she smiled. "And polite."

She batted Amelia on the arm.

"I like him, already."

"And these are his friends," Amelia added, "Simon and Harriet Debovar."

"Ah, hello," Cassandra said, offering her hand to whichever of them took it first.

Simon reacted first and took it, hoping he wasn't still shaking noticeably.

"I'm sorry, I hadn't realised you were a couple. I don't think Priest had either. We can organise you a double room instead of the two singles, if you like?"

Harriet snorted.

"Um, no, sorry," Simon stumbled, "we're not... she's my..."

"Sister," Bob finished for him.

"Oh of course, how silly of me," Cassandra said, reaching for Harriet's hand now. "I see the family resemblance."

"No problem," Harriet said, returning the handshake. "That's still funny."

Cassandra looked confused. Harriet smiled serenely, swaying slightly as she did.

"Harriet found this morning rather stressful, I'm afraid," Bob intervened.

"Oh, of course," Cassandra said, "It must have been awful. Come, let me get you all a drink. Priest is in the kitchen."

She turned to go.

"Harriet," Simon piped up, "didn't you have a gift for our hostess?"

Harriet looked blankly at him for a moment.

"Shit, yes!" she said. "I mean, sorry, yes, of course."

She fumbled with her wrist, freeing one of the makeshift bracelets.

"Oh, there's no need, really," Cassandra objected.

"No, no, please," Harriet said, proffering the jewellery. "We figured you have enough flowers here, so maybe something more unusual would be better."

Cassandra cocked her head and smiled again. "How thoughtful."

She took the bracelet and looked at it closely. Her face was difficult to read.

"Do you know, I think I used to have something like this," she said. "I can't remember what, though. Isn't that funny?"

She slipped it over her wrist, but she was so delicately built that what was almost tight on Harriet's wrist hung loosely around hers.

"Oh dear," she said, exhibiting how it slipped over her hand easily, "I'm not sure it will stay on."

Harriet stared. Her brain was clearly working, but slowly. Simon's was in panic mode. She'd given away half the necklace for nothing.

Now what?

"I'm sorry," Cassandra said. "And it is such a thoughtful gift."

She frowned sincerely. Simon could feel himself starting to shake again. Plan A had just gone dodo hunting.

"Would it fit as an anklet?" Amelia asked.

Simon resisted the urge to hug her. It would probably have been unseemly. And difficult to explain.

"Oh, good idea!" Cassandra answered.

She went down on one knee with the grace and ease of a dancer, lifting the hem of her floor length skirt to reveal that she wasn't wearing shoes. Her feet, Simon noticed, looked as smooth and soft as the rest of her skin, despite her apparent lack of inclination toward footwear. She carefully unclasped the gift and fastened it around her ankle.

"There," she said, showing it off. "Like it was made for me."

As she stood up, she wobbled slightly, staggered to her right and caught Amelia's arm. Bob instinctively moved to catch her.

"Ooh," she said, "head rush. I must have stood up too quickly..."

"We need to get you some food!" Amelia said, laughing slightly nervously.

Cassandra didn't answer. She was staring intently at Harriet, who smiled benignly back at her. Still swaying, of course. Cassandra looked like she was searching for something: a word on the tip of her tongue; a name for a face she hadn't seen in years.

"Do I...? Have we...?" She squinted at Simon now, who was doing his usual illuminated rabbit impression.

"Cass?" Amelia asked with concern.

Still no answer. Cassandra looked at Amelia as if she were a complete stranger.

"Cassandra?" Amelia asked, now urgently, shaking her arm gently.

"Yes, sorry," she finally answered. "What?"

"Are you all right? You're a million miles away."

"Of course, yes... just..." She looked at Harriet again and noticed the other bracelet. "Just feeling woozy. You're right, I should eat. We all should!"

With that, she freed herself from the supporting arms and led them towards one of the large doorways leading off the entrance hall.

"This way, ladies and gentlemen," she said with a flourish.

Amelia and Bob followed her directly, though Amelia watched her with concern. As Simon started to follow, Harriet caught his arm.

"What do you make of that?" she asked.

"I don't know. It did something, but I don't know what."

"Do you think she knows it was the bracelet? Anklet. Whatever."

"Well, it was obvious to me."

"You know about it, you halfwit!" It was a whispered shout, but still a shout. And a fair point.

"Right then," Harriet said, visibly bracing herself. "Into the lion's den..."

She walked ahead, more steadily than before. Probably the adrenaline, Simon thought in passing. He was definitely shaking now.

"Welcome!" Priest greeted them as they entered a spacious wooden kitchen with an appropriately huge, round, wooden table as its centrepiece. It was about eight feet across and only as he got closer could Simon see that it appeared to be a sliced section of a single tree.

"I hope you like chilli!" Priest boomed in that same resonant voice. He stood at a huge Aga, stirring a pot in which an entire cow could lose its way.

Harriet had stopped in front of Simon, staring lecherously at their chef and host. Simon tried his best to discern whether he was seeing the common, drunk-and-horny Harriet or if it was actually spellbound zombie Harriet.

It could go either way, he decided, and sat down, hoping to disguise his now trembling legs.

———

Certain questions asked around a dinner table are guaranteed to cause profuse sweating and numbness of the extremities.

"What are your intentions toward my daughter?" is one. This often causes men, and boys, to sputter incoherently and look piteously at said daughter, presumably in the hope that she will be holding up a placard with an appropriately witty yet respectful response, avoiding the need for later conversations about baseball bats and testicles.

However, this would have been far too easy and too predictable for Priest to really enjoy. Instead, he opted for, "So, how much is your wedding going to cost me?"

"Daaaaa-aaaaaaad!" Amelia protested.

Bob sat silent, half in shock and half of him, quite unexpectedly, rather intrigued by the idea. This girl was amazing and made him feel a way he'd last felt a long time ago; before he'd ever heard of immortals.

There was something about her. Every time he looked at her, he wanted to touch her. It was as magnetic as the time he'd seen her frozen in the garden, her dress rippling in the breeze.

Remembering that moment, it occurred to him that, contrary to Ingrid's assumption that he was taking advantage of her vulnerable position, no sexual thought had crossed his mind. She had seemed too perfect, too serene and beautiful. To think of her sexually in that moment would have been too base; too crude. She was so much more.

Looking at him now, her eyes sparkled with life. Life and embarrassment. Bob desperately wanted to kiss her. Not a reaction, he imagined, that Priest had in mind, and certainly not likely to be the best way to endear himself to a man who seemed to have positioned himself as his future father-in-law.

"I think your daughter is amazing, sir," Bob said, turning to Priest. "And if I was ever lucky enough to be her husband, I believe I would spend every day for the rest of my life being grateful."

Harriet looked at Bob with her mouth open and her eyebrows heading for the ceiling. She turned to Simon and the two exchanged a silent conversation, which consisted of:

"What the fuck?"

"I know!"

"Didn't see that coming."

"Me neither."

"I need another drink."

The final statement was made clearer with the assistance of Harriet swirling her empty glass.

Amelia beamed at Bob. Priest and Cassandra looked equally taken by surprise, however, Priest recovered and sat upright in his chair.

"Son, that's the best answer I could imagine to that question. Well played."

Cassandra put her arm on Amelia's.

"I *do* like him."

"Me too," Amelia answered. "And you know what else?"

She turned to her father.

"I don't stop when I'm with him. Not once. Well, except when mother was trying to kill him."

"Really?" Priest raised an eyebrow. "That *is* interesting."

He looked inquisitively at Bob, then cocked his head and stood up again.

"Who wants seconds?"

Simon nodded and handed his plate over. It was *damned* good chilli.

———

"So, I hope you will all accept this evening's meal as my sincere apology for the actions of Amelia's mother today." Priest spoke authoritatively as the guests sipped their coffee. Or liqueur.

Harriet raised hers in a salutary gesture.

"Don't mention it, sweets. I'd already forgotten."

She grinned widely at him. Priest returned her smile with a mix of appreciation and amusement.

"It's fine, honestly," Simon added. "We all survived it."

"You did indeed. Not least thanks to my new deputy, apparently. I have to say, I didn't think the old pirate still had it in him!"

Priest gave a deep, booming laugh, which was instantly infectious. Simon found himself, along with the rest of the table, laughing along, despite having absolutely no idea what was funny about that, and still being in desperate fear of being found out and bludgeoned to death at any moment.

"If you'll excuse me, I like to have a smoke after dinner." Priest stood up and made for the balcony door. "If anyone cares to join me...?"

Harriet stood up, wobbled slightly and followed him out into the night. She made no excuse or explanation, as if there had been nobody else in the room.

Amelia gave a concerned look after the pair for a moment, then at her stepmother. Cassandra looked... distant. She seemed to have retreated into herself several times during the meal and Simon wondered whether it was as obvious to everyone else as it was to him. He was watching her with particular care. Which was difficult, as he was particularly aware of not being caught staring at her.

Considering her natural beauty, it would not be hard to explain *why* he was staring but, as Simon was such a horrendous liar, the chances were that in the course of trying to lie about it he'd most likely have told Priest everything, including inappropriately intimate information about his recent Cherry-related activities. All in all, therefore, it was best he not arouse suspicion.

"Anyone for more cake?" Amelia suddenly asked, proffering the remains at Simon.

———

"Smoke?" Priest offered, a match lighting his face in the dark.

"No thanks," Harriet answered. "I don't smoke."

Priest looked quizzically at her. "So you came out here because..."

"You asked if anyone wanted to join you."

Harriet was attempting coquettish; it was more cock-hound-ish.

Priest smiled broadly. "You come out onto a man's balcony and smirt with him without even bothering with the pretence of smoking?"

"Smirt?"

"Smoking and flirting. Where have you been?"

"There's name for that? Jesus. Kids make up words for anything."

"Kids?" Priest inhaled deeply.

Harriet realised her mistake as soon as Priest questioned it.

"Um, yeah. I'm a little older than I look. Shh..." she pressed her finger to her lips coyly, "don't tell the owner."

Priest laughed and a cloud of smoke bellowed from his mouth into the night.

"Well, now, I'll see if I can get round that. I do have some sway with him."

Priest sucked in again, as there was a peal of laughter from inside.

"Your brother seems... nervous." He nodded toward Simon.

"Simon? He's always like that. He's a fud."

"That's harsh."

"It's accurate. Trust me."

"You are something else, young lady. You sure I can't interest you in a smoke?"

"I'm not a fan of cigarettes, sorry."

"Who said anything about a cigarette?"

Harriet cocked her head and smiled, before taking the little smoking bundle from her host.

"Well, I say," she said, smiling, "you are *full* of surprises."

"I like to think so. Makes life more interesting, don't you think?"

"Mm. Speaking of surprises, what about that Prisoner guy. What's with him?"

"He's hilarious, isn't he?" he replied.

"Is he?"

"You know the only reason we keep him locked up?"

"Why?"

"He told me to either give him the island or throw him in jail. I offered to let him leave, but he said no. I even tried to let him escape. The little bastard keeps coming back!"

They both laughed this time.

"Honestly?" she asked.

"God's honest truth – so to speak."

"So, *did* you steal his island?"

Priest stopped smiling.

"This island didn't *exist* before me."

"Hmm." Harriet blew out a plume. Was he being literal? Probably. "Your wife. She's... hot."

Priest's eyebrows raised again. "You have no idea."

"You guys into threesomes?"

He coughed and laughed at the same time. Recovering his composure, he smiled warily at Harriet.

"You serious?"

"Yep."

"I'll certainly ask..."

"What are the chances she'll say yes?"

"I usually get what I want."

Maybe.

Maybe not.

———

Calderon looked up the mountain. The idiot on the beach had finally told him where he could find the man he wanted.

The cable car was not an option. They'd know he was coming.

He grabbed hold of a rock jutting out above him, lifted a foot and began to climb.

271

CHAPTER TWENTY-EIGHT

Simon would not have slept well. He was terrified of how much Priest had figured out, and how much Harriet would end up telling him after she stayed up with Cassandra and him at the end of the night. Bob and Amelia had gone to bed at the same time, but to their own rooms. Simon liked how chaste their courtship appeared to be. It was a little beacon of decency in a sea of debauchery. Not that he was averse to a little debauchery, clearly, but it reminded him to feel a little bit bad about it.

He wouldn't have slept, but that he was really rather drunk.

And he wouldn't have woken up either, but for the knife at his throat.

"Right. What's the story?"

For a small, attractive blonde dressed in what appeared to be some kind of silk kimono, Cassandra was terrifying.

Simon gulped and felt the blade rub against his Adam's apple.

As a general rule, when Simon had no idea what to say, he kept his mouth shut. That didn't seem to be an option on this occasion, so he chose the next best thing.

"I don't know what to say."

Cassandra looked at him curiously. She drew the knife back and put her leg up on the side of the bed. In a Victorian novel, this would have been advanced foreplay. However, in this instance, it wasn't the forbidden flesh of her ankle she was showing him, it was the anklets around it.

Both of them.

"I woke up with these on. And the funny thing is, they seem to be made from a necklace I owned a long time ago. So where did you get them and why are you here?"

"Erm. OK." Simon's brain flailed desperately for an answer that would avoid him being filleted. If the necklace-cum-anklets was working, she was back to herself. Hopefully. That meant that the best course of action might just be, unthinkable as it was after the last 24 hours, the truth.

"Faunt sent us. To rescue you."

Cassandra's face went through a range of emotions that ran from pleasantly surprised to utterly gobsmacked via slightly perturbed. There were several tangents along the way.

"I don't believe you," she finally said. "That doesn't make sense."

Simon's head was reeling, and not only with terror. The hangover was already kicking in.

He decided on a course of action readily embraced by many intoxicated brains: when the truth fails, throw more truth at it. It's not a route to take lightly.

"I need you. I need to take you back to him so he can tell the angel and the demon where my carpet is so that they don't kill me and I can decide to give it to one of them."

Simon remembered to breathe in.

Cassandra sat down on the end of the bed.

"So... you own a carpet that heaven and hell both want. An angel and a demon came for it, but you didn't have it...?"

"I did when they got there."

"What happened to it?"

"It was stolen."

"When?"

"I was asleep."

Cassandra nodded. "Right. So they took you to Faunt to ask where it was. And his price for the information was... me?"

Simon nodded.

"And they threatened to kill you?"

"Well, not exactly, but Daniel – that's the angel – sort of let me know that he wasn't against the idea."

Cassandra stood, thoughtfully.

"The carpet; is it a relic?"

"I think so. It's part of a bet, apparently."

Cassandra sucked through her teeth. "OK. That does make sense, then."

She stood quietly for a long time. Simon realised he desperately needed the toilet.

"Erm, would it be OK if I went to the bathroom, please?"

Cassandra cocked an eyebrow at him. "Use the en suite. I need to think."

———

Simon staggered back to the bed. He'd splashed a great deal of water on his face and run it over his wrists in an attempt to sober up. It hadn't really helped. He hoped his impromptu decision to blurt out everything wouldn't get him, Harriet and Bob killed. It would be a disappointing end to the story.

"First of all, I need you sober," Cassandra said. "Drink this."

She handed him a small vial of red liquid.

"What is it?" Simon asked.

"You don't need to know. Just trust me."

That was definitely not what Simon needed to hear from the woman he was unsure would ever let him leave this room.

"Really?" he asked. "Can I trust you?"

Cassandra looked at him as if she'd forgotten he was there and had just been reminded.

"Look at you. You're like a lost puppy! You can trust me," she said, ruffling his hair. "I'm a very capable witch, and that's a potion to clear your head. There are a number of good reasons why Priest has kept me here. Very few people in the world can exert any control over him. I'm one of them. And I need to know why Faunt wants me."

Simon knocked back the red liquid in one gulp. His head, stomach and vision all cleared instantly.

"Wow. That's... wow."

"I told you."

"What did you mean, 'why he wants you'? You're his wife."

Cassandra smiled. "I suppose I am."

Clearly, it had been a while since she had seen him. One does not, Simon assumed, quickly forget being married to a deer.

"We need to get off this island," said Cassandra. "Tonight. Priest will stay asleep for a while, but I can't keep him that way forever. And we do *not* want him waking up. Come on."

"Wait," Simon protested. "We have to get Bob and Harriet."

Cassandra stopped.

"You realise how much is at stake here, right?"

Simon thought for a moment.

"No, I'm not sure that I do. But I do know that I'm not leaving without Harriet and Bob. They're... friends."

"You're sweet. Odd, but sweet. OK, I'll get Bob, *you* get Harriet."

There was something odd about the way she said it.

"Why that way around?" Simon asked.

"Because I left her in bed with Priest, and I don't think I can carry her."

Simon pushed the door open with all the bravery of a dormouse with a door phobia. The room was pitch black. Fantastic.

He slowly pushed the door further until the crack of light from behind him reached the edge of the bed. Cassandra had promised him that, short of anything highly abnormal, Priest would sleep for a few hours yet. He just wasn't sure exactly how abnormally Harriet would behave when he tried to pick her out of the bed and carry her outside.

Luckily, she was on the side of the bed nearest him. At least, he assumed the mountainous heap under the covers on the other side of the bed was Priest. The bed itself seemed to be tilting in that direction. Simon momentarily marvelled at the engineering of a bed that could keep itself in one piece at all with a man of his stature regularly indulging his clearly voracious appetites all over its poor wooden frame.

Simon crept as lightly as he could manage to the side of the bed. Her head was under the covers. He gently and slowly lifted the sheet to look down at her... feet.

For God's sake!

He couldn't entirely see the edge of the duvet, so he decided to follow it down to find her head. She was lying at an angle, which meant her head was further across the mattress than her feet. Of course. As he started to move further up the edge, a distinctly unpleasant thought occurred to him. The further he went, the worse it got, until finally, carefully, he reached her hip and confirmed it.

She was naked.

Simon suppressed his gag reflex, then froze.

Now what?

Simon was taking an inordinately long time and, frankly, they didn't have it. Cassandra had tired of waiting and crossed to the bedroom door. Poking her head around, she saw Simon standing frozen at the side of the bed with the edge of the duvet in his hands.

It was the kind of position she often found her step-daughter in, but *she* had a good excuse. What the hell was the man doing?

"Hoi!" she stage whispered. "What's wrong?"

Simon turned his head and peered pleadingly through the dark at her.

"She's naked!" he whispered back.

"So?"

Simon stoically continued to stare at Cassandra. She repeated the question with her eyes.

"She's *naked*!" he repeated.

Cassandra sighed. She turned back into the main room.

"There's a problem, apparently."

"What is it?" Bob asked, concerned.

"Apparently, she's naked..." Cassandra shrugged to show she had no idea why this was such an issue.

"Oh, OK. Yeah, that's a problem," Bob confirmed.

"It is?"

"Yes. She's..." He struggled for the words.

"Yes?"

"He's... never mind, I'll sort it."

Bob crept into the room, slowing his pace as he entered, and found Simon still stuck in position.

"She's naked!" he whispered again.

"I know!" Bob answered, quietly but urgently. "Stay calm."

Bob crept into the en suite and emerged carrying a huge, decorative dressing gown.

"OK. You hold up the duvet..."

"She's *naked*!"

"I know, you don't have to look, just hold up the duvet and I'll wrap her in this."

Simon nodded vigorously.

As he lifted the duvet, Priest stirred in his sleep, rolled onto his back and began snoring. They froze. The room vibrated gently. After a moment, they moved again.

Slowly, torturously slowly, Simon finished lifting the duvet, squinting through his eyelashes to make sure he didn't lift it too high and expose Priest to the cold air that might wake him.

As soon as he stopped, Bob began the even more delicate process of removing Harriet. After accidentally poking her in the eye and seeing no response, he decided it was safe and expedient to opt for speed, and simply rolled her towards him into the dressing gown.

"OK, you can let go and look," he whispered, after checking that he had covered anything that might damage Simon's delicate psyche.

They grabbed an end each – Simon taking the head, just to be safe – and moved to the door. Cassandra closed it after them.

They gently placed Harriet on a couch. She wriggled slightly, rolled onto her side and loudly farted.

Simon closed his eyes and went to a happy place.

When he opened them again, he was surprised to see an extra face in the room: Amelia's.

"As you can see," Cassandra said, "we have another hiccup."

"I'm sorry, but I had to wake her," Bob explained.

"I understand," said Cassandra, "but you boys are going to have to give me a minute to... explain some things to Amelia."

"Of course, but aren't we in a hurry?" Simon asked nervously.

"We *are*," Cassandra replied pointedly, "but this is important."

She gestured to the balcony. Simon shrugged and the boys moved outside. There was no point in them leaving without her, so until she was ready to go, they were stuck.

————

"So my father is basically a serial rapist?"

Amelia had listened with growing distress as Cassandra told her everything.

"Well, yes and no," Cassandra answered.

"Cass!" she pleaded with her step-mother.

"Not really, I suppose. I mean, look, he can have any woman he wants. So he has the ones he wants. It's not exactly right, but it's... understandable. Sort of."

Amelia was crying now.

"Your father is a very complicated man. You have to understand what he's been through... what they did to him. It was horrific. This island; his exception; his attraction for women — it's all to make up for it."

"Oh, God," said Amelia. "Oh, God."

"Yes, He has a lot to answer for. And so does She."

"What did they do?"

Cassandra visibly slumped.

"Honestly, I don't want to tell you."

Amelia's eyes begged for something to help her see her father as a decent man again.

"They used him," Cassandra finally relented. "They broke him. It was cruel."

Cassandra moved around the dinner table and sat next to Amelia, putting her arm around her shoulders.

"I'm sorry, sweetheart. If it's any consolation, I'd kill him if I didn't kind of understand him. And listen, I don't feel any differently about you. His ability only affects how people feel about him."

Amelia smiled through the waterworks.

"Really?"

Cassandra nodded. Amelia hugged her.

After a moment, the witch began again.

"So, listen: we have to leave. Well, *they* have to leave, and I should really go with them. But Bob wouldn't leave without you – without at least giving you the chance to come too."

"He wouldn't?" She didn't smile, but she did look less upset.

"I know it's hard, but you have to decide right now. Do you want to come with us?"

"Or stay here with my rapist father and sociopath mother?"

Cass shrugged to indicate that yes, that was pretty much the size of it.

Before Amelia could answer, a crackle of red light appeared on the table, which reached out to Cassandra with spidery red tendrils of lightning. She tried to move, but they quickly enveloped her and she was held in place, the red lights shimmering around her.

Amelia snapped around to look behind her, to see where the light had come from.

And stopped.

————

The scent of lavender was drifting up from the garden below and the air temperature was just at the stage where it was comfortably warm without being sticky. There was a gentle breeze now and again. Over the sea, the sky was just beginning to lighten with the first signs of sunrise.

"Do you really love her?" Simon asked Bob. "I mean, you hardly know her, really."

"I know. I know, it's insane, but I can't explain it. The time when I saw her in the garden it was like... like being filled with light. She radiated warmth and joy. Being with her is like sitting next to a furnace in the snow."

The giant appeared to have the soul of a poet. It was the second time Bob had left Simon dumbstruck. Then again, he'd only known him for a few days and already considered him a friend. Either that was a comment on what a good, decent human being he was or Simon was sad enough to befriend anyone who wasn't a total bastard.

In fact, he'd largely befriended everyone he'd met in the last week, which was odd. Daniel aside. He had seemed nice at first, but it only took one suggestion of painful murder to put Simon right off him. He didn't smell bad though. Not as good as Lily, but still...

Simon realised he had forgotten to speak again.

"That's lovely."

"What about you and Cherry?" Bob asked, yawning. It was their second late night adventure in a row.

Simon was glad that the low light hid his reddening face. How he felt about Cherry was nothing like Bob had described Amelia. It was much more... earthy, as Lily would say. He definitely liked her and absolutely lusted after her, but she was less a furnace in the snow than an oasis in the desert, if he was honest. Still, he was looking forward to seeing her again.

"It's not really the same as you, I don't think."

"Well, you and I have had very different lives. I think that makes us see things differently. Maybe it's not as different as you think."

"Maybe," Simon conceded.

"I agree, *mis amigos*; different lives make us see things differently."

The voice came from behind them, at the door. Simon turned. Bob did not. The colour drained from his face.

"Good evening, Robert. You are pleased to see me?"

Simon looked from the stranger to Bob. Sweat was beading on his forehead.

"I'm sorry, we haven't met," Simon said, stepping forward with his hand outstretched. In times of crisis, the British instinctively revert to polite niceties. It comes from being brought up on Victorian novels.

Bob grabbed Simon's arm, looked him dead in the eye and shook his head gravely. Simon retracted his hand, not least because he'd noticed the stranger's knife glinting.

Bob slowly turned.

"How did you get out?"

There was a hard edge in his voice that Simon had not heard before.

The man tossed his head as if shooing away a butterfly.

"The universe, she likes me, I think."

He smiled and Simon's stomach flipped. It was pure, undiluted evil.

"The girls!" Simon suddenly remembered. "Where are the girls?"

Bob glowered even more darkly. "No," he said, firmly. "No."

In the following silence, Simon thought he heard a distant, mechanical squeal.

"The ladies are fine," the stranger said. "Particularly fine, I would say. Perhaps you gentlemen would do me the honour of joining me in the lounge?"

"This is nothing to do with him," Bob said, stepping between Simon and Calderon.

The Spaniard smiled. "Do you imagine that letting me know you wish him unhurt is helpful?"

CHAPTER TWENTY-NINE

"It is a magnificent thing, I think, no?"

Calderon gestured at the crackling red light around Cassandra, which apparently held her frozen in place. Simon tried to gauge whether there was any recognition in her eyes, but it was impossible to tell. She may or may not have been aware of what was happening.

"It is a witch's trap," Calderon continued, imperiously. "When you come to an island inhabited by witches, it is best to come prepared, I think. I had another for the little one, but she is scared stiff! It is quite something, no?"

Calderon ran his hand down the back of Amelia's neck. Simon saw Bob stiffen, but he'd learned his lesson. He kept quiet.

"This one," Calderon moved to Harriet, "I thought was dead, until I heard the awful noise she makes!" He nudged her in the back with his leg. She grunted and one arm fell loose, dangling over the edge of the couch.

It was an understandable assumption. She smelled dead.

"What do you want?" Bob asked.

Calderon sneered at him, though Simon assumed it was

meant as a smile. His disfigured face was hard to read. Calderon produced a cigar, lit it, and sat down.

"First, I want you to tell your friend how we know each other, *por favor*."

Bob turned to Simon.

"Why?"

"Because it amuses me."

Bob seethed for a moment. When he spoke, it was in a dead, flat voice.

"Simon, this is Antonio Calderon. He tortures boys. I buried him in a bridge." He turned to Calderon. "That do?"

Calderon blew more smoke. "You missed the best part, my friend."

"Fuck you."

"Take off your shirt, Robert," the Spaniard smiled.

"No."

"Do it or I kill everyone," Calderon casually waved his cigar around the room.

Bob stood up, glaring at the intruder. He slowly lifted his shirt over his head. As soon as Simon could see the skin on his back, he knew why. It was a mass of scars. His stomach and shoulders were the same. There were cuts, burns and what looked like piercings. What the hell?

"What your friend is not sharing, Simon, is that I tortured *him*. A lot. And I *enjoyed* it."

A shiver ran through Simon's soul.

"And do you know what?" Calderon moved right in front of Bob, who defiantly stared back. "I think he did too."

Bob's right fist came up, swinging for Calderon's face, but the Immortal was already gone. He was fast. Insanely fast. Instantly, he was behind Bob, who went down, kneeling with his right arm pinned behind his back. Calderon's left hand held the cigar to Bob's cheek.

The sound of crackling flesh was nauseating.

Bob didn't make a sound.

"You see?" Calderon turned to Simon. A trail of saliva dangled from his mangled lip. "He likes it."

Something snapped.

Simon lunged at Calderon, aware someone was screaming. It was him.

Caught off guard, Calderon only partially dodged Simon's tackle, but he turned enough to put Bob between them, so that the three landed in an awkward dog-pile. The cigar rolled free from his hand and Simon smelt Bob's burnt cheek. It was acrid and caught the back of his throat.

With one leg trapped beneath them both, Calderon was at least constrained. Still, his speed was incredible. Simon struggled to swing punches at him as he ducked and wriggled to free himself. He landed a few glancing blows, but nothing solid. Bob was using his own body as a weight, reaching behind him in an attempt to grab a firm hold on Calderon, to give Simon a steady target.

Simon kept swinging as Bob tried desperately to keep hold of that leg. Calderon smashed a ceramic bowl over Bob's head. The giant reeled for a moment, but regained his composure and managed to keep his fragile grip.

Simon leaned back and reached for the cigar. He brought it round and stabbed at Calderon's chest, singeing his shirt a few times.

Calderon stopped trying to free himself and swung back – one direct punch connecting with Simon's jaw. Not having been in many fights, he didn't know how to roll with it. Instead, he took the full brunt and his eyesight went sideways for a moment, sending him reeling backward.

That gave Calderon time to concentrate on freeing his leg, but it also gave Bob a chance to shift his weight. He turned to face the Spaniard and, with a cry of rage and venom, rained punches on his chest and face. Calderon's speed meant most of them missed, but some hit – and Bob wasn't slowing down. He swung again and again.

Simon stood and grabbed the edge of the couch, catching his balance. He didn't have time to think, he needed to act. Quickly. He moved around behind Calderon and kicked him, hard, in the back of the head. Not seeing the blow coming, the Spaniard took it full force and his head lunged forward, towards Bob, who connected with his face at the same time. The combination made a sickening crack that reverberated in the room. But it was Bob's hand that had broken, not Calderon's face.

Bob reeled back as the pain registered. Calderon, seemingly unfazed by the double blow, lurched towards him and shoved him onto his back.

Simon grabbed a lamp and raised it to swing, but stopped when he saw the knife at Bob's eye.

Simon could see Calderon's warped face reflected in the dark window pane. The Spaniard grinned back at him. Blood ran from several cuts on his face.

"I told you, I came prepared. Now," he moved the knife to Bob's throat, "step the fuck away, *Simon*." He spat the name like a cobra. Simon stepped backwards, slowly. There was a pain in his mouth and an acrid taste. Was he bleeding?

Calderon stood and dragged Bob to his feet. He put his hand out, silently demanding the cigar.

"This must be a very good friend, that he is prepared to die for you, Robert."

Bob looked directly at Simon. "He's a good man."

Simon felt tears welling. He handed over the cigar, his hand shaking with adrenaline and frustration.

"Fuck you," he growled, staring at the Spaniard.

"I get that a lot," Calderon smiled and pushed Bob back into a seat. "I have a proposal for you, old friend."

Bob held a protective hand to his singed cheek.

"Sit," Calderon commanded Simon. He did.

"I wonder," Calderon said to Bob, "will he roll over too?"

Simon's face flushed. Of all the people in the world he had ever hated, this bastard was now top of the list.

Calderon moved back to the dinner table where Amelia and Cassandra still sat, motionless. Simon thought he saw Cassandra's eyes move.

Wait; Priest!

He could get them out of this. Simon just had to wake him up.

Ha. "Just." He was on the other side of the house, and under a sleeping spell.

If Harriet was awake, she'd know what to do.

Shit, shit, shit!

"So, my friend, here is my offer," said Calderon. "You choose which of these ladies I kill first."

"No!" Simon protested. Bob remained silent.

"I don't give a damn," the giant said, calmly. "They live here. They're nothing to do with us. In fact," he sat back in the chair, seeming to grow in confidence, "go ahead. Though when Priest finds out you broke into his home and killed his wife and daughter, I wouldn't want to be you."

Calderon paused. For the first time, Simon thought, he looked genuinely ruffled.

"Perhaps you have a point. There is no need to make life more complicated than necessary."

He moved to the couch, next to Harriet.

"Let's start again. I kill her or I kill him." He waved the knife at Simon.

"That would be a shame," said Bob. "Awake and sober, she'd eat you for breakfast."

"*De veras?*" Calderon looked down at Harriet curiously. "Sadly, she is indisposed." He looked up again at Bob. "So, which is it to be?"

"I'm not going to choose, you Spanish prick."

Calderon charged across the floor and held the knife to Bob's face.

"*Catalan* prick, Robert," he hissed.

Bob didn't flinch. "What do you *really* want?"

"I think you *know* that," he answered, licking the flat of the knife.

Bob closed his eyes.

"Fine. Take me. Leave everyone else. That's the deal."

"That's the deal? *That's* the *deal?*" Calderon's mask slipped dramatically as he stepped back towards the women. "I make the deals, you piece of shit!"

"Actually, no, you don't." Bob produced a pen from somewhere and lifted it to his temple. "I think you want me alive, because killing me isn't going to be enough for you. You don't want a quick murder; you want to inflict pain. Suffering. Right?"

Calderon was beginning to sweat.

"So?"

"So, *here's* the deal. I come with you, without a fight, and you leave everyone else alone. Or, I shove this pen in my brain and we see if I survive."

"You probably will, you know," Calderon drawled.

"Maybe. But if I'm a vegetable, how's that going to work for you?"

Calderon was simmering.

"I don't believe you will do it."

"My alternative is years being tortured by you again. You *honestly* don't think I'd do it?"

They stared at each other. Simon was acutely conscious of his own breathing.

Wait. What was that? Cassandra had moved; he was sure this time. If he could get her free, maybe...

"And you would choose to come with me, to protect your friends?"

Bob stared directly back at Calderon, as if he was trying to burn through him with his eyes.

"Yes. I would," Bob finally answered.

288

The Catalan waved the knife with a flourish, growing in confidence again. "It makes me wonder, you know, would it be worse for you if I just killed them?"

He dangled the knife casually towards Harriet's still sleeping body.

Out of the corner of his eye, Simon saw movement again. Was it Cassandra? Or maybe he was mistaken all along. Maybe it was Amelia. Maybe she'd come round and was playing possum, waiting to catch Calderon off guard. He needed to get the psycho near them. *One* of them was moving.

"So you're afraid of Priest?" he asked, hoping like hell that the next sentence would come to him when he needed it.

Bob and Calderon both snapped their heads to look at him darkly.

"I am afraid of nobody, *mi amigo*." There was an irritated edge in Calderon's voice. "I simply choose not to create... issues, where none exist."

"And you assume Bob gave you the right information, do you? About who everyone is?" Simon really wasn't sure where this was going but it was, at least, going.

"I beg your pardon?" Calderon stepped toward Simon.

"Simon, what are you doing?" Bob asked, with a significant edge of panic in his voice.

"Yes, *Simon*, what *are* you doing?"

"Maybe that's Priest's daughter on the couch. Or his wife. How would you know?" Simon asked.

Calderon smiled and moved towards the other women.

"This," he said, gesturing at Cassandra with his knife, "is Cassandra. Married to both Priest and your friend Bob's employer. Did I tell you, by the way, that it was he who told me where to find you?"

Bob's eyes widened.

"That's a *lie!*" Simon answered instinctively. "Faunt wouldn't do that."

"You know the old goat? Interesting."

"So?" Simon challenged him. He was on the back foot, now.

"Well, let me tell you: I had his teleporter – the punk? Your friend gave me Bob so that I would kill her quickly. Believe me now?"

Simon was standing before he had decided what to do. Bob grabbed his arm.

"No," the giant whispered.

"I will kill you," Simon said, in a voice he'd never heard before. "One day, I *will* kill you."

Calderon smiled again in return, his white teeth glinting. Simon sat – slowly.

"And this," Calderon continued, as if he had just paused for a breath, "must be his daughter, who is afflicted with a condition that causes her to – I believe they call it – 'stop'. Yes?"

Now was the time, he turned his back on the table to walk to Harriet. Simon steeled himself to act as soon as whichever of them was free moved. He tensed his muscles. If he could get to the knife...

...

Nothing.

Both women remained frozen in place. Surely, he hadn't imagined it? He'd definitely seen *someone* move.

"That, *mis amigos*, makes this young lady a nobody, who is simply sleeping off last night's excesses, no?"

"So, are we going or not?" Bob asked, urgently.

Calderon looked at Simon like a cow at a cattle auction.

"We are," he answered. "I think I will enjoy your suffering more if I am there to inflict it daily. You understand?"

Bob stood and walked to Calderon, hand held open in front of him with the pen.

"If you change your mind, if you harm anyone here, I'll find a different way to do it," he said, flatly.

"Robert, I think you have new steel I have not seen before. I think this will be even more fun than I imagined."

He turned Bob around and began to walk him to the door.

Simon trembled with rage and fear. He couldn't just sit there and do nothing. How would he live with himself? Every fibre of his being was telling him to stand – to do something; anything. He felt a chill on the back of his neck and imagined a voice in his ear, whispering, "Stop him. Now."

"Stop!" he shouted, standing and putting himself between the men and the door. "If you want him, you're going to *have* to kill me first."

"Simon, no," Bob pleaded.

"I can't, Bob. I can't," he answered, tears running down his face.

"What is a man to do?" Calderon mused, as if he were contemplating a choice of partner to take home after the last dance. "Perhaps I shall take you both? If I must, I must, I suppose."

He pushed Bob sideways to the floor and moved towards Simon, who steeled himself. He grabbed the lamp again and raised it like a bat, ready to swing.

Calderon slowed a moment, grinned lasciviously, raised his knife, stepped forward…

…and collapsed, face first, onto the floor.

Nobody moved.

Except Calderon, whose arms inexplicably bent themselves behind his back as his face pressed itself harder into the floor.

"*Que demonios?*" the rattled psychopath grumbled into the floor.

Bob regained his feet and looked down at his erstwhile captor. He and Simon exchanged looks of utter confusion. The giant finally took the lead.

"Hit him!" he ordered Simon, urgently.

Needing little encouragement, Simon raised the lamp and stepped forward, ready to bring it down on Calderon's head.

"Wait!"

The voice came from near Calderon, but it was clearly not his. It did sound familiar, though.

Simon duly stopped – as much out of surprise as obedience. A hazy figure appeared, kneeling on Calderon's back, with one hand held up in defence against Simon's lamp. His infectious grin slowly came into focus.

"*Prisoner*?" Bob asked, astonished. "You were... invisible?"

"Ain't that a thing?" their rescuer replied, smiling. "I did *not* know I could do that."

"*Yo mataria tu!*" shrieked Calderon, struggling to move.

Bob kicked him in the face. Hard. Blood sprayed across the floor.

"Shut up, you sick bastard or I'll drop you in another bridge," the giant growled, before bursting into nervous laughter.

Despite himself, Simon began to laugh as well – a quiet, uneasy, laugh at something that wasn't really very funny.

"I have a message for you, sir," Prisoner said to Calderon. "Maya says – and please excuse the language, ladies – 'Fuck you, too.'"

CHAPTER THIRTY

"This is an outrage!" Calderon screamed from the chair they had tied him to – for the moment, anyway. "He had no right! There are Rules!"

Cassandra frowned at him. It hadn't taken Prisoner long to defuse the witch's trap with Maya's instruction, and Cassandra, in turn, had been able to rouse Amelia. They had decided it was best for everyone to leave Harriet as she was.

"As I understand it, Mr Calderon, you attacked someone under the protection of Faunt. The spirit, Maya, is working for Faunt and is therefore entitled to protect his interests."

The witch took Bob's broken hand between her own, which glowed slightly.

"She acquired the temporary services of our prisoner to act on her behalf due to her incorporeal situation – which I believe you are responsible for. Where do you think the Rules were broken?"

Cassandra had seen everything, as Simon suspected. But the movements he had seen, he assumed, were actually from the invisible Prisoner creeping into the room.

"I have a claim over Robert!" he screeched. "A right to revenge!"

"It wasn't Bob she was protecting," Cassandra answered. "You were, arguably, within your rights until you threatened Simon. *He* is under Faunt's protection. If you wish to try to take revenge on Bob now, be my guest."

She took a step out of his line of sight and released Bob's hand. "Nobody will stop you."

Bob stretched and contracted his fingers tentatively, smiling at the apparent lack of pain. Calderon glared at Simon instead. It was uncomfortable. He turned away, nervously, to speak to Prisoner.

"So, you can turn invisible?" he asked. "That's... brilliant."

"Ain't it?" he answered. "Made it a lot easier to get out of them dungeons this time, too. Imagine if I'd known..."

"How did you find out?" Simon asked.

"Well, the young lady, Maya, told me what I could do and helped get me up here."

"Who *is* Maya?" asked Bob.

"She is a good friend of Faunt's – and *mine*," Cassandra answered, directing the last part at the intruder. "She was murdered by this man and is now a spirit."

"Oh. Is she still here?" Simon asked, skipping over his brain's instinctive response: "A *ghost*?!"

"No," Cassandra and Prisoner answered together.

"She needs a person to act as an anchor for her spirit or she dissipates. She has to return to them often. She's gone there now," Cassandra explained.

"Oh, OK. That makes sense," said Simon.

"I'll thank her later," Bob added.

"Madam, if you're now in control here, would you mind if I leave?" Prisoner asked. "I have... things to do. You understand."

"Of course, thank you again," Cassandra smiled. "And good luck."

Prisoner turned to leave.

"This is not over!" Calderon was throwing spittle everywhere as he ranted at everybody.

"Now," Cassandra addressed Calderon again, "you have broken into my home, attacked me and, at the very least, inconvenienced my guests. What, would the Rules say, is an appropriate recompense for that?"

Calderon breathed heavily.

"Kill him," Simon suggested, suddenly hit by what the bastard had told him in the midst of the chaos. "He murdered Cherry."

"Oh, hell," said Bob. "I forgot. Simon, I'm sorry."

Bob put his hand on Simon's shoulder.

"He's right," the giant added, "*can* we kill him?"

"Not easily," Cassandra answered, "And not without a price."

"Cass?" It was Amelia. She had sat quietly watching ever since she came round. "Don't we need to go? The sun's up. Won't Dad wake up soon?"

"You're coming?" Bob asked, his voice cracking.

Amelia smiled and nodded, tears running down her face. She stood up and Bob grabbed her into a joyful embrace.

For Simon, it was bittersweet, but he smiled for them anyway.

"Yes, but we need to make a decision about *him*," Cassandra said. "If we leave him here, he'll come after us. If we take him with us... that would be dangerous."

The room fell silent. Calderon grinned.

"*How do you solve a problem like Maria?*" he sang quietly, taunting them.

Bob walked out of the room. Simon and Cassandra both looked to Amelia, wondering where he was going. She shrugged.

"He is scared," Calderon drawled, before spitting blood on the floor. "He knows he cannot escape me."

Was he right? Bob had left him inside a *bridge* and he

295

came back. How could they keep him permanently out of the way?

The door clunked open again as Bob re-entered. He moved so quickly towards Calderon that it took Simon a minute to realise what he was carrying. He'd been to the woodpile.

"Wait!" Calderon cried in panic.

He had no time to say anything else before Bob brought the axe around in a huge arc and, with one blow, took the Spaniard's head clean off.

———

"OK," said Cassandra, after everyone had come to terms with Bob's somewhat spectacular course of action, "here's the plan. I'll carry his head in this." She lifted a bag from a drawer. "Bob, can you carry his body?"

"Why?" he asked.

"If his body is destroyed, he will grow a new one. But not if the old one is intact. It's best we keep it safe and separate from his head. Priest will burn it. We have to take it with us."

The thought of Calderon growing an entire body from his head stunned the room back into silence.

"OK," Bob eventually answered.

"Excellent," Cassandra turned to Simon, "That leaves Harriet to you, Simon. Is that OK?"

Simon quickly decided that if Bob could carry the headless body of a man who had tortured him for years, he could probably manage his drunk great-aunt.

"Yes," he answered, "but I need to do something first, so can somebody please dress her?"

Cassandra looked at her watch. "You understand Priest will wake up soon? He's been nice to you because you're guests. You do *not* want to be here when he finds out what's really happening."

Simon nodded. "It's important."

"It's your life, I guess," the witch conceded. "OK. I have three things to do anyway."

"What?" asked Amelia.

"Cauterise that neck so that it doesn't make a mess of Bob and get rid of the blood on the floor."

"Won't that take a long time?" Bob asked.

"Not the way she's going to do it," Amelia answered for her.

"You said three things?" Simon reminded her.

"Yes." She lifted Calderon's head off the floor. "We need to gag this thing in case he starts shouting again."

———

Simon knocked at the door. It was louder than he'd intended, but he needed to make sure he woke the occupant.

The door finally opened after he knocked a second time.

"Morning," said a bleary-eyed Sean. "Isn't it a bit early?"

"Yes. Sorry."

"What's up?"

"I have to be quick, and I'm sorry, but so do you. We're leaving. Right now. In a hurry. And Priest is going to be very angry. That's why we're in a hurry. Anyway, we have to go. But I wanted to ask if you want to come, too. I mean, it seems like you went to a lot of trouble to save us. And I think you like Harriet and maybe she likes you too and so you should come."

Sean looked shell-shocked.

"So, you got what you came for, then?"

"Yes."

"What is it?"

"Cassandra."

"Fuck me. Seriously?"

Simon nodded.

"Right, then. Give us a minute."

Sean opened the door and waved him in. Simon could feel his heart pounding. This had been a big risk, but it was the right thing to do. Sean deserved it. He just hoped he'd judged the situation correctly.

After a few minutes, Sean stood, fully dressed and carrying a rucksack over one shoulder.

"Fuck it. Who wants to live forever, right?" the Irishman asked.

"Ha, yeah, like Queen," Simon answered, as they walked up the corridor.

"Does she?"

"Who?"

"The Queen?"

"What about her?"

"She wants to live forever?"

"Does she?"

"Isn't that what you said?"

"No..."

"Oh."

"I meant the song."

"What song?"

...

"Never mind."

————

They arrived at Harriet's room to find everyone ready to go, including – unexpectedly – Harriet.

"She woke up," Amelia explained, helpfully.

"I've woken up before with men trying to undress me," said Harriet, "but women trying to dress me is new."

She sounded remarkably clear-headed.

"I fixed her," Cassandra explained, answering Simon's unasked question. "We need her to be able to walk. We've also brought her up to speed."

"Yeah, I hear the nutjob turns invisible," said Harriet. "That would have been good to know yesterday."

Sean looked at Simon questioningly.

"I'll tell you on the way," he answered. "We need to go."

"We?" Harriet asked, surprised. "You're coming?" she asked the pirate.

"If that's OK..." Sean answered.

An odd look crossed Harriet's face momentarily, before she shrugged and said, "Why not?"

"So, where *are* we going?" Simon asked.

"The beach, for the boat," said Cassandra. "It's the easiest way off the island. It should be in dock. We need to *move*."

They all moved aside to let Cassandra lead, followed by Bob – still carrying most of Calderon – Amelia, Sean and Harriet.

Simon brought up the rear. He was suddenly struck by the thought that these people were all here because of him. They were all, one way or another, helping him.

How had that happened?

Harriet dropped back, grabbed Simon's elbow and slowed him down.

"You brought him for me, right?"

"I suppose so," Simon answered, nervously. "Sort of."

"Nice thought. But has it occurred to you how happy he's going to be when he finds out he gave up this life for a pensioner?"

No. It hadn't.

"Didn't think so. Here's hoping he's a granny grabber, eh?"

She stalked forward again, leaving Simon wondering whether the nice thing he thought he'd done had actually been deeply, deeply stupid.

There was a good chance.

CHAPTER THIRTY-ONE

Halfway down the rocky steps to the beach, Cassandra suddenly put up a hand. Everyone stopped.

"There's somebody down there," she whispered to the group. "It's probably Carlos. Stay here."

She handed the sack with Calderon's head in it to Amelia and carried on down the steps.

———

Cassandra moved quickly, but not so quickly as to appear to be in a hurry. She needed to be rid of Carlos as soon as possible, but without raising suspicions. He surely knew how Priest went about keeping his women on the island, and was exactly the type she'd expect to call his boss the minute anything seemed unusual.

As she got closer, however, she could see that it was not Carlos at all. The man was wearing the same white suit he'd had on when they saw each other less than an hour ago. He was staring down at the ground, fixated on something she couldn't make out. It looked like a pile of red blankets.

Ten feet away, she snapped a shell beneath her feet and he turned.

"I did not do that!" Prisoner yelped.

Cassandra looked at him quizzically. He stepped towards her, holding his wrists out as an offer for handcuffs.

"Didn't do what?" Cassandra asked.

"That!" he answered, pointing at the pile he'd been standing next to.

Cassandra moved past him to get a better look.

It wasn't blankets.

She didn't have to worry about Carlos calling Priest.

———

It didn't take the rest long to get down the rocks once Cassandra waved them on.

"This was you wasn't it?" Cassandra held the sack up with one hand and hit it with the other.

Simon had thrown up as soon as he realised what he was looking at. It was the nice man who'd welcomed them to Paradise. He didn't look so nice now.

"Jesus," Harriet said. "Is this normal for him?" she asked Bob.

Bob nodded, silently.

"We should bury him," Simon said.

"We don't have time," said Cassandra. "But I do need to let him know this wasn't me."

She took a pen and notebook from her bag and quickly scribbled a note on it, then placed it near Carlos, pinning it down with a rock.

It read:

Not me. Calderon.
Cass.

"What are you doing down here?" Bob asked Prisoner.

He smiled and shrugged.

"Escaping. 'Cept I been caught again, huh?"

He nodded at Cassandra expectantly.

"Actually, we're leaving too. You want to come with us, come now," she answered.

"What?" Prisoner was clearly surprised. "Well, sure, but I warn ya, I got a habit of..."

Before he could finish, Cassandra waved her hand. There was a clicking noise and the steel monitor around Prisoner's ankle dropped out of his trouser leg.

"Oh." He stopped. "So this is for real?"

Cassandra nodded, then turned on her heel. "Come on."

Everyone moved to follow her, except Prisoner, who was rooted to the spot.

After a moment, the roots came free and he ran awkwardly down the beach towards the dock, shouting, "Wait!"

"Christ, are we leaving anybody *on* this island?" Harriet asked.

A siren wailed like a lost dog from back on the island. A big, demonic dog. Prisoner stopped in his tracks and began searching himself frantically for some missed device.

"It's not you!" Cassandra yelled back at him. "Priest is awake! And he knows we're missing!"

Prisoner resumed running for the boat.

————

They all clambered onboard as quickly as possible. There was blood there too, and a blood-soaked shirt. Chances were they'd find Captain Alexander's body somewhere at the other end.

"Right, who knows how to drive this thing?" Cassandra demanded.

They all stopped. Harriet and Simon looked at each other. This was a really bad plan if nobody could drive the boat.

Sean rolled his eyes and pushed his way forward.

"'Scuse me ladies, ancient mariner coming through."

He looked around the wheel and on the dashboard nearby.

"Keys?" he asked, turning to Cassandra.

She waved a hand and the engine rolled into life. Sean moved back and began to untie the mooring rope.

"Come back here!" boomed a voice that Simon could feel in the pit of his belly.

They all looked up to see Priest bounding down the steps they'd just come down. He really was huge.

"Get out of the boat!" he bellowed again.

Simon really did not want to do that. In fact, it was an odd thing to say. Who, when escaping from someone, would just stop and come back when they were told to? It was... He stopped mid-thought.

Harriet was climbing out of the boat.

"Shit!" Simon yelped and grabbed for her legs. He caught one, but the other wriggled free. Sean had managed to start reversing the boat, but they were still alongside the pier for the moment and Priest was reaching them quickly. Very quickly.

Bob clambered over Calderon's body, lying in the middle of the deck, and caught her other leg. She flailed like a fish on a hook, desperate to reach the water again. Prisoner reached across, getting a hand-hold on her belt.

Predictably, with so much weight on one side, the boat began to tip.

Cassandra and Amelia quickly moved to the other side to keep the boat in balance. They were in very real danger of capsizing.

Harriet was unusually strong. Had she been in her own mind, she most likely could have escaped from all three of them and dived back onto the pier herself. Her fighting, though, *was* rocking the boat. Literally. Sean was doing a decent job of backing them out, but they kept bumping the pier. Thankfully, they were almost at the end. Less thankfully, Priest was at the other end – and advancing.

Simon felt someone clambering over him and the boat ditched heavily towards their side. It was Cassandra. What was she doing? They were going to go over! Simon threw himself backwards to compensate for her weight and landed next to Amelia.

Cassandra reached over the edge and grabbed Harriet by the hair. Yanking her head back, she pulled her upright. Harriet shrieked with pain and fury, and clawed at the witch's face. Calmly, as if swatting a fly, Cassandra punched her in the face. She was out instantly, and collapsed into Prisoner's arms.

"Gun it!" Cassandra shouted to Sean, who duly obliged.

They reversed more quickly now and Sean took them off at a right angle from the pier, giving him room to turn and start moving forward at speed.

"Cassandra!" Priest roared from the end of the pier.

Cassandra gave him a not-remotely-magical gesture, with a smile.

With a grunt, Priest leapt off the pier and landed... *on* the water. He continued running towards them, his feet splashing slightly as he did.

This was *bad*.

The boat turned left and picked up speed. Priest lunged for it, trying to catch the edge, but his fingers only scraped the side. Having lost concentration as he jumped, he belly flopped into the sea. Sean accelerated and the island faded away behind them.

Simon looked back to see Priest climbing up, back onto the water's surface again, as if out of a hole in the ground. He still looked huge. And very, very angry.

"Jesus," said Simon. "That was scary."

"We're not out of the water yet," Cassandra warned.

"What do you mean?" asked Amelia.

A distant booming noise was followed by an increasing whistle and, finally, a huge splash just off the side of the boat.

"That," Cassandra shouted over the roar of the engine, "was a cannonball."

"You don't think he'd kill *us*, do you?" Amelia asked, horrified.

"*Us*, he can bring back if he wants to, sweetie," her stepmother explained.

"I really thought I was done with this shit," Sean grumbled, before shouting, "Right, everyone hold on to your bollocks!"

The boat began to bob and weave as cannonball after cannonball smashed into the water nearby. Simon grabbed hold of Harriet with one hand and a bar on the side of the boat with another. Then he ducked.

They weaved and turned as the whistles came again and again, growing and growing until they banged into the water.

Simon wondered if this was what war felt like. Certainly, he was terrified, and he'd always imagined that's exactly how he'd feel in a real battle.

Boom. Whistle. Splash.

Boom. Whistle. Splash.

Boom. Whistle. Splash.

Again and again.

The weaving of the boat was starting to make Simon feel sick. But if he threw up now, God knows where it would end up. Surely, they'd be out of range soon?

Then, suddenly, it stopped. Simon looked up. The engine had stopped too. Were they out of range? Then he realised.

Where Calderon's body had been, there was a gaping hole torn in the base of the boat; water flooding up through it.

They were hit.

They were going down.

Sean was frantically strapping a lifejacket on to Harriet. She was still out cold, which might have been the only thing stopping her from swimming back towards Priest. Bob was holding Amelia, who was crying. Could she swim? Surely, living on an island like this, she would be able to swim. Prisoner had already begun to swim away from the boat and Cassandra appeared to be floating just above the water – which was weird.

Jerkily, the boat lurched to one side and began to sink. Simon braced himself to begin swimming. He hadn't been in anything deeper than a bath for 20 years, but how hard could it be? He kicked away from the boat with his leg.

But it didn't come away. He kicked, but it wouldn't move.

His foot was caught. *Bloody hell, his foot was caught!*

With a yank, he was under water and sinking. He looked up to see the legs of his friends above him, fading away quickly.

Frantically, he tried to reach down, grabbing at his foot, but he couldn't work it free. What the hell was he caught on? He hadn't been prepared to go under so he hadn't taken a deep breath. He could already feel the urgent pleading of his lungs to breathe out, expelling the poisonous carbon dioxide and sucking in more precious oxygen. Now.

Now.

Now!

He looked up in panic. Was someone swimming down towards him? Was it Sean? He seemed to be trying to reach him, but Simon was sinking as fast as the boat. Could he reach him before they both ran out of air?

How ironic. After all the things he'd survived this week, with the fate of the world on his shoulders, Simon Debovar was going to drown, here, stuck in a speedboat sunk by a cannonball.

At least it would look interesting in the newspaper. 'Tourist drowns in speedboat accident' would be better than

'Rotting corpse found in bath after stench causes local dogs to howl incessantly'.

Ha.

After years of shutting himself away, Simon had finally come out into the sunshine. He'd made friends. He'd got closer to his family. He'd had sex. Several times. He'd learned to love a shower. He'd had a grand adventure. All the things he'd been avoiding for all those years, he'd actually enjoyed.

And look where it had got him: drowned!

As the light started to fade, Simon's resistance to his lungs' constant pleading became weaker and weaker. He began to hallucinate. Well, he assumed he was hallucinating. It was hard to tell.

Lights danced around him in the darkness of the abyss. Hands beckoned him downwards; down to join the others. Merchant seamen; lost fishermen; executed pirates; they all gestured to him with open arms.

"Come, join us in a watery grave," they called. A lobster sang to him.

It was over in moments.

As the lights faded completely, Simon's lungs finally gave out and the bubbles that represented his last hope, his last breath, escaped forever. Even if Sean reached him now, Simon would never make the surface alive.

An odd calm came over him. At least it was over. No more weight of the world on his shoulders. No more responsibility. No more worries. Just quiet. Cool, dark quiet.

The last thing Simon Debovar saw before his eyes closed was Death's bony hand reaching for him. The pale white claw grasped frantically at him, searching for his soul to drag away. The fingers were tipped in red; the red of blood and death and the end.

Simon's end.

CHAPTER THIRTY-TWO

Jean-Claude had very quickly gotten used to the luxury afforded him during his brief stay in Faunt's home. Cooking for him was a pleasure – he had excellent taste – though it was always odd serving breakfast in a bowl on the floor.

He'd slept soundly, but something had wakened him. He wasn't sure what, but it was a strange, wailing noise. Wondering if something was wrong, he'd crept out of his bed, pulled on a dressing gown and opened his door, slightly, just to get a better listen.

It was hard to say for sure, as it wasn't a noise one heard often, but now it sounded less like wailing and more like something possibly even more disturbing.

Laughter.

The hysterical laughter of a small deer.

―――――

Simon awoke in heaven. Clearly, it was heaven, because everything was soft and nothing hurt. He was warm and felt the heat of the sun on his face. Opening his bleary eyes, he saw a figure in silhouette. The head was surrounded by a circle of light, which seemed to be the source of the heat.

It must be an angel. So, whatever else he'd done, it seemed he'd ended up in a good place. Ah well, all's well that ends well.

"Hello," Simon said, peacefully, "I'm Simon."

"I know who you are, you bloody idiot."

The angel sounded disconcertingly like Harriet.

Simon sat up and rubbed his eyes.

"Harriet?" he asked, confused. "Did you drown too?"

She roared with laughter.

"You're not dead, you nipple!"

"I'm *not*? Why not?"

"Because your teleporter hottie saved your arse, that's why!"

"Cherry? *Cherry's* not dead?"

Simon bounded off the bed like a giddy labrador.

"What the hell is wrong with you? Nobody's dead! Everyone's alive! Well, except for the boat guy with the vomit shirt and the nice guy who met us on the beach. They're both mince."

"Yeah, I knew that. Scary Spanish guy. Did you hear about him?"

"*Hear* about him? I've met his head."

This, finally, stopped Simon's bouncing. He sat back down.

"So, everyone is here? Everyone made it?"

"Yep. Cassandra fished out most of us and Cherry got you. The ghost directed Cass to get us back here to the boat."

Simon looked around as if the room had just appeared about them. Only then did he notice that the halo of light he'd seen earlier was, in fact, a porthole.

"Oh yeah. We're on a boat. Cherry has a boat?"

"No, it's the other pair's. The stuck up one and the tart."

"Daniel and Lily?"

309

"There you go."

"Oh."

Simon sat back on the bed.

"Oh my God. We did it. Harriet, we did it."

Harriet smiled broadly.

"We did indeed, twinkle-toes. We fucking did indeed."

"Where's Cherry?" he asked after a moment.

"In her cabin, resting."

"Why? What's wrong?"

"Apparently she can't teleport into water, so she had to teleport above you and swim down. To get up speed, she teleported pretty high up. Even then, she almost ran out of breath getting to you. Once she got hold of you... well, she didn't have a lot left. And she still had to poof you both back here, so..."

"So... what?"

"It took a lot out of her. She's pretty wiped out."

"Can I see her?"

"I imagine she'd like that. But hoi, you take it easy too, sunshine. You nearly copped it as well. And then where would we be, eh?"

Harriet showed an uncommon sense of decorum by leaving the room and allowing Simon a chance to get dressed in private.

He looked out the porthole at the water and the sun. It was a beautiful day.

———

Simon knocked lightly at the door and opened it tentatively.

"Hello?"

Cherry was sitting up in bed, raised up on pillows. She seemed to be asleep.

He came in quietly, shut the door, moved over to the bed and stood looking down at her. He'd never before experienced the feeling that comes when the only girl you've been intimate with in the last 15 years risks her life to save yours. He reached out to touch her face, but stopped short, afraid to wake her.

She smiled.

"Hey, Aquaman, how ya doin'?" she asked, quietly.

She opened her eyes to see him grinning widely.

"I'm great," he answered, honestly. "Thank you so much."

He stroked her cheek gently. She winked weakly at him.

"Well, you know, Faunt would be pretty pissed if I brought you back all dead and bloated."

"I suppose he would. Can I do anything for you?"

"Well, I hear we have a few hours on this boat. Wanna get some popcorn and watch a movie?"

She nodded to the remote control on her bedside table. Simon couldn't see a TV in the room. Cherry nodded upwards. It was on the ceiling. It very nearly *was* the ceiling.

"I would love that," Simon smiled. "I'll get some popcorn."

"You're on top of the blanket, though. No taking advantage of me in my weakened state."

Simon crossed to the door.

"I promise," he grinned back at her.

"You're at least going to have to buy me dinner first, next time."

Simon closed the door and smiled.

"Next time."

———

Harriet came up the stairs, back into the sunshine on deck. Daniel, sociable as ever, had opted to pilot the boat. Lily was deep in conversation with Cassandra. Bob and Amelia were doing 'Titanic' up at the front of the boat. Sean was sunbathing. Prisoner was at the back, watching the island disappear in the distance.

She sat on the lounger next to Sean's.

"All right, sexy?"

It was an apt description. Even with a few interesting looking scars, Sean looked good.

"All right, love? If I'd known this was the lifestyle you were accustomed to, it would have made it an even easier decision to come with you, I tell you."

"Yeah. About that: listen…"

Sean sat up and raised his sunglasses.

"It's OK. Look, I'm not asking anything from you. You want to call this a holiday fling, that's fine with me, love. I didn't just come for you. I like Bob and Simon, and Amelia's an old mate. You guys are sorta fun to hang out with, if a little dangerous. So don't stress. You're a free woman. You want to come find me and have some fun, a few beers, you know where I am. Now, it seems like an awfully nice day to be wearing as much as you are. Don't you think?"

Harriet smiled and stood up to leave.

"Where ya goin'?"

"To get us a couple of margaritas, Cocky O'Bighead. I'll be right back."

"Margaritas?" Sean said to the sky. "Deadly."

"You know what?" Prisoner had appeared at his side.

"What's that, mate?"

"Looking back now, I think I may have been mistaken."

"How d'you mean?" the Irishman asked.

"That ain't my island, after all."

———

Gabby woke up to an empty bed. She was aware Luke had had a fitful night. He hadn't wanted to sleep, but she insisted. They were both exhausted, and Debovar was hardly going to steal Priest's wife from under his nose in one night, was he?

Luke had woken her several times, moving around – first in bed, then around the room. He must have gone for a walk.

It was early. The sun was up. It was a new day. Today,

they started again, with a new plan to prevent Debovar and his friends from kidnapping Cassandra.

She'd already decided, for herself, on a nuclear option, if necessary. She would tell Priest everything.

It was risky. Priest was a law unto himself. He could go either way. They could all end up dead. Or just some of them. Or, he could be an ally, who would help them solve the problem. Unfortunately, it really was like firing a gun in a dark, crowded room; she had no idea who might die.

But she had to do it. Luke wouldn't. He'd probably thought of it, but he was already carrying so much guilt...

No, it had to be her. And she would do it, happily, if they couldn't find another way. The decision, the knowledge that she had a backup plan, was calming. She decided to go out and pick up some coffee and croissants for when Luke came back.

Or maybe that's where he had gone?

She got up and found some clothes to throw on.

As she was on the verge of leaving, Luke returned. He was, indeed, carrying coffee, but he looked as though he'd forgotten it was there. His face was pale and drawn. Bless him, he'd clearly hardly slept at all.

"Sit down," he said darkly.

"Why?" Gabby asked, doing it anyway.

"Because I wish I'd been sitting when I heard this."

He handed her a coffee and sat beside her.

"We've blown it. It's over. We've lost."

"What do you mean?"

"They're gone. It's all over the island. They escaped last night; with Cassandra *and* Amelia."

Gabby felt the world tilt beneath her. She was indeed glad to be sitting down. With no other options available, she did the one thing that came instinctively; she hugged him.

"I'm so sorry," she said.

"Me too."

They sat like that for an age, in silence.

Finally, Luke sat upright.

"There is one last option."

"What?" Gabby asked, intrigued.

...

"We run."

CHAPTER THIRTY-THREE

"Good afternoon, everyone. And welcome back."

Faunt opened the door wide. It was quite a sight. The last time he'd seen Simon here, he'd been hunched over and practically hiding behind Daniel and Lily. Now, there he stood, proudly front and centre, flanked by nine other people.

"Quite an entourage you've collected, Simon."

Faunt spread his arms and welcomed the ex-hermit with a bear hug worthy of an old friend. Simon gladly reciprocated. He was very pleased to be back. The smell of pine was comforting.

"It's crazy, isn't it?" he whispered to Faunt. "I'm not sure how it happened."

Faunt held him out and smiled at him. "I know you're not." He held his gaze for a moment, before welcoming the remaining guests in, one by one.

Cherry got an especially long hug; Daniel a polite handshake.

"Cassandra, my love, I never thought I'd see you again."

She stepped up to him and hugged him, with a kiss on each cheek.

"I can honestly say I didn't think I'd be seeing you again either."

They smiled at each other. There was something old and familiar about that look. Who knew what unspoken messages were passing between them? Simon had reunited them. Well, with a little help.

Cassandra stepped inside to allow the last of the guests to enter.

"Good afternoon, Prosper, it's a pleasure to meet you."

Prisoner stepped back a pace.

"Come again?"

Faunt smiled. Your name is Prosper Delassixe, and you are an excellent chef, specialising in Creole cuisine. I'd love to try your jambalaya."

Prisoner's eyes opened wide.

"Now ain't that the kind of thing a man ought to know about hisself? They weren't lying when they said you knew everything, Mr Faunt." He took Faunt's hand and shook it vigorously.

"I don't suppose you would be kind enough to tell me where my island is, would you?" he asked, conspiratorially. "I seem to have... misplaced it."

"I'm sure we can come to an arrangement. Do you play Yahtzee?"

"I have no idea," Prosper answered, stepping inside. "Prosper!" he announced to the group with a satisfied flourish. "I told you it started with a P!"

———

Pleasantries concluded, the group stood in the entrance hall, milling slightly aimlessly.

"So, Faunt, you know why we're here. Can we get down to business, please?"

Of course, it was Daniel who was in a rush.

316

"First, it would be bad manners for me not to offer you all some lunch," Faunt said. "After all, it is lunch time."

Simon had secretly hoped they'd get to eat here. He wasn't sure what he was in the mood for, but Faunt's meals were always perfect.

"We don't really have time," the angel objected. "It really would be better if we could just get going."

Faunt opened the doors to the dining room, where a dozen chairs were also milling around a huge table laden with a veritable banquet of food. Meats, cheeses, breads, pastries – everything one could conceivably be in the mood for, for lunch.

"It would be a shame to waste Jean-Claude's efforts, don't you think?" Faunt asked.

Before he could answer, everyone with an appetite had crowded into the room and was busily catching themselves a seat. Faunt followed them in and took his place at the head of the table.

"What difference does it make?" Lily asked the distinctly huffy Daniel. "Right now; after lunch – you expecting the apocalypse at any moment?"

She went in to join the rest. Daniel followed, with a sigh. Patience was clearly not his virtue of choice.

———

After a lunch that was largely spent recounting tales of what had happened on the island – ostensibly for Faunt's benefit – the host, Daniel, Lily and Simon retired to the library for coffee and a private chat.

"OK," Faunt began. "Simon, you have fulfilled your end of the bargain. And may I say you did a remarkable job; you and your friends."

"Thank you," Simon answered.

"Now, your payment is the location of the Holy Rug of Djoser, correct?"

Simon looked uncomfortably at Daniel and Lily. In all honesty, he'd be very happy never to see that rug again. Though he did rather miss looking down at it, in the way that you miss a childhood friend you haven't thought about in years when you find a photo of the two of you eating ice cream in the sun. Perhaps, really, it was the lack of responsibility he missed; the innocence.

He sort of missed home, too. Only sort of. While the familiarity of it was appealing – in the same way people who have spent all year looking forward to going on holiday are bizarrely desperate to get home after two weeks – there was something now... *mundane* about it. In his mind, it was grey; grey and cold.

He raised his coffee to his face and breathed deeply. Hazelnut.

"Honey, you need to actually say 'yes'."

Simon had forgotten he had been asked a question.

"What happens if I say 'no'?" he asked, sipping the coffee.

Faunt sat back in his chair, smiling. "That's not up to me, I'm afraid."

"I beg your pardon?" Daniel asked, like a headmaster whose student had just asked him whether or not his mother had ever tried to claim a refund.

"What if I say no?" Simon repeated.

"You can't say no," Lily answered. "You just can't."

The cold, hard edge in her voice made it very clear to Simon that this may be the last choice he ever made, should he choose to make it. Fair enough. At least he knew where the cards had fallen.

He turned back to Faunt. "Yes. Please."

Manners cost nothing, after all.

"OK." Faunt sat forward again. The Holy Rug of Djoser is currently on Queen's Drive, Edinburgh, Scotland."

The room remained stoically silent.

"Pardon?" Simon asked.

"Queen's Drive, Edinburgh," Faunt replied.

"No, no it's not," Simon answered. "See, it was there, but now it's... not."

"Forty-three Queen's Drive," Faunt added.

"Across the road?" Simon asked, bewildered. "My neighbours stole it? Why would my neighbours steal it?"

"*That* is not the question, Mr Debovar," Daniel interrupted. "The question is," he looked at Lily, "*who* are his neighbours?"

Lily nodded sagely. Clearly, that *was* the question.

"There you have it," Faunt stood up. "You have your answer, I have my payment. Now if you'll excuse me, I have guests to attend to."

He turned to Simon. "*Mr* Debovar," he mimicked the angel's tone out of sheer devilment, "you are welcome to stay as long as you like."

Simon gulped. He looked at Daniel and Lily.

"Thank you. Honestly, I think I'd really just like to get this over with, if you don't mind. But I'd be very happy to come back sometime, if that's OK?"

"Anytime you want to come, I'll send someone for you," he answered.

"Faunt, would you be kind enough to lend us your teleporter?" Daniel asked, smiling.

Faunt turned at the door.

"I'm afraid not, sorry. I need her to do something else for me this afternoon."

Daniel furrowed his eyebrows. He really was used to getting what he wanted.

"Your car is still parked outside though, and I have had it washed and valeted during lunch." He bowed slightly and left the room, backwards, closing the door behind him.

Daniel gave Lily a look which Simon interpreted as 'suspicious'. Was Faunt up to something? Simon very much hoped so.

"Would you mind if I say goodbye before we go?" he asked.

"Sure, honey," Lily answered. "We'll be in the car."

Simon followed Faunt out the door.

"What's he doing?" Daniel asked.

"He's not *obliged* to help us, you know," Lily answered. "Chill out. What can he do?"

"If there is anyone on this bloody planet who is capable of finding something to do, it is *him*. I don't trust him."

"OK. Tell you what. You stay here and try to figure it out. I'll be in the car. First one there gets to drive, right?"

Lily left Daniel alone in the room. He looked up at the portraits Faunt had on the wall. All these irrelevant people immortalised in oil.

What a waste.

———

"Of course I'm coming. So's Sean, aren't you?" Harriet had seemed genuinely surprised that Simon hadn't realised she would want to go with him. It simply hadn't occurred to him.

"Sure, if that's OK," the Irishman confirmed.

"I guess," Simon said. He assumed that since Daniel and Lily would each want him to choose their respective offer for the Rug, they'd be unlikely to refuse to let his friends come if he asked.

"Ace," said Sean. "When do we leave?"

"Erm, now, I think."

"I'd come, but Faunt needs me for something," Cherry said. "But I'll come see you soon, huh? There's some cool places I want to show you."

"I'd like that," said Simon.

She kissed him gently on the cheek. "Take care of yourself."

"We're staying here, for now," Bob said. "Until we figure out what else to do."

"But good luck," Amelia added. "I hope it all works out for you."

"Me too," Simon said – stating, he felt, the bleeding obvious. He wasn't good at goodbyes. He wasn't used to them.

"Right then, shall we go?"

"Come on then," Harriet said, downing the last of her drink. "Once more onto the beach!"

———

Faunt closed the door behind him. Simon and the others had been gone only a matter of minutes before he and Cassandra had found an excuse to slip away. It hadn't been hard for the long-estranged couple to explain a desire to be alone.

"So, do you want to tell me why I'm here?" she asked, grabbing a chair and placing it next to Faunt's straw bed.

"You mean you don't understand why a man would want to rescue his long-estranged wife at a time like this?"

"You could have rescued me a long time ago. And don't think I don't realise that. So..."

"Priest does present a unique challenge. Even for me."

"Uh huh. So when you finally decide to save me, you send a baby? That boy can barely look after himself! How he got off the island in one piece, never mind brought me with him, is a mystery. There are plenty of others you could have sent. Calderon, for a start!"

"Ah yes, Calderon. What *shall* we do with him?"

"I don't care. Use him as a bloody ornament."

Faunt snorted. "There is a certain appeal to that, yes. I'd certainly know where he is and he couldn't accuse me of violating our mutual non-interference pact. Of course, he'd be free to leave whenever he liked..."

Cassandra laughed.

"But seriously, why am I here? You planning to ask me to lift your curse?"

"You told me not to bother when you cast it," said Faunt. "Have you changed your mind?"

"Not really. Just curious if you're tired of it, yet."

"The transformation is... inconvenient, but I can live with the rest. In fact, I'm not sure what I'd do with myself if I didn't have the curse, now. I'm not much good at anything but this and Yahtzee."

"OK, so what then?"

"I need you to deliver an invitation," he said.

"An *invitation*?" Cassandra looked incredulous. "Is that all? You went to all this trouble to ask me to be a courier?"

"Essentially."

"You could have used anyone for that. Your teleporter could have done it days ago!" she protested.

"Ah, but you don't know what the invitation is *to* yet. Or who it's *for*..."

CHAPTER THIRTY-FOUR

Simon woke up leaning on the palm of his hand. He couldn't tell if he'd woken naturally or with a snore. He could, however, tell that he had drooled on his own hand, which was undignified at the very least. He 'casually' wiped it on his thigh. Also, since he'd been leaning close to his left eye, it felt weird and wasn't focusing very well, which meant his balance was a little off kilter. As his mind cleared he realised he had no memory of arriving at, or going through, the airport. In fact, he felt entirely discombobulated.

He looked around.

First Class. Lovely.

Daniel and Lily sat across the aisle from him. Harriet and Sean were nowhere to be seen, but judging by the gentle, repetitive rattling of the toilet door, he had an indecent idea where they were.

Other than them, First Class was empty. Simon wondered whether they had booked out the whole section, or if those who had held First Class tickets for this flight had been convinced of the error of their ways and chose instead to travel in the back with the rest of the hoi polloi.

He could hardly blame Harriet – in this instance at least –

for her carnal impatience. After all, how much longer was she going to get as her youthful self before Daniel and Lily changed them back? He couldn't help but feel sad at the thought that such a perfectly matched couple were on the verge of being separated when one of them involuntarily aged 60 years. He also felt guilty about bringing Sean, who would begin ageing at a normal rate again, now he was off Priest's island.

Hang on.

Why did it have to be that way? Simon had a little leverage right now. What harm would it do to use it a little?

"Excuse me," he said, clearing his throat.

"Welcome back, Mr Debovar," Daniel answered. "How are you feeling?"

"OK, thanks," he lied.

"That's nice, honey," Lily looked up from the in-flight magazine she was reading.

"You know how Harriet and I are... well, younger, at the moment?"

"Ah yes, of course. You'd like us to put you back. No problem." Daniel began to gesture, but Lily grabbed his hand.

"Not now!" she yelped, nodding towards the vibrating toilet door.

Daniel smiled. Simon had a sneaky feeling he had known exactly what he was doing.

"Actually, no," Simon continued. "I wondered if, well, when all this is over, I wondered if you could... sort of... *leave* us this way?"

Lily looked at him in surprise. Daniel raised an eyebrow.

"I'm surprised you ask," said Lily. "You were so against the idea."

"As am I, Mr Debovar. I have to say, despite our differences, I have taken you to be a man of some conscience; the kind of man who believes in earning his rewards," said the angel.

Simon sat upright in his seat.

"Earn it? You don't think I've *earned* it?"

Daniel recoiled slightly.

"Have you been *asleep* for the last week?" Simon ranted. "Have you not *noticed* the number of times I have nearly been killed just to get you *my* carpet? What is it that you need me to do to *earn* it? Hack off a limb? Cough up an organ?"

Simon cricked his neck. Whatever came of it, that had felt fan-bloody-tastic.

"He's got a point," Lily said to Daniel.

The angel shrugged.

"Whatever," he said, dismissively. "You can stay. You'll still age and get that spare tyre back if you keep to your normal diet, though."

Lily had gone back to her magazine already.

"Thank you," Simon said — but it wasn't them he was thanking. It was the universe, which he felt had finally realised that karma was more than a little out of balance in his case and, in fact, he was perfectly entitled to something nice about now.

He tried to convince himself that his delight was entirely on behalf of Harriet but, really, he was happy for himself too.

Which was nice.

———

Sean was missing something. He didn't know what, but it was, apparently, pretty bloody good.

When the pilot had announced they'd be landing in Edinburgh soon and that the toilets were no longer in use (which, at that precise moment, had not been entirely accurate), he and Harriet had emerged to re-take their seats and Simon had gestured Harriet over to him.

He'd whispered something to her that had clearly been unbelievable, as she had immediately turned to Daniel and

Lily for confirmation. When Daniel nodded in affirmation, she had nearly torn Simon out of his seat to hug him, kissed him somewhat more passionately than a sister should kiss her brother, told him he had always been her favourite, then dropped him and did much the same to Daniel and Lily, who both looked a little disconcerted by the whole thing.

When she'd returned to sit beside him, he'd asked what was up and she had simply answered, "Later." But the smile she said it with and her entire attitude made it clear to him that, whatever it was, it was the best news she'd ever had. And he had seen her pretty happy. She wasn't even bothered when the stewardess refused to bring them a bottle of champagne because they were about to land.

And something was fundamentally different. From the time they'd left the island, there had been a melancholia about her. He'd been prepared for her to tell him at any time that the game was up and she wasn't interested in making any more of this than they already had. Which would have been a shame, but he'd certainly have survived. He was an old man; he'd been rejected more than once. Not much more than once, but still...

But now, for the first time he could remember, she was holding his hand; and stroking it; and smiling.

Whatever Simon had done, Sean was pretty sure that he owed him a pint.

———

"Hurry!" Gabby called frantically up the ladder.

With the boat sunk, they had chartered a helicopter off the island. When their flight home was delayed, it had almost been too much to bear. They were running out of time.

"I'm coming!" Luke's voice echoed in the attic above her. "But this thing is heavy, remember?"

"I know, I'm sorry. It's just..."

"I know."

Accompanied by much grunting, the edge of the Holy Rug of Djoser appeared in the hatch, sprinkling dust down into Gabby's face.

She sneezed.

"Sorry!" Luke called. "You ready?"

"Yes," she answered, bracing herself.

Luke's head appeared next to the Rug.

"What are you doing?"

"Getting ready to catch it."

"What?" he asked.

"What?"

"It's far too heavy. It'll crush you!"

"Oh. Well, why did you ask me if I was ready, then?"

"I was checking you were out of the way. So it doesn't crush you!"

"Oh," she answered, stepping out of the way. "That does make sense."

With further grunting, the Rug tipped and slid down the ladder into the hallway, landing with a thud. Luke peered down from the gloom to see Gabby spluttering in a cloud of dust.

Oops.

"You'll need to tip it over, so I can come down the ladder," he called down.

Gabby nodded and, with one hand over her nose and mouth, shoved the thick roll until it fell free of the ladder. As it landed with another dull bang, it unrolled slightly, and Gabby could see the edge of the intricate patterns.

It really was very pretty.

CHAPTER THIRTY-FIVE

Simon wasn't sure what he had expected to see when they turned into Queen's Drive. He had been overcome with a nervous kind of nausea as they approached. He was not good with conflict, and he had a feeling that conflict was unavoidable here.

At the same time, he was curious. Who were his carpet-thieving neighbours? And, now he came to think of it, how had they known to steal it just then, at the very point where he would otherwise have given it to, in all likelihood, Lily? It was really rather improbable. Unlike the rest of the week, of course.

What he had certainly not been prepared for was to pull up in front of the house to find a couple frantically trying to put what he could only assume was his carpet on top of a car that was barely bigger than the floor-covering itself.

"What in heaven do you two think you're doing?" Daniel demanded, getting out of the car.

"You can't *have* it," the man replied forcefully. "Back off."

Simon was extremely confused. There was something vaguely familiar about the pair. In fact, he was relatively certain he'd seen them recently, but he didn't recognise them at all in the context of here and now.

Lily walked over to the car, which the woman was desperately trying to start.

"Stop that," said the demon. "You know it's not going to start."

The woman looked pleadingly at her and kept turning the key. The engine made a deeply unhappy grinding noise and spluttered into absolute quiet. She put her head on the steering wheel.

"I'll ask you again: *what* are you doing?" Daniel repeated.

"We're stopping you. And *them*!" he answered.

"I'm sorry," Simon interjected when it became obvious nobody was going to explain anything to him. "Do you know each other?"

Daniel turned as if he'd forgotten Simon, Harriet and Sean were there. "Ah, of course, Mr Debovar, how rude of me. Allow me to introduce you to two old friends of yours."

"Of *mine*?"

"Indeed. This 'gentleman'," Simon could hear the quotation marks in Daniel's voice, "is Lucas, and the lady in the car is Gabrielle."

"Erm, OK. But I don't know them."

"Hang on," Sean interrupted. "I do. You were on the island."

"Were they now?" Daniel asked, turning to Luke.

"So?" answered Luke.

Daniel smiled at him with a malevolence that sent a chill down Simon's neck.

"Honey, the thing you need to know about these two is that prior to Daniel and I being given the Holy Rug of Djoser to find, Lucas and Gabrielle had been looking for it for a long time," Lily finally explained.

"Why?" Simon asked.

"Because, Mr Debovar, until about 15 years ago, Lucas

was an angel and Gabrielle a demon. Just like us," Daniel finished, with a clear sense of satisfaction. "Unfortunately for them, Lucas broke some rules in the search and was punished. He was made *mortal*."

The final word dripped with derision.

"And I'm grateful every day." Luke stepped toward Simon, but paused when Daniel held up an arm in warning.

"Simon... Mr Debovar... you can't give them the Rug. If you do, it's the end of everything," Luke said, pleadingly.

"What are you talking about?" Lily asked.

"You know what will happen when this is over!" Luke was shouting now. "Once one of them wins the bet, it's over. They'll forget this planet even exists! And without them to hold it together, the planet will die in – what – a decade? Less?"

He turned back to Simon.

"If you give either of them that Rug, Simon, it's the end of the world. Literally, the end of the world."

"You don't know that," said Daniel, dismissively.

"Yes he does and so do you!" Gabby had climbed out of the car. She turned to Lily. "She hasn't even bothered to send Her envoy, has She? She was due in 2000. Where *is* she?"

"She's here," Lily answered, evasively.

"But does she know who she *is*? Does she know *why* she's here? Has anyone bothered to *tell* her?" Gabby was barely pausing for breath now.

Lily looked back darkly. "That's not my decision to make."

"But doesn't that tell you everything? If She's not interested in *her*, then how interested is She going to be when this is done?"

Lily looked at Daniel, who rolled his eyes.

"Sorry, who are we talking about?" Harriet asked.

Gabby approached her, pleading.

"Mother! She gave Him a 2000-year head start. Her envoy was supposed to reveal herself in 2000. But she didn't. That was when Luke and I were sure. Sure that this Rug," she pointed back at the car, "is the only reason the world still exists. Without this bet, without a reason to compete, they'll move on to a new playground and leave Earth to collapse into the Sun!"

Simon looked at Luke, who nodded in confirmation.

"It only works because they make it work," he said. "The reason physics doesn't make sense in space is because they're forcing it. Without them, it collapses."

"Fuck me," said Harriet.

"Jesus," Sean added.

Simon swallowed hard. Suddenly it was so much worse.

"You don't know that any of that is true," said Daniel, walking towards the Rug. "And anyway, it's all redundant. Mr Debovar has already agreed to give it to one of us, once we make him our offers. Your arguments are academic."

"No," Luke looked piteously at Simon. "Please, no."

"Mr Debovar," Daniel said, lifting the Rug free of its ropes with one hand and balancing it on his shoulder, "it is time for us to adjourn to your house and make you offers for this relic, and for you to make a decision."

...

"No," said Simon.

"I beg your pardon?" the angel asked.

"No. I won't give it to you."

"Is that right?" Daniel put the Rug on its end. "Perhaps, as you are so keen to trust the word of your neighbours, you should know exactly why it is that they are no longer in the employ of our Parents."

"No," Gabby begged, tears streaming down her face. "Please, no." She looked at Lily. "Don't let him. Please. It's not fair. He won't understand."

Luke was pale and trembling slightly.

"Wait a fucking minute."

Harriet stepped in front of Simon.

"Wait a *fucking* minute. Fifteen years ago? You broke rules?"

Harriet's voice was gravel on glass. Simon had never seen her so angry. What was wrong with her?

Daniel smiled. "I think she's figured it out."

"What rules did you break?" she looked at Daniel. "What *fucking* rules did he break?"

Simon and Sean exchanged a confused look. Sean shrugged.

"Fifteen years ago," Daniel spoke slowly and calmly, "Lucas murdered your family, Miss Debovar."

Time stopped.

————

Simon's head was spinning. Had he blacked out? He still appeared to be standing up. There was a noise, like screeching. He shook his head slightly to see if it cleared. It didn't. After a moment, he realised it was coming from outside his head; from Harriet.

She ran at Luke, who made no move to protect himself. He looked sad; resigned. Accepting.

But she didn't reach him. Gabby had covered the same ground and reached him first. She tackled him to the ground and turned to put herself between Harriet and her lover.

"No!" she yelled. "You can't have him! You have to kill me first! And I'm a *really* nice person!"

Harriet stopped in her tracks – more out of surprise than anything else.

"Get off him," she growled, "or you're *both* dead."

"No! You don't understand. When you're like them," she waved frantically towards the angel and demon, "it's different! They're not human! They see things in black and white. No emotion. No empathy. They just do as they're told. We just did as we were told!"

"I'll count to three," Harriet said. "One..."

"No, please! Since we were made human, we're different. We feel love. Passion. Sadness. Regret. Luke has spent every day trying to make up for what he did. We've lived here for years, protecting Simon and the Rug. We're good people!" Gabby pleaded.

"I have spent fifteen years believing I was at least partially responsible for the death of my family," Harriet said quietly. "What do you think I'm prepared to do to get to the person who actually was?

"Two..."

"Please!" Gabby pleaded. "We're trying to save the world!"

"Three."

Simon put a hand on Harriet's arm.

"Wait," he said.

She turned to look at him, tears streaming from her red eyes.

"Why?" she asked, confused.

"Just... wait. Please? For me?"

She was shaking with anger. But she stopped.

"For *you*," she said and stepped away, back to Sean, who put a hand on her shoulder. She stared venomously at Luke.

Simon put his hand down to Gabby. She took it, hesitantly, and allowed herself to be pulled up. Then Simon offered the same hand to Luke. He looked up, incredulous. After a moment, he took it and got back to his feet.

Simon took a deep breath. He was inexplicably calm. Something had been turned off in his head.

"Explain it to me," he said to Luke.

"I can't," he answered. "It's like she said. We were *different*. *They* are different. They don't understand being human. Their drive is to please their Parents. Their only drive. My only drive. This world is barely real to them. It's like... role-playing. No consequences. The whole planet dies; they still live."

"You're not *human*," Daniel said, mockingly. "You have to be *born* human. *You're* an angel; *she's* a demon. The only difference is you're mortal. You're going to die."

"Is that true?" Simon asked.

"No," Luke answered. "It's not the only difference."

"Once a servant of Father; always a servant of Father," said Daniel. "You made your choice."

"I had no choice," said Luke. "Neither do you."

"Why did you kill our family?" Simon asked.

Luke somehow looked Simon in the eyes. But he couldn't answer without looking down.

"For the Rug."

Simon took a deep breath. "Why didn't you defend yourself? From Harriet?"

Luke shook his head, sadly. "Simon, I was trying to kill you too." He glanced at Harriet. "Both of you. I deserve to be punished."

"No you don't! That's not fair!" Gabby sputtered through her tears.

"Why were *you* punished?" Simon asked her. "Why were you made human?"

"For me," Luke answered. "Our Parents took pity on me when I begged them not to leave me alone. She was my gift from them."

Gabby smiled and touched his cheek.

Simon looked at them silently for a moment, then calmly turned and walked to Harriet. He looked deep into her eyes.

"I never realised you blamed yourself. I'm so sorry." He hugged her. She hugged him back, sobbing something into his neck that was probably swearing.

After a long, awkward silence, Harriet lifted her head off his wet shoulder.

"You're a good boy," she said. "You always were. *I'm* sorry."

"Thank you," he answered.

After a moment of steeling himself, Simon turned to Daniel and Lily. "Now, I believe you two need to make me offers. First, I want some answers."

"OK." Lily stepped up. "What do you want to know?"

"Is what they said true?"

"Not necessarily," she answered.

"I mean the stuff about physics not working. Is that true?"

"Yes, that is true."

"So, if they abandon us, the planet will die."

She hesitated. "Possibly."

"We are all here at their whim, Mr Debovar," Daniel interrupted. "And we are all lost without them. It is... the way it is."

"Right. What happens to them?" Simon nodded at Luke.

"Nothing," Lily answered. "We're forbidden from harming our brothers and sisters – mortal or not."

"OK. One more thing. When we started all this, you offered me a night to sleep on things. After your offers, I want a night to sleep on it before I make a decision."

Lily and Daniel looked at each other. Daniel shrugged in resignation.

"OK, honey, we agree to that, too."

"Don't call me 'honey'," said Simon. "What are your offers?"

"Maybe we should go inside, Mr Debovar?" the angel suggested.

"No, thank you. I'd like to hear your offers and then I'd like you both to leave, please," said Simon.

"OK," Lily began. "I'll go first?"

Daniel nodded his assent.

"Simon," she began. "You're not aware of this, but you have a hyper-sensitive sense of smell. It's dozens of times more sensitive than a normal person's. In one way, it's a bonus, because pleasant smells, to you, are amazing. However, the opposite is also true. Bad smells are awful.

"This is why you think people stink. You can smell everything about them: the smallest amount of sweat or a hint of coffee on their breath. It's one of the main reasons you find people so difficult to be around.

"My offer is this: I will amend your sense of smell so that only the good smells are amplified, and the bad ones go back to the level of a normal human. You will experience the world as an entirely new place."

Simon was silent.

"Holy shit, kid. Is that true?" Harriet asked.

"You do all smell pretty bad," Simon confirmed. "I thought everybody smelled things the same way I do."

"Well, that's the thing, honey – sorry," Lily faltered, realising her mistake, "you have nothing else to compare it with."

"Wow," he said, flatly. "OK, Daniel, what about you?"

Lily seemed a little taken aback at how quickly Simon dismissed her, which made Daniel smile.

"Well, Mr Debovar, I think it's fair to say that you and I have not, perhaps, gotten off to the best of starts. I assure you, that was never my intention and I apologise for any offence I may have caused you."

"OK," Simon said when it became clear the angel had paused for some kind of answer.

"However," he continued, "In my estimation, you have certainly formed more of a relationship with my colleague and this, I think, puts me at a very probable disadvantage when it comes to your decision. With this in mind, my path has become very clear to me.

"My offer is this, Mr Debovar. I will give you..." He swept round dramatically and gave a flourish with his hands. "...Lily."

"You'll *what*?" Lily asked, agog.

"You heard. We did both agree to abide by *whatever* each other offered. Correct?"

"But I didn't... you can't..." She couldn't find the words.

"I most definitely can." He grinned so wide Simon thought his face might split. "And I will."

"What do you mean, I can *have* her?" Simon asked, entirely unsure whether he was even vaguely understanding this.

"She will be yours for the rest of your life, at your beck and call, to do whatever you please with, Mr Debovar. Imagine the possibilities."

Simon looked at Lily. She was ridiculously attractive, even without obvious nipples.

"OK," he finally spluttered. "Thank you both. Can you leave now, please?"

Daniel's smile disappeared from his eyes, despite remaining on his face.

"Of course," he answered, formally. "Shall we say seven o'clock tomorrow morning?"

"No," Simon answered, "Let's say ten. I'd like to have breakfast and a bath first."

"Ten it is," Lily answered. She nodded to Daniel, who joined her in walking to their car, which was still abandoned on the street.

The two got in and drove away without exchanging a word.

Simon turned to Luke and Gabby, who were now sitting, quietly, on their doorstep.

"Are you sure? The world ends if I give them the carpet?"

Luke nodded. "I'm sorry Mr Debovar. I really am."

"I know," said Simon.

"Tell him," Gabby nudged Luke, "about Faunt."

"What about Faunt?" Simon asked.

Luke was hesitant.

"He sent us after you. To the island. He said we could stop you," Gabby blurted out.

Simon thought he'd had as much paradigm-shifting as he could get in the last twenty minutes. Apparently not.

"Did he hell!" Harriet barked. "That's a lie! Why would he?"

"Because he believes it too," said Luke. He looked up at Simon. "He told us we couldn't hurt you. Said he'd kill us if we did. But he said we could stop you, if we could."

"I don't understand," said Simon, "Why would he do that? Why send us there and then let you try to stop us?"

"It's all the Rules, mate," Sean interjected. "These lot, they live by some seriously mad set of rules over who can and can't do what. It's mental."

"It's true," said Luke. "He wasn't allowed to interfere, but he didn't want to give you the information, so he let us follow you, hoping we would find a way to stop you. If you didn't bring back Cassandra…"

"Then he didn't have to give us the location of the Rug," Simon finished. "So if we'd failed, we'd actually have been better off," Simon observed. "How ironic. Why didn't you just tell us?"

"Rules," Luke answered. "You had to do everything in your power to get the Rug back. If we'd told you to fail and you had chosen to, you'd have been in breach of contract. And then the Rug is up for grabs again."

"See?" said Sean. "Mental."

"OK," said Simon, "OK. So what if I refuse to give them the Rug? They kill me, right? And if I amend my will and make sure that Harriet gets the Rug, then she knows not to let them have it, right?"

"That what happened with Marvin?" Harriet asked Luke, accusatorially.

He closed his eyes and nodded.

"He said it wasn't for sale. At any price."

Harriet looked up. "Good boy, Marvin."

"I'm afraid that won't work either," said Luke. "You've agreed to give it to one of them. You're under contract. If you breach the contract, your ownership of the Rug is null and void. Their claim would come before your will."

"So who would get it?" Simon asked.

Luke shrugged.

"They'll fight over it," Gabby answered for him.

"What, you mean an actual fight?" Simon asked.

"She means an actual war," said Luke. "Angels and demons. On Earth. It's the final artefact. They'll kill each other for it. No question."

"So, basically, there's no way out of this, is that it?"

"I can't see one," Luke answered.

Gabby shook her head in agreement.

"Well, in that case, I'm going to get hideously drunk," Simon said. "Anybody care to join me?"

"Hell, yes," said Harriet.

Sean nodded and smiled, weakly.

"Coming?" Simon asked Luke and Gabby.

They looked back at him, astonished.

"Seriously?" Gabby asked. "You want *us* to come?"

"Why not?" Simon asked, "Seems like we're all pretty much buggered, doesn't it?"

Luke stood and offered a hand to Simon.

"It would be an honour to get drunk with you, Mr Debovar."

Simon shook his hand. "Call me Simon. If you don't mind, I'm just going to have a shower and put on some clean clothes first. Shall we say an hour?"

"Sure," Luke nodded.

"You two are welcome to come back with me, if you like," he said to Sean and Harriet. "I don't have much to offer, but you can at least sit inside while you wait. And either way, would you mind helping me carry this rug?"

CHAPTER THIRTY-SIX

Simon opened the door. It was odd to see it from the outside. It had been a long time since he'd come in through it. A very long time. The front garden could do with some attention.

Now that he was aware his sense of smell was unusual, he was hyper aware of every scent. The house smelled of home. It smelled of him, his cooking, his shampoo and deodorant. But all of that was overshadowed by the sharp, earthy smell of the exposed living room floorboards.

Also, something was rotten. He'd been away a week, so who knew what was festering in the kitchen?

"Christ, boy, you live *here*?" Harriet asked. "Do you not understand 'loaded'? *My* house is bigger than this!"

"I like it," he said. "It's easy to clean."

They put the Rug down in the hall. There was no point putting it anywhere else. By this time tomorrow, it would be gone.

Simon walked straight into the kitchen. It was the bin. He'd left chicken offcuts in there. They were rank. He began tying the bag to lift it out.

"Simon?" Harriet called from the living room. "You need to come here. Now."

Her voice sounded strange. Now what?

Simon put the bag back in place and washed his hands. He walked through to the living room. He'd been distracted as he came in before, or else he'd have noticed, as he passed the entrance to the room, that there were three people sitting in it.

"Hey sexy," said the first.

The second stood and offered a hand.

"Erm, hi. Long time no see."

But it was the third person whose presence had Simon rooted in place, wondering how fast he could run and whether or not he had already wet himself.

"Good afternoon, Simon," he boomed. "We have a lot to talk about."

CHAPTER THIRTY-SEVEN

Simon had woken up with the alarm. It was slightly foreign to him but, actually, quite refreshing somehow. He'd got up and woken his guests, who had slept on inflatable beds with sleeping bags that Cherry had provided before she left.

He had heated up some blueberry muffins in the oven and served them, buttered, with hazelnut coffee, using crockery borrowed from his neighbours – who had been more than a little surprised to see him.

They had all been suffering slightly from the previous evening's excesses. Simon had stuck to Rioja, so he wasn't feeling too bad. Good wine was like that, for him. But still, a good host will always have sachets of Resolve on hand. A little paracetamol and stomach settlers never hurt.

At ten o'clock exactly, the doorbell rang. Simon actually chuckled to himself. He would have to get that fixed, he supposed. Eventually.

He answered it and, stepping over the Holy Rug of Djoser, showed his guests into the living room.

———

"What are *they* doing here?" Daniel asked, suspiciously. "And who is *that*?"

"Harriet and Sean are here because I asked them to be," Simon answered. "And this is my cousin, George."

George stood up and offered a hand, which Daniel took, slowly.

"Hello, nice to meet you," said George. "And you must be Lily," he said, turning to the demon.

"Yes," she answered, equally confused by his presence.

"Please, sit down," Simon said, gesturing to the two free chairs.

Daniel and Lily took one each, surveying the room. Daniel was unused to not understanding what was happening. The presence of the aunt and the pirate was not wholly unexpected, but why the cousin?

"So, Mr Debovar," he asked, taking control of the situation, "have you made a decision?"

"I have," said Simon, "but first, George would like to clarify a few things with you on my behalf, if you don't mind. He's an international contract lawyer."

"*Is* he?" Lily asked.

"Can I offer either of you a drink?" Simon asked.

Daniel and Lily both paused. Who was this confident man who had taken the place of their hermit?

"Have you got a Guinness?" Lily asked.

"I'm sure I do," Simon answered. "Anything for you, Daniel?"

"I'm fine," he answered, an unmistakable tone of irritation creeping into his voice.

"Harriet, would you mind getting a Guinness for Lily?" Simon asked.

"I'd be delighted," she answered, getting up and heading for the kitchen.

Something was definitely not right.

"So," George began, looking up from the laptop he had opened while Harriet was in the kitchen, "just a few things to be absolutely clear about before Simon gives you both an answer."

"Yes?" Daniel was running out of patience.

"Lily, for your offer: you have advised Simon that you will partially correct his olfactory issue, whereby he will no longer find offensive odours any stronger than normal people, is that correct?"

"Yes, that's right," she answered, cheered by the fact that Simon wanted further information on her bid.

"And who decides what a good or bad smell is?"

"What do you mean?"

"Well, what I'm asking is: will it be your choice which odours he does and doesn't smell more strongly, or will it be his?"

"It'll be a trigger in his brain. If he doesn't like a smell, it will be weaker; if he likes it, it stays the same."

George looked at Simon, who nodded thoughtfully.

"And can you confirm," he carried on, "if this is a genetic trait? Will Simon's children be likely to have the same problem?"

"Yes, it is genetic, but it's a quirk," she answered. "Simon's children, if he has any, will be no more or less likely than he was to have it."

"Interesting," answered George, typing. "Now, onto you, Mr... Daniel."

"Yes?" the angel asked, clearly going to great pains to remain 'aloof'.

"You have offered, as I understand it, Lily. Is that correct?"

"That is correct."

"And what services will she be obliged to perform?"

"Anything Mr Debovar wants her to."

"So, would I then be correct in saying that, if he chose to,

Simon could order her, as his – what will we call it, is servant OK? Yes? – as his servant, to grant him anything that it is in her power to perform? Up to and including the change to his olfactory system? This would effectively give him both her offer and yours, in return for the Rug?"

It was Daniel's trump card and he was extremely pleased with it.

"Yes," he smiled triumphantly at Lily, "that's absolutely correct."

"OK," George said. "Just a few more formalities before Simon gives us his decision. I've taken the liberty of drawing up a formal contract regarding the purchase of the Rug, using the original wording."

"Fine," said Daniel, "whatever." He was impatient for this to be over, and he'd clearly won. He'd outmanoeuvred Lily beautifully. And she knew it. Her face was a storm of anger and depression. She was about to become a human's servant for the foreseeable future and there was nothing she could do about it. It was all perfectly valid. All she could hope for was that the world would end quickly.

"I just need to use more specific language than the original, for the avoidance of doubt, OK?"

Daniel nodded his assent again.

"Now, my understanding is that the original words used were that you asked Simon to, I quote: 'choose to give your living room carpet to the one of us whose offer is most attractive to you.'

"I'd just like to amend that to read: 'choose to give the *Holy Rug of Djoser* to the *angel or demon* whose offer is most attractive to you.' Is that OK?"

"Yes, yes, fine," Daniel agreed. He was so close to victory, he could barely stay seated. Father would be pleased.

George clicked a button and paper started to run through the little mobile printer he had next to him on the floor. When it had come out completely, George handed a copy each to Daniel, Lily and Simon, asking them all to sign each copy.

"Just for absolute clarity, you understand, to make sure there are no unexpected ramifications for my client. You'll also see I've inserted a clause on page 2 to record the fact that you have both agreed to allow Simon and Harriet to remain in their current, de-aged state, regardless of the final decision. Also that there will be no repercussions for Simon or any of his friends or family associated with the choice that he makes."

Daniel quickly scanned and then signed all three and handed them on to Lily. She took a moment, before signing them too, and handing them to Simon, who signed them himself and handed them back to George.

"Excellent, thank you all," said George. "Now, I'll hand over to Simon, who will give you his decision."

Daniel sat forward in expectation.

"So," Simon began, standing up. "I've had time to weigh up the offers and they each have a lot of appeal. Lily, your offer is very attractive and I can see a great deal of benefit in taking you up on it. It's a very thoughtful offer and one which I believe would improve my life greatly. Thank you."

Lily smiled and nodded. Was she still in with a chance?

"Daniel, your offer is, frankly, amazing. The thought of being able to have Lily in my service for the rest of my life is truly... amazing. However, I do have the moral dilemma of whether or not it is right to force someone into servitude, and that is something I have struggled with. I am, I like to think, the kind of man who makes the decision he believes to be the right one, regardless of my own personal desires."

Daniel started breathing heavily. The bastard was going to choose her!

"But, then again, Lily is not human. She is a demon and therefore is in service to someone, whether me or not. So am I better off choosing to take her into my control and therefore be able to have a positive effect on the world?

"As you can see, it's been a difficult decision."

Simon paused.

"Yes." Daniel said eagerly. "So...?"

"But I have made a choice, as I promised I would," Simon continued. "I have made the choice that I feel leaves no moral ambiguity and therefore leaves me free of any burden of guilt or any question of impropriety. I have chosen to give the Holy Rug of Djoser to..."

His dramatic pause hung in the air for an eternity.

Then he smiled.

"Lucas and Gabrielle."

———

"What?!"

Daniel and Lily both stood upright.

"Is that supposed to be funny?" Daniel demanded. "Your choice is her or me. Now stop pissing about and make a decision!"

Despite his certainty that he was on solid ground, Simon felt his legs tremble beneath him. Daniel looked murderous. Even Lily looked a lot less appealing than usual. Were those fangs?

"No," Simon said confidently. "I'm giving it to Luke and Gabby."

"Simon, listen, you can't do that," Lily said through gritted teeth. "There are Rules. You agreed."

"Actually," George interrupted, his previously calm voice trembling slightly, "I think you'll find, on reading your versions of the contract, that my client is entirely within his rights."

"Contract?" Daniel spat. "*Contract?* Your contract is worthless! We had an agreement under the Rules."

An acoustic guitar version of the introduction to Stairway to Heaven interrupted his rant. George took his phone out of his inside pocket.

"Hello? Yes, of course. It's for you. He asked me to put it on speaker."

George handed the phone to Daniel after tapping the screen a few times. Daniel held it at arm's length like a freshly laden nappy, disgusted by the need to touch it.

"*What?*" he barked.

"Hello Daniel... Lily," the voice came from the phone. "I'd ask how you both are but, as we all know that I already know, it would just be a silly formality, wouldn't it?"

"What are you doing, deer? This is none of your business," Daniel sneered.

"Ah, but it is. You see, George and I have entered into a mutual agreement, whereby he does some work for me and I advise him on legal matters relating to the Rules. I am acting in that capacity now."

Everyone turned to look at George, who smiled agreeably.

"OK, so what?" Lily asked, irritably. "Simon agreed to give one of us the Rug. The Rules say he has to do it, or we can take it. There's no wriggle room here, Faunt."

"Actually, I think you'll find there is." Faunt was in his deer stage of the day, made evident by the high pitch and vaguely nasal sound of his voice. The combination of this and the serious nature of the conversation tickled Simon and made him snort involuntarily. He hoped nobody noticed. He also hoped he hadn't just snotted himself. Casually, he wiped at his nose, scratching an imaginary itch, just to be sure.

Daniel was glowering at him. He lowered his hand, slowly.

"In your original agreement," Faunt continued, "you asked Simon to 'choose to give your living room carpet to the one of us whose offer is most attractive to you'. Correct?"

"Yes," Daniel answered.

"That was a fundamentally flawed agreement from the start. You may have known what you intended, but you had no right to assume Simon did. For example, you didn't ask for the Holy Rug of Djoser, you asked for his 'living room carpet'. It is not a carpet. It is a rug. And Simon has two spare carpets in his attic, one of which used to be in his living room. We could easily have argued that giving you that was a fulfilment of his agreement, had we wished."

Daniel was turning red. Lily sighed and sat down.

"Shit," she said.

Conversely, Harriet looked like she might explode with glee at any moment. Daniel had also noticed this. It wasn't improving his mood.

"Moreover," said Faunt, "you asked him to give it to 'one of us'. 'Us' is not a specific term is it? 'Us' could easily be misunderstood as a term for any of a certain group to which one belongs; for example, angels or demons. Could it not? This is why George decided to be more specific in the terminology, prior to the agreement being fulfilled; so that there was no need for us to argue that point after the fact."

"Fine. Then choose the angels or choose the demons, but choose one. Lucas and Gabrielle have been banished. They no longer count among our number."

Daniel turned menacingly back to Simon.

"This is between you and me, Mr Debovar. *Choose.*"

Simon swallowed hard. He'd feel a lot better if Faunt were actually here.

"Back off, Sparky, or I'll rip you a new orifice just so I can shove your head up it."

Simon turned to see Harriet standing behind him. Sean stood too. That was better. He could feel his feet again.

Daniel's eyes flared. He began to reach for Harriet.

"Ah," George raised a finger. "Page 2: 'No repercussions for Simon, his friends or family...'"

Daniel lowered his hand. Lily shook her head.

"If I may continue," said Faunt, "we were also prepared to argue that point, but then, yesterday, you very kindly did it for us, Daniel. You said to Luke: 'You're not human. You have to be born human. You're an angel; she's a demon. The only difference is you're mortal. You're going to die.' Correct?"

Daniel closed his eyes and bowed his head. He muttered something inaudible and slumped in his chair.

"Wait," he said, raising his head again. "Wait a minute! Faunt, you are not allowed to interfere!"

He stood again, shouting at the phone.

"There's no possible way that the humans came up with this alone. This is *your* plan. You *must* have told them and that means you interfered! Nobody is allowed to intervene. The agreement is null and void! The Rug's ownership is annulled. And you, deer, are in serious trouble."

Daniel was triumphant. There was even a faint glow about him.

"I did no such thing," Faunt answered, calmly. "By coincidence, my wife and I did have coffee yesterday with a mutual acquaintance, and we did happen to discuss what I would do, were I allowed to do so, but I also made it clear that interfering would be entirely against the Rules. For *me*."

"Well *somebody* did! And they weren't allowed!" Daniel ranted.

"Daniel, stop," Lily said, calmly. "Think about it. We're beat. And we walked right into it."

"How?" he demanded. "*How?*"

"Who's the one person who could have told Simon what to do without breaking the Rules?" she asked.

Daniel looked confused, then realisation grew across his face. "No. No, it's not fair."

"You may not think it's fair," boomed a voice from the hall, "but I don't give a crap about your Rules."

"The Exception," said the angel, bitterly. "The damned Exception."

Priest's huge frame filled the archway.

He stepped in, making space for Luke and Gabby to come in behind him. They'd stayed in the kitchen until now, letting it all play out as Faunt had suggested. The deer had a flair for the dramatic.

"So you see," said Faunt, "everything has happened exactly according to the Rules. Lucas and Gabrielle are now the rightful owners of the Holy Rug of Djoser. You are certainly welcome to try to negotiate with them for it, but I suspect you will find them unwilling to part with it."

Daniel stood and tossed George's phone back at him.

"Fine," he said, fixing Simon with an icy stare. It didn't seem 'fine'.

The angel looked down. A low rumble gathered in the ground beneath him. Nobody spoke. Simon was barely breathing.

"I think you'll agree," Daniel said to Lily through gritted teeth, "that our agreement not to use our abilities is at an end."

"No," Lily said mournfully. "Don't."

Daniel looked back up. His eyes burned with a blue flame. His face was contorted in anger. A huge pair of eagle's wings spread from his back, knocking over furniture. He seemed to fill the entire room.

"Daniel!" Faunt's electronic voice squealed from the phone, "Daniel – you *can't* harm them!"

"We'll see," he growled.

With barely noticeable exertion, the angel burst upwards, through the ceiling, through the upper floor and out through the roof. Debris and dust clattered to the ground as Simon and his guests dived to find whatever cover they could.

When the masonry had stopped falling, they crawled out of their hiding places. Lily had not moved at all, standing amidst the debris as it fell around her – seemingly avoiding her. She looked upwards, sadly.

Priest had moved only a few feet out into the hall.

"Where's he going?" he asked the demon.

"I don't know," she answered. "But I don't think it will be good."

"Oh God! No!" It was Faunt's voice again. "Daniel, no! You're making a huge mistake!"

Crashing sounds came through the phone's speakers, before it suddenly went dead.

Everyone in the room looked at each other for answers.

"He can't... he can't hurt Faunt. Right?" Simon pleaded.

Nobody answered.

———

The guitars played again.

George held out the phone, silently pleading for someone to take the responsibility from him.

Harriet lifted it.

"Hello?" she answered, holding it to her ear. Her face quickly turned thunderous. "OK, hang on."

She held the phone out and switched on the speaker again.

"OK, you're on," she said, loudly.

"Hello everyone," Faunt said. "I have bad news. Daniel has taken Amelia."

"What?" Priest bellowed, stepping toward the phone. "I'll *kill* the son of a bitch!"

"Wait," Faunt said. "There's more to it. His logic is sound – in a way. He is not allowed to harm any of Simon's friends or family. His thinking is that while Bob could be considered a friend, Amelia's status is unclear. Simon barely knows her. He also reasons that killing her will gain him the most revenge, as it will hurt Priest, Cassandra, Sean and Bob. He also believes, Simon, that hurting Bob will hurt you and I. And you, he believes, are the way to get Harriet. It's almost elegant. It's also, arguably, within the Rules."

"She's innocent," Simon said, flatly. "It's not fair."

"No, it's not," Faunt replied.

"Where is he?" Priest demanded. "Where is he *now*?"

"That's not as important as this: he is prepared to spare her," Faunt continued, "in return for something else."

"What?" Priest asked, agitated.

No answer.

Glass fell from a broken window and shattered on the floor.

"It's me, isn't it?" Simon asked, in a tiny voice.

"Yes, Simon, I'm afraid so," Faunt replied. "If you give up your protection under the Rules, he will spare Amelia."

"Like hell!" Harriet barked. "Tell us where the bastard is! For Christ's sake, we've got a demon, a witch and whatever the hell Priest is. He can't beat us all!"

"I can't fight him," Lily said, ruefully. "It is expressly forbidden."

"And Priest's power is substantially reduced off his island," Faunt continued. "As powerful as Cassandra is, she couldn't take on an angel alone. It would be suicide. Though, understandably, she is prepared to try..."

Silence.

Simon quickly ran through the options in his head, but it was pretty clear it was Amelia or him. He didn't want to die. He hadn't wanted any of this. But Amelia was just a girl. A sweet, innocent, happy girl, who deserved a life.

How would he live with himself if he was too much of a coward to let her have it? He was the kind of man who did the right thing. At least, he wanted to be...

"OK," he finally said, "OK. I can do it. We saved the world, right?"

He gave Harriet a watery smile, tears filling his eyes.

"He gets you over my dead fucking body, son, and no other way." Harriet put a hand on his shoulder. "Tell me there's another way, Faunt."

"I'm glad you asked, Harriet," the deer replied. "I do have an idea..."

353

CHAPTER THIRTY-EIGHT

Daniel hovered above the cliff face. He held Amelia out at arm's length. Initially, she had struggled and wriggled to get away from him. He wanted her to stop. So she did.

Now, she dangled like a lost statue, her dress crackling in the wind. He'd told Faunt that Debovar had an hour to meet him here, or the girl dropped. It had been fifty-nine minutes. Either he'd misjudged the man, or he was eking out every last minute of life.

Two people blinked into sight on the cliff top below him. After a moment, one disappeared. Debovar had been delivered. About time too. Daniel lowered himself to ten feet above the ground. He was going to savour this.

"Mr Debovar!" he called over the wind, as if Simon were a guest of honour, "I was beginning to think you weren't coming!"

Simon said nothing, looking back blankly at the angel.

"I take it you agree to my terms then?" he continued. "You surrender your protection under the Rules, and I release the girl."

"No," Simon replied. "I don't."

What? Why was he here, then?

"I'm not an idiot," Simon continued. "If you 'release' her, she'll drop down there," he pointed to the cliff face, "and die. So let's be clear."

Damn. Ah well, that would only have been a bonus. Debovar was what he really wanted.

"My terms are these," Simon shouted over the howl of the wind, "I will waive my protection under the Rules if you agree to safely return Amelia to the ground and not to harm her in any way, or allow her to be harmed by any inaction on your part."

It was fairly watertight. The deer had probably given him the line. Ah well, he had no real problem with the girl. He'd find another way to get back at the Exception.

"Fine," he answered, "I agree."

Simon nodded. "Then so do I."

Daniel lowered himself far enough to place the girl gently on the grass.

"Now," the angel said, towering over Simon, the blue flame flickering with glee in his eyes, "it's just you and me."

Simon smiled.

"I never agreed to *that*."

———

Cherry was pacing.

"What's happening?" she asked, impatiently.

Lily and Cassandra sat cross-legged on the floor, facing each other, their hands held up together. They looked like they were meditating – except for the weird golden glow around them.

"He's put her down," Faunt said calmly. "It's working. Be ready."

Cherry turned to look at Priest, who nodded gravely at her. Bob sat on a stool, wringing his hands. He could barely sit still.

They were ready.

"What?" Daniel asked, gliding forward.

Simon stepped back, giving himself a little breathing space. He looked up at the huge angel bearing down on him.

"I said, 'I never agreed to that'," he answered.

Daniel paused and looked around slowly. There was nobody else to see, and even if there were, nobody could lay hands on him if he didn't want them to. He was literally untouchable.

And yet, he had learned to be wary of this odd little man.

"Oi! Bell end!"

Daniel spun around to face the direction the voice had come from. From Simon's perspective, a pair of bat wings appeared either side of his erstwhile attacker's head. He fleetingly remembered his earlier desire to be rescued by Batman.

This was even cooler.

"What in Heaven?" Daniel sputtered as Harriet rose above him on what was clearly a pair of demon wings. Her eyes burned with red fire.

This was not in the plan.

"OK," Faunt said. "Go, now, for Amelia..."

Cherry blinked out.

Simon took Daniel's distraction as an opportunity to back away from the angel. That was as much space as Harriet needed.

She swooped down towards him, ramming him hard in the chest and scooping him up into the air with her. He was momentarily shocked into inaction, but quickly recovered. He pushed her back, hard. She flew away from him, staying in mid-air.

Regaining her composure, Harriet caught herself and hovered, about fifty feet away from him and a hundred feet above the cliff below.

"All right, posh bollocks," she grinned, "you've been asking for this."

Harriet flew at him again. Daniel's eyes burned bright. He barrelled towards her. The two battered into each other at speed and an explosion of purple flame sent them both careering back in the directions they had come. Harriet went out over the sea and disappeared below the cliff edge. Daniel flew back inland, dropping to earth out of Simon's sight.

He heard a sucking noise and turned to see that Amelia was gone. OK, part two complete – she was safely away with Cherry.

Now for the hard part.

———

Priest hugged his daughter, confirming that she was mobile again. She was confused, but mostly glad to be alive.

"You'll only get one chance at this," Faunt warned. "If he realises what we're trying to do, you won't catch him out again."

"Don't worry," Priest growled, "he's mine."

———

Simon rushed to the cliff edge. He couldn't see Harriet, but Faunt had assured him that while Cassandra was channeling Lily's powers into her, she couldn't really be hurt. Still, he'd be happier if he could see her.

A hand grabbed him by the back of the neck and lifted him off the ground. A long way off the ground. He struggled to free himself, but he couldn't even touch the fingers gripping his throat.

And he couldn't breathe.

"Mr Debovar, I am very tired of you," Daniel sneered. "And while I had decided it would be enjoyable to beat you to death, I think perhaps now I will just go for the simple option."

Simon felt the wind picking up around them, but most of his attention was on the fact that he couldn't breathe. Shit. Where was Harriet?

Simon lurched as the arm holding him was jerked backwards. Then, suddenly, it let him go.

He fell.

———

Harriet had thought she could take the angel out by sneaking up behind him. Unfortunately, she'd been more successful than she'd planned and he'd lost his grip on her nephew. She released his head from the sleeper hold she had grabbed him in and dived towards Simon's plummeting body. He was going to miss the edge of the cliff, so she had a little more time to get to him than she might have done.

But as she prepared to pass the edge herself, the angel slammed into her from behind, carrying them both screaming past Simon's plummeting form and splashing into the ocean.

———

"No!" Faunt howled.

"What?" asked Cherry.

"The cliff!" he shouted. "Simon! *Go!*"

———

Simon was close to blacking out. He thought he'd seen Harriet

358

coming towards him, but then she disappeared. The wind rushed up past his ears – he knew what was coming.

The rocks at the bottom of the cliff.

The last week flashed through his mind as he prepared himself for the end. It was still hard to breathe as the air whipped past him. But even through the roaring, he could swear he heard a faint popping noise.

———

Harriet burst up out of the water. It had only taken her a moment to free herself from Daniel after they went under, but it might have been a moment too long. She looked around to get her bearings, to see where Simon had been. There was no sign of him – either in the air or on the rocks below.

He better not be dead, or she'd kill this bloody angel if she had to face God himself for doing it.

Daniel burst back out of the water toward her. Turning, she swung a punch which connected perfectly with his chin and sent him further upwards. She flew after him, fists glowing red.

The two met again in the air and immediately rained blows upon each other – sparks of red and blue flame flying off them as they rolled across the sky, locked together.

———

"What was *that*?" Amelia asked. An almighty crash had resounded around Faunt's house.

"Cherry's bed," the deer answered. "She can't remove kinetic energy by teleporting, only take it to a new location. She landed them on her bed. They're both OK. It was designed to collapse and spread an impact like this – just in case."

Amelia stared. That was one hell of a just in case.

Gesturing to Bob, she raced up the stairs toward Cherry's room. He followed.

By the time they got there and swung the door open, Cherry was already gone again, leaving her passenger confused and disorientated on what was left of the bed.

"What happened?" Simon asked.

———

Harriet was still swinging and still connecting with every punch. But so was Daniel. They were evenly matched, but the angel had spent his entire existence with these abilities – Harriet had spent less than an hour learning how to use them.

She was tiring.

As she tried to reorientate herself to deliver a big hit to her opponent, he caught her by the leg, swung her around over his head, and slammed her down into the earth below them. Before she could adjust, he rammed his feet into her back, forcing her, face first, into the soil.

Flying up and down at speed he repeatedly rammed into her back, forcing her down, down, down into the earth. She couldn't breathe, but frantically reminded herself she didn't need to – she was immortal as long as Cass kept up that spell.

Theoretically.

Eventually, the pounding stopped. Harriet slowly pushed up on her aching limbs and turned over to see Daniel's silhouette standing triumphantly above her impromptu grave, the sun burning bright behind him.

"You thought you could beat me? *Me?*" he asked, glowing blue from head to toe. "I'm an *angel.*"

Harriet gave a low, guttural laugh. "You're an idiot."

"What?" He reared up again, ready to strike another blow.

"I wasn't trying to beat you, moron. I just needed to distract you long enough for this to happen," she said.

"For *what* to happen?" the angel demanded.

"This," Priest's deep voice answered from behind him.

Before Daniel could turn to see the new arrivals, Priest had grabbed his arm and the two of them, plus Cherry, blinked out.

Harriet slowly lifted herself to her feet and stretched.

That was fun.

———

Simon followed Amelia down the stairs, supported by Bob.

"How's it going?" he asked as they entered the library.

"They've got him," Faunt answered. "It's in Priest's hands now."

"How's Harriet?" Simon asked.

"On her way back," he answered. "She's fine. And she rather enjoyed herself."

Faunt handed a sleek, silver smartphone to Simon.

"Hit redial and you can let George and the others know," he said, smiling.

———

"Where are we?" Daniel demanded, looking around at the lush, green grass that surrounded him. "How did we get here?"

"This young lady brought us," Priest answered, indicating Cherry, who had collapsed to her knees on the grass. She'd done a lot of teleporting in a hurry, and she'd finished with a major one.

"Is that right?" the angel asked. "Let's deal with that.

"*Die,*" he commanded the girl.

Cherry looked up, smiled and flipped him a finger.

Daniel was confused. Why wasn't she dead? He *wanted* her dead.

"Bad news, angel," said Priest. "You've been lied to."

"By *whom*?" Daniel demanded imperiously, still trying to get his bearings.

"Your father."

The angel's eyes widened. Not because of what Priest had said, but because he'd finally realised where he was.

He wasn't supposed to be here. *Ever.*

"Why are we here?" he asked, an unprecedented hint of fear in his voice.

"You probably think I banned you from my island because I didn't want you in my home," Priest continued. "That's not true."

"All right. Why did you?" Daniel asked.

Priest smiled. "I didn't. *They* did."

The Exception suddenly strode towards him. The angel put a hand up in defence, but Priest swatted it aside, grabbing his lapels and lifting him off the ground.

Daniel instinctively tried to spread his wings... but they weren't there. The angel began to panic. What was happening? Had Father forsaken him?

"They didn't want you coming here because your powers don't work here, Daniel."

Daniel stared wide-eyed. He'd had no idea Priest's deal was so extensive. What *could* he do?

The man mountain pulled the angel down towards him, head-butting him hard in the face. There was a sickening crunch as Daniel's nose collapsed.

Priest dropped him to the ground. Daniel held his hand up to his broken face, confused and in *pain.*

Priest calmly circled behind his captive. "What do you know about me?" he asked.

Daniel shook his head, trying to think clearly through the panic. "They chose you," he answered. "You were their champion. That's why they rewarded you."

"They *chose* me," Priest repeated the words, but there was

something about the way he said them, as if the idea was almost amusing.

Priest crouched down in front of him.

"I had a family, Daniel. A home. I was a *farmer*."

"They didn't choose me. They *took* me. They took me, and made me a murderer."

Daniel looked at him wide-eyed.

"They tortured me. Took everything I had. Everything I was. They broke me; remade me as their weapon. To punish the disloyal."

Daniel knew his Father could be unforgiving. His temper had softened with time, but in the beginning, his wrath had been... legendary.

"What happened?" Cherry asked, quietly.

Priest stood and turned away from them both.

"I *loved* it," he answered. "I didn't stop with the faithless. I killed everyone. Everyone I could find. Humans, angels, demons... *everyone*.

"I was called 'Plague'. 'The First Evil'."

Daniel didn't speak to fill the silence. Cherry was trembling.

"They wanted me to stop. I think they may even have felt... regret. So they 'fixed' me."

"That doesn't make sense..." Daniel began.

Priest continued as if he had never spoken. "Do you know what *still* pisses me off?"

"No," Daniel answered, carefully.

"When they play games with people's lives," Priest answered, suddenly grabbing the angel by the throat and lifting him off his feet, again. "And I can't think of a better way to repay that than with a dead angel. Can you?"

Daniel's eyes bulged as the huge hand tightened around his neck.

"Nobody touches my *family*," Priest growled.

Cherry recoiled as the crack of the angel's neck echoed off the mountain.

Priest dropped the lifeless body to the ground and stood over it in silence. The wind gently whispered through the palm trees and the ocean lapped against the beach. Butterflies fluttered around them – in paradise.

Cherry stood and walked cautiously to him. Now she understood why everyone was so afraid.

"You're *him*?" she asked, gingerly. "The *real* one?"

Priest smiled sadly at her.

"Not anymore."

CHAPTER THIRTY-NINE

Simon looked up at his living room ceiling. It was nice to have it back again. Lily had kindly agreed to 'repair' it. Which was nice.

"What now?" he asked.

She shrugged. "You get on with your life. I guess it might be a little different now, huh?"

Simon smiled and nodded. Yes, it probably would be different – in lots of ways.

"Can I ask you something?" he asked, after a moment.

"Sure."

"Not that I don't appreciate it or anything, but I was just wondering why... well... you took this all a lot better than Daniel did."

The demon smiled.

"I did, didn't I?"

"Quite a bit."

"We have very different perspectives. His boss is... let's say 'uptight'. Mine is more chilled out. Plus, I actually quite like it down here. It's fun. My Mother is big on fun – it's important. And, to be totally honest, Faunt was right. Chances are, if we had taken the Rug and decided the bet..."

"Oh."

Somehow, it was scarier to have their worst fears confirmed – even now that they'd avoided them.

Lily walked to the door.

"Plus, as much as I like you, life as your slave is not as appealing as you might imagine, so thanks for turning that down." She laughed and he joined her. "Now, if you'll excuse me, I probably have some questions to answer. And you have a dinner appointment."

"Of course," said Simon, before adding, "Thanks. Really."

Lily beamed back at him.

"Simon, for a hermit, you have an uncanny knack of attracting friends. I'd never have believed it. You're like a child; all indignant and uncompromising, but scared and vulnerable."

"Thanks," he said. "I think."

Stepping out, she turned and faced him. He was reminded of their first meeting. Had it really been just a week?

"Two things," she said, "before I go."

"Yes?"

She stretched up and kissed him on the nose.

"You deserve it," she said, smiling.

"What?" Simon asked.

He breathed in. He could smell the grass, the fresh, crisp air, a hint of vanilla and not a lot else. The stale, sweaty, lingering human odours were gone. His head felt clearer than it ever had. It was as if a light had come on. It was actually easier to *think*.

"Thank you," he said, tears welling in his eyes again. "My God. Thank you."

"You're welcome," she smiled. "And secondly: Lucas and Gabrielle had to make you an offer, right? For the Rug? What was it? I'm curious."

Simon smiled, opened his palms wide and shrugged.

"Free pizza for life."

———

"*Slainte mhah* and up yer bum!"

Harriet raised her champagne glass high. Everyone else around Faunt's dining table joined her and knocked back their drinks.

Simon looked around. Cherry sat to his right. She was not back to full strength, but she looked amazing. She'd even put on a dress for the occasion – though with her own style, of course. The ripped bottom of it revealed her striped tights and trainers.

Harriet sat next to her. The two had spent most of the evening chatting and it seemed like they had known each other for years. Harriet was educating her in the ways of good single malt, and why bourbon isn't real whisky. Next to her, Sean and Bob were deep in conversation about something.

Amelia was next to Bob, holding his hand on her lap, while she spoke to her step-mother at the end of the massive oak table.

On the other side, Gabby and Luke sat together, seeming happier every time Simon looked at them. They had asked Faunt to keep the Holy Rug of Djoser here for them, to protect it, and he had happily agreed. He had also advised them that they might want to start thinking about creating a new generation, in order to have someone to inherit the Rug and look after it in future. Gabby had made a very cute squeak and hugged Luke.

Next to them was Priest. There was no small amount of tension between Cassandra and him, but Faunt had asked them to put aside their differences for the evening in order that everyone who had played a part could be there to celebrate. Interestingly, he and Prisoner, or Prosper, as Simon was going to have to get used to calling him, had become quite friendly once the former had confessed his error over the ownership of the island, and they were currently swapping chilli recipes. In fact, Prosper had spent the day preparing the Creole feast they had just finished. Faunt had, of course, been right about his culinary abilities.

Next to them was an empty place and then, deliberately placed opposite Simon, was George. He looked about as uncomfortable as Simon assumed *he* probably had when he first came here, but he was joining in as manfully as he could. Simon was making an effort to keep him involved, while revelling in not being the most socially awkward person in the room for a change.

At the head of the table was Faunt; the man they all had to thank for their lives. The man *everybody* had to thank for their lives. And they'd probably never know it. He sat back in the chair, smoking a Cuban cigar and smiling like Santa Claus on Christmas Day.

And, of course, there was Calderon's head, placed on the sideboard amongst the drinks and currently being used as a candleholder. His black, thunderous eyes were visible through the streams of hardened wax.

It was very funny, if a little creepy.

Simon stood.

"Excuse me, please, everyone. I'd just like to say something."

The room fell silent as everyone turned their attention to him.

"We saved the world today. All of us. We all helped and I think we should all be proud."

There were murmurs of "hear, hear" and nodding.

"But, I think it is important that we recognise two people in particular. Firstly, Maya, whom I assume is here?" Simon gestured toward the empty place across from him.

He had directed the question at Faunt, but it was Cherry who answered, "Yeah, she's here."

"Good," Simon continued. "Because she lost her life and,

without her, we'd all be dead too. I think that's worth noting and saying 'thank you'." He raised his glass. "Maya."

"Maya," the room joined him.

"Secondly, our host and benefactor. Without him pulling the strings; without his knowledge; without his cunning, we'd all have been lost. I would *never* have come up with those plans. He is a genius and we all owe him our lives.

"To Faunt: an immaculate host and a genuine hero."

Again, he raised his glass; again the room echoed him. After drinking, he sat down.

Faunt stood.

"Thank you all. There is also a specific thanks *I* would like to make."

He turned towards Luke and Gabby and raised his own glass toward them.

"To Lucas and Gabrielle. If you two hadn't stolen the Rug, I'd never have had the chance to make a plan in the first place. You had *absolutely* no idea what you were doing, but you two saved the world. Congratulations."

"Lucas and Gabrielle," the rest of the room said.

Gabby hugged Luke again, while he smiled through the tears streaming down his face.

———

After dinner, when everyone had descended into jovial and rather inebriated conversation, Faunt asked Simon to step away with him for a moment, into the study.

"You have questions to ask," Faunt said plainly, as they entered.

It was true. He did.

"Would you like to ask them, now?"

"I suppose so," Simon answered, "if that's OK?"

His host nodded indulgently. Simon was aware Faunt

already knew what the questions were, but was respectfully allowing him to ask them out loud.

"Why did you tell Calderon where we were?"

Faunt's eyes darkened. "It was a calculated risk. He was going to kill Cherry. I risked Bob's life, and yours, I suppose, to save hers. I hope you can forgive me."

Simon had already lost count of how many times Cherry had saved his life. He definitely didn't object.

"Nothing to forgive. Honestly. Did you know that you were going to send Maya after us when you told him?"

"No. I confess I was making that part up *ad hoc*. It was... challenging." He said the final word with a mixture of fatigue and excitement.

"OK, I guess," Simon paused. "Why did you *really* want Cassandra back?"

"I needed her to invite Priest here under the pretence of peace-making. He and I have not been allies. If *I* had asked him, he wouldn't have come. I knew he'd come for Cass. And I needed him. He was the only one who could tell you how to get out of your contract without breaking the Rules. And in order to tell him without breaking the Rules myself, I needed him here for another reason."

"So that was all? You didn't really want her back?"

"What *I* want isn't as important as what *she* wants, in this instance, Simon."

"Oh," he shrugged, feeling a tinge of sadness for his friend and a little guilt for asking the question. "I guess that's everything."

Simon turned to the door, but Faunt put a hand on his arm.

"Before we go, I wanted to show you something," he said.

"Sure," said Simon, bumping into a stool that moved across his path and wondering what could be left to see that he hadn't already seen.

"It's this," said Faunt, gesturing to the wall.

Where Faunt's portraits hung, there was now a new, large drape, with tassels hanging down.

"Pull it," he said.

Simon stepped forward and tugged at one of the tassels. The drape fell to reveal a new addition.

"That's what I needed a space for," said Faunt.

At the front, looking, he thought, rather impressively heroic, was Simon. Behind him, in a sort of ragtag vanguard, stood Luke and Gabby, Harriet and Cherry, Sean and Bob, Amelia and Prosper, Priest and Cassandra, George and a beautiful black woman with ice blue eyes. It was... awesome.

"Yes, that is Maya, and yes, she is beautiful." This time, Faunt answered Simon's unspoken question.

"But..." Simon began to object. Faunt put up a hand to stop him.

"Simon, it's *my* gallery. I already know what *I* look like."

———

Simon's footsteps were still audible in the hall as she stepped out of the dark corner.

"So. What *do* you want?" Cassandra asked.

"Honestly, Cass, I don't know," said Faunt. "But it's nice to see you."

She looked him up and down.

"Have you changed? You look different."

"It's been a long time. I've seen things."

"You look tired."

Faunt's eyes trembled.

"It's hard."

Cassandra grasped a chair that was passing behind her and sat down.

"You hurt me," she said.

"I know."

"You don't, though, do you?" Her smile was pure ice.

"That's the deal. You're not allowed in here." She tapped her head, then her chest. "Or here."

"Cass, I know. I know I hurt you, because I'm human. And I was an idiot. And I deserve it all."

"But you still brought me here to ask if I'd remove the curse."

"No. I brought you here because I needed you."

"Priest would have come for other reasons. You could have got him here without me."

"I couldn't be sure..."

"You damn well could have!"

"All right. All right. I wanted to see you."

"To ask me to..."

"No. To see you. I miss you."

Cass snorted. "But not so much that you couldn't wait for sixty years?"

Faunt's head dropped.

"I had no right..."

"He *kidnapped* me! He took me against my will and kept me on that island for sixty years!"

"I know, but..."

"Why didn't you *rescue* me?!"

Faunt staggered, steadying himself on the mantelpiece. "Rescue you? You wanted me to *rescue* you?"

"Well who *else* was going to do it?"

Faunt fell to his knees in front of her, grasping one hand between his.

"Cass, I swear, I didn't know. You hated me. I thought you wanted me to leave you alone. You did... *this* to me."

"For God's sake, Faunt, I was *angry*. I'm a witch!"

Faunt shook uncontrollably.

"Cass, I swear, if I'd known, if I'd even thought... I'd have done *anything*."

The witch smiled through her own tears.

"But you *didn't*, did you? I gave you knowledge of everything, and you're still a damned idiot."

Cassandra stood, gently pulling her hand from Faunt's. Silently, she crossed to the door and opened it. Without turning, she quietly spoke.

"I'll remove it. If you ask me to."

After a long silence, he answered.

"I'll never ask."

Cass nodded, and closed the door behind her.

CHAPTER FORTY

Simon teetered gracelessly into the room. At best count, he'd had at least a bottle and a half of Rioja to himself, and then there was whisky. It was smoky and rich and sweet, and it burned the back of his throat. But it had left him feeling really rather merry. Which was nice. He was also relatively confident he would escape a hangover, knowing his host's capabilities.

What he was not expecting was for his bed to be other than empty.

"Hey, sexy," she said, pulling the duvet up to her neck.

"Hello," he slurred, equally surprised and delighted. "Why are you here?"

On immediate reflection, it seemed an awful lot like checking a gift horse for cavities.

"Well, technically, you didn't buy me dinner, but we did have dinner together." She smiled and lifted the duvet invitingly, just enough for him to see a line of naked thigh.

"Best day ever," he whispered to himself as he struggled with his clothes.

Simon lay back, exhausted and happy, with Cherry nuzzled in against his chest. It was almost perfect.

"Can I ask you something?" he asked.

"What's up?"

Simon did not have a full grasp of the subtleties of American English.

"Does that mean 'yes'?"

"Course it does. Ask away."

He took a deep breath.

"Well, not that I want to ruin anything but, I was just wondering, you know, what with everything that's happened and, you know, I mean, I know I called you a prostitute... but that was before I knew you, and...'"

Cherry put a finger to his lips.

"Do you think you could ask the question without insulting me again?"

Simon nodded sheepishly, and she removed the finger.

"What is this?" he asked.

"What do you mean?"

"Well, do you do this with a lot of people, or just me?"

Cherry sat upright.

"Are you asking if I'm easy?"

Simon desperately racked his brain for a way to not make the next thing he said another insult, but since Cherry's breasts were now between his face and hers, it was very hard to concentrate.

"Umm, no... I just meant, erm... are you my girlfriend?"

After a moment, Cherry's face broke into a wide grin.

"Are you asking me to go steady, Billy Joe? Are you gonna give me your pin?"

Simon was fairly sure he was being ridiculed, but he didn't really care.

"*Will* you be my girlfriend?"

"Don't you think we're moving a little fast? I mean, we've only had sex like, what, eight or nine times?"

"Oh, really?" Simon fumbled. "Erm, sorry, I didn't know..."

"Shut up you idiot." She slapped his chest playfully and smiled.

"Sure, I'll be your girlfriend."

She laid her head back on his chest and stroked his stomach affectionately.

Simon grinned like the king of the world.

"One thing, though." She lifted her head to look at him.

"What?"

"We're going to have to teach you some social skills."

EPILOGUE ONE

The doorbell rang.

"You expecting anyone?" Luke called upstairs to Gabby.

"Nope!" she called back. He lifted his coffee and went to the door.

He opened it, and stopped dead.

"What do you want?" he asked, a tremor of fear in his voice.

"I... I'm sorry, I don't know where else to go."

Luke realised the visitor looked rough. He had stubble and smelled terrible.

"How do you survive? Nothing... nothing *works*. Where do I go?"

Luke smiled and stepped back.

"Come in, Daniel. You're going to be OK."

The former angel stepped in, tentatively.

"I made a terrible mistake," he said.

Luke put his arm around the newly mortal shoulders of his brother.

"You've got time to make up for it."

EPILOGUE TWO

There was a knock at the door.

Simon went to answer it. It was probably the new living room carpet. They were a little early, though.

"Hello," he said, when he saw who was actually at the door. "*Déjà vu.*"

"Can we come in?" Lily asked. "We could do with your help."

"We?" Simon asked. He could only see the demon.

She gestured to her side and a woman stepped into sight.

"*Sabrina?*" Simon asked his cousin. "What are *you* doing here?"

"Hey," Sabrina said. "Lily said you might be able to help me with some stuff."

"What kind of stuff?" he asked, bemused.

"Well, apparently," she answered, "I'm some sort of envoy."

ACKNOWLEDGMENTS

There are a huge number of people who've contributed in some way to making this book happen: friends and family who have been unwaveringly supportive and patient; writers who've offered helpful advice and constructive opinions. But a number need specific thanks for really going out of their way in one way or another.

Lots of people have been kind enough to read full drafts of the book at different stages, and their feedback has directly contributed to the final story. In no particular order, thank you Kim Curran, Steve Rapaport, Hannah Henderson, Keith Shaw, Mandy Ward, Elizabeth Bank, Cat Macdonald-Home, Simon Hemmings, Jess Naylor, Avril Hofman and Jaqueline Wheddon. I think I've remembered everyone, but if I've missed anyone I'm deeply sorry.

One person not only read an early draft and gave me great feedback, he also created the beautiful artwork for my first cover. Martin Lennon, you are an amazing talent and a good friend. Thank you.

Ross Garner was the last reader and it was his edits and observations that finally got me to a finished product I was proud of. Thank you.

Poppet's unwavering support, encouragement, patience and tolerance were all invaluable and, without her, there's a good chance I'd still have a work in progress, not a published book. Thank you.

Without Rod Glenn and Wild Wolf Publishing, I might literally still be unpublished. Thanks for your faith and for taking a gamble on me.

Nathan Dornbrook's friendship, belief and support has not only enabled this new edition to be published, but also allowed me to write full-time, for which I will be eternally grateful. Thank you.

And finally, the person who has supported me for years, made sacrifices to give me time to write and edit, read the book multiple times and believed in me when I didn't believe in myself: to my wonderful wife, Juliet, without whom this book simply would not exist. Thank you.

ABOUT THE AUTHOR

Born in Edinburgh, Justin spent a decade of his childhood bouncing around the US, following his dad's professional football (soccer) career. He returned to the Scottish capital in his teens and, after a few brief sojourns to Dundee (for an English degree) and the South of France (for his family), settled back in the city that's always been 'home', where he lives with his Brady Bunch family in a permanent state of happy chaos.

In two decades of writing and editing for a living, he's done everything from restaurant, theatre and comedy reviews to training manuals and magazines, including four years as the writer, editor and photographer for an Edinburgh guidebook.

He has the same initials as the Justice League of America, and his favourite writers are Neil Gaiman, Aaron Sorkin, Joe Abercrombie and Joss Whedon, in no particular order.

He misses *Firefly*.

 facebook.com/justinleeandersonauthor

twitter.com/authorjla

 instagram.com/justinleeandersonauthor

Made in the USA
Middletown, DE
18 January 2019